WAYWARD

AS THE

WIND

TABLE OF CONTENTS

MAP

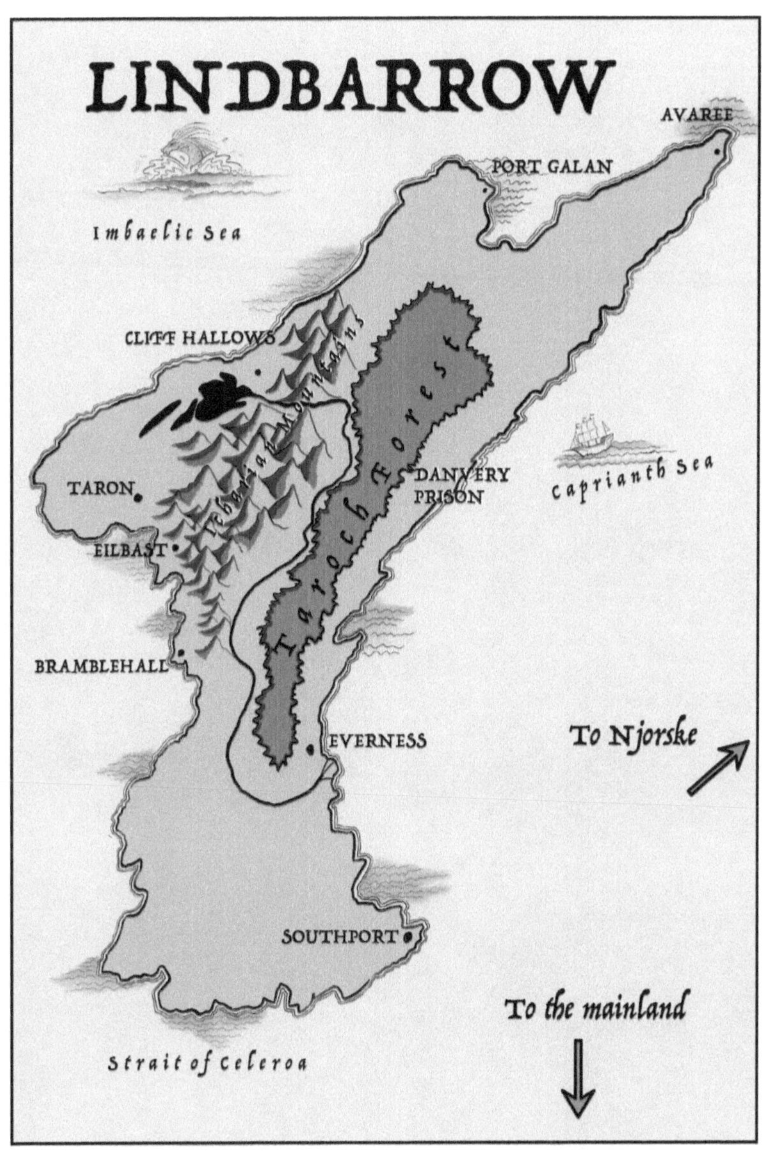

LINDBARROW
AVAREE
PORT GALAN
Imbaelic Sea
CLIFF HALLOWS
Tebariat Mountains
Taroch Forest
DANVERY PRISON
Caprianth Sea
TARON
EILBAST
BRAMBLEHALL
EVERNESS
To Njorske
SOUTHPORT
To the mainland
Strait of Celeroa

PROLOGUE

He could tell she was nervous. Not only that, but she didn't quite know why she was nervous. He had once found her restlessness charming, endearing. Now that he knew the truth, it was easy to dismiss it as a bothersome habit he was glad to be rid of.

"Zare? Did you hear what I said?" she asked from across the table.

"Sorry, love." He let an easy smile drip honey-smooth over his features, and watched her soften at it.

She had no idea what was about to happen, that he'd learned her secret.

"Wine?" He reached under his chair, wrapping his fingers around the neck of the bottle he'd selected just for this occasion.

She nodded, swallowing the bite of slaw she'd just put in her mouth. "What's the occasion?" Her lashes fluttered over her mismatched blue and green eyes.

"I suspect… I am about to come into a great deal of money," he said, lazily uncorking the bottle. She didn't even notice the little vial he'd emptied into the bottle from within his cuff, a quick sleight of hand. "Cheers, love."

She frowned, set down her fork. "You didn't tell me we came all this way for a trade deal."

"It was a sudden change of plans," he shrugged. "Regarding some new information brought to light in Kalassa."

She paused, mid-drink, uneasiness darkening her features. She took another sip and the door to his cabin swung open. Two of his sentinels, Mitch Romal and Petir Danske, stepped in. He nodded silently to them as Gillian turned in her chair.

Only she wasn't Gillian. Gillian wasn't a real person, and *she* was a liar.

"Boys," she raised her glass in their direction. "Did you want to join us?"

The two men stood stone-still, expressions hard and unreadable.

She turned back towards him, brow furrowing.

"Captain," Danske cleared his throat. "The Lindbarrian Navy approaches. Shall we prepare to be boarded?"

"Tell the men to stand down," Zare nodded, setting down his glass. "They won't give us any trouble."

Her half-empty wine glass fell to the floor with a clatter, rolling away in a trail of red.

"What—"

He turned back to his lover.

"—the hell," she gasped, sucking in a pained breath, "is going on, Zare?"

"It has come to my attention, Gillian," he sighed, "or… I suppose I shouldn't call you that anymore."

She winced, doubling over. He would take the furious glint in her eyes as nothing other than blunt realization. Oh yes, her more feral side would be making an appearance.

"What the hell did you give me?" she lurched forward.

"It has come to my attention, love," he repeated, standing, "that you have been lying to me. For quite some time."

"No—"

"I don't enjoy being lied to, and I certainly don't enjoy being stolen from." He paced around the table.

"I *never* stole from you!" she exclaimed. She tried and failed to stand, the drug taking effect quickly.

He watched her fall to the floor. Funny, how he'd once thought her so beautiful. "It took me longer than I'm proud of to figure out, you know," he continued. "You're clever, I'll give you that."

"You *bastard,*" she snarled, curling her arms around her knees, the poison working exactly as calculated.

"She ought to pass out soon enough," Zare said to his sentinels. "Bind her hands and meet me above deck."

"Yes, Captain."

"I trusted you," Gillian groaned into the floor.

"I should be going, Gill," he said, kneeling beside her to tuck a strand of hair behind her ear. "It's been lovely, really," he said with a wink, leaving her there on the floor.

PART ONE

CHAPTER ONE

She opened her eyes to a dark, unfamiliar room. With a start, she jerked up, head pounding, mouth dry.

Where the hell am I?

Her heart leapt into her throat as she felt the sea undulating beneath her. She was on a ship, yes, but not *her* ship, certainly. Her thoughts were hazy as she squinted into the dim room with dry, itchy eyes. A nagging, jabbing pain in her stomach told her something was most definitely not right.

"What the hell?" she muttered under her breath, voice raspy and hollow even to her own ears.

It took a few tries to peel herself off the floor, and she nearly went over sideways when the ship crested a wave, lurching beneath her. Swallowing, she grabbed the door handle and tugged.

It was locked.

She felt her pulse quicken as it hit her. Where the hell was she? What had Zare gotten her into this time?

With a frustrated grunt, she yanked the handle again, the only fruits of her effort the sound of the bolt clanging against the inside of the lock and a harsh jolt to her shoulder. She stepped back, running a hand through her rat's-nest of hair. *Gods*, she smelled.

Then it came back— the wine, the poison, the crippling pain in her stomach, Zare looking down at her on the floor.

He'd sold her. He'd learned the truth of who she was and sold her to the highest bidder.

"*No*," she muttered to herself, rushing back to the door again, this time bracing a foot on the wall as she tried to wrench the cursed thing open.

Whose ship was she on? Had Zare set her up to take the fall for another of his schemes? For all she knew, she was halfway to Khalim to be sold on the flesh-market.

She gulped down air, trying to clear her thoughts. Panic nearly had her in its grip when someone pounded on the door. Her eyes locked on it as she heard the jangling of keys and she hurled herself to the back of the room, searching for anything that might be a useful weapon. Her hands shook as she pressed her back to the far wall.

The bolt clicked to the side and the door swung open, revealing three men: one well-dressed official, flanked by two well-armed soldiers.

The air was thick and her chest heaved as she tried to catch her breath, her throat raw and dry. Her gaze flitted frantically between the three of them.

"On behalf of the Lindbarrian Royal Navy, welcome aboard His Majesty's Ship, *The Valiant*, Your Highness."

The sea churned violently as the ship raced towards the line on the horizon. They were only minutes from succeeding in dragging her back to the place she'd been running from for years— home.

"We're making excellent time," the primly dressed captain said, tucking his little watch back into his breast-pocket.

"Fancy that," Ferrin said, worrying the skin under her fingernails, unable to be still as the island grew closer.

When she'd awoken, they'd provided her only with a bucket of seawater, a pile of old clothes, and barked, "*clean yourself up, we're nearing land!*"

Whatever drug Zare had spiked her wine with, it had taken a toll on her stomach. Remembering the look on his face had left a bitter taste in her mouth, and she quickly batted away the rising despair in her chest before it could drag her under.

"If you have anything you wish to report to the Navy, it may grant you some form of clemency from punishment," the captain said, turning to her, his chest puffed out.

"And what exactly are you hoping I'll say to that?" She clenched and unclenched her fists before laying her hands on the varnished rail of the ship. "That I'll give up every last detail on the fortifications of Old Orini? That I'll know all of the routes of the Black Trade? Who makes port in Meroya? Unlikely," she scoffed. She may have been sold out by everyone she knew, but that didn't mean she would become a traitor to everyone making a living in the southern pirate ports.

He cut her a stern look. "I was thinking more along the lines of Bourjon outposts in the Meddemara."

She bristled. "Why?"

"Conflict stirs within Bourjony. They test their borders with Efel, and they block our sea-trade at all angles. Some say we'll be at war by summer's end."

She frowned. "What should Bourjony want with Lindbarrow, all the way out here?"

"I thought perhaps in all your travels you'd have learned something of use."

"Well," she huffed. "Terribly sorry to disappoint, I know of no Bourjon outposts north of Khalim."

"Perhaps you spent time on Calixta, learned something of use?"

She shook her head dismissively. She'd spent time on the Bourjon colony of Calixta, yes, but she'd been busy selling contraband liberated from over-funded trade ships.

"His Majesty will not be pleased at that," he said with a *hmph.*

"His Majesty surely has better ways to spend his time than dragging me back from across an ocean," she quipped.

The captain gave her another sidelong glance, shaking his head. "He had the entire crew of the ship you ran away from sent off to Danvery Prison, you know. None were heard from again."

Her grip tightened on the railing, her throat threatening to close.

"Your father is not taking this lightly."

"I know," she swallowed.

"Approaching the harbor, sir!" called out one of the men up in the riggings.

"Looks like we'll be getting you home sooner than expected, Princess Ferrin."

And then, in the final throes of the poison, she heaved her guts over the side of the ship.

Before they docked, the soldiers aboard the ship allowed her back into the tiny little room that had served as her cell on the journey from the south so she could wash up again. Gods forbid she appear unpresentable when they dragged her off the ship under guard.

She looked awful. Her face, paler than usual, was sunken with hunger and dehydration. Her dark eyebrows were grown in, thick and angry. Beneath her mismatched green-and-blue eyes were dark circles, and her black hair was matted and tangled.

She had spent a few days in and out of consciousness, sick out of her mind from the poison or drug or whatever Zare had used to knock her out. Her joints ached, and a thin layer of grime seemed to cover every inch of her freckled skin.

The seawater had done little to help with detangling her hair, and they hadn't thought to provide her with a comb, so she raked her fingers through the knots, trying to make her long, dark hair more presentable. Finally, once it was un-matted, she pulled it back and secured it at the nape of her neck, making the harsh edges of her face even more pronounced. She huffed, releasing the swath of hair and letting it fall back around her face. If she were to choose, she'd rather look like a half-wild creature than a tightly-strung shrew. Growing up, she'd always thought her face too sharp, too angular, and she'd learned that pulling her hair back, as was fashionable, only seemed to emphasize that severe look.

With a resolute sigh, she splashed the cool seawater on her face once more before patting it dry with a cloth rag. She could only keep her mind from returning to the betrayal for so long. Her old clothes lay on the floor in a pile in the corner, each item with a story of its own. The blue shirt she and Ash had picked out at a shop on Corsovena, the breeches Tabka had shown her how to mend. The boots with a hole from the bullet she'd shoved Pierre out of the path of, as it narrowly missed taking a chunk out of her own calf. The necklace Zare had given her a year ago, on the warm shores of a secluded inlet on Tunis.

She hoped the soldiers would just burn them all.

CHAPTER TWO

"Sorry, sorry!" Her new lady-in-waiting, Soviel, winced in the mirror as she dragged a comb through Ferrin's hair.

"It's fine," Ferrin said through gritted teeth as the snarls yanked at her scalp.

"So… how are you feeling about being back? After so many years?"

Soviel was a gentle girl, perhaps a year younger than Ferrin's nineteen. She wore her fine white-gold hair in a neat, simple bun, tied away from her soft-edged face.

Ferrin wasn't sure how much Soviel knew of the circumstances of her return. "Not terribly pleased, if I'm honest."

"Why's that?"

"Well… how much do you know?" She grimaced as Soviel snagged a particularly nasty tangle.

"I've heard some rumors… that you never made it to the university and instead ran off with a crew of pirates."

Ferrin bit her lip. "That about sums it up."

"And I take it… you never planned to return?"

"No. At least," she sighed, "not for a long while."

"I see." Soviel's heart-shaped face twisted in concentration as she pulled the comb over Ferrin's scalp, creating a neat part down the center. Her cream-pale hands shoved half of the dark mass of hair out of the way while she detangled the other side.

Five years ago, before Ferrin had run off, she and Soviel had been friends, and Soviel had visited Everness in the winters. She'd always gone back to her parents' small estate in her homeland of Njorske. She hadn't changed much since then; her almond-shaped damp-earth eyes still exuded a gentle warmth that seemed to put everyone around her at ease, and she still spoke softly, as if trying to soothe a startled fawn.

"How did you manage it? Slipping away from all those soldiers, I mean."

"Stole a lifeboat," Ferrin replied, trying not to think of the fate of those sailors. "Escaped a few miles off the coast of Efel… pre-blockade, of course."

"*Escaped*?" Soviel chuckled. "You make it sound as though you were a prisoner."

"Hmph," Ferrin grunted as she pulled a silk stocking over her knee.

Unprompted, Soviel handed her a ribbon garter. "I suppose it must have been difficult after…" she trailed off, stiffening at the expression on Ferrin's face. "I'm sorry, I only meant if my mother disappeared… well, that it would be awful," she clarified.

"It's alright," Ferrin assured her, the pit in her stomach growing. Ever since her mother had vanished without a trace, and her father had acted as if nothing was wrong, erasing every trace of her… well, she simply wasn't ready to face him.

"Are you nervous?" Soviel asked, almost reading her mind.

"Yes," she admitted.

"Right. Let's talk about something else. How did you manage to find a pirate crew willing to take you on?"

"Well—"

"Let's hope these will fit you!" A young red-haired girl carrying a folded pile of blue fabric swept into the room.

"Ah, this is Nimhe," Soviel introduced, the old-fashioned Caelish name *Neev* rolling in one syllable off her tongue.

"We've met briefly," Ferrin smiled politely at the girl. Another familiar face from before.

"Your Highness," she curtsied. "Here's the dress, and the stays and petticoat."

Soviel took the underpinnings from Nimhe and gestured for Ferrin to turn around so she could be laced into the stays. They were faced with blue silk and trimmed with gold.

"So… how furious is my father?" Ferrin asked Soviel.

"He looked… quite livid." Soviel tucked the cord into the first eyelet of the stays and begun lacing the stiffened garment up Ferrin's back with deft fingers as she spoke.

Ferrin grunted. "Not too tight, I'm still feeling a little ill from the journey."

"Of course," Soviel said, tying off the lacings.

"Here's these," Nimhe said, passing Soviel two layers of skirts to be pulled on and tied around Ferrin's waist.

"Well, after you speak with your father, if you don't want to face the great hall this evening, I'll have your meal sent up to your room and dine in with you."

Gods, she hadn't even thought of that. "Is Rhi home?" she asked.

Soviel shook her head. "He's on a hunting trip. Should arrive back tomorrow morning."

"I'll take dinner in my room then."

Seeing her brother would be bittersweet. On one hand, his presence would make the royal table a thousand times more bearable. On the other, she'd spent the last few years with the growing, gnawing shame of having left him behind.

"And the stomacher," Nimhe said, handing over the stiffened triangle of decorative fabric.

Soviel and Nimhe were in similar positions at the court. Both had relatives who'd been exiled as part of the Unification after the Island War— Or the Barrian Civil War, depending on one's point of view. Their families had been supporters of the Caelish side, fighting against the Lundi occupation. With the arranged marriage of Ferrin's parents, Arabella of the Caels and

Henrik of the Lundis, some twenty years ago, the fighting had ended. Soviel's parents had retreated to their home estate in Njorske, but Ferrin wasn't sure where Nimhe's parents had ended up.

Many children of the exiled were permitted standing at court for the sake of opportunity, Soviel and Nimhe among them. They became ladies-in-waiting, companions, poets, and painters.

"These were sent up as well," Nimhe said, producing a little velvet box. Inside were a pair of gold earrings and a strand of delicate, white pearls. "Should be lovely with your new, sun-touched complexion."

The finery was exquisite.

Exquisite, but false. Veneer and gilt over decades-deep decay.

While the palace itself was adorned in the most beautiful marble and gold, painted delicately with pastorals and lined with crafted tapestries, those who lived in the outlying villages surrounding the capital struggled to maintain their roads, fences and houses. There was only so much an arranged marriage between monarchs could fix.

Finally, she was dressed, bejeweled and polished; the perfect image of what she represented here, the marriageable product of the Unification. *Look, see! Caels and Lundis can get along! Everything here is fair and good!* she mused glibly before tearing her gaze from the mirror. She needed to get out of here before she became trapped in the politics of it all.

"Ready to see your father again?" Nimhe chirped.

"Not in the least," Ferrin groaned.

*   *   *

The walk to the throne room revealed that not much about the castle had change. The most notable difference in decor was the new portrait of her brother hanging in the hall beside her father's. That had once been the place her mother's portrait was displayed, but much like the queen herself, the portrait had vanished.

The white and pink doors of the throne room were still edged in gold, the little blue pockets of sky painted on the ceiling with the cherubs and winged lions were bright as ever, the stone floor polished and spotless.

Some years ago, the older part of the castle had been given a new crust to cover the old bones of the fortress it had once been. Massive funds had been diverted to bring it up to current fashion and standards. Polished silver chandeliers, paneled walls with gold trim, pastel paint, and scenes of divinity rendered on the ceilings. Meanwhile, less than a mile away, the rest of the country rotted around the edges.

Two elegant servants in green velvet coats and perfectly coiffed powdered wigs opened the doors to the throne room, bowing as they did. Ferrin exhaled sharply through her nose as she tried to still her nerves.

Once inside the throne room, standing on the marble tiles in front of her father, her chest tightened. Soviel and Nimhe had left her at the door, and the enormity of everything hit her. She was here, facing the man who had hunted her down across land and sea to drag her back to this place.

Her father stared down at her from the dais as if she were a puddle of spilled ink, a stain on his desk, a bug under his shoe. Something irritating and inconvenient that he couldn't quite decide how to get rid of.

Her stare was unblinking as she watched him, her own rage simmering below the surface. She *hated* him, hated how he'd driven her mother away, how he'd ripped her from the life she'd created and had her dragged back.

She waited, her fists clenched.

Finally, he spoke. "Do you have," he paused with an aggressive exhale, "*any* idea of the severity of your little excursion?" he spat, color rising in his face as his temper, palpable in the air between them, bubbled up and over. "Do you know the implications— how this reflects on this House, this nation? What message this sends other rulers? My own subjects? To have a child in the royal line run away from school for *five years?*"

"I didn't run away, I never got there," she mumbled under her breath as she fidgeted with the edge of one sleeve, dropping her gaze.

"And to find out, only months ago, that while you were supposed to be studying in the countryside, you were gallivanting across the sea with a criminal!" he continued, his expression melting into something cruel and smug as he added, "of course you trusted him."

Icy rage and pure unadulterated shame twined within her. "I wasn't *gallivanting*." It sunk in just how meaningless her voice was. She'd been made a pawn — traded back and forth between two greed-driven men. That's all she was to them, an expensive bargaining chip.

"You know," her father mused. "It didn't take much for him to give you up. After he contacted Admiral Nash, I was prepared to pay a much higher sum. But he didn't haggle it half as far as he could have."

She said nothing, knowing if she opened her mouth she'd only find herself in more trouble.

"You will be punished for this," his business-like tone returning. "Make no mistake. You can start by helping clean the stables in the mornings. Don't get too comfortable, though." He leaned forward. "If you step out of line once more, I will not hesitate to send you west to the Cliff Hallows, where you can live out your days in quiet contemplation and hard labor. And this time, you'll be sent in a *locked carriage*," he growled.

Her eyes widened in surprise. That was extreme. It had been decades since a member of the royal family had been disowned to a monastic life, and *she* had drowned her own child in the bathtub during a fit of madness.

"But, until I decide the best way to handle this matter, you will stay here as if nothing is wrong. You will do what you are told."

"Fine."

"You'll start stable duties at dawn tomorrow."

"Do whatever you want with me. Ship me off to the damn blockade for all I care, as long as I'm not bringing shame to *your* great name," she snapped. The lump forming in her throat was dangerously close to making her voice break.

She would not wait around while her father picked through foreign princes and nobles to be her unwelcome suitors, she would not wait around to be imprisoned in a nunnery. She was getting out of here. She just needed to figure out how.

*   *   *

That night, Ferrin took Soviel up on her offer to dine in with her. The idea of diving straight into the Great Hall, potentially facing dozens upon dozens of questions and faces of friends and foes alike was too much. She needed at *least* a day before diving into that particular lion's den. Back on *The Gravedigger*, problems had been sorted out face to face, sometimes with fists. In polite society, things were entirely different. Besides, she wasn't sure what rumor her father had decided to circulate about her disappearance, but it couldn't be good.

Worst of all, her stomach still wasn't feeling right. Whatever she had been poisoned with had made a mess of her insides.

When she returned to her rooms, Ferrin was hot with rage and holding back tears. Soviel took one look at her, disappeared and came back twenty minutes later with half a loaf of bread, a bottle of wine and a dish of chocolates.

"You might be a fortune-sprite," Ferrin laughed when Soviel set the items down on the table.

"Dinner will be brought up within a half hour," nodded Soviel, uncorking the bottle and pouring the wine into one of the glasses.

"Thanks," Ferrin said, taking the glass from Soviel, who then filled the second.

"Cheers." Soviel clinked her glass to Ferrin's and they sat, the chocolate truffles between them on the table. Soviel had a sweet, nurturing way about her that Ferrin was sure won her friendships easily. This evening, her pale hair was pulled back and up into a loose knot, showing off a pair of dainty pearl earrings.

"Oh, that's good," Ferrin said, taking a swig.

"Swiped it from the dining room before it got too busy," said Soviel, with a wicked twinkle in her eye.

"Thieving, now?" Ferrin asked with a wry grin, "I see I'm not the only one who's changed since the days of playing faeries in the courtyard."

"Alas, it's true. When I'm not helping you to dress, I am a highwayman," Soviel joked, looking over her glass.

"*Highwayman*? Nonsense. Run away and become a pirate," Ferrin said with a laugh that didn't quite reach her eyes.

"You never did finish telling me how you made it onto a vessel," Soviel said, tipping her glass to her lips.

"Cut my hair, stole some breeches from one of the smaller sailors on the ship, escaped," Ferrin shrugged as she took a small bite of bread, testing herself for more nausea. "I sold my jewelry once I got to a small town, and pocketed the coin. Worked on a pig farm a few weeks while ducking into taverns at port until I found someone willing to bring me further south, then found a crew willing to take me on."

The servants arrived with two platters of roasted potatoes, buttery asparagus, and sliced chicken.

"You disguised yourself as a boy?" Soviel's eyes widened. She probably thought it terribly scandalous and unseemly.

"Well, not the whole time…" Ferrin adjusted her dress. "It was for safety purposes. And only for a few months. The first mate figured out I was a girl and offered me a deal: Help him overthrow the captain and he'd raise my station on the ship."

"And when the rest of the crew found out?"

"A few didn't like it so much at first," Ferrin admitted between bites of chicken. "They learned their lesson, though."

Soviel's eyes bulged again with shock.

"Women on pirate crews aren't as rare as you might think. There was another girl on the ship a bit later. Ash."

"Were you friends?"

Ferrin chewed her lip against the hollow pang in her chest. "We were."

"So," Soviel said, cutting into her chicken with delicate grace. "Tell me about the Meddemara. I've never seen anything south of the Veiran border."

"Mm," Ferrin nodded, chewing and swallowing a bite of potato. They were seasoned perfectly. "*Warm*. The whole year long it's like summer. It's windy, but not in the bone-chilling way it is here. There're little ports everywhere, and they're all different. And there's so much trade going on that you can get almost anything at any port," she recalled fondly. "And the water is so blue. Like a sea made of jewels. And so much food and drink of all flavors— seafood, fresh fruits, Meroyan rum that you can drink right out of a coconut."

"Out of a nut?"

"A really big nut. It's more like a fruit," Ferrin explained.

Soviel's eyebrows shot up. "So… how come you're back now?"

Ferrin exhaled, feeling her mood deflate. "It's a long story."

"Someone recognized you, then?" Soviel wondered.

"No. Someone betrayed me. I'd really rather not speak about it now."

"Oh, I'm sorry. I didn't mean to bring it up."

"It's alright," sighed Ferrin, determined to leave it at that. She was in no mood to relive her relationship with Zare out loud. She'd done quite enough of that in her own head ever since her father had divulged how little it had taken for Zare to hand her over.

Her heart sank as Ash crossed her mind again. Ash, with her big heart and wicked sense of mischief. Ash, who'd been her best friend in the world. Had she been complicit in Zare's betrayal? Had she taken coin in agreement to sell Ferrin out? The thought sent her mood plummeting once more. Time for a change of subject. "How have things been here? Has anything strange happened?"

"Well," Soviel began, "things are tense, to say the least. Efel continues to buffer us from Bourjony, but it's no secret that full-on war with the Bourjons is on the horizon. In the next five years, certainly." She paused to take another sip of wine. "And things are not helped by the growing disparity between the poor and the nobility. To say nothing of the tension between the Caels and the Lundis."

"My mother would have stopped that from happening if she was still here," Ferrin frowned.

"There's more rules and laws and regulations that seem to affect Caelish businesses disproportionately. It's *Kraushiik*."

Soviel's annunciation of the guttural, sharp syllables of the Veiran curse word took Ferrin by surprise. She was fairly sure the word meant something like *nonsense*. Ferrin shook her head. Things had been strained when she left, but not like that. Or maybe she simply hadn't been paying close enough attention.

Some eleven-hundred years ago or so, she'd learned from her old governess, the tribes of Lundo, a region snuggled between what were now the nations of Efel and Bourjony, had been driven from their land. They'd found themselves on the shores of the Barrian Isle, which was inhabited by several tribes of its own. Those tribes eventually gathered into one, and that formed the initial ancestry for those of Caelish descent.

Eventually, as most peoples do, the two groups, the Lundis and Caels, clashed and fought over land. For hundreds of years they split the island in half, the Lundi tribes in the south, and the Caels in the north, divided by Mairan's Wall. From that point on the conflict had ebbed and flowed from eras of long-lasting peace to bloodshed and back again. The issue was always the same: Who's island was it?

The conflict dragged on for so long that it seemed the gods — even Strata herself, who had so long smiled on the Caelish people— were turning away. Both sides were decaying. So finally, the Unification was achieved, and the last bloody, violent push between the two peoples was renamed 'The Barrian Civil War'. To deter any further conflict, a handful of people from both sides were exiled or executed.

"If things keep going the way they're going, Bourjony will have little trouble overpowering our people — they'll all be too busy fighting each other," Soviel said mournfully, as she crossed her arms.

"I wish my father would *understand* that," Ferrin said. If her mother was still here, she was sure things would never have deteriorated so.

Soviel went on to detail some of the worse, newer laws: Those found guilty of treason to the Unified Lindbarrian Kingdom would have their property seized and given over to the crown and the military. And from there the witch hunt had begun, more and more crops, livestock, businesses and land had been seized from supposed traitors and seditionists. Though the war was long over, it seemed it was still easy to sniff out rebels when their capture benefitted those in power.!

CHAPTER THREE

Sometime in the night, Ferrin awoke with a start. Perhaps it was the lack of motion— when did the sea become so still? Or perhaps it was the cool, wet breeze coming through her open window. Shouldn't it have been warmer? A tree branch scraped the windowpane.

She couldn't place where she was as she came out of the haze that sleep had left. Somewhere ashore, perhaps inland?

At last the clouds rolled out of the way, parting like dreary curtains in the *Drama Macabre,* and the moon and stars took their places, illuminating her bedroom at Everness Castle. Then she remembered — they'd brought her home. Dragged her here against her will. And Zare…

Something moved in the dim light, materializing out of the dark corner of her room and coming to stand beside her bed. She blinked and he came into focus. Lidded silver-blue eyes flashed above her, brown hair with a glint of copper, a knife-sharp smile.

"Zare?" she croaked. Her throat was dry as sandpaper.

"Shh," he crooned softly, gazing into her face in that affectionate way he had, assessing her state. Slowly, he dragged the back of his knuckles gently down the side of her face in a familiar gesture, then cupped her chin.

"Is it morning?" she asked, unable to break his gaze. There was something she was supposed to remember.

"It's time to go," he whispered, leaning in close. His mouth slanted over hers, sensual at first and then claiming, possessive, smothering. That nagging feeling grew inside her and she turned her head away.

She moved to put her hand up between them, to push him away, ask what was going on, but she found she could not move.

Slowly, he brought his hand from her chin down to her neck, where he wrapped his palm over her throat and squeezed. She tried to scream, tried to pry his hands away from her neck, but she was completely paralyzed, completely helpless…

She gasped as her eyes flew open to the sound of the rooster crowing and the light of day on the horizon.

*   *   *

The stable doors were already open when Ferrin arrived, but upon entry, the barn appeared to be completely empty of humans. The sun was just peeping over the horizon to the east, and the golden light of early morning spilled over the concrete floor of the barn, casting her shadow long as she crossed the threshold. The gentle sound of animals moving about kept the air from growing too still.

"You're late," a familiar voice said from a half-open stall door. It was lilting and gruff, and she couldn't quite place it.

As she stepped in the direction of the door, Ferrin was nearly knocked over by a big, dark shape — a horse who'd poked his curious head out of his stall. "Oh, hello there." She gently patted him on the nose before continuing down the hallway. "Uh, sorry I'm late — I overslept," she explained as she tried to figure out who's voice she was hearing.

"Glad to see you back, Ferr." The man stepped out of the stall and leaned the pitchfork he was holding against the wall.

"Alick!" she blurted as he pulled off his dirty gloves and embraced her in a bear hug. His dark hair was greying into salt and pepper, as was his beard. The slightly rosy complexion he'd always had was unchanged, and his dark green eyes were crystal clear as he squeezed her shoulder. "I'm surprised you're *only* this late. Your mum always joked that you slept like the dead," he snorted.

"Here I am," she said sheepishly. "Reporting for duty."

Alick had been her mother's childhood friend. When Arabella had married Henrik, she'd brought an entourage of people with her from her home, including Alick, who'd been a young blacksmith.

"It's good to see you, lass," he grinned.

A calm, safe feeling that she didn't know had been missing warmed her chest.

"Well, don't just stand there," he waved his hand at her as he stepped back into the stall. "Go get a pitchfork and start on the opposite row. I hope you remember how to muck a stall," he teased.

She did as instructed and grabbed a pitchfork. As she hauled a rusty wheelbarrow into the stalls, she was greeted with a variety of reactions from each occupant. Some offered a gentle headbutt, some sniffed at her with curiosity, and others completely ignored her. When she was a little past halfway finished with the row, she entered a stall that housed a gentle mare. Her grey, dappled coat looked like raindrops on a windowpane.

"Hey there, girl," Ferrin ran a hand over her side.

"That's Aster, retired championship jumper," Alick told her on one of his trips down the aisle.

"Retired?"

"Lord Nalmont is her owner — he's got a breeding program for Fairbreds."

"Oh," Ferrin nodded, looking back at the mare. She was an expensive horse. Fairbreds ran the elaborate jumping races in

Corsovena every summer. Ferrin herself had been party to many a ruse among those betting pools. "She's a beauty."

"Take her out for a ride later, the girl could use some exercise. I'll count it towards your duties here," he said with a wink.

"It's been a *long* time…" Ferrin shook her head. There'd been a time when she thought of nothing *but* horses and riding. She'd been competitive and driven and pretty damn good. But that was years ago.

"Don't worry yourself, you won't have forgotten how to ride," reassured Alick, resting his arms on the ledge of the stall door. "Finish up the row and take a break to eat."

After a few more trips to the waste-dump to empty the wheelbarrow, she was finally finished. When she returned, Alick was sitting on the edge of the concrete step with a loaf of bread in a checkered cloth balanced on one knee. He ripped off half and held it out to her.

"I should wash my hands first," she said, examining her palms. They were *filthy*. At least she still had good callouses from the ship. The morning's work would have left unworked hands raw and shredded.

"Water pump is out to the left," he jerked his thumb in its direction.

When she returned, she took the hunk of bread from him and devoured it. The ache from hours of shoveling was already seeping into her shoulders, and she knew she'd be *beyond* sore tomorrow.

"So," Alick began, ripping another bite of bread off and popping it into his mouth. "You gonna tell me what happened? Or were you just gonna eat my breakfast?"

"Sorry," she mumbled, her mouth full of bread. "I didn't realize I was so hungry."

He shook his head with a laugh. "How bad must it be that the *princess* is put on stable duty? Aren't your punishments supposed to be more domestic? Regal?"

"Not this time," she laughed, trying not to think about her father's threats.

"He must be livid, then," Alick nodded, raising his eyebrows knowingly.

"He better get over it or get on with it," she grumbled. "He'll probably try to foist me off on an advantageous suitor before he resorts to sending me to the Cliff Hallows, though."

Alick nodded. "So…" he said, "I've heard a few different stories. Tell me what *really* happened." His tone was earnest and gentle.

"Well…" she began, fidgeting as she told him the same parts of the story she'd told Soviel. "The first mate figured out I was a girl after a while, and we, along with about a dozen others, mutinied. He took the captaincy, and eventually made me first mate." Ferrin shook her head. Poor Captain McGidrew, she now realized in hindsight, had been another victim of Zare's manipulation. The night they'd taken the ship had been calm, and under the cover of night and the moonless sky, they had snuck into the captain's cabin. Zare had tied him up, and Ferrin had never been clear about what exactly had happened to old McGidrew. She'd been so blinded by Zare's charm, and his interest in her that she'd barely stopped to question things. Shame crept up the back of her neck.

Alick listened quietly, allowing her to continue.

"Then, they found out who I was and ransomed me to my father," she said, her voice tightening.

Alick nodded, expression forlorn.

"So," she said abruptly, anxious to change the subject, "When did you get promoted to stable master?"

Alick turned and looked at her, as if examining what she'd become. His expression softened and he turned back to his bread. "A few years ago. The last one was a drunk and I found myself doing his duties in addition to my own as groom and farrier. When your father realized it, he gave me the job."

"Really?" she snorted derisively. "That's progressive of him. Wasn't the last one some handpicked favorite of the nobility?"

"Yes, but he was costing them a lot in damages and loss of property. We never found two of the horses that got out while he was indisposed."

Ferrin grimaced. The horses had likely been eaten by something in the forest — most times, the animals came home after an impromptu frolic, back to where fresh food and shelter awaited them.

"Ready to get back to it?" Alick stood and dusted off his hands.

"Sure," Ferrin agreed. "What's next?"

*   *   *

They spent the rest of the morning bringing the horses out to their assigned paddocks, which reached far back on the land surrounding the castle. As the sun climbed higher in the sky, they brought feed around to the stalls and paddocks and refilled water troughs as needed. Alick gave her a tour of the stable property and a brief lesson on how to close up for the night if she was the last one there. She was hoping he'd mention where the keys were kept so she might sneak back in and make her escape on horseback, but he didn't bring it up, and she didn't want to draw suspicion. At the end of her shift, they'd gone on a brief ride through the woods, taking the horses on a peaceful loop past the stream.

When the day's work was done, Ferrin was sore from ass to ankle. It had been years since she'd ridden, and clearly the muscles used to muck stalls were different from those used to hoist sails. She felt like she'd been trampled by every horse in the barn.

With a grunt, she flopped down on her bed, dusty, dirty clothes and all.

Though it still stung, being busy in the stables all day had distracted her from thinking too long about Zare. A day of hard work had made her feel incrementally better, at least on the inside.

She decided to rest her eyes for just a moment before planning her escape.

*　　*　　*

When she awoke to a gentle knock on the door, it was dark out. She bit back a curse. She hadn't meant to fall asleep for so long.

There was another knock on the door. "Your Highness?" It was Nell, the chambermaid.

"Come in, Nell!" Ferrin called.

The woman bustled in, a bundle of soft fabric in her hands. "I'll run the bath for you. I've brought fresh towels."

"Thank you," Ferrin said gratefully, shifting onto her elbows on the bed. She was unused to someone waiting on her, and it felt awkward to do nothing.

Once she was out of the bath and dried off, she slipped into the clean shift Nell had brought her and tied the patterned dressing gown around her waist before combing out her hair.

Soviel and Nimhe arrived minutes later, each carrying a big box.

"Oh, no, *what* is in there?" Ferrin groaned.

"A dress for dinner," Nimhe said.

Soviel shot her an apologetic look.

"I'm not hungry," Ferrin lied. She was starving. But she'd rather hide in her room than head into the wolf's den.

"Well, it's an order from the king…" Nimhe said in her clear, loud voice.

"Well, why don't you tell the king to shove it where the Northern Vampires could survive," Ferrin grumbled.

Nimhe squinted in confusion.

"You know, *where the sun doesn't shine*," Soviel explained to Nimhe, referencing the age-old myth.

"Thanks," Ferrin smirked, grimacing in pain as she plopped herself into the vanity chair. "Alright, fine. I won't have you two getting in trouble over me not wanting to go to dinner. Do your worst," she closed her eyes and put out her arms, submitting.

Over the next thirty minutes she was brushed, powdered, tweezed, bejeweled and shoved into all the appropriate underpinnings that went with the bright blue silk dress. This one had white lace at its wide square neckline and matching flounces at its elbow-length sleeves. The skirt was drawn up and tied with tapings into a fashionable puff.

"One last touch…" Soviel said cautiously, as she took out the last box.

"No. Absolutely not, that has to be a lark," Ferrin said as she saw the box.

"Your father ordered it," Soviel winced.

"He also spoke of disowning me, I hope he makes up his mind."

"It's only a piece of jewelry."

"No, it's a *crown*."

"Technically, it's a diadem," Soviel said as she tipped the box open. The white gold glinted with pearls and diamonds as she carefully removed it from the velvet pillow.

Ferrin's mother had been painted in this crown. It was from the Caelish collection. What game was her father playing by making her wear this?

"Fine," she growled.

Soviel placed it on her head, positioning the little combs in place. The cold metal pinched the sides of her head. In the mirror she looked an even further cry from Gillian the Pirate. She looked like a portrait of Lindbarrian royalty, almost like her mother.

"And… there," Nimhe finished, dabbing perfume across Ferrin's collar bones. "You look perfect."

"Thanks," Ferrin said distantly, taking in her reflection.

"Ferrin, there's something else you should know, before you go down there," Soviel said, her voice edged with stress.

"What is it?" She swiveled from the mirror to face Soviel.

"It's your father, he," she paused, as if searching for the words. "He's remarried. A couple of years ago."

Ferrin jolted to a stop. He'd remarried. He'd given up on Arabella ever returning. Her pulse ratcheted up and her throat went dry. "Oh," she said weakly.

"I meant to mention it earlier, it just slipped my mind. I didn't want you to find out at dinner tonight." Soviel shook her head.

"Thank you," Ferrin said, feeling a thousand miles away once more.

Soviel nodded and gave her shoulder a squeeze. "Let's get you down to dinner. I'm told the Lady Denison has returned from school on the continent and is being honored with a toast for her accomplishments on horseback."

Ferrin felt a pang of annoyance, drawing her out of her spiraling thoughts. Before she'd run away, she had competed in many equestrian events, and Denison had been her sworn rival from age eleven on. Though they'd been friends before, the constant competition had turned their girlhood friendship bitter.

CHAPTER FOUR

The finely dressed servants gave a well-rehearsed bow before opening the filigreed double-doors to the Great Hall in perfect unison. As she entered the room, Ferrin halted momentarily, glancing down the wide hall of tables with caution. She was still off balance after hearing Soviel's revelation of her new step-mother.

Her brother caught her attention first. According to Soviel, he'd just come back from a week-long hunting trip. Rhi was laughing and chatting with a red-faced man in blue who was clearly in his cups. His brown-black hair, the same shade as her own, was tamed and tied neatly at the back of his head, and his chocolate-brown eyes were warm as he conversed with those around him. It wasn't unlike him to float around the dining room, greeting and conversing with people at all the tables rather than just at the royal table, which rested on a raised plat-form at the far end of the hall, perpendicular to the others. He stood from where he'd been speaking with the sanguine man, bronze goblet in hand, and looked as if he were going to contin-ue mingling before he caught sight of her. A wide grin lit up his handsome face as his eyes locked on her, *"Ferrin!"*

She met him halfway down the aisle and he wrapped his arms around her, picking her up in a crushing embrace. He was taller than he'd been the last time she saw him, and had grown out of any youthful gawkiness he'd had. Just two years older than her nineteen, he'd become a fine young man.

"Oof. Can't breathe," she wheezed.

"I've missed you!" He gave her shoulder a squeeze as he set her down. "You're all grown up, you little mushroom."

"I was grown up the last time I *saw* you!" she smacked his arm lightly. Then, with a smile, she admitted, "And, I missed you too."

"Yeah, but now you're really grown up. We'll probably be sending you off to some Dromatan War Lord's harem soon," he joked as they walked together to the royal table.

Ferrin choked, and for a moment considered letting it go. "You know, Dromata hasn't allowed its rulers to keep harems for decades now," she said as she slid into her seat. "Though, I can't say the same for the *popava* lords. But they seem to operate outside the law."

A hint of astonishment crossed Rhi's face as he looked back at her. "You really *are* grown up," he squinted, furrowing his brow. "Tell me more."

She was taken aback by his interest, but she supposed she shouldn't have been surprised. Rhi loved people. He knew how to listen, and converse, and just *be* in a way that made others feel important and seen. No matter who. He loved to learn about how other people lived all around the world.

Rhiach kept her talking about the Dromatan system of governing, their cities at the edge of the desert and more. It wasn't until the second course had been served that she realized he was keeping her distracted so she couldn't fret over people staring, and was keeping her engaged in conversation so no one would approach and bombard her with questions.

By the time the servants came around to refill the wine a second time, their conversation had drawn to a close, and at last, a dainty *ahem* caught Ferrin's attention.

To the left of the king, who still hadn't acknowledged Ferrin's presence, sat the Lady Denison, tonight's guest of honor. While Denison wasn't high-ranking in title, she did come from one of the wealthiest, if not *the* wealthiest family on the isle. She was a picture of polished perfection in her cream-gold gown. Her golden-blonde hair was curled and coiffed into a fashionable high roll, showing off her big pearl earrings and matching necklace. How she could hold her neck so straight with all that hair piled on top of her head was a mystery to Ferrin. Her complexion was rosy and doll-like in its blushiness, and her big caramel-brown eyes were doe-wide under her groomed eyebrows. To Ferrin's dismay, her old rival had not grown ugly in the last years; if anything, she'd grown more poised and lovely.

"I see you're back from your… vacation," Denison said, her smile far too pleasant.

"Hello, Lady Denison," Ferrin greeted, offering her best courtly smile. "I see you are tonight's guest of honor, does that mean you've enjoyed many victories in the saddle in my absence?"

Denison's bristled expression was barely perceptible. "Well, none of my competitors are any match for you, *Your Highness*. Though I wonder, are you still as skilled as you were when you were younger?" She tilted her head innocently and Ferrin's blood boiled.

"Perhaps we'll have a chance to find out," Ferrin replied curtly.

From the corner of her eye, she could see where Soviel and Nimhe sat below. Soviel met her eyes and pulled a face as if she'd eaten something sour, and stuck her tongue out at Ferrin, who returned an ugly grimace of her own. Soviel quickly composed herself as the gentleman sitting next to her turned back from his food to finish their conversation. Ferrin stifled her giggle.

She wished she could go sit down there instead.

When she looked back to Rhi, he had twisted around in his chair, speaking to a hooded figure who had seemingly appeared out of thin air in between courses.

They finished speaking and Rhi returned his attention to the table as the hooded man retreated, vanishing through a sliding wall panel.

"What was all that about?" asked Ferrin, ablaze with curiosity.

"Oh, just a friend. A personal Tradesmaster, you might say," Rhi explained with a coy smile.

"*Tradesmaster*?" she repeated. "What on earth for?"

"This and that," Rhi shrugged, clearly amused.

Ferrin nodded and looked out at the room. It was nearly time for dessert, and she was ready to make up for all the days of retching up her guts. She caught sight of Soviel again, who was now talking with a couple, lesser nobles, if Ferrin was correct, who owned a small farming estate just a few miles outside of the capital. They were both middle-aged and dressed in very well-coordinated shades of blue and green. Nimhe had disappeared from the table, but then Ferrin noticed her returning from the outside hall.

At last, dessert was brought forth: a creamy, eggy, golden cake with berry-preserve filling and a sugary glaze poured over the top. No chocolate in sight, but nonetheless, Ferrin helped herself to three pieces. Halfway through the third, she realized she could not fit anything else in her stomach without having to rip off her stays.

The seat to the king's right had remained empty throughout the meal — when was she to lay eyes on this mysterious woman who'd apparently swept in and married her father?

As if on cue, the wide doors were thrown open and every chair in the room scraped the floor as the crowd scrambled to stand. A woman crossed the threshold. Her black hair was swept up and back, off of her porcelain face, and her midnight-blue and gold jacquard dress swished as she walked gracefully down the central aisle, every step assertive as she ascended straight up to the royal table. Up close, Ferrin recognized the circlet of gold and sapphires woven into her hair. Her eyes were as light blue as a frozen mountain lake, and a little freckle punctuated the smooth skin below her left eye.

What happened next had Ferrin white-knuckling her fork. The woman stooped, kissed Ferrin's father on the cheek, and sat herself down in the chair beside him.

*   *   *

That night, as soon as the door shut behind Soviel and Nimhe, Ferrin sprung out of bed, flinging the covers to the floor. The candle, which she'd left lit to read by, offered more than enough light to dress in the clothes she'd worn to the stables, which had already been cleaned and dried for tomorrow.

She flung her nightshift onto the bed and laced up her boots before grabbing the beaten-up green coat from the back of her armoire. It was one of Rhi's from years ago that she'd borrowed and never given back. Once, it had been loose and awkward. Now, it fit perfectly.

She shrugged it on and shoved her small coin purse into a pocket before dropping to the floor by her bed. With a little effort and a push in the right place, the floorboard she'd loosened a decade ago popped loose. The long, sheathed hunting knife was still there. Of course, it had gone dull long ago, but it was better than nothing. She strapped it to her hip.

Tonight, she was getting out of here. Before she could get sucked back into her old life, or worse, be confined to a temple for the rest of her days. Ferrin tried not to think about the new queen, about how eerily she resembled her own mother. She didn't want to think about what it might mean.

She let out a sigh of relief when she found the hallway deserted. She'd half-expected there to be guards ready to bar her from leaving her rooms. The hallway was quiet, considering it was not yet midnight, and only the flicker of the oil lamps moved in the still night.

She tiptoed through the hallways to the stairwell. She wasn't foolish enough to believe there wouldn't be guards at the front doors, so she'd have to settle for climbing down from the second story. The night was pitch-black. When she reached the ground, she waited for her eyes adjust to the moonlit exterior of the castle before striding off towards the barn.

The early spring air chilled her face as she jogged past the field house and past the apple orchard, at last reaching the withering oak tree where she had long ago hidden a key to the stables. When she dislodged the cobblestone from its roots, she swore. The key was gone.

She should have expected that.

"Damn it," she cursed under her breath and sat back on her heels. Who could have known it was there? She paced a moment, wracking her brain. How was she supposed to leave this place behind without a horse?

She checked under the brick by the door, which seemed foolishly obvious. As expected, there was nothing. At last, she walked to the side of the barn by the central window and craned her neck to peer under the eave. Nothing.

"Shit," she rubbed the back of her head in frustration, then ran a hand along the tall ledge under the eave. Something cool and metal brushed her fingers and a grin spread across her face as they closed around what was unmistakably a key.

Restraining herself from crying out in victory, she took it from the ledge and returned to the barn door, where she inserted the key into the lock. Before she even had a chance to turn it, she felt something hard and metal on her shoulder.

The tip of a sword.

"Stop right there." The voice was low and deep and all hard edges.

Ferrin let go of the key and slowly spread her hands.

"Who are you?" he demanded.

She closed her eyes, trying to steady her racing pulse and breathing as she braced herself for the inevitable. Whoever this guard was, he'd recognize her, and turn her in to her father, and she'd be on her way to the Cliff Hallows by dawn.

"Turn around," he commanded. "Slowly."

"I'm *just* trying to—"

"Shut it. I said turn around." The flat of his blade was insistent on her shoulder.

Exhaling deeply, she turned and straightened her back, and got her first look at the man who was holding her up.

He *wasn't* a guard. In fact, he wore no uniform, just nondescript dark clothes. Plain, but of high quality. The lantern light revealed dark brown hair, thick and curly and pulled back in a knot, leaving his face in full view. His skin was a warm honey-brown, almost gold in the firelight. He was handsome in a coarse, unvarnished way, with two-day stubble on his jaw, and that fearsome look he'd fixed her with.

To her surprise, no flicker of recognition crossed his face.

"Who are you, and *what* are you doing stealing my spare key to the stable?" he asked angrily.

He had no idea who she was. It took effort for Ferrin not to let out an enormous sigh of relief. "I'm a relative of the horsemaster's," she answered.

"And?"

"I was only visiting. Have to be getting home tomorrow."

"Oh, really? Where's home?" he asked, as if testing her.

Her mind went completely blank, as if every map she had ever looked at had melted into one big, unlabeled mess. "Uh, I'm from—"

"Right," he said, a smug, self-satisfied grin beginning to take shape on his lips. "Why leave so late? Seems suspicious to me."

"I meant to leave earlier in the day, back to Lochdale, you know," she said, trying to play it off casually. Lochdale was where she'd claimed to hail from when she'd been Gillian. It was perhaps a few hours ride. "I got caught up. If I could just get my horse, I'll be out of your way."

"Really, which horse is yours? I was here earlier and I didn't see any new boards."

"Dandy," she bluffed.

"Dandy belongs to Duke Hadringston of Bramblehall and has been here training for over a year."

She cursed inwardly. This man just had to know *everything*.

"Look, just let me leave on foot, you can have your key back. I'm sorry."

"So you can double back and break in?" He laughed derisively. "Not likely, sweetheart. Besides, you're a suspicious, unaccompanied civilian walking around the palace at night who won't say who she is. For all I know, you're a Bourjon spy."

Her eyes went wide, and she was about to tell him who she really was, if only to wipe that smug expression off his face. But then it occurred to her, "Wait. *You're* a suspicious unaccompanied civilian," she said, looking pointedly at his unmarked clothing. "How do I know *you're* not a Bourjon spy?"

"I'm under orders from the crown," he replied curtly.

She froze completely.

"I know," he said, seeming to ponder his next move. "I'll bring you down to the barracks, and tell my good friend in the Guard *all* about how I found you attempting to break into the stables in the middle of the night, and let him decide what to do with you."

"You don't want to do that. Please," she beseeched him.

"Oh, don't I?"

"Truly, it will only end horribly for both of us, I assure you."

He slowly lowered his sword, narrowing his eyes and assessing her as he asked, "who are you?"

"No one important," she promised, eyeing the blade as she backed a half step away.

He lowered the sword the rest of the way, apparently deeming her no threat. "Consider yourself lucky I didn't catch you with a stolen horse. Now go back to wherever you came from."

She laughed drily at that.

"Get out of here before I change my mind," he said, quickly glancing to his right. What was he anticipating?

She backed away another step, eyeing him suspiciously. He seemed awfully keen to get her away from here, and her curiosity was burning. She opened her mouth to ask what was going on, a truly unwise decision, she realized. He shot a pointed, expectant glare at her as if to ask, *Why aren't you running*?

"Fucking bastard," she muttered not-so-quietly as she turned and began to jog back to the castle.

"Back at you!" he called after her.

She knew she'd have a chance at finding a horse below in the village, but after her narrow escape, she didn't want to push her luck. She'd just have to try again tomorrow.

By the time she returned to her hallway, it was well after midnight. She slowed her pace from a jog to a fast-paced walk, and as she rounded the corner by her rooms, she nearly collided with a girl who was stumbling down the hall in a bright orange gown.

"Sorry," the girl muttered. Her eyes were half open and glazed as they settled on Ferrin. "Your Highness," she slurred as she sketched a pitiful bow that nearly sent her tumbling before she carried on down the hallway.

Ferrin raised her eyebrows. She'd always known Rhiach to prefer men, but perhaps there was a different explanation for why a fancily-dressed young woman was leaving his rooms in the middle of the night. She paid it no mind, and let herself back into her rooms, not bothering to change out of her clothes before flopping into bed. She'd be cleaning the stables in the morning anyway.

CHAPTER FIVE

The days went on much the same, and by the end of the week Ferrin hadn't gotten better at waking up before the sun. Her attempts at escape had been halted for now, as she really didn't want to get Alick in trouble for a missing horse, but that didn't mean she'd given up.

When she rolled out of bed, the sun was leaking through the trees in dim, pale swaths as the rooster crowed and continued to do so for far longer than seemed necessary. She was going to be late again.

Dawn was in full swing as she rounded the corner of the field house, so she broke into a jog as the sun appeared over the tree line and she was standing on the concrete barn floor not a second before the eastern sunlight touched the steps.

"Ha!" she cried, pointing gleefully at the light cast on the stones. "I'm on time!"

"Barely," Alick shot her a pointed glare from the office before sliding his wire-framed reading glasses off his nose. "You'll get used to the early hours."

"I hope so, this is already wearing me down. And it's only been three days," she moaned. She crossed her arms and leaned on the doorway, then winced and straightened when the pointed edge dug into one of her sore muscles.

"Maybe you aren't drinking enough water," he said contemplatively, then clapped his hands together in front of him. "Well, these stalls won't clean themselves. Get to work, kid."

She rolled her eyes as she turned to procure a wheelbarrow, grumbling, "You are *way* too cheerful for this hour."

"I see you are not a morning person," Alick fell into stride beside her.

"No, and I got *no* sleep," she rubbed her eyes.

"Ah, I thought I heard something about a late-night revel that was to take place in the royal wing. How was it?"

"What?" Ferrin asked, then remembered the drunken girl she'd seen staggering out of Rhi's rooms in the wee hours a few nights ago. Maybe it was a regular occurrence.

"Yeah, I heard some of Nalmont's trainers talking about it early yesterday evening."

"Well, no one invited *me*," Ferrin said, crinkling her nose. She'd been up late reading. "So, what's the plan for today?"

"Same as yesterday morning, then breakfast, then some of the tack needs cleaning, then I'm going to put Kela on the lead rope. You can sit in if you want," he said with a grin.

"Sure!" She perked up at that.

"Great. I'll fetch you from the tack room before I go in."

She started on the stalls, and ached every time she squatted or lifted a particularly full pitchfork-load, but once she fell into a rhythm her sore muscles were easy enough to ignore. She finished up her side of the hallway a little after Alick, and then they set about refilling water buckets and bringing all the horses out to their paddocks for the day. A cloud cover had rolled in around midmorning and blotted out any trace of the golden light of dawn.

They took a respite to eat and Ferrin grabbed the cloth-wrapped bundle she'd requested Nimhe fetch her yesterday.

"I brought some croissants," she said, extending the bundle to Alick.

He eyed the package and let out a low whistle, "You're not trying to bribe your way out of cleaning tack, are you?"

"What? No!" she cried. "You let me eat half your bread the other day, so I figured I'd repay the favor."

"Well, aren't you nice," he said, as he unwrapped the parcel, unadulterated glee consuming his face as he saw that they were *ham* stuffed croissants. "Oh, you've done it now."

He handed her one of the croissants and picked one up himself, biting into the buttery, flaky layers. "That is good," he groaned.

Ferrin giggled as she took a bite of her own croissant, which could only have been better if they were still oven-fresh.

"Right," Alick said, finishing his in a few bites, "finish up and then polish the saddles on the back wall. There's a few tins of leather polish on the shelf just inside the door. Should be some rags, too."

"You got it," she nodded as she shoved the last of the pastry in her mouth.

The tack room only had one high, tiny window, so she lit a candle to set about the task of polishing. The busywork was a welcome distraction. With her escape plan thwarted, she knew she'd have to wait a while to try again, and so far, that had left a surplus of time for *what ifs*? The task of polishing streamlined her chaotic thoughts.

In the time she'd allowed her mind to wander to Zare and everything that had happened, she'd found herself full of rage. But it was not as before, when that anger was directed at her father for buying her back from him, or even for Zare at selling her out.

No. She was furious with herself.

She had never been complacent before, had never allowed someone to have so much control over her. And yet, Zare had wormed his way in with pretty words and soft kisses and she'd flung the door wide open for him. Slowly, bit by bit, he'd worn away at her until she was wrapped around his finger. Shame filled her at what she'd become. What she had *let* herself become.

She snapped out of her thoughts and realized she'd been furiously polishing one spot on the saddle in front of her without moving on to the next area. With a sigh, she rotated it and began on the other side, dabbing the polish onto the cloth and onto the supple leather, burnishing it into the material.

It had been maybe an hour when Alick came to collect her. "Ready to go?"

She looked up, coming out of her daze. "Oh. Yes."

She followed him out of the barn, wiping her stained hands on the front of her pants. Little good it did her; the stuff always took forever to clean off.

They entered the circular arena where Eonan the stablehand was standing, patting Kela gently on the nose.

"All ready to go," the boy said, giving a curt nod of the head.

"Thanks, E," Alick nodded, taking the green lead rope.

The colt was still gangly, but it was clear that in time he would be a magnificent beast. His chestnut coat gleamed, despite the clouds above, as Alick uncoiled the rope, coaxing him into a trot around the circumference of the ring.

Kela made a few loops at a gentle trot, warming up his muscles.

"Here, hold this," Alick said, handing Ferrin the rope.

"Right," Ferrin nodded, focusing on the colt as she pivoted to track his gait around the ring.

"Now, try and see if you can coax him into a canter *without* using the tail of the rope."

She narrowed her eyes on the colt and made a few clicking, smooching sounds with her lips, and soon enough the colt shifted his gait into a canter.

"Not half-bad," Alick said, impressed. "Look at that, he's even on the right lead."

Sure enough, Kela's inside-front leg was leading the three-beat gait.

"I'd like to think I pick these things up quickly," she boasted.

"So I've heard. Sailing, shooting," he grinned, "not to mention embroider—"

She smacked him lightly in the arm. "I'm gods-awful at embroidery and *everyone* knows it."

Somehow, to her great chagrin, the *embroidery incident* had become public knowledge.

"You know, I heard they were going to display—"

"Not another word!" She exclaimed, with an embarrassed laugh. She should have burned that cursed stitching sampler years ago.

There was a knock at the gate.

"Yes?" Alick called. "Here, halt him."

Ferrin obliged, reeling Kela in at a gentle walk.

"Excuse me," a stout man with a timid voice appeared in the doorway. He looked most uncomfortable when his eyes landed on Kela, who was ambling along slowly.

"Hello," Ferrin nodded, the lead rope still clutched in her hands.

"Your Highness, the king requests your presence in the great hall in a half hour," the man stammered, his gaze shifting nervously as Kela approached him, the colt curious at this new visitor.

"Did he say why?"

"No," he stumbled back a step as the colt sniffed him, "no, Your Highness. But you are to wash and change and-and go."

Ferrin gave Alick a puzzled look.

"Alright," she said to the page. "Thank you, I'll be there."

"I'll have Eonan help me finish up here. Go," Alick said, taking the lead rope from her.

"Right, I'll see you in two days, then."

"Good luck!"

*   *   *

A million thoughts raced through Ferrin's head as she sprinted through the castle. What could be *so* important to relieve her of her stable duties halfway through the day?

A horrifying thought dawned on her. Perhaps the mysterious sword-wielding man from the other night had realized who she was and snitched. She felt her throat tighten. Perhaps she was walking right into her own life-sentence to the Cliff Hallows.

Or, she reasoned with herself, perhaps it is just a marriage prospect visiting Rhi.

A visiting suitor always meant a big procession, and much celebration. The visiting nation would bring merchants and dancers and goods to promote the sharing of cultures. Maybe it would be a procession from further south. Aliya, the Akhatan princess, had come of marriageable age recently, and was said to be unrivaled in beauty. Or perhaps it would be a delegation from Kalassa. That would mean good food. Maybe even a visitor from further east, like Veira or Marak. Though since the tension with the Bourjons had heightened, visitors from further east along the continent had stopped venturing out to the coast and islands.

She hoped that was the case, rather than the alternative. Her thoughts soured at what it would mean for Rhi. Though he could tumble whomever he wanted, since even their rigid father knew Rhi preferred men and was fine with it, as the heir to the throne, he was still expected to marry a woman and produce heirs. Progress, it seemed, was only fashionable if it didn't stir up too much change.

That didn't seem fair at all to her.

When Ferrin rounded the corner into her rooms, she nearly collided with Nimhe and they both let out little shrieks of surprise.

"*Strata*, you're in a hurry," Nimhe exhaled, hand on her chest. Steam was pouring out of the washroom.

"We've had Nell run you a bath," Soviel announced as she popped into the room, a big garment box in her arms. "What do you think of the dress?" she asked as she pulled it from the box. There were yards and yards of deep crimson fabric, silk by the looks of it.

"It's *huge!*" Ferrin exclaimed as she stripped off her boots.

"Yeah, that's what these are for," Soviel said, setting down the dress and holding up a set of wire and linen panniers with a wicked smirk.

"I didn't realize we'd be sailing me down to the Great Hall," Ferrin frowned. "That is ridiculous."

"It is to accentuate the hip-to-waist ratio," Soviel wiggled her eyebrows suggestively.

"If anyone *believes* that I have hips four feet across, then our educators have truly failed." She shucked off her coat and the rest of her clothes and hopped into the bath.

"I heard the Duchess Hadringston wears them with three feet on either side. How do you imagine she dances in them?" Soviel asked as she placed a big towel on the table beside the bath.

"Her husband probably can't even reach her."

Ferrin was in and out of the bath in a handful of minutes, and as expected, the leather polish still stained her hands. She folded them in her lap against the fabric of her dressing gown. Soviel wrangled a brush through her hair by the fire, hoping the heat would dry it out in a timely fashion. She hadn't meant to wash it, but after a minute of soaking in the tub she realized it smelled of manure, so under the surface she'd gone.

Once she was brushed out and mostly dry, she pulled on a clean linen shift that rustled against her bare skin, the fabric cool and crisp. They piled her dark hair into a sizable hedgehog roll atop her head, but there was no time to do much else with it. She squeezed her eyes shut as Nimhe applied powder over her freckles. Next she rolled on a pair of silk stockings, clocked at the heel with a little red floral pattern, and tied them with matching red ribbon garters.

"Shoes, then stays," Nimhe said, holding up each item. Ferrin laced herself into the delicate little heeled beige slippers. The blue set of stays she'd worn the day before went on and laced up the back, yanking her spine straight. She hadn't even realized how much she was slouching, but she felt some of the soreness leaving her back as the stays braced her. Next, she pulled on a slim white linen under-petticoat and a set of big pocket bags.

"Arms out," Soviel instructed, shimmying the sleeves of the gown over her arms, then pinning them in place at the front over the gold and cream stomacher. By the end, Ferrin was sure if any more pins were stuck into her clothing, she could fight a wild porcupine and win. The crimson skirts of the gown draped over the panniers and stayed open in the front to reveal the cream and gold pattern on the petticoat beneath, offering fashionable contrast.

"Perfect," Nimhe said, adjusting the pleats of the gown over the hoop skirt.

"Right, we have ten minutes to get you down to the Great Hall," Soviel clapped her hands onto her hips, the light pink fabric of her gown swishing.

"And how do you plan to do that, roll me?"

"Oh, hush," Soviel chided, "it isn't that huge."

"I could fit so many rolls of bread in here," Ferrin said, testing out the opening to reach her hidden pocket bags, "and no one would know."

"Good, take a few for me," Soviel quipped.

*   *   *

Lukas checked his pocket watch. It still didn't give the right time, no matter how many times he'd had it fixed and tinkered with. The funny thing about it was its inconsistency. Some days it ticked forward at a regular pace. Other days it sped along, passing hours in seconds. Today it was going backwards, and fast. It was only minutes from speeding back into the morning hours, even though the sun told him it was far past noon.

He had no idea why he kept the damn thing. He would have probably been best off taking it apart and selling the parts as scrap. But for some reason, he'd hung onto it after it had come to him in a stiff match of cards with a fur-trader from Njorske and a Kalassan apothecarist.

With a sigh, he tucked the senseless thing back into the pocket of his tailored coat and straightened. The clothing he'd chosen for the day was nice, but poorly broken in. He almost never wore court-appropriate attire, and the dark teal coat and matching waistcoat had sat unused in the back of his closet for months now.

Next to him, Prince Rhiach looked bored and distant. According to his sources, the royal family was holding some ridiculous court today to impress the wealthy prospects visiting not just one, but both royal children, though Rhi's mysterious sister had not yet arrived.

Lukas had never seen the princess, as he'd only begun doing work for Rhi *after* her notorious departure. He'd heard plenty of rumors surrounding her apparent alter-ego, Gillian, though.

Today, he would stand in as Rhiach's personal guard, which put him front and center for the festivities. It wasn't how he usually spent his time. When he wasn't procuring this or that for Rhi, he was running other odd errands in the shadows. If you needed something illegal brought into the country, he was the one you asked. Lukas could get you just about anything — for a price.

Just a few nights ago, in fact, he had been preparing to make a drop for the horsemaster when he'd heard noises at the stable door. He'd been sure the Royal Watch was going to bust him with about ten kinds of illegal items on his person, but it had just been some girl trying to break into the stables for gods-knew-what.

At last, the doors to the Great Hall swung open and a young woman in lavish red swept in, flanked by two ladies in pastel gowns. *The runaway princess*, Lukas thought to himself. He'd heard all about her adventures, be it through the king's seething anger, her brother's animated regaling, or from sailors in taverns along the coast who'd traded tales of *The Gravedigger*. He supposed it wasn't common knowledge that Gillian and the Lindbarrian princess were one in the same, but he and Rhi had put together weeks ago that it was possible. Then, out of the blue, she'd ended up back here.

As she neared the dais, Rhi smirked beside him. "I see you're late as usual," the prince teased.

"Oh, you know me," she winked, wrapping her arms around Rhi fondly.

When she pulled back, she turned to survey Lukas.

Gods above, he bristled.

It was *her.*

Every bone in his body tensed as he took in her face. Yes, she was cleaned up and bejeweled in silk and gold, but the girl he'd caught breaking into the stables mere nights ago stood in front of him with a *crown* on her head. The same sharp lines of her face, strong, angled brows, the haughty tilt to her posture. The same intriguing eyes, which he noticed now that they weren't hidden in shadow were two different colors – one blue, one green. He cursed himself for not suspecting something like this the other night.

Recognition flickered across her face, then shock and dread. It vanished in a flash and was replaced by a saccharine smile dripping with deadly venom. She fixed him with an assessing, cat-like, glare.

"Why hello, sir," she offered him her hand to kiss. "I'm not sure we've met."

"*Gods above*," Lukas muttered under his breath, rubbing the back of his neck.

Rhi arched an eyebrow at him, "Do I want to know?"

"*You're* the princess, and I'm an idiot," he groaned.

Something in her mismatched eyes told him to keep his mouth shut about what had happened at the stables.

"Both of those statements are true," she smirked, her hand still hovering expectantly before him. "And you are?"

Stifling a grunt, he took her hand and leaned down to press a formal kiss atop her knuckles. "Lukas Mazrihn, Rhi's uh… guard."

She shot Rhi a questioning look, to which her brother shook his head lightly.

"Well," she said, turning her gaze back to him, "It is a *pleasure* to have made your acquaintance, Lukas."

He looked down and realized he hadn't dropped her hand yet. "Is that…" he squinted at her hand as she pulled it away.

"Leather polish," she smiled sweetly. "I spend a lot of time in the stables."

His face burned at her innuendo. One of the ladies who'd accompanied her, the blonde one, skittered up and passed the princess a pair of satin gloves with an apologetic wince.

He had truly been lucky the other night. If he'd turned her in, if she'd told anyone how he'd threatened her at sword point… he could have been in a lot of trouble. The last thing he needed was to draw attention to his late night comings and go-ings at the palace. *Why hadn't she just said who she was?*

Lukas rubbed his temples. Last night had been a long night, too. He'd won a few matches in The Pit, then shortly after, lost a third of his earnings in a bad game of cards. On top of that, one of his clients hadn't shown up for an exchange, and now he was sitting on a three-pound tin of specialty *arimopo* that he'd painstakingly acquired from beyond the blockade. Lady Caswich would be paying a steep holding fee.

He took out his pocket watch again. Checking it had become somewhat of a habit, like picking one's nails or chewing one's lip. Funny, the hands now ticked steadily forward at an even pace.

Ferrin was positive her face had reddened to a shade that matched the crimson of her dress. That man had held her against her will —at the tip of a sword, no less— and now he was here as her brother's bodyguard? He hadn't even been wearing a uniform, and he wasn't wearing one now, either.

Rhi's dismissive shake of the head had confirmed that they weren't lovers, but they did seem to be more than acquain-tances. Friends, even.

She tried to calm herself. It was fine. He could have spoken up about their encounter then and there, but he hadn't. If he was going to rat her out, he'd have done it already. He'd had days to do so.

The wide doors of the Great Hall burst open, and the first procession began to make its way in. Dancers swept through, each draped in flowing white swaths of fabric, crowned with golden branches as they danced up the hall. Every dancer held a different attribute of one of the gods.

This must be a delegation from Kalassa, Ferrin thought. The Kalassans worshipped the entire pantheon. Spirituality and god-ly-worship was everything to them. Every single deity, no matter how minor, was honored as such, whereas other countries seemed to pick and choose which deities they revered as gods and which were considered different beings, like tricksters, nymphs, muses, sprites or fates.

Ferrin's very sporadic attendance to the temples and ceremonies would be seen as unacceptable if she were a part of Kalassan high society. Long ago, some had even believed in using magic for spiritual practices only, and those who used it for their own purposes were persecuted.

Most of what she knew about the nation had been from Tabka, who was half-Kalassan on his mother's side, and half the time she was convinced he was pulling her leg.

That debate didn't matter anymore, though. Not with magic so scarce and diluted across the world.

Kalassa was still a highly spiritual place, despite the fact that it had retained only a negligible speck of magic, just like the rest of the world. A memory flashed in her mind of a time when a Kalassan spirit reader had come to Meroya, the more lawless of the two free pirate ports in the Meddemara.

The spirit reader's tent was made up of dyed purple and blue canvas draped and drawn over wooden poles in the ground. Like most of the structures on the isle of Meroya, it was temporary. The floor was covered by a round, patterned rug with a little low circular table in the center, and cushions on the floor at its north and south points. Inside the tent, incense smoke writhed and fluttered, and eventually dissipated out the open flap at the top of the tent. On the far cushion sat an old woman. Her black hair was loose and curling from the heat, and she ran a wrinkled, sun-tanned hand through it before raising her chin to Ferrin, who stood in the doorway.

"Come in and sit down, girl," the old woman commanded.

Ferrin — Gillian, she'd been at the time — obliged. She crouched down, tucked her legs up and sat cross-legged on the cushion opposite the woman.

"Do you have something for me?" the woman crooked an eyebrow.

"Yes," Gillian had said, reaching into her pocket. She set the two silver coins on the table between them.

"Very well, then." The woman tucked the coins into a pocket hidden somewhere in the folds of her dress. "Hold these," she ordered as she took six little bones from somewhere underneath the table and dropped them into Ferrin's palms. They were a collection of small bones from various creatures— bird, fish, rat. "What is your name, girl?"

"Gillian," she'd replied.

"Your true name," the spirit-reader said, her tone flat and raspy.

"It is Gillian."

The woman uttered an unconvinced hmph before taking Ferrin's hands in hers. She breathed in deeply, shut her eyes and leaned forward.

With an exhale, she began, "I see… storm clouds on the horizon and a herd of running horses, a crown beneath a bare, muddy foot. Blood on hands, a monster that devours from within. I see… a smoldering field in the distance and a hand rising from the ashes." She opened her eyes, releasing Ferrin's hands. "Cast the bones," she directed.

Ferrin dropped them onto the patterned table and stared down at them.

"Hmm…" the spirit reader said, viewing the scattered bones.

"What does it say?"

The woman's dark eyes snapped up and met Ferrin's, "Divination takes time, sweet."

"Sorry."

"Here… you will not be able to escape the beast you so desperately wish to run from. Your departure, it will not be permanent." She squinted at another grouping of bones on the table, "You will have your revenge but you will never find what you are seeking if you keep running. You will be free of the shackles you hide, only to find yourself in a new set of chains."

None of that sounded good. Ferrin scooted away from the table slightly. "What in the name of the gods does any of that mean?"

"I suppose that's up to you, sweet."

"But—"

"Oh, and you will face a betrayal, one that will change the path of your life forever."

Of course, most of that had been complete nonsense, wise-sounding vagary meant to trick travelers out of their coin. The betrayal part, however, had come to pass. Less than a year after that reading, Zare had sold her out. She wondered which other odd premonitions foretold in that tent might come to pass in their own strange, unexpected way. Perhaps the Kalassan procession had brought along a spirit-reader. The Lindbarrian nobility would surely find it a fascinating pastime.

The gilded chariot that entered next was pulled by two white horses that marched right through the outside doors into the Great Hall. Inside it sat a man, presumably the Kalassan king. He was handsome, perhaps in his late forties, with well-groomed mahogany hair receding from his temples, olive skin and a neatly trimmed beard, accented by the bright gold trim on his black coat. Next to him was a young woman who shared his coloring and good looks, though she was far more slight in build. Her hair was swept off her face into a loose knot at the back of her head, with romantic wisps falling on either side of her face, her nose was slightly hooked and she wore a swipe of translucent gold paint across each eyelid. Ferrin assumed this was the princess.

Across from them sat a stern, red-haired woman. She wore a fine, plain dress, a kerchief tucked modestly into the neckline, and her red hair slicked into a severe bun. Perhaps a governess or chaperone.

The parade organized itself into the left side of the Great Hall, which had been cleared for the day. There would be no grand feast tonight, but rather a small, intimate wine tasting, where each country displayed some of its wines and shared them. The following day, the tables would typically be brought back into the Great Hall and an additional, smaller table for two would be added so everyone could gawk at the prospective young couple as they got to know each other over roast duck, or whatever the kitchens deemed most impressive. That part of the tradition would last anywhere from a few nights to a month, depending on how they got on.

The atmosphere was already filling with a cheerful buzz. The people were excited to go out on the lawn and browse the little market that the procession had brought from abroad.

A horn sounded — a second procession?

Ferrin shot Rhi a look. If she was to watch two princesses compete over her brother who had no interest in them beyond politics, she would need something to snack on. He returned her look with a subtle shrug.

When the doors opened again, more dancers spilled in, this time clad in saturated jewel-toned frocks and coats. They erupted into a series of acrobatic twists and flips as the musicians followed them. Next came a flock of men dressed in red and gold military uniforms, each holding the leash of an orange tiger cub.

Finally, a golden litter, carried by eight servants, entered. Aboard were two men, one old and one young.

Oh, no.

Her fears were confirmed. There was a second royal suitor arriving, and this one *was* for her.

The line of merchants followed the litter, parading through, then back out to the marketplace, carrying pots and pans that clanged with the music. All of it became a dull roar in Ferrin's ears. The litter was set down.

She couldn't do this, she'd *just* gotten back, just had her heart ripped out. Her last lover had *poisoned* her, and now, not two weeks later she was to be courted by a prince she'd never met before? Her throat was closing and her breathing was quickening. Gods, was it just her or were these stays getting tighter? She was seconds from breaking out in a sweat…

Rhi elbowed her lightly in the side, and she looked at him. He nodded. *You can do this.*

The two sets of royals approached the dais, the Kalassans first.

"Her Highness, Princess Khianie of Kalassa, and His Majesty, King Yonis of Kalassa," announced the herald at the bottom of the dais.

Rhi met Ferrin's eyes once more with a slight inclination of his head before heading down the steps and plastering a smile on his face.

"Your Highness, you are even more radiant than the rumors say!" he exclaimed, sweeping into a shallow but courtly bow and taking her hand.

"It is a pleasure to be here, Your Highness," she replied with a curtsy.

"His Highness, Prince Havian of Efel, and His Majesty, King Alban of Efel," the herald said with another sweeping bow.

All she had to do was exactly what Rhi had done. Go down those steps, act cheerful, polite and charming for a few minutes. She could do that.

Her heart hammered in her chest as the Efelians approached the dais.

The prince looked like he was Rhi's age, early twenties. He had thick, dark brown hair, cropped short, but it looked like it would curl if it grew longer. His face was finely boned, broad plains and angles almost calculated, as if chiseled by an artisan. His skin was lightly tanned.

She trained her features into a pleasant, dull expression as he neared. Her heart was still racing.

"Your Highness," Prince Havian swept into a regal, practiced bow before her and gently took her hand and kissed it.

Ferrin nearly sputtered over her words as she said, "welcome to Lindbarrow, Your Highness," she smiled, composing herself. "Thank you for coming all this way to visit."

Efel's nearest coast was about a day and a half away by boat, but it was far more likely that the royals had boarded at their main port on the south coast, where their capital was, and sailed the long way around, which would take closer to a week.

She had been there only once, but she knew the Efelians had a similar history to Lindbarrows. A hundred years ago they had joined two warring regions under a marriage: Stebania and Alavar. From what she had learned, their unification had been far more successful than had Lindbarrow's.

"The pleasure is all mine," he replied, his hazel eyes crinkling as he offered a charming smile. He was clean-shaven, and his light green and silver jacket complemented his tan complexion.

"I do hope the weather is agreeable for your stay," Ferrin expressed.

"It is a little colder than I expected, for springtime," he said, dropping her hand.

"Yes, our spring tends to be nothing but rain and chill, I'm afraid." Efel was nestled at the northwest edge of the Meddemara, and therefore caught the warm currents that swept through seasonally. It didn't get very cold there at all, even in the winter.

"Well, I shall have to dress more warmly, then," he responded. "May I accompany you on a turn about the grounds later on?"

She was almost about to decline and feign a headache, until her father caught her eye from where he sat at the side of the room, fixing her with an expectant glare.

"That sounds lovely, I would be happy to show you around," she said sweetly.

At that moment, King Alban approached. His grey hair was unbound and fell over the velvet of his maroon coat as he clapped his son on the back. "Well, well, the infamous Princess Ferrin of Lindbarrow." His voice was jovial— amused, even.

"Is that how I am known in Efelian Court, Your Majesty?" Ferrin inquired.

"Only by those who have heard of your journey," Havian interjected.

"Yes. Who would have thought a young girl like you could be kidnapped by pirates and live to tell the tale!" Alban was incredulous.

For a moment, Ferrin lost her words. Her father certainly had flooded the rumor mill.

"Mm, yes, it was terrifying, I'll admit," she nodded, biting her lip. "And how did you come by this story?"

"A Njorskan duke… some Holvstram or someone…" The king scratched his head, "Well, a nobleman from Njorske enlightened me at a joust in our capital last week."

"Oh, my. Word certainly travels fast," she laughed nervously.

"A true feat of bravery, highness." Alban gave her an amused grin.

"Thank you, Your Majesty," Ferrin replied.

"Wonderful, wonderful," the old king said as he teetered away, mumbling something about today's youth.

"Well, I would love to hear more about your adventure later this evening," Havian said, turning back to her.

"Of course," Ferrin answered, her voice jumping perhaps an octave too high. She wanted to limit her contact with him as much as possible.

"I look forward to it, but I must now retire and wash this journey off my skin. It's been a long day and the sea does not seem to agree with me."

"Yes, I will see you later," she tilted her head as she bid him farewell.

As Havian retreated to the palace with his valets and entourage, Ferrin excused herself and made her way out to the little marketplace that had sprung up on the Palace Green.

The tent-filled courtyard set-up reminded Ferrin painfully of the beachside dwellings on Tunis. Old Orini had been an abandoned Efelian settlement of long ago that the pirates had taken over. Huts and shanties had been built along the beach outside the old town and most crews hung around in tents when they weren't at sea or at one of the inns or taverns. It was lively and mottled and loud.

She missed it.

The Kalassans and Efelians had brought artisans and merchants of every kind. There was cutlery, pottery, a leatherworker, spice sellers, metalworkers and even a coiffeur. Ferrin was running her hand over a skein of carmine-colored silk when something moved in her periphery. Instinctively tensing, she whirled around.

"That was quite the display." It was Rhi's friend, the one who'd thought she was a horse thief. *Lukas*. Yes, that was his name. He was leaning against the wall, trying to light the pipe he held between his lips.

"At least Havian knows how to treat a *lady* when he sees one," she retorted.

"Sure he does," Lukas said, trying again to light whatever was in the pipe's bowl. He pulled a drag off the pipe, and then immediately exhaled it with a cough. "Gods, that is *awful*."

"Then why are you smoking it?" She raised an eyebrow. Realizing she was still holding the silk, she placed it back on the cart and turned to him.

"Testing it out—" he coughed again. "To see if it's worth introducing to one of my clients."

"*Clients*? What are you, a traveling apothecarist?" She rolled her eyes.

"No." He set his jaw and put the pipe out, emptying its contents onto the ground. In the daylight, she noticed that his eyes were a startling sea-green. The color was striking beneath his thick lashes and brown skin.

"What *do* you do? Other than threaten ladies with swords," she crossed her arms, waiting.

His answering laugh was just shy of derisive. "Not sure I can tell you that, princess." He winked as he stuffed the pipe back into his coat.

"Try me," she glared.

"Fine, but if you get me in trouble, I'll let His Majesty know about your stable visit," he threatened.

"No you won't."

"Won't I?" His expression was smug and arrogant. She wanted to wipe it off his face.

She stepped closer to him, tilting her head and letting a viciously sweet smile spread across her face, "Because if you do, I'll tell everyone how you held me up and threatened me at sword point when you had no reason or authority to do so. After all, you're not a palace guard, are you?" she asked in her most innocent voice.

His self-satisfied smile disappeared and he crossed his arms, mirroring her body language. "I buy and sell and move things that are… difficult to come by around here."

"Carry on," she tilted her head to the other side, skeptical.

"…for a profit, to wealthy buyers who value discretion," he continued. "Things one can't just hobble down to the docks, or the market to find. Certain herbs, drinks, ordinary items that come out of certain locales."

"So… you're a *popava* trafficker?" she narrowed her eyes suspiciously.

"No." He looked taken aback by this.

"But that's what you do. You just said as much."

"Among other things. Many, *many* other things," he clarified.

She stared at him expectantly. "Are you a mercenary?"

"As I said, I do many things."

"Hmf. You're not nearly as mysterious and intimidating as you think you are."

"I'm really more of a smuggler."

"Well, Lukas, *smuggler*," she emphasized. "Who buys these items of value?"

"Did you not hear the bit about discretion?"

"I wonder if you might be able to track something down for me," she said softly. Before she could elaborate, they were interrupted.

"Ferr, this scoundrel isn't bothering you, is he?" Rhi's playful voice drew both of their attention to the other end of the cart. His warm-chocolate eyes twinkled with mischief.

"I was just about to leave, actually," Lukas said, taking a step back. When had she come so close to him?

"So soon? They've just set up the market."

Lukas looked back and forth between brother and sister. "I'll see you later."

Ferrin eyed him skeptically, his broad shoulders shifting under his teal coat as he wove through the market and disappeared amongst the smoke and tents. Her question was still burning in the back of her mind.

"*Popava*, Rhi, really?" She turned and smacked her brother on the arm. "I can't believe you're paying *that* man to bring you that vile stuff."

"We're friends, you know. And I hire his services for other things, too. Do you know how difficult it is to get your hands on Veiran silk nowadays?"

Ferrin groaned. "You need to spend some time away from here, truly."

"You're probably right. But why leave the comforts of home when everyone is just so desperate to come to me?" he joked. Something like loneliness flickered behind his eyes, but it was gone almost immediately.

"Be careful, Rhi. I know it seems harmless, but I've seen *popava* turn deadly."

"Highness!" a shrill voice sounded. Another one of the king's pages. Did her father only hire ridiculous caricatures as pages, or did the job and uniform simply make them all seem that way?

"Yes?" Rhiach and Ferrin said in unison.

"Princess Ferrin, you've been summoned by the king."

Now what? she wondered.

CHAPTER SIX

Ferrin followed the squeaky-voiced page through the alabaster halls of the Royal Administrative Wing to her father's quarters. The walls were lined with portraits of Lundi kings and queens going back generations. Most of the portraits of former Caelish rulers had been removed. Porcelain figurines of nymphs and heroes, and gilded glass vases punctuated the hall. Inside her father's office, pewter sconces cast a dim glow through the room, though daylight still poured through the windows onto the green and ochre patterned rug.

When the doors shut behind her with a loud thud, Ferrin stiffened. Her father sat at the head of his huge office desk, pawing through the pages of an old, yellowing ledger. An advisor to his right spoke in a subdued tone while gesturing to the open page. King Henrik picked up the steaming cup of tea next to him and drank, some of it dribbling down his chin. The smell of it hit her, it wasn't a spice tea or a green tea, but something else she couldn't quite place.

"You summoned me?" she offered a shallow curtsy.

"Yes," said Henrik, not bothering to glance up from the papers he was studying, giving her a view of his full head of greying blond hair. "You are, of course, aware of the position we are in with the Efelians?"

"Well… if I remember correctly, they are in a growing conflict with Bourjony, one which we will likely soon be a part of?"

"And?"

"And," she swallowed, "they're our sole trade partner in many goods now. Due to the blockades and all."

"Indeed," the king confirmed, raising an eyebrow. Why wasn't he yelling? He seemed so calm, rational. A far cry from his red-faced lividity the last time they'd spoken. "And since the Efelians have become the middleman and our path to all of our southern imports, we now pay more for sugar, olives, *arimopo*." He opened the tin of dry, fragrant leaves and shot her a pointed glance.

Arimopo was an herb commonly smoked or chewed. It had a musky smell on its own that Ferrin liked, but tasting it second hand or getting a whiff of the smoke was bitter, earthy and revolting. Zare took to chewing it to stay awake, and she remembered how awful kissing him had been if he didn't rinse his mouth out afterwards.

"I understand," Ferrin clasped her hands in front of her. "You think that if I am married to an Efelian prince, they might become more agreeable in regard to their tariffs."

"Precisely." He shut the tin. "And allow me to make this even clearer, *daughter*." There was not an ounce of affection in the word, only possession. "The Efelians are an important geographic stepping stone into the Meddemara, and by extension South Hallan."

"Yes, I'm familiar with the map," she snapped. She'd only spent the last five years in the damn Meddemara.

"Then you understand perfectly," her father smiled, no, bared his teeth, and leaned forward. "If you ruin this, I will make your life miserable here."

"I do understand, Father," she said, her face heating and heart racing as she searched for the words. She couldn't be courted, she simply couldn't. Her chest grew tight again as images of ruddy-brown hair and too-cool words, eyes that saw into her soul and read just how to control her flashed in her mind. "I'm just not sure what to say if they ask about… where I was."

"I've circulated appropriate rumors."

"Could you at least tell me what they are so I can have my story straight?"

An hour later, she had changed into yet another gown, this one requiring far less underpinnings. It was a simple linen day gown, in cream with a fashionable floral pattern on it. Around her shoulders was a shawl, which she clutched with both fists so Havian couldn't try to hold her hand. She'd tied a woven, flat brimmed hat over her hair and was enjoying the cool breeze.

"So, how did you finally manage to break free from the pirates?" he asked lightly as they strolled the grounds.

"Oh, I simply bided my time — I think they meant to ransom me — but one night they were all drunk in a port," she explained. The story made some kind of cock-eyed sense. "And the one guarding me fell asleep on watch. So I managed to steal his keys and escape, then I found some navymen and they…" she swallowed, "rescued me."

The story was plausible, but not probable. It was more likely that if a girl in a ripped dress came screaming up to the navymen, they'd call her crazy and return to their drinks, or worse.

"Goodness," said Havian. He was the perfect gentlemanly suitor; he knew when to sigh, gasp and ask questions, he nodded at all the right times, and seemed to be respectful of her space, though a chaperone was never far off, trailing them through the orchards.

They had been walking for about an hour when she weaseled her way out. "I have some reflection to do, by the chapel," she said apologetically. "But I'll see you when we uncork the wine?"

"Of course, can I walk you to the chapel?" he asked.

"Oh, I'm visiting," she began somberly, "I'm visiting a grave, so I'd prefer the solitude. You understand."

"Certainly," he said with a dip of his head. "Until later then, Princess."

Once he was out of sight, she relaxed. She felt awful and dirty using her mother's grave as an excuse to be rid of him, but was it really sacrilegious if her mother was still alive? The casket they'd buried had been empty, since the queen had simply vanished without a trace. Ferrin *knew* she wasn't dead.

She wandered around a little longer, enjoying the sun that had finally peeked out from its covers, the light golden and slanting in the late hour. She was just entering the sour part of the apple orchard when she realized she was being followed through the trees.

She turned casually, making back towards the castle as if she'd simply tired and decided to return. She maintained a casual pace, so as not to clue in her follower that she'd sensed their presence.

She quickened her pace a little, cursing herself. Why had she sent away Havian? Why couldn't she have just tolerated him and the lie she had to tell for another few minutes? Now there was no one around, no one to help her and no one to even hear her scream when the bag went over her head.

She kicked and thrashed but lost contact with the ground when she was hoisted over someone's shoulder. With a hard swing, she brought her elbow down on what she could assume was their back, confirmed by the resounding *oof*. It wasn't enough for them to let her go.

"Hey!" She kicked and elbowed and swung. "Put me down!"

There was no one around. *Gods* how stupid had she become? That was what she got for wandering the grounds unaccompanied. Oh, how she had not missed being recognized as royalty.

"Help!" she pounded on her assailant's back again, hollering.

"Shh!" the voice admonished. Definitely male. There were at least two of them.

"Quiet," the second one commanded. She felt something hard and round press against her shoulder. A gun?

As they thumped along, she tried desperately to gather her thoughts. Where were they bringing her? What did they want? How many of them were there? She tried to slow her breathing, but given the hard edge of the man's shoulder digging into her gut, it was a difficult task.

It felt like they were traversing down a hill, thumping along until they finally stopped. She heard what sounded like a door hinge creeping open, and her carrier stooped, presumably stepping through the door.

She heard the door shut, and she was set down rather gently, considering the situation, in a chair. Then they pulled the hood from her face.

Two men and one woman stood around the front of her chair, with neutral expressions and no instruments of torture in sight. Behind them, a few figures stood along the wall, masked and cloaked so she couldn't see their faces or even discern their build.

Though there was no table with an array of surgeon's tools or mallets or saws, a dark room in the bowels of a compound in Kalassa flashed in her mind.

"Last time this happened to me I was interrogated by Calomba Herotis." She jerked her chin at the closest man, the blond, and asked, "this going to be be anything like that?"

She still had the scars to remind her of the olive trade's most infamous enforcer.

"No," he said coolly, his arms crossing over his blue waistcoat. He had a clean-cut look about him. His short blond hair was wavy, but not a single strand of it fell out of place. His silken cravat was knotted with impeccable precision at his throat. The only unpolished thing about him was the red scar cutting through his lightly tanned skin on the lower left side of his face.

"Then what is it you've brought me here for?" she asked, almost demanded, as she looked from person to person with increasing agitation.

There were two masked guards by the door, one male and one female as best as she could tell. Two more masked figures were hunched at the table behind her hosts, and another three skulked along the wall, all of varying heights.

Who are they?

"You are Princess Ferrin, are you not?" the man standing in front of her asked with one eyebrow raised.

"Yes."

"And also Gillian, first mate of *The Gravedigger*?"

It took considerable effort not to balk. "Did Zare send you? What, is he after more gold?" she scoffed, trying —and failing— to keep every trace of terror and dread from her voice. What if he came back? What would she do?

"We are not affiliated with Captain Zare," the woman answered, stepping around the blond man. "We are from the north." Her sleek, red-gold hair fell in a loose braid over her shoulder, swept off her pale face. She was in her late thirties and she had a no-nonsense way about her, clad in clean, brown breeches, boots, and a dark green vest laced over a white shirt.

"So you're… tired of the snow?" she quipped. "Why am I here?"

"I didn't believe the rumors about you being a mouthy little shite. I see now I was wrong," said the third man, the dark haired one.

"Please, both of you are insufferable," the woman waved the two men back. "My name is Helene."

Everything about the room had Ferrin's nerves screaming at her to get up and run.

"Well?" She braced her hands on her knees, determined to keep up the fearless front. She'd come close to breaking down once already today. She'd be damned if she let it happen again. At least they hadn't bound her hands.

"We mean you no harm," the woman assured her, dragging a chair across the floor. She sat in front of Ferrin, surveying at her at eye level. "Unless you threaten harm to us."

"*You* brought *me* here. At gunpoint, I might add," she snarled. "I don't even know where we are, so…"

"Gunpoint?" the woman shot the blond a scathing look.

"She wouldn't stop kicking and screaming," he shrugged. "It wasn't even loaded."

"Right. Sorry about that. As I was saying, my name is Helene, and I'm from Avaree. Your mother's city, if I am not wrong?"

"That's right," Ferrin nodded warily.

"Well, I am also a captain in the army. In the Caelish Resistance."

"You—" Ferrin squinted hard at Helene. "The *what?*"

"Give it a minute," the blond man rolled his eyes.

Ferrin shot him a seething look. "Well, what do you want with *me*? I've been here a grand total of five days."

"We have a proposition for you, depending on where you stand," Helene explained. "But first we have questions."

"How do I know you're telling the truth? How do I know you aren't some agents of my father trying to sniff out just how rebellious I really am?"

"For now, I suppose you'll have to trust us."

Ferrin had fallen for honeyed words and poetic waxing on trust and faith from another cool-tempered, pretty face before. And she had paid dearly for it. "No, not good enough. Prove to me that you are who you say you are or I'm leaving."

"You're the one surrounded in an unknown location. Don't you think if we wanted to hurt you, we'd have done it by now?" Helene asked.

"I really need more than your word to go on," Ferrin said defiantly.

"Fine," the woman's nostrils flared ever so slightly, and she held out a hand. "Darian, the seal, if you don't mind?"

The fourth unmasked figure, the dark-skinned man in the green coat stepped forward. His black hair was cropped close and his shoulders were broad under his coat. He looked Alick's age or a little older. From the inside pocket of his coat he produced a little silver object.

It was a ring— tarnished and thick. It did indeed have the old Caelish crest, three geese and a falcon silhouetted over a full moon on the rise.

Ferrin nodded. "I will hear you out," she conceded, though she knew it wasn't outside of the realm of possibility to fake the seal of a dead nation.

"As you may have heard rumored, there is a growing force in the north, people who want to push for Caelish independence," Helene began.

"How many?"

"I am not at liberty to discuss those specifics just yet. Almost enough to pose a significant threat."

"Right," Ferrin narrowed her eyes, "*almost.*"

"In the future, it would be immensely helpful if you and your brother would come north with any others who are sympathetic to the cause. As the last of the Caelish royal line, the two of you could be seen as a beacon to rally support."

"What you're saying could get you strung up for treason. Surely you had to believe I'd be of the same mind as you. Why?"

"Yes, we took a calculated risk in bringing you here, in showing you some of our faces," Helene cast a furtive glance to one of the masked figures behind her. "But we had reason to believe you would be interested in what we have to say."

"Princesses don't run away because of their loyalty," the blond man added sarcastically.

Helene shot him another glare.

"We also know that the queen's disappearance was something more than what the king tried to pass it off as."

Ferrin stiffened.

"Arabella worked with us for a short time in the months before she vanished," Helene revealed.

"What else do you know?" Ferrin sat forward, her curiosity burning.

"She suspected someone was trying to remove her from power."

Ferrin nodded, chewing the inside of her cheek. "Well," she swallowed. "I don't know how much I can be of help to you, I don't have much power here."

"Power is taken, never given," Helene crossed an ankle over her knee. "As I'm sure you already know."

"And I don't know how receptive my brother will be to any of this," Ferrin continued.

"Why don't you find out? Take a few days, maybe look around and see if you can find anything of interest. In a week, we'll find you again."

"Can't you just tell me where to meet you? And who are they?" she gestured to the masked people at the back of the room.

"We can't risk compromising our agents. Some work undercover around the palace," Helene explained as she swept an auburn tendril behind her ear.

"I've learned my lesson on trusting blindly, and I don't take kindly to being blindfolded and manhandled," Ferrin complained, crossing her arms resolutely. "I'll be in the apple orchard at dusk in ten days. Meet me there, or don't."

The blond man sighed, "I'll meet her."

The words were directed at Helene but the exasperated sigh was *definitely* directed at her.

"Fine, then. Can I get a name, at least?" Ferrin looked pointedly at the man, noticing how perpetually irritated he seemed to be.

"You can call me Grey," he replied drily.

PART TWO

CHAPTER SEVEN

By the time Ferrin made it down to the Great Hall for the wine tasting, she was sweating. Her little foray into the rebel safe house had cost her time she needed to change and bathe. Of course, they'd insisted on bringing her out hooded, but this time they let her walk on her own, at least. When they removed her blindfold in the orchard, the sun was nearly setting. She'd had to sprint back to her rooms to prepare for the next step in her courtship.

Once again, she nearly plowed into Nimhe, who was laying out yet another gown on Ferrin's bed.

"Sorry!" Ferrin exclaimed, screeching to a halt. "Lost track of time."

"No time to bathe," Nimhe scolded. "the uncorking is in twenty minutes!"

"Shit," Ferrin panted. "Fine, I'll brothel-rinse."

Nimhe looked at her with horror.

"Oh, don't give me that look. You know what I mean," Ferrin said as she shucked off her hat and began untying the tapes of the day gown. How many outfit changes would this courtship require? Once she was undressed, she moved to the wash basin to sponge off her face, under her arms, and anywhere else that was sweaty.

"Where's Sov?" she asked as she shimmied into a clean shift.

"Here!" Soviel announced, scrambling into the room with uncharacteristic chaotic haste. Her cheeks were flushed, and she smelled faintly of grass. "Sorry I'm late."

"Where have you been?" Nimhe asked.

"Oh, uh, library," she answered, sounding abashed.

Ferrin raised an unconvinced eyebrow.

"I had some things to research, for Madame Leone at the infirmary. Botanicals. Plants that are suited for healing magic," explained Soviel, still breathing hard.

"Really?" Ferrin asked, rolling on the same silk stockings she'd worn earlier. "I once met a woman in the south of Bourjony who could reattach a man's severed foot with healing magic… or so she said."

"That is very advanced. I'm only learning to mend broken bones and close up cuts, but I've been improving a lot," said Soviel. "Madame has been teaching me."

"You have healing magic?" Ferrin asked. She didn't know why she was surprised. Soviel came from Njorske, which historically hinted at an affinity for flame, or would have, long ago. But her mother was from Veira, where magic was once tied closely to the earth.

"Some," nodded Soviel. "It started presenting itself when I was fifteen and I've been working at it ever since. Though, I couldn't do much with it until recently."

"That's incredible," Ferrin said sincerely. "I can't do anything like that. Though I suppose that's to be expected nowadays." Long ago there'd been… more. Then a hundred or so years ago, magic had faded fast everywhere, with the exception of a few regions where healers were still born, though with a fraction of their original strength. There had once been Stormriders in the cliff-speckled northern islands, flame wielders in the frostbitten tundra of the continent, water witches in every desert village in the south, Earthshakers scattered across the land bordering the Meddemara.

"I heard of a village bursting into flames outside of some city in Njorske," Nimhe shared. "But I suppose that could have been from anything."

"You know, I heard about that too," Soviel added, her focus narrowing in on the braid she was winding around Ferrin's head. "I also heard rumor of a young boy in the desert, a village in Dromata, I think, causing a huge rain storm during a month of bad drought. And this was at the height of the dry season."

"That is interesting," Ferrin's eyes widened. "But no more Stormriders," she added with a small pout. She'd have loved to meet a Stormrider, would have loved to be one. True, they couldn't necessarily fly, but their control over air currents allowed them to ride the breeze if it was strong enough, and tailor it to their need.

"Well, you never know," Soviel shrugged, patting Ferrin on the shoulders to let her know she was done with her hair. "Let's get you dressed."

They pulled her into the blue dress she'd worn to dinner her second night back, and wove the same little tiara into her hair.

"So, how's the Efelian prince so far?" Soviel asked as Nimhe left to find Ferrin's gloves.

"Oh, fine," Ferrin shrugged with a tight-lipped smile.

"That hair? He's gorgeous," Soviel giggled.

"He certainly is handsome," Ferrin agreed mildly.

"And that's a bad thing?" Soviel asked, handing Ferrin a pair of sapphire earrings.

"No," Ferrin said ambiguously as she wiggled the earring through her ear lobe. She'd taken out the extra jewelry that had adorned her ears, but the holes were all still there. "I'm just not used to it, being back here, being courted by suitors and all."

"Ah, because of the young captain?" Soviel asked lightly.

"Yes—" she froze, "Sov, I don't think I ever told you about him."

Soviel's face flushed. "You must have."

Ferrin racked her brain but she was sure she hadn't yet told Soviel the romantic extent of her relationship with Zare. She hadn't wanted to discuss it with anyone. Perhaps she'd mentioned it when they shared the bottle of wine and it had slipped her memory. "Hm, I suppose." Strange.

"Don't worry too much about it, everything is so rigid with these things that the most you'll have to do is dance with him. At least for a while."

Ferrin sighed in agreement. "Hey, where'd Nimhe go?"

Soviel sighed, "I sent her to find gloves for you because of that damn saddle polish. She probably got distracted."

Ferrin caught a touch of annoyance in Soviel's voice and wondered if Nimhe becoming distracted and disappearing was a common occurrence.

"I got most of the polish off, I'll just hide my palms and no one will notice," Ferrin suggested.

"Alright then, are you ready?"

Ferrin stood, straightening her gown and glancing in the mirror. "At least it's not a whole dinner."

CHAPTER EIGHT

The rows of green canvas upholstered seats within the chapel filled up quickly. Families filed in, taking their usual seats, visitors milled around the edges, unsure of where to sit, young couples happily plopped down next to each other amongst the rows.

The royal box, corded off by a golden rope, was placed right beside the altar at the longest point of the triangular building. The seats were adorned in gold, painted porcelain with blue velvet cushions. It was empty save for Ferrin and Rhi.

Rhi's guards, silent and sturdy, flanked the box. Ferrin was fidgeting with the knitted grey mitts on her hands, and the sun was filtering through, illuminating the fabric of the empty seats in front of them.

"I can't believe you dragged me to the chapel on my only day off from stable duties," Ferrin huffed.

"I told you, the new attendant is good. He's actually *interesting*. Much better than old Teager."

Ferrin stifled a laugh.

Sir Teager, the last attendant, had been ancient and spoke in such a slow monotone; he had even put himself to sleep a few times.

"I could be *sleeping*. My head still aches."

"It's not my fault you sampled every single wine the Efelians brought last night," Rhi chided. Usually, it was he who was unwell after a late night. Last night he'd politely conversed with Khianie over dozens of tiny flutes of different wine. She was enjoyable enough to be around, but he had no desire to do anything more than converse and share wine. Yet still, she'd been leaning in and dropping her gaze to his lips in a telltale *kiss me* manner for the entire last hour of the event.

"I don't know how you deal with these women for whom you have no interest in all the time," Ferrin said, incredulous. "It's exhausting, and this is only the first time I've been officially courted."

"It's called being cordial for the sake of politics. Just wait until you get invited to another court to do the very same. It's even more exhausting than hosting," said Rhi. "At least when they visit us, our time is our own when we're not entertaining."

"It isn't fair. For anyone involved," Ferrin grumbled. "Doesn't it bother you?"

"What, pretending to be enchanted by the batting eyelashes and cleavage of a foreign princess? Yeah, it bothers me, but it's temporary." He shifted uncomfortably in his seat. It was far too early for this conversation.

"I don't see why you have to go through it. Father knows you don't want women in that way, I don't see—"

"Him knowing and accepting that, Ferrin, and him actually altering the politics around succession are two very separate things." An easy way for the leaders of the world to laud themselves on their progress, on their tolerance without having to lift a finger to change a damn thing, he didn't add.

"I'm just saying, you're his favorite, everyone's favorite. Traditions are always changing, why not this one?"

"The crown passes through the bloodline. Just drop it for now, alright? It's not as if I'm getting married tomorrow."

"Sorry, I know it isn't really any of my business."

"No, it's fine. Now hush, the ceremony is starting."

Ferrin leaned back in her seat beside him, her light blue frock shifting as she tried to get comfortable. She'd always been too restless to sit through ceremonies at the chapel, but Rhi loved them.

He loved the stories, the music, the candlelight flickering on the stone carvings in the walls. Every story seemed to connect to another. When he was young, he'd tugged on his mother's sleeve before bed every night, *begging* to be told just one more story before lights out.

The candles within the chapel dimmed as the attendant swept down the central aisle, holding a large metal-bound book with an eye embossed on the front cover. Rhi sat forward, adjusting his blue and white embroidered waistcoat.

The new attendant was younger, maybe in his late forties. His brown hair was graying at the edges, and his build was slight under the enveloping folds of his dark wool robes. His complexion was ruddy and contrasted by his easy expression, a trace of a smile on his face as he gently set the big book down on the altar.

"Good morning, all. Truly met," he said in greeting.

And then he launched into a story Rhi had never heard before.

"In the beginning, and also the end, there was a great, wide chasm of untold depth and breadth, containing nothing. Or rather, the absence of nothing. And in this not-nothing, dust between stars intermingled with something far more potent: magic. Magic in its earliest and rawest form.

"A mother from another beginning, and also another end, fell into this chasm. And she wandered day by day, floating on the stardust, gliding through the not-nothing. She searched day and night to find her lost children, certain that they must be among this chasm of dark and dust, but she could not find them. In her path she left suns, stars, young planets and drops of magic so dense they became life.

"Out of loneliness, dust and not-nothing, she crafted him — her new son, who would be king over all that was suspended in the not-nothing. Together, they would care for all things in the chasm.

"But he grew greedy and wanted to rule every drop of magic and life. So he picked a world and crowned himself their god.

"In the same fashion as his mother, though, he grew lonely and wished to have companions in this state of godhood, so he poured essence of his divinity into eight cups and shared it with his most trusted subjects. A gathering of sprites, wisps, nature spirits, beasts and even humans.

"They became gods, bright and powerful and true. The power of creation at their fingertips.

"When they realized his true intent for the life on their world: to harvest the magic and life for his own use, the new gods met in secret, under cover of darkness on a starless, moonless night.

"They moved to kill him when the sun was high in the desert land, where he planned to perform the ritual, and they fought valiantly.

"But in the end, he realized he could not win the day, so he blasted out a lash of his life-magic power and created a grove of ancient trees, sealing himself inside of it, safe and asleep, the earth around him heavy and blanketing. There he would wait, until he could rise up and finish what he'd started in this world."

The king and queen watched from the wings, standing silent as they listened to the newest attendant relay the ancient and forgotten story. The queen leaned in and whispered something into the king's ear. He nodded in agreement.

The next day, the temple attendant did not arrive for morning prayers.

CHAPTER NINE

Between the unpleasant meeting with her father and the rattling interaction with the supposed rebellion, Ferrin spent the days leading up to the grand feast nervous and jumpy.

The night of the grand feast was when all eyes would be on her and Havian, and it was only two days away.

She had tolerated his presence the last few days, through the wine tasting, walks around the orchard, billiard games, and the welcoming feast on his second day here. She was juggling stable duties, a royal suitor, and being approached by the rebellion, so it had clearly been a busy week.

The grounds had been crawling with extra guards since the arrival of the Efelians and Kalassans, so she hadn't even bothered to try another escape, but with every passing day she grew more and more anxious and restless. She needed to get out and do *something*.

At least snooping around had given her something to focus on. So far, she hadn't been able to uncover anything useful, and she was to meet Grey in the orchard in a few days. It was hard to find out much of anything when she was forced to drag a foreign prince along with her everywhere she went.

She'd been let out of stable duties early, at noon, for the last few days so that she could maximize her time with Havian, but truthfully, she'd have rather spent her afternoon hours dozing off the morning's work, or riding, or even mucking more stalls. She'd at last managed to wear out Havian and he'd decided to retire early after dinner.

She had snagged Rhi away from Khianie, claiming they were going to visit the family chapel to reflect in the presence of their ancestors. The princess pouted and squeezed Rhi's hand in her own, which he chivalrously kissed before bowing and waltzing out of the foyer.

When they were in the hallway leading to their own rooms, Ferrin pulled Rhi to a stop with a hand on his elbow.

"Let's go do something fun," she suggested. "I'm off from stable duties tomorrow so I want to stay up late."

A grin slowly spread over Rhi's face. "I have just the place, but we have to wear disguises. Unless you fancy getting pick-pocketed."

Her answering grin was devious. "Oh, now that sounds like my kind of place. Should I throw on breeches or just a plainer dress?"

Rhi considered, humming as he did, "throw on breeches. Meet me at the oak tree in the courtyard in half an hour."

With a nod, she stepped into her room. Soviel was there laying out her nightgown and a cup of tea.

"How was dinner?" she asked.

"Delicious," Ferrin replied, striding to the closet.

"Are you not going to bed?" Soviel asked.

"No, actually, I'm going out with Rhi…" she paused, pondering. "Do you want to come?"

Soviel looked initially surprised at the invitation, but then said, "sure, where?"

"I don't know, but it's somewhere a little rougher, from what he told me. You can borrow some of my riding clothes if you want."

Ferrin expected Soviel to balk and excuse herself. Gentle, sweet Soviel who cared for dozens of different species of plants in her room, and whom little fawns would probably approach in the woods.

"Yes, I'll go. Thank you!"

"Here," Ferrin tossed a pair of breeches at her from the closet. "I don't know how well those will fit, but try them."

They got dressed quickly, pulling on riding attire and waistcoats over their loose shirts.

Soviel pulled on the breeches and tugged the buttons shut. With some effort, they closed. The fabric was significantly tighter in the hips and thighs, showing every curve, so Ferrin offered her the longer of the two coats she had pulled from the closet in case the other girl felt the attire was too immodest.

With her rust-colored short coat draped over her arm, Ferrin strode to the door, Soviel behind her in the longer green coat. Ferrin had been surprised to find that her old dusty hats were still at the top of her closet. She'd worn them for riding, back before she'd run away, and both of her parents had absolutely hated the look of them.

They turned the corner into the hallway, letting the door slide shut behind them.

Rhi was waiting by the oak tree as promised, a little metal flask uncapped in one hand. He raised the flask in greeting when he saw them.

"I brought Soviel, I hope that's alright," Ferrin said.

Soviel curtsied, "Your Highness."

"Oh, no. None of that tonight. Where we're going, there are no titles and certainly no curtsies."

"Right," Soviel nodded apologetically.

"So, where are we off to?" Ferrin asked, linking an arm through both of their elbows as the trio strode off.

"Well, ladies, we are going to the finest establishment that the lower market has to offer: The Pit."

The Pit was aptly named, Ferrin realized when they arrived. It was an old warehouse on the outskirts of town, past the docks and close to the back road. It didn't look like much of anything other than *abandoned,* but when they went inside, a staircase led them down into a literal pit.

The Pit was lined with seats, tapering and descending in concentric circles before reaching the bottom level, where there was some sort of fighting ring. A large crowd of onlookers made a dull roar, but no one was fighting yet. People laughed loudly and drank ale from tin flagons and whisky from flasks, coins changed hands as people placed bets amongst themselves. Around the top rim was a bar, if you could call it that. A huge, big-muscled bruiser of a man stood with his arms crossed beside a keg at a long, high table. Behind him was a shelf of cheap whiskey bottles. On the other side of the top rim, there was a betting station with a board full of names and match numbers.

"*How* did you find this place?" Ferrin asked. She had to shout to be heard over the din.

"Through the grapevine," Rhi replied.

"Meaning your top smuggling-man?" Ferrin asked.

"How did you—" he began, but stopped short when he saw Ferrin pointing to the ring, where Lukas was up first.

"I didn't realize he had a match tonight," Rhi said, "Usually he only does this once a week or so."

"Is it just fists, or are there matches with weapons too?" Soviel asked, her eyes fixed on the men who'd just entered the ring.

Ferrin's eyes widened.

"No, it's just fists. Too many casualties and this place would get busted by the City Watch," Rhi explained.

Lukas stood, chatting with some man outside the ropes and shaking out his shoulders, while the other man gestured some signal with his hands. Then, Lukas shucked off his shirt.

He was over six feet of muscle, a tattoo of some symbol Ferrin couldn't make out on his shoulder blade, visible when he reached up to tie his hair behind his head. The muscles in his back rippled as he wrapped a cord around his hair. Ferrin forced herself to look at something else as he began wrapping his hands with long, thin strips of linen.

"That's a lot of muscle," Soviel observed, staring.

Lukas' opponent was similarly built, big and brawny, his pink skin and light golden-brown hair shimmering with sweat.

Ferrin's eyes skipped back to Lukas just as his gaze landed on their group of three. He sketched a mock bow, complete with a dramatic flourish of the wrist.

"I thought you said no curtsying," Soviel laughed to Rhi.

"Yes, won't they think him a fool, now?" Ferrin asked a little bitterly.

"Somehow, I think he'll manage to preserve his fearsome reputation," Rhi said confidently with a smirk as he crossed his arms and leaned back in his seat.

The match began.

It wasn't the same as the *suldura* fights in the *stadia* of Khalim, the Akhatan capital, but the energy of the crowd surely matched those, if on a smaller scale. She'd seen those fights. They ended bloody most of the time, and every drop of red that stained the sand seemed to make the crowd hunger for more. In those fights, they used weapons, though, even if every match wasn't 'to the death'.

Lukas moved much faster than she would have expected him to be able to, considering his size. He slipped a punch from his opponent and caught him with an uppercut, knocking him back a few steps. When his opponent caught him with a left-hook to the ribs, Ferrin winced. She knew how much that hurt.

But it didn't seem to slow him down.

"He's rather good," Ferrin observed after a minute.

"Why do you think I bet on him?" Rhi chuckled, taking a swig from his flask. "Drink?"

Ferrin took the flask, drank and passed it to Soviel, who knocked back a mouthful. It would be empty soon if the three of them kept sharing it.

"I'm off to buy us a bottle. Tell me if I miss anything," Rhi said as he hopped up, clambering around Soviel to the main aisle.

The first round was drawing to a close when Rhi returned with a bottle of whiskey. When they passed it around, it became evident that what was in Rhi's flask had been of much higher quality than what was available at the Pit.

"Och," Soviel grimaced as she swallowed.

"This is… not good," Ferrin announced, taking a second sip anyway before passing the bottle back to Rhi.

After another few rounds, it seemed Lukas had won his match, earning Rhi a small sum of coins. Ferrin wasn't sure why Rhi bothered making bets in places like this when he already had gobs of money and riches as a prince.

"I like winning, and I'm showing *support* for a friend," he explained when she asked. "Half the pool goes to the winner."

"That was exhilarating!" Soviel exclaimed after the next match had finished. The second match had been between two women, and the crowd had gone wild when the victor, a Caelish girl with ash-blonde hair braided tightly down her back, knocked out her opponent in the second round.

The trio had migrated to the upper rim of the Pit and were clustered around the railing a few steps from where Rhi had picked up his winnings.

"I would not have guessed you'd enjoy this so much," Ferrin said to Soviel, surprise in her voice.

"Why not?" Soviel cocked her head, leaning her elbows on the railing.

"Well, it's so violent and you're always so gentle and—" Ferrin gestured, searching for the words, "you take care of your plants like they're babies."

Soviel broke out laughing, "Oh, Ferrin, you'll have to stop by the infirmary someday and you'll see just how much violence I can handle." She took another pull from the bottle.

"Alright, I will," Ferrin said, eyebrows raised.

"You ladies in for a drink at the pub? I'm a rich man now," winked Rhi, holding up his small winnings.

"Mind if I join?" Lukas had appeared beside them, his hair wet and pulled back, and a small, bandaged cut visible on his cheek. He wore a clean shirt with an unbuttoned waistcoat haphazardly tugged over it, his coat draped over the crook of his arm.

"Nice hit in that second round, I thought you'd knock Ivans out for sure," Rhi said, clapping Lukas on the shoulder.

"So did I," he admitted. "He nearly caught me off guard right after."

"How's that cut?" Soviel asked, peering at his face.

"Not too deep, why?"

"Soviel here is an expert healer," Ferrin shared, gesturing with the bottle.

"I can take care of it if you want, speed up the healing so you can ditch the bandage," offered Soviel.

Ferrin straightened, intrigued. She'd never seen healing magic up close before.

"Sure," Lukas said, hefting his satchel onto his shoulder. "But can we move this party elsewhere first?" He glanced over Ferrin's shoulder, as if looking for someone.

"Are you always in this much of a hurry?" she asked, recalling how he'd scrambled to get her out of his way at the stables.

"Only when I'm avoiding someone. I'm sure you understand what that's like," he replied with a wink.

She narrowed her eyes at him. *What a scoundrel.*

Soviel and Rhi exchanged a glance.

"Right, so... to the pub?" Soviel said cheerfully. Her cheeks were tinged pink, either from the drafty building or the whiskey.

"Yes! I'm *starving*," Ferrin said, looping her arm through Soviel's and leaving the boys to follow.

"Do you know where we're going?" Soviel laughed.

"Not remotely, but I'm sure one of them will strut up and insist on leading the way."

"Hey!" Rhi gave an indignant cry as he stepped forward.

Ferrin and Soviel halted and raised their eyebrows at him.

"Let's go to the one on Baker Street," Lukas said, eyeing the trio like they were all crazy. Come to think of it, he was the only sober one in the group. "I know a guy, we can go in the back and skip out on paying anything at the door."

"They charge you just to go in?" Ferrin asked with surprise.

"Only on fight nights. Gets busy out here," he said.

"Do you think they have fried potatoes?" Soviel asked.

"Let's split a basket if they do," Ferrin giggled.

*   *   *

The pub was packed, and Ferrin was glad of their plain clothes. Not only would the full skirts of a gown take up loads of space, she'd have stood out like a sore thumb with a target on her back.

The atmosphere was dim and smoky, with plenty to look at. The walls were decorated with various odds and ends, ranging from a pair of elk antlers to a few sets of scanty lady's stays and frilly stockings draped up on the rafters.

They crammed into a booth near the back corner, again thanks to whoever Lukas knew (or more likely, whoever owed Lukas money) who worked here. A red-haired woman bustled over with a pitcher of ale, a stack of tin cups and a little notepad.

"Any food for the table?" she asked, setting down the four cups and topping them off.

They ordered three baskets of fried potatoes to share, and Lukas ordered himself a plate of chicken wings.

"Here, let me see if I have anything on me that I can use to heal up that cut," Soviel said, rooting around her pockets.

"Will it hurt?"

"Eh, it depends," Soviel said.

"On what?" Ferrin asked, sipping her watered-down ale.

"On what plant is used, how deep the cut is and how messy, how much other tissue is damaged, how precise *I* am," she rattled off.

"Here," Lukas said, reaching up to his face and carefully peeling back the bandage. The smile-shaped gash was just an inch or two under his left eye. It was red, wet and bloody and when he pulled the skin below it, it opened like a mouth.

"I'm going to lose my appetite," Rhi said, returning his attention to his drink.

"That is nasty," Ferrin grimaced in agreement.

Lukas pressed the skin down again, a wicked glint in his eye as he made the wound pop open once more.

"Sweet *Strata, stop* doing that!" Ferrin demanded, sitting back and scowling.

"You're going to make it worse," Soviel chided.

"It's not so bad," Lukas said, stilling under Soviel's touch, allowing her to fully examine it.

Her focus was knife-sharp, honing in on the skin and the underlying tissue of the wound. Ferrin had never seen someone transform so quickly. Soviel's expression had become stern, determined, as if she were figuring out how to fit the last pieces of a puzzle together, except the pieces were made of flesh.

"This might feel a bit odd," she warned, pulling some green leaves from her pocket. "Ferrin, make sure no one is watching too closely."

Ferrin obliged, scanning the room. She wasn't sure why; it wasn't as if Soviel was doing anything illegal. When her eyes settled back on Soviel and Lukas, there was a faint glow where Soviel had touched Lukas's face, and a leaf was withering and dying in her hand.

"Why does it do that?" Ferrin asked, watching as the cut pulled itself closed.

"The magic comes from me, but the energy, the cost, has to be supplemented. I essentially draw the power out of the plant and channel it into fixing the tissue. Life and growth and healing are all interconnected. Parts of the same system."

"How's it feel now?" Rhi piped in.

Lukas touched the healed skin, moved his jaw in consideration. "Itchy."

"That's pretty standard for small injuries," Soviel sounded professional as she tucked the rest of the little green leaves back into her pocket. She must have carried them with her everywhere.

"Is that why you have all those little plants in your room?" Ferrin asked with sudden realization. She'd stopped by Soviel's room a few days ago when prolonging the inevitability of afternoon stroll with Havian.

"Um, sort of. I just like being surrounded by them; it makes me feel good. Something to do with the power, I think," she said.

"Incredible," Lukas was still running his fingers over the now unmarred skin.

"You're welcome," Soviel smiled.

The waitress returned with their fried potatoes and topped off all their ales.

"Oh, these smell divine," Ferrin inhaled deeply, letting the savory, herby smell wash over her.

"I'm *starving*," Lukas said, plucking one of the slices out of the basket and popping it into his mouth.

"Splendid," Rhi added, nodding at the baskets.

Lukas swallowed another mouthful of potatoes. "Hey, I have cards."

"Oh, let's play Stacks!" Rhi leaned forward excitedly as Lukas took out a little deck of cards.

"Gods, Rhi, I don't think I even *have* money to lose to you," Ferrin groaned.

"Oh, nonsense. We can play for…" he ran his eyes over the table, searching for something to substitute for currency but came up short. "Bragging rights."

"Here…" Lukas said, shuffling and dealing out cards to each of them. "Everyone knows the rules?"

They all nodded.

"Wait," Ferrin held up a hand. "Do you all play Njorske or Southerly style?"

"Njorske," Soviel answered.

"I know both," Lukas said.

"Right, so I just try to get rid of all my cards?" Ferrin asked, raising her eyes from her hand of four.

"Exactly," Lukas answered, meeting her gaze.

Rhi won the first round, and the second, then Soviel smoked him on the third. Lukas was winning the fourth, until Ferrin at last had some luck and managed to beat him for the nonexistent prize.

"At least you won your fight," Rhi said with a cackle as he set down his final card on the fifth game.

"Yeah, I didn't need any more bruises to my pride, though," Lukas said, tossing his cards down. "That was brutal."

Ferrin turned one of the cards over in her hand. There was a stamp on it, Bourjon words, something in blue ink.

"Where'd you pick these up, Lukas?" she asked.

"Ah, a fellow I know gave them to me in exchange for a smokes' worth of some high grade *arimopo* I had a while back."

Ferrin nodded. His net cast far indeed if these cards were from where she suspected. Emblazoned on the back of each was a blue lily, mirrored over a pool of water. The symbol of *Lelia Blu*, an upscale brothel in New Larais. *The Gravedigger* had visited Calixta, an island colony of Bourjony, often enough, and some of the sailors would save their gold to visit the high-class brothel. Ash had had a particular fondness for one of the blue-clad women who loitered on the ivory steps. Ferrin and Zare had typically gone off to enjoy the city's other entertainment, which led to them tangling on the shore of a remote cove until the wee hours.

"Do you trade like that with a lot of people?" Ferrin asked, treading lightly.

"All the time, Princess. You got somethin' in mind?"

"No," she shrugged, "I was just curious."

"Speaking of," Rhi shifted the subject easily, "what's the time frame for my latest, ah, order? I have some very eager pals waiting."

Lukas raised an eyebrow. "Soon, hopefully. The checkpoints are getting stricter, so moving anything across the Strait is becoming harder and harder."

"Checkpoints?" Soviel asked with mild interest.

"Anything coming or going from the coast is subject to search," Lukas explained. "It's just a matter of packaging things in a way that won't draw attention, and usually that means small items only."

"Right," Rhi nodded as he leaned back in his chair with obvious frustration. "And you can't go around them?"

"If we go around," Lukas said, cutting the deck again, "we have to take the road down the coast after dark. Last time I tried to move something that way, I was stabbed, and I'd very much like to avoid repeating that incident."

"Fair enough," agreed Rhi sheepishly.

The next few rounds of cards went by much the same, with Rhi winning the majority of the games and Ferrin finally getting the hang of the Njorske style. Some time after two bells, they made their way back to the castle. When they neared the gates, Rhi removed his hat so the guards on duty would recognize him and wave them in, and when they reached the end of the main entry hall, they split off toward their different rooms, Lukas heading to the left, Soviel, Ferrin and Rhi to the right. Soviel took one of the branching hallways close to Ferrin's room.

"Night, Rhi," Ferrin whispered as she opened the door to her suite.

"See you tomorrow."

She tried not to dread the upcoming grand feast too much as she passed out cold.

											CHAPTER TEN

It was early evening and Ferrin was letting Soviel and Nimhe put the finishing touches on her hairstyle, a romantic half-up half-down look with little curling tendrils around her angular face and little pearl-topped pins woven throughout her thick dark hair.

Stable duties had been brutal, and after she'd finished up at the barn, she'd gone on yet another walk around the grounds with Havian, who'd been trying harder and harder to steal a kiss, despite the portly chaperone trailing them. She should have eaten some pickled onions before they met up.

When it felt like it had been an appropriate amount of time, she claimed exhaustion, which was no ruse, and retired to her rooms. She'd dozed off for an hour or so before Nell roused her and drew a bath in the big copper tub.

Now she was minutes away from the big event of the courtship visit — the grand feast. Eyes would be on the couples, who'd be seated at their own private tables. It would be the first time they'd be able to speak to each other without anyone within ten feet listening.

With a yawn, Ferrin stood from the vanity table, midnight-blue silk swishing around her.

"Did you get up to anything interesting today?" Soviel asked, handing her a delicate lace shawl, and a pair of sheer muslin mitts that would cover the space between wrist and elbow-length sleeves. They hadn't discussed it, but after the first dinner Soviel had given Ferrin's thieves' brand a knowing look and ever since had supplied her with something to cover it.

"Nothing out of the ordinary," Ferrin shook her head. "Moved some hay down from the loft, walked through the vineyard with Havian. Read up on Efelian history."

"Impressive," Soviel nodded. "You're taking this whole courtship seriously, then?"

"Only as far as my father can see," Ferrin explained with a sly expression as Nimhe returned from the closet with a ribbon that matched the shade of Ferrin's deep blue dress.

Salmon fillets glazed in honey, lemon and butter gleamed on the server's tray. Ferrin had him set two on her plate.

"Thank you," she nodded with a slight smile.

She was doing her best to remain fascinated with what was on her plate rather than letting Havian's endless stream of questions annoy her. She might even have enjoyed herself if it hadn't begun to feel like an interrogation. After all, he was handsome. She supposed over time she'd move on from the twisted, gnashing wound deep in her chest. And then what? Havian was a better option than many, better than being confined to the Cliff Hallows, better than being paired off with a much-older husband. Efel was a country with plenty of beautiful coastline, after all, and it wasn't uncommon for royal wedded pairs to come to agreeable arrangements. They could lead mostly separate lives, interacting only when necessary. Perhaps she could eventually take to the sea again.

She examined him thoughtfully.

"And while you *were* at University, what did you study?" he asked.

"Rendering wildlife, sketching, history," she answered with a curt smile, raising her glass of light, summery white wine to her lips.

He squinted almost imperceptibly, then nodded. His Meddemaran tan accented his hazel eyes, and his thick hair gave him the look of a painted god.

She wondered what he thought of her, if he had any true interest or if this was strictly political. Did he think her too shrewish in nature and looks? Were her eyebrows too unkempt? Was he put off by the strangeness of her two differently colored eyes?

She sighed, setting down her glass of Efelian wine. She couldn't remember what it was called, but King Alban had claimed it was their best.

At the other private table, Rhi laughed at something Khianie said, and raised his glass to her yet again. How was he so good at this? He seemed genuinely enchanted by her presence. Rhi was a much better actor than she.

"So you must have traveled around to sketch different wildlife, yes? Where did you go?"

Ferrin removed her gaze from her brother's table. "Oh, a few places. Um… the countryside, and some places near Marana. We were given opportunity to travel to different climes to study different birds and animals there."

"Really?" Havian's voice had changed completely. He sounded wholly unconvinced.

"Indeed," Ferrin replied lightly, again picking up her glass, if only to occupy her hands.

"And how long were you held prisoner by the pirates?" he asked, the concern in his voice edged with something darker.

She swirled her glass, pretending to be fascinated by the color of the wine. "I'm not sure, I was knocked unconscious at first," she revealed. "Less than a week, I think."

"Did they know who you were from the beginning, or..."

"I don't know, I was unconscious," she repeated.

A loud drumroll interrupted their conversation as dancers swept up the aisle between the lower tables, flipping and waltzing their way along, swathed in bright golds, blacks and magentas.

Havian turned back to her. "But you must have had some idea what they meant to do with you, no?"

She frowned, taking another bite of the salmon.

"Did they take you for ransom, or to rob you? Perhaps to sell you to the flesh market?" His curiosity was making her deeply uneasy and Ferrin did *not* appreciate the direction in which the conversation seemed to be heading.

"Well, I didn't stop to ask them," she joked tightly. "But... I assumed for ransom."

"My apologies, I did not mean to bring up unpleasant memories," he said, holding her gaze. "But this is something I must know."

Ferrin looked at him expectantly, waiting for elaboration.

"I may be a second son, but legitimacy of my heirs is just as important to my nation as those of my older brother's," he said coolly.

"Of course," she agreed, feeling the heat rising in her face. *What is he talking about?*

"So, you understand why I must know. When you were... ehem...*captive*..." he uttered the word as if he didn't quite believe it. "The pirates, did they damage you in any way?" He looked away and took another sip of his wine.

She froze, tightening her grip on her half-full glass. "I'm not sure I understand your meaning."

"As a suitor, it is of political importance, you understand. I must ask," he said defensively. As if *she* were the one questioning *his* worth.

"Then ask me directly," Ferrin said, gritting her teeth.

Havian carefully set down his wine and sat forward slowly. "How, as a suitor, can I be sure that your virtue is intact when you've been running about with sea-ruffians?" This was a calculated question, a challenge she could see in his cold eyes. He clearly knew more than he'd let on, and wanted her to slip up.

"Excuse me?" Ferrin said, aghast.

"I need to know," he continued. "After all, unlawful men will do what they like. And runaway girls cannot always be trusted. Even with their own chastity." He paused, then added pointedly, "even royal ones."

"Prince Havian," Ferrin began, barely restraining herself from shouting in his face. Was he really doing this? In public? "I don't believe this is an entirely appropriate subject—"

"Tell me whether or not you played *whore* for those pirates, or I will leave this parasitic backwater island nation to the mercy of our tariffs," he hissed, something self-righteous and full of fury burning in his eyes.

Ferrin jumped up, nearly knocking over her chair.

"How dare you!" she slammed her hand down on the table, and the room went quiet. She leaned in close, pleased with the shock that registered on his face, though his expression quickly turned to a satisfied sneer. He'd meant to rile her. "Nothing was done to *taint* me. You're a guest in my family's house, and you've insulted me, *and* my country," she seethed under her breath.

She picked up her glass again and swirled the wine. "And I'm afraid your 'best wine' is rather dry." With that, she tossed the contents into the prince's face. "I'll not continue a courtship with a man so lacking in honor." She turned and stalked down the aisle and out the door, skirts billowing behind her as she became acutely aware of exactly how much trouble she was about to be in.

Ferrin was at the edge of the orchard when the anger and adrenaline finally wore off, and she halted, bracing herself on the big tree in front of her, gulping down air as the reality of what she'd just done hit her.

The orchard would be blossoming soon, but for now the branches were bare, knobby and gnarly. Damp and dark with spring rain, twisting like skeletal arms, clawing their way towards the night sky. The big oak tree that had grown by accident decades ago at the edge of the orchard was a comfort in its familiar out-of-placeness. The swing suspended in its branches was mostly dry, and the wooden plank creaked as Ferrin sank into it, her heart still racing as she slouched, grasping the ropes like they were the only thing tethering her to the earth. They bit into her hands in a familiar way, as memories she'd been trying to avoid spilled into her mind.

Sea air, Zare's laugh, the click-clack of the butterfly knife he was always whipping around, his nimble fingers too quick to be caught by the blade. His cool gaze leveling at her the day before he'd sold her out.

She took a deep shuddering breath and tried to release the tension from her body, to still her shaking hands.

"Not sure a glass of wine to the face is the way *I* would go about winning over a suitor," a voice drawled from the trunk of the oak. *Lukas.*

She was so taken aback, she snapped out of the downward spiral into which she was descending. "What in the name of *Heleion* are *you* doing out here? Can't I get a moment alone?" she barked, turning in her seat to face him.

He was leaning on the side of the tree, arms crossed, smug expression fading from his face, replaced by something that might have been concern, or even surprise. "Well, after all hell broke loose in the Great Hall, I figured it was as good a distraction as any for me to slip out for some fresh air."

"Fascinating," she sniffed, then straightened, composing herself. "This is my apple orchard, please leave me alone."

"Is it?" he asked, pushing off the tree and circling in front of it to the other side, "I thought it was your father's. And isn't he speaking of disowning you? Especially after all *that*," he gestured toward the castle.

"Oh, bite me," she fired back at him. "Wait. How did you get out here so fast? I thought you were still at the feast when I left."

"Servants don't just materialize out of the woodwork, you know," he laughed. "They have tunnels, secret hallways."

"Show me them."

"No."

"Well then, how about you leave me alone?" she snarled.

Silence.

"So, now you've angered the king, and the Efelian royals who are here as guests," he sighed theatrically. "I'm wondering, why would someone who seems to want to escape this place risk drawing so much attention to herself? What could dear, sweet Havian and his ungodly lashes have said to cause such an uproar?"

"Mind your own damned business," she snapped.

"Do you insist on biting everyone's head off when they ask you a question, or am I simply lucky?"

She was silent for a moment, wholly drained and exhausted from the last two weeks. "I want to run, but I have nowhere else to go," she quietly confessed. It was what had been plaguing her for days. Maybe she *could* escape again, but then what?

"I see," he nodded.

"Why are you here?"

"I told you," he repeated with an impish grin, "Fresh air."

"There's fresh air just about everywhere else on the grounds, you know. Are you following me?"

He whistled. "Well, we think awfully highly of ourselves, don't we?"

She glowered at him as he stalked forward.

"I'm here for this, Princess," he said, stepping towards the swing. He halted less than half a foot from her knees, eyes locked on hers with a devilish smirk as he reached up into the thick branches above and pulled out a brown paper-and-twine wrapped parcel. How it was hidden there was beyond her. He slid it into the inside pocket of his coat and retreated to the chopping stump a few feet away.

"Truly, your stealth is unparalleled," she rolled her eyes.

"I'm trusting you won't mention this," he said pointedly.

"Who would I even tell? It's probably *for* Rhi, or am I mistaken?"

He huffed. "Perhaps your crafty friend."

"Who?"

"Your blonde friend."

"Soviel?" she asked. "You think Soviel is *crafty*?"

"I know card-counting when I see it," he replied. "The only reason she didn't win every single round of cards last night is because Rhi does it too."

Ferrin frowned. She'd been too busy adjusting to the different set of rules to notice. Perhaps she didn't give Soviel enough credit.

"Fine, I won't say anything." She leaned back in the swing, letting it sway. "What's in there, anyway?"

"That's confidential," he said with mock primness.

"Oh, come on. I know you're dealing in *popava*. What is it, Veiran Red? Or Maraki Blue?"

"Alright, first," he said, reaching into one of his pockets and pulling out a little brass pocket watch. "I am *not* a *popava* seller. I just move it. Among other things. Second, it's a blend."

She sighed. "I know Rhi likes to get wild. You don't need to behave so suspiciously about it. That does seem like an awful lot for one person, though."

"He likes to distribute it to his friends when he has his revels," Lukas shrugged. "Not my business."

"And do you attend these revels?" she asked.

"I pop in every once in a while. It's a good way to meet new clients, see who might have an itch only Meroyan rum or Veiran silk can scratch. Who might be invested enough in the polishing of their soul to pay for a reliquary to be transported from a *venaculta* in Bourjony."

"Right," Ferrin said. "So, Lukas, what else is it you do around here? Besides pit fighting and hiding illegal substances in trees."

"I told you before — a bit of this, a bit of that." He slipped the watch back into his coat and took out a silver flask. "A blockade run every now and again."

"Blockade runs?" she asked, her voice skeptical.

"You might not know it in your ivory tower, Princess, but a lot of people on this island are simply 'going without' because of the high taxes on everything coming in off the continent."

"I do know that," she said haughtily, with no small pang of guilt. "How do you manage it?"

"Every so often I'll take a skiff across the strait at night and load up on food on an island off the coast of Bourjony, then come back and sell it for cost in the village." He unscrewed the flask. "It's risky, so I can't go often."

Ferrin blinked. "That's noble of you… what's the catch?"

"Your skepticism wounds me, highness." He placed a hand over his heart.

"I am skeptical," she frowned. "You're quite a suspicious character, you know."

"Ah, of course, coming from the runaway pirate, *I'm* the suspicious one."

"What is that supposed to mean? And how do you even know about that?"

"It's my business to know things." He took a sip. "What were you doing out by the stables the night we first met?"

"You already know the answer to that," she said sarcastically.

"Then why are you out here tonight? Why draw all that attention from the king, in front of a crowd of nobles, no less? Why not just gather some jewels and slip away in the night? Surely you could liquidate some heirlooms to buy passage off the island."

"I tried that, remember? Some scoundrel thwarted my plans," she said drily.

"Right," he said, once again lifting the flask to his lips.

"What's in there anyway?"

"The tears of small children."

"Very funny. I'm serious."

"Tell me what you're not saying and I'll give you some."

"Plying a lady with alcohol? You really *are* a scoundrel."

He said nothing, only jerked his brows up and stared expectantly.

"You do realize I can get myself expensive whiskey and wine whenever I please?" she continued.

"I do, but you can't get this," he wiggled the flask. "This is good, hard Savikian stuff. They don't even sell it over here."

"Fine," she sighed. "State your query."

"So. Why did you run away in the first place?" he asked.

"Strata above, really?"

"I genuinely want to know."

She paused, then took a long and tired breath as she fidgeted with the fabric of her dress. "Every minute I'm here feels as if… I don't know, as if I'm wasting time. I can feel myself dissolving and settling like sand at the bottom of a river, like I'm somehow anchored down and adrift in a storm at the same time. Nothing I do here matters, and it never has."

Lukas extended the flask wordlessly.

"When my mother disappeared, it just felt like my father was trying to erase every trace of her from the palace, the country even," she shared, surprised at how easily she could talk about it. She'd kept that bottled up for so long. She sipped from the flask. "I wonder if it's why he tries so hard to suppress the Caelish ways. In the country and his children."

"Prejudice against Caelish folks has gotten a lot more harsh recently," Lukas told her, accepting the flask back.

"That stuff is strong," she choked, swallowing against the burn still in her throat. Savikian Deathwater indeed.

"I'm sorry about your mother," Lukas offered softly.

The accursed Savikian liquor must have greased her vocal chords, because she found herself admitting, "ever since she disappeared I've been waiting for my father to finish stomping out the dying remains of her legacy, of everything she loved, and taught Rhi and me to love."

He passed her the flask again, and she knocked back another swig.

"Careful!" he threw up a hand, urging her to slow down. "It'll hit you like a ton of bricks if you drink too fast."

She lowered the flask and rolled her eyes, "Don't be ridiculous. I lived with pirates for five years, remember? I can hold my liquor."

"I'm sure you can, but Savikian Deathwater is twice the strength of whiskey. Keeps them from freezing to death out there."

"The name seems misleading, if that's the case."

"Well, it also doesn't taste as awful as it should, so it wouldn't be hard to drink yourself to death without noticing."

"Lovely."

"So… what did His-Royal-Pomade have to say that elicited such a response?" Lukas asked, reaching for the flask again.

Ferrin bit back a laugh. The prince *did* seem to use an awful lot of pomade to keep his perfectly styled hair in place. "Why do you want to know that?"

He shrugged his broad shoulders, swirling the flask. "I've done some business with the a few Efelian nobles before. Call me curious."

"Well… if you suspect that he made a ridiculous and insulting comment regarding things that may or may not have happened while I was 'captured', you would be correct," she said, looking down at her hands, and again fidgeting with the trim of her gown. She knew color had risen to her cheeks, and hoped it was too dark for him to see. "I believe the words used were 'tainted virtue' ,'backwater nation', and 'whore'."

Lukas chuckled, and she thought for a moment he was going to point an accusatory finger in her face and tell her she was a fool or a whore. "Maybe you should've thrown your dinner at him too," he laughed.

She snorted mildly. "What about you, Lukas, grand smuggler and valiant blockade runner? Tell me something surprising. Where do you come from?"

"Not much to tell, Princess," he shrugged and took another sip of Deathwater.

Ferrin just glared at him and waited.

"Fine," he exhaled. "My mother was a spice seller living in the slums of Khalim, and my father was a Caelish sailor stationed there, before he was called back to fight for the Caels in the 'Barrian Civil War', or whatever you prefer to call it," he said, passing the flask back to her. "I grew up on and off the streets of Khalim with my mother and older sister, and eventually my younger sister. Well, half-sister. My older sister moved to a farming estate with her husband, my younger sister disappeared. After that, my mother left the city to my sister's farm."

"I'm sorry," Ferrin said quietly. "You never found out what happened to her?"

"No," he shook his head, sorrow flickering behind his eyes. "Khalim is… it's a big city. Girls disappear off the streets a lot there, and she wandered off by herself all the time. My sister and I tried to prevent it, but you can only cage someone in so much before it becomes futile." He sighed deeply, and reached absentmindedly into in his pocket. She caught a glint of brass as he closed his hand around a mystery object. "After that, I joined up with the Akhatan insurgency to purge the Veiran occupation. Led a guerrilla troop for a while before… before I came north to find my father. That was about two years ago."

"Did you find him?"

"Nope," Lukas said simply. "The records from that time are imprecise. But there's nothing showing he went with the exiles to Njorske, so he probably died in the war."

Ferrin felt her heart ache at hearing that. Not knowing what had happened to two of his family members, not knowing whether they lived or died… she knew what that felt like. She almost wished they were sitting closer so she could reach across the space between them and lay her hand over his. Sitting there saying 'I'm sorry' felt shallow and empty.

"Then I ran out of money, started running odd jobs. Met Rhi soon after," he added.

"Ah, yes. How *did* you meet my brother?"

"He actually caught me in the servants' hallways with *many* illegal objects in my satchel, I thought I was done for. Then he handed me a bag of gold and gave me a list."

They both snickered at that. Ferrin may have been the one with a reputation for getting into trouble, but that was only because Rhi was better at not getting caught.

"So what was on the list?" she asked.

"The usual. A bundle of fancy Calixtan *arimopo* cigars, Maraki Blue *popava*, a certain kind of chicken that lays only double-yolked eggs and a beat-down on someone who was giving his current beau trouble."

"Oh, so you're a smuggler, a birdkeeper *and* a hitman?" she joked.

He gave a low whistle. "No need to sugar-coat it for my sake, Highness."

"Hmph. How have you *not* been thrown in jail yet?"

"Well, for one thing I'm very good at what I do, and for another I have a lot of connections," he said. "If I get thrown in jail, my good friend in the Guard doesn't get to write letters to his sweetheart in Calixta, and another doesn't get his pre-wrapped cigarillos, and another doesn't get his bathtub gin sold for a profit overseas. Plus, if I'm really in a bind, I could always flash Rhi's seal."

"I see," nodded Ferrin. She rolled her eyes and passed back his flask.

"Well," he braced his hands on his knees and stood. "I reckon you're going to be in for it tomorrow. Any idea what you're going to say to your father?"

She exhaled, deep and slow. It felt good. "No," she admitted. She had no idea what was to come. "To be honest, I haven't ruled out making a break for it."

"He'll probably spin some excuse for you, and then make you apologize to the Efelians," Lukas surmised as she stood.

"I do not think my pride could bear it."

"Then fake it," he shrugged. "If you want a chance at getting out of here again, wouldn't it be worth it?"

"I doubt I'll have the chance. They're probably readying the prison wagon to take me to the Cliff Hallows as we speak."

"You think he'd really send you there?"

"He's threatened it already," she shrugged sadly.

Lukas bristled. "I think that would be worse for his reputation than anything else."

"I agree, but he isn't known for his rational, calm thought."

Lukas grinned. "You seem to have that in common."

She narrowed her eyes at him but said nothing.

He gave her a wry sidelong glance, "Come on, let's get back before they send someone looking for you."

*   *   *

The two parted ways shortly after passing through the front door. Lukas said he had a few things to take care of, but Ferrin wasn't ready to go to sleep, so she found herself in front of Rhi's door. She was there partly because she wanted to find out what kind of trouble she was in, and partly because the Savikian liquor had put her in a sociable mood.

"Rhiach!" she banged on the door with the soft side of her fist. "Open up!"

After a long moment, the door swung open, and Rhi braced a hand on the doorframe, his shirt half-open.

"Ferrin!" he exclaimed. "What a surprise!"

"Oh, shit. Are you with someone?" she asked, peering around him.

"What? Oh. No." He tugged his shirt closed. "Just me."

She nodded. "Right then, I'm coming in."

"Want a drink?"

She declined with an open palm and a shake of her head. "Already had some of that stuff Lukas had."

"Well, I'm going to," he said, popping the cork on a vintage Bourjon red, likely also compliments of Lukas. "That wine at dinner was awful. There is no way that was their best."

Ferrin chuckled, and then sobered at the thought of how much trouble she was in. "How was the Kalassan dessert?"

"Surprisingly good. Imagine if a croissant had children with a sugar-nut cookie."

She arched her eyebrows thoughtfully. That did sound good. "Do you have anything to eat?"

"There's a bowl of fruit *right* in front of you — oh wait, never mind. I moved it. Here." He set the wooden fruit bowl in front of her on the table.

"Thanks," she said, plucking a ripe orange from the top of the bowl. "So, where's the wild revel?"

"Oh, I'm taking a little break, but fear not! The festivities will resume later in the week."

"I may drop in," she mumbled as she peeled the orange. "I could use a little fun."

"I'll drink to that!" Rhi proclaimed, swirling his glass.

"So…" she began. "How bad was it from where you were sitting?"

"What, your extreme display of 'hard to get'?" he joked.

"I'm serious, Rhi."

He blew out a breath and set his wine glass down. "It was not good. But I'm sure it will pass; new scandals happen every week and it always seems like the end of life as we know it. Until the next one comes along and everyone forgets that your pants ripped up the back during a particularly vigorous waltz."

"That," she said, "was very specific."

"And yet, no one really remembers it. Besides, my coat hid it well," he grinned, reaching for an apple. "I digress, it will pass. Father turned red as a summer tomato, but Nerena got him to calm down."

Ferrin grimaced. "I don't like her."

"Who? Nerena? Have you spoken to her?"

"Well… no, not so much," Ferrin admitted. They'd had a brief, formal introduction in passing a few days ago, nothing more. Maybe she was being unfair to the woman. After all, it wasn't as if it was her fault that Ferrin's father had driven away their mother. "She just seems… off-putting."

"I know, she's a little young for him, I thought. She's what, thirty? Thirty-five, maybe?" Rhi bit into the apple. It sounded juicy.

Ferrin chewed the inside of her cheek. "When did she turn up here anyway?"

"Oh," Rhi sighed contemplatively, "perhaps two and a half years ago? She's the daughter of some wealthy iron tycoon from Njorske. Some province I'd never heard of. Why?"

"I get a weird feeling from her, is all." She chewed her cheek. "And don't you think it's strange how much she looks like Mother?"

"Everyone has a taste for something," Rhi shrugged, knocking back another swig of his wine. "Obviously, father's is for dark-haired ice-queens."

Ferrin frowned. She didn't think their mother was an 'ice-queen'.

Rhi reached across the ornate couch to the little carved end table, where he opened the drawer and pulled out a delicate box. It was silver and enamel, decorated in swirling patterns and symbols of blue and white. He opened the box to reveal blue-grey powder and a tiny snuff-spoon. He withdrew a tiny pinch and held it to his nose, inhaling sharply.

"Want some?" he offered, holding out the box.

"No, I don't really like it," she said. *Popava* came from the fields of *Popavium* blossoms on the continent. She'd tried it in a tea and it had made her dizzy. She knew there were different strains and that it could be ingested and inhaled, and it made a good painkiller if one needed a large quantity of stitches or to set a broken bone, but she had seen a few of *The Gravedigger*'s crew take too much of a liking to the stuff. No one had worried about it, until they'd run out, far from any supply. Then they'd spent days sick, shivering and vomiting.

"Rhi, are you sure you know what you're doing?"

"Absolutely," he promised, shutting the box. She noticed the pupils in his warm chocolate eyes had become pinpoints.

"You know what that stuff does to you over time? And what happens when you stop?" she asked, trying not to sound too judgmental.

"I know," he said evenly. "But that's only if you take too much of it. This stuff is mild, it's not even full-strength. Completely harmless."

"Just… be careful," she said, reaching out and squeezing his hand. "Even mild *popava* can be intoxicating."

"Oh, Ferr. You worry too much," he winked. "I can handle it."

"I know, I know," she said, not fully convinced. "So, what do you think I should say tomorrow? Do you think Father will pack me off to the temple?"

Rhi considered carefully, "No, I don't think so. Not immediately, at least. I'll talk to him."

"And say what? 'Please don't send my shrew-tongued, wayward sister to be confined'? He doesn't listen to anyone."

"Like I said," he bit into the apple again, chewing and swallowing. "Nerena was able to calm him. He may be more amenable than you're expecting."

CHAPTER ELEVEN

There was nothing more unpleasant than awaking with a dry, stale taste in one's mouth, Ferrin decided when she came to the next morning. Maybe it was the Savikian Deathwater. Maybe it was the days of limited sleep and laboring in the stables.

"Shall I draw the curtains?" Nell asked.

Ferrin sighed, sitting up. A servant was waiting outside her room the night before to tell her she was to report to her father's throne room first thing in the morning, and to not bother going to stable duties. She sat back in her bed, picking at the breakfast of toast and eggs that Nell had carried in for her, and poured a glass of water from the pitcher by her bed. Her hair was a mess, she realized as she ran her fingers through it. Soviel and Nimhe had arrived to dress her, this time in a modest, dark grey frock. They walked her down to the throne room in tense silence.

"Father, he was insulting and rude and improper," she explained, gritting her teeth. Her face was warm with remembered rage. "I have nothing to apologize for, he should be apologizing to *me* for questioning my honor in such a public setting."

As it turned out, no one else had heard what Havian had said just before Ferrin's outburst.

The king had turned an even more violent shade of red than Ferrin had thought possible, and by the time he'd finished hurling admonishments at her, the vein on his forehead was popping out. Now, he sat fuming upon the throne, burning holes through her with his eyes.

"*Nothing to apologize for*?" he spat. "You've cost me everything. My reputation with the Efelians, your reputation with any suitor, the easing of tariffs this was supposed to bring about! Did I not make myself perfectly clear when I told you what you were expected to do?"

"Father, believe me, if you'd heard what he said, the *way* he implied it—" Ferrin attempted to interject.

"'*Believe you*'? You're a liar, Ferrin. A liar and a criminal."

She choked. "I'm sorry it happened so publicly," she said, feeling her throat tighten.

"Stop talking," he snapped.

At that very moment Nerena swept in unaccompanied.

"Good morning, Ferrin, it's lovely to see you again," she said with a placid smile that did not reach her ice-blue eyes. Her straight black hair was swept over her shoulders and accented with a crown in a surprisingly youthful look for a married woman of her station.

"Good morning," Ferrin said politely.

"Darling, stop yelling at her," Nerena swooped down and placed a kiss on King Henrik's cheek. "I'm sure Ferrin will find a way to make things right, won't she?" Nerena fixed her cool gaze on Ferrin.

The sentiment was not as comforting as it should have been.

The queen took her seat beside the king, that not-quite-a-smile still on her face, "I know we can come up with something."

"I'll summon you again when I decide what to do with you," growled the king, though it did seem his temper had cooled significantly since Nerena had arrived. "You are dismissed."

Ferrin offered a small curtsy and turned to leave. She was halfway down the aisle when the doors burst open and a frantic man in glasses and an unbuttoned waistcoat tumbled in. He looked like he'd never seen the sun, his skin was so pale. There were papers all but coming out of his ears as he scampered down the aisle. When he passed her, a slip of paper flitted out of one of his folios and landed in front of her.

She stooped to pick it up, turning the sheet over in her hand as she turned to tell the man he'd dropped it.

"So sorry, Your Majesty!" he said in a panicked voice.

"Jensen. Your meeting isn't until twelve o'clock," the king said with a grunt.

"Oh, Gods above, I've been up half the night drafting the blueprints for the garrison. I'd forgotten you moved it back, my deepest apologies," he babbled, scrambling to gather his things from a table at the side of the room.

"Jensen, shut up and show me the plans, you're here now." Her father stood and stalked down the dais to the table.

Ferrin froze, forgotten at the edge of the room, the paper clutched in her hands. It was a proposal with plans of where to allocate the lumber and space for building a new defense and guard tower to the south.

Her eyes skimmed the paper; the first option denoted that the lumber would come from Taroch Forest. It was an old, old forest that stood a mile or so from the castle walls, just past the town, and reached most of the way up the coast.

Two more men burst through the doors, falling over themselves with apologies, brushing past her as if she were a piece of furniture as they groveled to the king and queen. "Your Majesty! We are so sorry to be late—" They stopped cold when Jensen shot them a frantic-eyed glare.

One of them cleared his throat, straightening his cravat as they both stepped forward, "Right, yes, the plans."

If her father noticed that she hadn't left, he didn't care, for he said nothing as she stepped closer to the table, waiting to overhear what exactly was going on.

"The Companies of Labor and Resources: Malgram, Forsyth and Biert have surveyed and inspected the land to be used for the installation of a new guard station, watchtower, and wall." Jensen named the location, describing what was currently there. "The allocation of lumber to the correct amount will take between five and seven acres, with an additional three to six acres to be taken for fire and fuel. The Companies have surveyed and cordoned off a portion of the southern edge of Taroch Forest..."

Ferrin sucked in a breath and stepped closer.

"Brush and scrub will be burned, and the lumber will be transported by way of barge through the harbor, circumnavigating the difficult journey over the cliffs."

"That's a terrible idea," Ferrin uttered without thinking, stepping forward. "Father," she shook her head, turning to face him. "Think on this, the destruction, the loss—"

"Did I not make it clear you were on thin ice, *girl*?" Her father growled. "A new wall will be magnificent. Years ago, the old wall kept the wildmen of the north at bay, and this one will keep the damned Bourjon hedonists of the south from our fortress."

"But, father, think on it—" she pleaded, coming around the table to him.

He slapped her across the face. It only stung, but the shock of it was jarring enough to stop her in her tracks. She raised a hand to her face in disbelief. He had *never* raised a hand to her, even in the worst of fights.

"You were not brought here to give your opinion. I can have the carriage brought round in a minute's notice and ship you west to The Cliff Hallows," he seethed.

Nerena looked on calmly.

"Father, please just *consider*." Her voice sounded hoarse.

"Get her out of here," he ordered the guards, without deigning to look at her as his sentries approached. "Leave before you further anger me."

The guards closed in and marched her from the room.

Still reeling from all that had happened in the throne room, Ferrin paced the halls. She couldn't return to her chambers or she'd explode. She needed to go do *something*. As she stalked through the courtyard, her heart raced. Where were those damn rebels anyways? Shouldn't they be trying to stop this?

The whole proposal was senseless, and she'd been kicked out before she'd heard any dates, or whether or not it was a sure thing. She let out a frustrated sigh as she stared off towards the bit of forest she could see poking out over the village below. Maybe, just maybe, she could win some influence… with Rhiach's help. Maybe they could change the course of this foul plan. They could try, if she stayed instead of running away again.

She knew she had nowhere to go, nowhere to run, but that feeling persisted nonetheless. It was under her skin, the constant need to *go*. Like she had somewhere she was meant to be, but she couldn't remember where it was or how to get there. It was out there. Perhaps it was the motion in itself, not just in the open seas and endless sky full of clouds whisking across it to parts unknown. Perhaps it was just restlessness she couldn't seem to shake.

Her attention was drawn to two figures standing in the courtyard, hovering beside a marble fountain carved in the likeness of Marras and Merriye, the twin sea gods. It was Rhi and Lukas.

She considered Lukas as she approached, and wondered if *Rebel Insurgent* was one of his 'many talents'. After all, from what he'd told her the night before, it wasn't a far cry from what his life had been like before he left Akhata. She had to admit, she was intrigued by the thought of him leading a guerrilla troop during the Veiran occupation.

As she approached them, she saw Lukas pass yet another linen-wrapped package to Rhi, who folded it into the pocket of his dark blue frock coat and nodded before turning and striding towards the castle.

"Cake delivery?" she joked as he passed her.

"No," he said, turning. "Apricots, actually." He then proceeded to withdraw the package, while still walking backwards away from her, and popped out a small, orange-colored fruit. He bit into it with a silly grin.

She laughed in surprise. "What's next, a tiger for a pet?"

"Oh, sure, it's on the way," he called over his shoulder, tossing the bitten apricot from hand to hand.

She shook her head with a chuckle and turned her attention to Lukas.

"You know, when you said you got anything and everything for a price, I really didn't consider exotic fruits as part of that— hey, what happened to your eye?" she asked as he turned towards her. She stilled her hand, some strange reflex urging her to reach up and brush his hair away so she could better see the fresh bruising around his eye. "Bad round in the Pit?"

"What? Oh. No, actually. I broke up a bar brawl in the middle of one of my deliveries late last night." He rubbed his jaw. He looked like he'd skipped shaving that morning. "Then it just turned into an even bigger brawl. Probably should have minded my own business."

She found herself wishing she could somehow ease the bruising away like Soviel had with his cut the other night.

"Does it hurt?"

"Only if I touch it. Or squint really hard."

His eyes really were striking, that bright sea-green lined by thick lashes and desert-gold skin.

"That's unfortunate," she said. "Must have been a late night. Do you ever sleep?" When they had parted ways, it was near midnight. It was now only a little past eight in the morning.

"Oh, on occasion," he smirked. "I had a meeting with some private representatives of *arimopo* farmers out of Kalassa who are here with the delegation. It's been difficult to get anything by way of Efelian trade, since they only want to sell from their own colonies. Not to mention, their fat export fees."

"Ah," she nodded. *Arimopo* was grown mostly on farms further south, in the rich soil bordering the *Meddemara*. That was the land that earth magic was said to have blessed.

"I used to move it with the *popava* shipments out of Dromata, but the latest blockade has all but stopped that."

"Ah, the Dromatan *popava* trade. I knew it well, once, you know," she said wryly. Why couldn't she keep her mouth shut?

"Did you, or did Gillian?" he asked her pointedly.

"Oh, hush," she crossed her arms. "It was a long time ago. I was going by Gill, then, actually."

"Now *that* is something I must hear," he bit his lip impishly.

"Oh, wouldn't you just love that," she waved him away. "At least ask nicely."

"Please, royal highness Ferrin, master embroiderer and seafaring scourge, do tell me about your cross-dressing run-in with the Dromatan *popava* trade."

She scowled at him, especially at the embroidery part. "Are you mocking me, good sir?"

"Oh, I would never," he said, placing his hand over his heart.

"I could have you beheaded! Thrown in the stocks for your insolence!"

"Could you, truly, oh-disowned one?" he crowed.

"I'm not disowned yet, I'm a proper lady. The pinnacle of royal society!" She smacked him playfully on his well-muscled arm.

"I wouldn't believe that even if I *hadn't* seen you toss a glass of wine in a prince's face," he laughed, batting away her hand.

"Well, they haven't shipped me off to the Cliff Hallows yet," she shrugged. Escape crossed her mind again, but was quickly swept aside by the overwhelming need to stop the potential destruction of the Forest.

"Good thing for those poor nuns," teased Lukas. "They wouldn't know what to do with you. Although," he said, stroking his chin contemplatively. "Maybe the vow of silence would be good."

"Take that back, you scoundrel!"

A grin spread across his face. "I'm an honest man, Princess."

"You're incorrigible," she said.

"Incorrigible and still curious about that story," he said, shaking his finger at her like a scolding schoolmarm.

"It's a bit of a long story. What are you doing this morning?" she asked.

"I have some errands to run," he replied, looking curious. "Why?"

"Well, I suppose I'll have to accompany you."

"Don't be ridiculous. I'm not bringing you to the black market—"

She opened her mouth to protest, but he continued on.

"—dressed like *that*." He gestured at her fine frock. It may not have been a jewel-toned silk ball gown, but it was an ostensibly fine garment nonetheless. "I have some things you can borrow at the cabin, if you really must."

"You do?" She eyed him skeptically. "Did you *also* once have a cross dressing altar-ego?"

"What? No." He shook his head as she fell into step beside him. "I have some of my older sister's things for when she visits."

"Is that often?"

"No, but her husband used to trade in the north every so often, and she comes with him when he plans to stop on the island. They own a small farm."

"Ah," Ferrin nodded. She wondered if his sister was as tall as he was. "Well then, we'd better be going," she said playfully.

"Fine, fine, come along, then." He rolled his eyes with a sigh, though she had a feeling his exasperation was only theatrical.

The little cottage in the woods on the edge of the grounds was, well, surprisingly homey.

"This is your *house?* I thought you had rooms in the castle."

"I do. Last door in the west wing, second floor," he said from where he stood digging through a shelf in a closet. "This place is for meetings that need to be in private and can't happen inside the palace."

"Again, how?"

"It was just sitting here falling to ruin, so I asked Rhi if I could use it. He said fine, I fixed it up, and here we are. I think it was once used for guard lodging."

Ferrin surveyed the interior. It was small, only two tiny rooms, but it looked well cared for, which was another surprise to Ferrin. She wondered if he had a lover who'd made it feel so cozy. She quickly dismissed the thought and picked up a little tin dolphin from the mantle, turning it over in her hand.

"Here you go," he tossed her some clothing.

"Thanks," she said.

He left the room, giving her some privacy to change. She stripped off her gown and tossed it onto an armchair. It was a boring, colorless thing that fell into a crumpled heap of stiff gray. That left her in her shin-length shift and stays, which laced down the back. *Right... that might be a problem,* she realized. With some contorting of her shoulders and elbows, she managed to find the knot at the back and undo it before wriggling herself free.

She quickly slipped out of her shift and into the breeches and undershirt, then pulled the stays back on over the shirt. *His sister couldn't have kept a spare set of jumps or a lady's waistcoat around?* She considered going without any additional support. Her chest was relatively modest in size, but it still wouldn't be comfortable. And she might pop right out of the loose, flowing shirt.

"Lukas?" she called from the doorway to the other room, "Could you give me a hand?"

"What is it?" he said, turning from the window.

"Um," she felt her face flush as she clutched the front of the blue stays. "Would you lace these back up for me?"

His eyes widened almost imperceptibly. "Oh. Sure, yes. I can… do that."

She passed him the little blue cord, and turned around, sweeping her hair off her back and over her shoulder.

"Is it supposed to be like little X's? I'm not sure how…"

She fought a chuckle. "No, you just tie it to the bottom hole and then go from side to side, in and out, like a spiral."

"Alright," he nodded. His fingers brushed her spine through the thin fabric of the shirt as he secured the cord. She felt the tug of the stiff, boned panel hug and press lightly against her waist as he drew the cord through the next eyelet and the next.

"How tight is it supposed to be?" he asked, pulling the excess taut.

"That's fine," she breathed.

She could feel the warmth of his body as he pulled the lacings shut over her back, and shivered when his knuckles brushed the space between her shoulder blades as he tucked the excess cord into the top of the stays. Her breath caught when she felt his, warm and faint, on the back of her neck.

Suddenly the air in the little cottage seemed much too quiet, and she knew she must be breathing far too loudly. Had it gotten warmer? She swallowed, turning to face him and nearly bumping into his chest. They stood like that for a second too long, eyes locked, all but sharing breath. "Thanks."

He stepped back and ran a hand through his hair. His bronze skin showed the barest hint of a blush. "Well, uh… ready then?" he asked awkwardly. "I think I have a coat laying around that you can throw on…" He went to search the coat hook by the door.

"Flustered by ladies' underthings, are we?" she teased, cocking an eyebrow at him as he returned with a tattered, rust-colored coat looped over his arm.

He stopped just short of her and ran his eyes over her stays with a small smirk, "Maybe, I'm just more used to removing them, Princess."

Ferrin stifled a choke.

And with that, he handed her the coat, winked, and headed out the door.

The walk down to the town in the daytime revealed a far grimmer view than the one Ferrin had made out the other night. At its edges, the town was a mess. Buildings were crumbling. Kids begged at the side of the road. Contents poured from chamber pots lingered in divots on the streets because no one had properly finished cobbling the road.

They passed through the thick of the slums and past a pale woman surrounded by three skinny children dressed in yellow-ing, torn clothes, breastfeeding her too-tiny baby. A man blinded in the war, the way so many had been, was seated on the side of the unpaved street. His cane lay on the ground beside him, a metal cup extended in his hand to beg coins off of passersby. Ferrin fished the lone two copper coins out of the bottom of her coin purse and dropped them in his tin cup with a hollow clang. The houses were all in shambles, with thin roofs and cracked windows. Everything was falling apart. A few places were selling food. Every person's face held the same hunger, the same soul-deep exhaustion. Dark circles ringed their eyes.

The pang of guilt she felt in her gut was sharp and demanding. There she was, living up in the castle, well-fed, sheltered from the cold and hating her life, when there were people down here starving and wearing threadbare clothes through the winter. These were *her* people, her family's people. Who was looking out for them?

She had been in such a hurry to leave her father's corruption behind, but had she thought about the rest of the people his actions affected? Her own inaction, even? Shame flickered through her again, and she did not like how familiar she was becoming with the feeling. It was cloying, nagging and scraping, and it came from within. It demanded to be felt, the sensation all dirt and grime.

Towards the center of town, things began to look up a bit. The merchant quarter was still kept prim and tidy, as was the strip of expensive shops and the block of business offices. A few apartment buildings of modest size were scattered here and there.

But even on the fully-cobbled street of high-end shops, Ferrin held the images in her head of the blind man, the mother, the cracked windowpanes.

"How long has it been like that?" she asked Lukas.

"What?"

"Back there… the slums. How long has it been that bad?"

He exhaled through his nose as they trudged up a side street, "Since before I arrived, but it's gotten much worse in the last year, really."

"Why did I never learn of this? I knew there were problems but I never realized the extent," she wondered aloud.

He turned to look at her as they stopped in front of a fabric shop. She suddenly became very aware of her own ignorance.

She'd always thought herself worldly. Now she felt like a fool. Not a mile from her ivory doorstep, people were dying.

"Awareness sparks change," he said finally. "From what I heard, that whole district back there used to be full of Caelish businesses. Dress shops, pubs, bookstores. According to one of my contacts in the merchant's square, after the queen disappeared, things started getting bad for the whole neighborhood. Break-ins, robberies, threats."

She remembered then, there had been a small Caelish neighborhood in town. Nothing like the huge Caelish quarter in Avaree, but dense with Caelish shops and homes. She'd gone once or twice as a child with her mother. Had it truly fallen so hard in just five years?

"Ready?" Lukas asked.

She nodded, following him into the shop. *Madame Lana's Fashionable Headware,* read the pink and white sign above the door.

"We're… hat shopping," Ferrin said in deadpan disbelief.

"No. Follow me." He nodded at the shopkeeper, "Good morning, Cora."

She nodded back and returned to her morning paper, wire-rimmed glasses resting on the bridge of her nose.

"Upstairs there are actually rooms to rent, but it's by the hour, if you catch my meaning," he explained. "And down here…" he stepped into the back, behind a large pile of hat boxes, where there was a painted, taupe changing screen. He tapped the floor with his foot to draw her attention before dropping into a squat and rolling the small rug out of the way, revealing a trap door. "…is the entrance to the black market."

"No shit," Ferrin breathed, her expression incredulous.

"There's a way into the other end from the bottom level of the Pit, but you didn't hear that from me," he winked before yanking the door open.

Down she followed him. At first, she felt pressure all around her and her nerves buzzed at the thought of so much rock and earth closing her off from open air, but then the narrow stair opened into a wide, well-lit cavern and her jaw dropped.

"Don't tell me all this has been under the village this whole time," Ferrin said, eyes wide with disbelief as she surveyed the entirety of the cavern. There was *actually* a market underground. "This is striking me as very literal."

"They considered painting the walls and booths black, too," Lukas smiled.

"Good one."

As she took in the surroundings, she was relieved she'd changed clothes. Men and women milled around, all in rough, work attire, save for a few people scattered around in skimpy dresses or shirts with the sleeves torn off to show some extra skin. Free agent prostitutes who weren't affiliated with any brothel, she'd guess.

"Don't let anyone know who you are. Just say you're my cousin," Lukas said.

"Relax, *cuz*," she smiled as they approached a market stall selling bars of silver. "This isn't my first time." She picked up one of the bars marked at two-thirds market value, and the stamp and crest had been filed off.

"Wreck salvage," Lukas nodded. "Any cargo that washes up after a wreck is by law property of the crown, no matter what ship it comes from. Salvage crews who get there first sell the goods down here."

They'd want to get rid of the stolen goods quickly and without a trace. Interesting.

"What if it sinks?"

"Some unlucky — or very lucky — bastard goes over the side of a skiff and has a look around. It's cold, tiring work."

"You speak from experience?"

"I do."

"How deep can you dive?"

"I don't know," he admitted. "Thirty feet? Forty? Maybe more."

She let out a low whistle and they continued on.

"I believe I was promised a story?" he suddenly said, turning to her with a smirk.

She shot him a wry smile and recounted the time Zare and she, while still disguised, had dared to cross Rahl, one of the biggest bosses of the *popava* trade, with the help of the ship navigator's wife, Azara.

Eventually they came to a sort of open-concept pub with a few tables scattered around a bar, and a half-partition separating the seating area from the bustle of the market. A woman in her late thirties was buffing the surface of the bar with a rag and told them to sit wherever they pleased. Apparently, whoever Lukas was meeting there had already arrived.

They slid into the seats opposite two men — one old, one young.

"Good day, gentlemen," Lukas greeted.

"Luk, so very good to see you," the younger one responded in a tight voice. His sand-colored hair was pulled back and his chin sported a matching goatee.

"Who's your friend?" the older, bald one asked.

"My cousin," Lukas explained.

"Cousins," the bald man repeated quietly, looking back and forth between Lukas and Ferrin, unconvinced.

"*Distant* cousins," Ferrin added helpfully. "My name is G… retcha." She'd nearly used Gillian, but thought better of it.

"Pleasure to make your acquaintance… Gurretcha."

"Gretch," Lukas said sweetly, bracing a hand on the table as he turned to her. "This is Oren and Phelipo."

Oren, the older one, was gruff and tough, with a dark brown beard, a silver stud in one ear and a permanent scowl on his sun-tanned face. Phelipo, the younger one, looked a little more polished, if in a lazy, arrogant way.

Lukas leaned back in his chair to signal to the barkeep, holding up four fingers. A few moments later, she appeared with a tray of four glasses of ale and a basket of rolls.

"Ah, that's the good thing about morning business," Oren said, his voice deep and rocky as he leaned forward to grab one of the rolls. It steamed when he broke it open. "The bread's still fresh."

"Cheers to that, gents," Lukas said, lifting his glass.

"It's eleven in the morning," Ferrin laughed.

"It's a business meeting, that makes it acceptable," Phelipo said. His voice was accented and pretty, it reminded her of her friend Pierre. The thought soured her, and she tried to bat it away before the sting of that particular betrayal could pull her under again.

"Well, alright then," she agreed, raising it and clinking it with the others before taking a sip. From the corner of her eye, she noticed the level of Lukas's glass hadn't gone down much. He must have wanted to keep his faculties sharp for this exchange.

"Shall we get down to business, then?" Lukas suggested.

Oren sipped his drink. "The shipment is on its way, it'll be ready for pickup on Rochmere at dawn."

Ferrin had never heard of Rochmere. It could have been a smaller port town on the coast.

"And it is the agreed upon quantity? I'm not going to get all the way out there again and find you've shorted me a bundle, am I?" asked Lukas, a hint of ice creeping into his voice.

Oren tensed. Phelipo studied the table, fascinated by a water stain.

"You know once it's on the boat, it's out of our hands."

"Maybe you should be hiring better sailors," Lukas said sarcastically.

"Six bundles. Dawn tomorrow. Take anything that's missing out of their cut," Oren said, grinding his jaw.

"It would be a shame if you had to start moving your product through customs, I hear they take a thirty-percent tariff on all crops coming out of the Meddemara now. And that's not even including the export toll in New Larais harbor. The one you'd have to present Proof of Payment of upon arrival in the Everness customs house."

"The whole thing will be there," Phelipo said, his lips thin and face pale. "On Rochmere. At dawn."

"Very well," Lukas said, taking a narrow leather folio from his coat. "The agreed-upon half-amount up front." He slapped it on the table.

"I'm sure you won't mind if we count this?"

She would have done the same.

"By all means," Lukas said, gesturing his acceptance.

Once everyone was more or less satisfied, they stood to leave. Ferrin hadn't said much, but it had been oddly comforting to be amongst thieves again. Her stomach turned, though, knowing that at least some of the *popava* coming in was going to her brother.

"What is Rochmere?" she asked Lukas as they made their way to the next destination.

"A little island north of here."

"I've never heard of it," she admitted.

"That makes sense, given that it's not on any map. It's a glorified pile of rocks that's submerged during high tide. It'll be uncovered enough tomorrow morning for me to row out there, dock my dingy," he shot her a glare when she snickered, "and get my shipment from the men who will meet me there. Then I cover it over with a fishing haul, and kill two birds with one stone. Or, gut two fish with one knife, if you prefer."

"Full of wit today, I see?" she chuckled.

"Only every day, Grrrrr-etcha."

She stifled a laugh, squeezing his elbow as she halted in front of a shop selling patterned skeins of fabric. Different inter-locking designs of knots, woven plaids, checked or striped wools.

"I almost said Gillian. *Almost*," she said, examining a cut of fine wool. "But then I realized it was time for a new alias."

"It sounds like a noise a cat makes when it's throwing up a hairball," he snorted.

"Hey! I thought it was pretty."

"It is. For a hairball," he teased.

"Yuck," she frowned disapprovingly at him. "What are you fetching from this glorified rock pile anyway?" she asked.

"A few bundles of Calixtan *arimopo*, and some specialty *popava*."

"For Rhi? He worries me with that," she shared.

"He's a grown man," Lukas said. "He's sharing it among his inner circle of young nobles."

"I know, I know, he can take care of himself," she said, again feeling that pang of guilt for having abandoned him five years ago. "I just worry for him."

"Maybe you should drop in on one of his revels and see what it's all about."

She shot him a sidelong glance before returning her gaze to the fabric in front of her. "Why is this here? Is it stolen too?" she asked in a hushed tone, though the shopkeeper was nowhere to be seen.

"No," he replied, his brow furrowed in confusion. "You don't know?"

"Know what?"

"Caelbarrian traditional fabrics were banned. Two years ago."

"What?" Ferrin asked, her hand stilling on the wool as her eyes widened with shock. "They're just *clothes*, though."

"Anything considered to be in opposition of the Unification was banned. After the riots at the mill?" he asked, his tone expectant.

"What riots?"

"It was discovered that there was pay disparity between people with last names that sounded Caelbarrian versus those that sounded Lindbarrian." He looked at her expression. "You didn't know?"

"No, I was half a world away, remember?"

"A married couple realized it. They both worked there, and the wife had taken her husband's last name. He was Caelish, she was Lundi. She took the job at the mill, made friends with all the Lundi ladies working there as weavers and realized she was being paid less than all of them. She started asking around and found out it was almost entirely split by nationality."

Ferrin dropped her hand from the skein of fabric. It was a blue and red, shot through with accents of bright yellow.

"She was Lundi but she was infuriated, raised all kinds of funds, got the mill shut down for a week when she damaged equipment. Then there was a strike, and somehow it devolved into a riot. People went wild with panic, some were trampled, some shot by guards or anyone else who was crazy enough to bring a rifle into the mob. Two guards were killed, and that led to a lot of outrage on the Lundi side of things, and then the ban passed days later with almost no resistance."

"That seems convenient."

He shrugged. "Ask your father."

She frowned, looking back at the fabric and thinking of her father. *What was his goal here?*

CHAPTER TWELVE

The next day, Ferrin headed down to the apple orchard to meet with Grey regarding what she had learned, which was not a lot. Between her time entertaining Havian, her duties in the stable and her father's wrath, she hadn't had the time or the courage to go snooping through his office.

But the rebels could help stop this insane forest plan. They had to have *some* resource on the inside, someone who could influence how the order was received.

The sun was getting low in the sky, slanting gold and buttery through the fresh spring air, and dancing on the rustling branches. She leaned against one of the trees, enjoying the feel of the sun on her face as she waited for Grey to fetch her.

She rubbed at her eyes, which were threatening to droop shut. Her stomach was grumbling too. If only the rebels would meet up with her at a tavern or a bakery. With a sigh, she wished she'd specified a more exact meeting time. For all she knew, Grey wouldn't show, just to make her sit here all night. She drew another long sip from her canteen and crossed a leg over her knee.

Finally, when the sun was good and fully set, a rustle through the grasses caught her attention. A man's shape appeared out of the orchard.

"You," Grey asserted, halting with a hand on his hip. He was dressed like a nobleman, blue frock coat embroidered with threads of green, pristine breeches, knee-high boots and a silk cravat at his throat.

"*You,*" Ferrin replied, raising an eyebrow in the dying light.

"We don't have all night to sit about and chat. Come," he jerked his chin at her.

"Well forgive me for gossiping," Ferrin muttered snidely under her breath as she stood. "I have new information," she said, jogging to catch up with him. "You'll certainly find it interestin—"

"Shh! What are you doing?" He spun to face her, scolding. "Wait until we're in a secure location, *gods above.*"

"Sorry," she muttered. "Long day."

He gave an exasperated *hmph.*

"Are you always like this?" Ferrin asked.

"Like what?"

"Grumpy and moody."

"I take my line of work seriously," he replied curtly.

Ferrin crossed her arms. "Where's the coat from? Do you lot have a closet of undercover-wear?"

"It's mine," he frowned.

"I didn't realize the wages for rebel insurgents were so high. I'd have joined up sooner."

"My father is a minor lord," he admitted hesitantly.

Ferrin tilted her head, examining him, "That's not the answer I was expecting."

"That's the usual reaction," he said without looking at her.

"I always thought nobility were cordial and pleasant all the time," she couldn't help but mock him.

"Maybe that's just when they have to ingratiate themselves to spoiled members of the royal family."

"Well, I walked right into that one," she nodded.

They reached a worn brick house in the residential district, and Grey looked pointedly at Ferrin.

"Close your eyes and cover your ears."

"Oh, come now, you can't be serious."

He glared at her, waiting.

"Fine." She turned around and pressed her fingers to her ears. A moment later, he slowly led her into the house.

Again, people were gathered around tables and milling about the common area. This time there were only a few masked figures present. The front room let out into a narrow hallway with a warren of doors on both sides. At one end was a stairway and at the other a narrow, green door.

Grey stalked to the door, back straight as a knife as he knocked. A wisp of short, gold hair fell into his face.

Ferrin stood behind him, feeling awkward as she fidgeted with her sleeves.

The door opened, and Helene stood, dressed in a deep plum-colored coat over a clean shirt, her hair down.

"Grey," she said with a sliver of a smile as she walked back around her desk and sat down. "It's always lovely to see your smiling face."

"Captain, I've brought the princess," he replied dully, still scowling despite Helene's attempt to lighten the mood.

"Yes, I see that. She looks just as happy to be here as you do," said Helene, shoving her empty dinner plate to the side. "Come in, Ferrin, have a seat."

"Thanks," Ferrin smirked, biting back a chuckle about Grey's disposition.

"She says she has new information," Grey said from the door, "which she nearly blurted out in the middle of the apple orchard, by the way."

"Grey, do sit down. You're not a sentry."

"It's protocol—"

"I have no taste for people hovering in the doorway of *my* office. Sit, Lieutenant. Or get out." Helene's voice was sharp and commanding as she gestured to the chair on Ferrin's left.

Begrudgingly, Grey obliged.

"Now," Helene sighed, straightening in her chair. "What have you learned?"

Ferrin took a deep breath. "Today, some men arrived to show my father plans he ordered — plans to build a wall and a garrison south of the castle and village. They want to source it from the southern part of Taroch Forest, the part that wraps between here and the rest of the island."

Helene listened intently and looked thoughtful for a moment, her hands pressed palm to palm, fingers to her lips. "We suspected he was looking to build a new garrison out there. The wall is a bit of a surprise, I'll admit. As is the lumber source. Has anyone from the Companies bothered to look into that? I mean," she looked back and forth between Grey and Ferrin. "That forest is as good a natural defense as you're likely to get from that side."

"My father seems to have no care for the harm he will do."

"Well, we knew that," Grey snorted.

"There are invaluable resources in that forest, yes?" Helene asked.

Grey nodded.

"A mole of ours in the castle has mentioned land surveyors scouting the fields to the south, and has noted the extra soldiers who have been arriving over the last few weeks," said Helene. "Between this and the foreign royalty visiting, I think we can assume that's why they're here." She looked to Grey, "I want you to continue looking into that."

"Ferrin," she said. "I need you to get a good look at those plans, copy them or take notes, and bring them to me. Anything you can find out is important."

"You're giving her a *mission*?" Grey scoffed, his tone cold and condescending.

"Yes, *Lieutenant*, I am. Is there a problem?" Helene asked.

"How do you know we can trust her? How do you know she isn't just going to sell out our names and location?"

"She knows better," Helene slid her gaze to Ferrin. "And she's got no reason to. We're all on the same side here."

"Captain, really," Grey said, standing up defiantly. "We have moles in the castle; if she exposes them they'll be tortured and killed."

"*She* is sitting right here," Ferrin snapped, a little sick of Grey's attitude by now. "And if I were going to rat you out, I'd have done it already. Besides, I have no idea who your moles are. I'm in this with you until I can get out of this place again."

That morning, the wind was wet and biting as Lukas rode up the coast. It was still dark out, and all that could be heard over the wind were the crash of the waves on the rocks below and the steady thud of horse hooves on the road.

Behind him, Ryder Berry, a bruiser he knew from the Pit, kept pace. He didn't always bring along help, since it usually meant having to split the pay, but the Calixtans had shorted him once already, and he didn't want to be out on that rock alone if it happened again.

They reached the spot along the Coast Road, marked by a little dip in the side, that led to the steep path down the cliffs.

They tied their horses on the other side of the road, behind the tree line, and began the descent down to the shore, where Lukas kept a wooden dingy and oars in one of the many caves dotting the coast. They'd have to catch a decent haul of fish to bring back to town with them, lest anyone question where they had gone so early in the morning.

"Think we'll get a storm later on?" Ryder asked.

"Could be," Lukas said as they shifted the boat out of the cave. "Hard to tell with the sky so damn dark."

It would take them at least a half hour to row out to Rochmere, maybe more, since the waves were so rough.

"Sure is dark out there," Ryder said a little nervously, jerking the lantern towards the black, churning sea.

"Sun'll be on the horizon in a few minutes," Lukas assured him. He knew better than to acknowledge the big man's nerves. Ryder might have been six-foot-seven, all muscle and tattoos, but the ocean didn't give a damn about that. The ocean did not give a damn about anything. It was a thing to be respected, and not approached foolishly, especially on days when it was churning with storm.

Lukas relished the smell of the sea air and inhaled deeply. It reminded him of summers spent diving in Khalim's Harbor, salvaging anything he could hock for a few coins. He loved the water. Loved how it connected the whole world. No matter what part of the sea you stood in, all that water and all that power would flow home at some point.

"Right, let's get on with it before I lose my nerve," Ryder said, dousing the lantern. Its measly light would only make it harder to see in the dark.

They shoved the boat into the water and hopped in, knives strapped to their legs and guns wrapped in oilcloth on the floor of the skiff. Each of them took up an oar and pushed out to sea.

Rochmere was barely a speck in the distance from up on the road, and from sea level it was nearly impossible to locate. Especially in the dark. The waves slapped the bottom of the boat, jarring them at each crest. They were more than halfway across when the sun began to peep over the horizon, and Lukas set down his oar to stand and take a look. By some grace of the twin sea gods, they'd stayed on course, Rochmere still a little blip surrounded by breaking water in the distance. He sat back down and they kept rowing.

Finally, they reached the island and secured the dingy, both stretching their sore shoulders and wiggling out their stiff knees. The schooner they were meeting, on its way up to Avaree, was visible in the distance, white sails full and purple flag of Efel flying.

Ryder set about harvesting some of the little oysters and mussel shells off the rocks while they waited, and Lukas took the guns from the oil cloth.

The schooner dropped anchor just beyond the rocks and a longboat with three men in it was lowered. Lukas kept a flintlock ready at his belt should they decide to keep both payment and prize.

A few minutes later, the sun was up and the trade was underway.

The schooner departed, leaving Lukas with the *proper* amount of goods this time. As promised, he had the bundle of specialty *popava* that Rhi had paid a small fortune for, and the earthy, spicy Calixtan *arimopo* that Lukas would turn a massive profit on, even after paying Ryder for his help.

"That *pop*?" Ryder asked as they shoved back out to sea.

"Yeah, specialty from Khalim. This little bundle has been through more ports than I can name at this point."

"Hope it's good stuff. My girl got a bad batch of Maraki Blue last month," Ryder sniffed and spat over the side of the boat. "We both ended up seeing things for hours before getting sick with the shakes. She threw up all over our bed."

Lukas looked concerned. "Where from?"

"Picked it up off some guard who said it fell off the back of the cart between Everness and Lewich."

"Good to know," Lukas said as he organized the bundles underneath a sheet of cloth, and then covered it with their little fishing haul. "Do you know the name of the guard?"

"No. Odd fellow, I didn't recognize him. And I've been arrested enough times to know most of the ones who have town duty."

"Well, let me know if you see him again. It's dangerous shit when it's been tampered with."

"Will do," Ryder gave a mock salute, then paused, squinting off at the horizon. "Hey, you see that?"

Lukas turned back towards the horizon, where the sun was peeking through a gap in the cloud cover.

"Is that…" he squinted. "Here, hand me the spyglass."

He opened the brass instrument and stood, bracing one leg up on the dingy's bench as he peered through the glass. In the distance, a three-masted ship was heading north. Its sails were white, but…

He rubbed the glass on the sleeve of his shirt and raised it back up to his eye.

"It looks like a frigate. And the flag, it *looks* like it might be Bourjon," Lukas said with deepening curiosity. "What are they doing up here?"

"Are you sure?" Ryder asked, halting his rowing.

"Those certainly look like blue circles on the sails. Can't quite make out the flag, though."

"Maybe the storm blew them up this way," Ryder suggested. It wasn't out of the realm of possibility.

"We're going to have to report it to someone. Good thing we've got these fish as an excuse for why we're out here."

They were still out far on the water. Lukas couldn't be sure, but he thought if they were on land, even with the height of the cliff, the ship would be just over the horizon. Out of sight.

"That's odd, isn't it? Warship with Bourjon colors so far from the front?"

"It is indeed."

"Maybe they don't like us Barrian's cozying up to the Efelians," Ryder said with a huff.

"Whatever the reason," Lukas responded, taking up his oar, "it can't be good."

*   *   *

The library was quiet and warm as late afternoon light slant-ed through its wide, high windows, and dust motes floated gold and bright, swaying through the air. Since no one had come to throw her into confinement or fetch her to grovel at Havian's feet, Ferrin found herself with a free afternoon when Alick re-leased her from stable duties after lunch.

She'd come to look for some kind of documentation regard-ing the Forest of Taroch, and how it had been part of their de-fense in the past, but after a few hours of searching in vain, she found herself running her fingers over the old spines of her fa-vorite novels.

Dusting off the first book of one particular series, she smiled down at the worn cover. It was an adventure romance about an epic war, and a band of odd misfits who had to travel across the continent to rescue the king's children amidst a succession cri-sis. She felt a warm sense of familiarity as she thumbed through its pages for the characters that felt like old friends.

She closed the book with a smile and slid it back onto the shelf. It caught, and bumped. With a frown, she tugged it out and wiggled it back in. Again, she met resistance, so she pulled the book out and peered into the gap. There was something back there, partially hidden by the other books.

Sighing with exasperation, she pulled out the entire series. "Well, I guess I might as well reread the whole thing again," she huffed, not all that disappointed by the prospect. In the dark nook, she could make out the gleam of metal, dust and paper. She squinted, peering at it as she reached in and pulled the ob-ject from the cranny.

Objects, rather. In her hand, she held a ring with a paper note rolled up inside of it.

She gasped when she turned the ring over; she'd have rec-ognized it anywhere. A thin silver band, set with four round di-amonds and three little square rubies, turned on the diagonal so their corners faced each cardinal direction, the central ruby far larger than the rest, and surrounded by a complex knotting of dullish silvery metal.

This ring was her *mother's*. It was a family heirloom from the Caelish Keep. She'd never seen her mother remove it for more than a few minutes.

With trembling hands, she slid out the rolled up paper from inside the ring, unrolling it as she held her breath.

H.G. Serengath, 24.

Who or what was H.G. Serengath? And 24 what? she wondered. The writing was plain, not recognizable or memorable.

"Oh, no!" The muffled voice came from two aisles over, and was followed by some curse words in a language Ferrin was only partly familiar with. The expletives were punctuated by several loud thuds and an *ow*.

She shoved the ring and note deep into her pockets and went to investigate.

"Are you…" she turned the corner and found Soviel on the floor with a heap of books, including *Botany and Your Health,* and *Poisons and Pigments: an A-Z Encyclopaedia on Plants*, strewn on and around her. "…alright? Soviel!"

"Oh, hi, Ferr," Soviel said casually, scrambling to her feet and bending down to gather up the fallen books. "What's going on?"

"Nothing," Ferrin said, setting down her pile of novels. Her hands still felt shaky from her mysterious discovery. "Do you need some help?"

Soviel rubbed the side of her head. "Yeah, actually. Thanks," she said sheepishly.

"What are you looking for?"

"Doing some research for Madame Leone, about regenerating skin to look smooth after severe burns. A lot of the soldiers at the hospital… well, some of them were severely disfigured on the battlefront in Efel."

The convalescent hospital was attached to the infirmary on the palace grounds, and part of the alliance with Efel was contingent on their housing and helping wounded soldiers.

"*Shrubbery and Bowel Health*?" Ferrin read one of the titles aloud.

"That author has an entertaining way of making even the lengthiest of expositions on flora comical," Soviel smiled, nodding at the volume. "But unfortunately, he specializes in disease and internal functions, not healing of traumas to the skin."

"Interesting," Ferrin said, sliding it back onto the shelf.

"What do you have there?" Soviel asked, gesturing to the pile of books Ferrin was clutching in one arm.

"Ah, an old favorite of mine. It's a series. You'd like it!"

"Actually, I think I read that a few years back," Soviel tilted her head to look at the front cover, where an engraving of a dragon-riding priestess was embossed into the leather. "Oh, I remember that cover."

"It's been a while since I read it, I want to see if I still enjoy it as much."

"I love rereading old favorites," Soviel said with a satisfied smile.

"I think I'll have more time on my hands until my father's next attempt to marry me off," snorted Ferrin.

"Only if you're lucky," smirked Soviel.

"So. Regrowing skin, huh? That sounds rather intense."

"It takes meticulous, delicate work. Hence, the books." Soviel slid the last of the pile back onto the shelf, cradling two of the volumes in her arms. "Actually," she looked at Ferrin, "would you mind giving me a hand with something?"

"Sure, what is it?"

"Would you let me practice on that brand on your arm?"

Ferrin had been hesitant to let Soviel altar her in such a way, though she wasn't sure why. It wasn't as if she was *proud* of having a thieve's brand on each arm. She had one from Khalim, and one from the dungeon of a private estate, courtesy of the Kalassan olive-trade boss's favored enforcer, Calomba Herotis.

Soviel's rooms in the south wing of the palace were modest, just a bedroom with an adjoining washroom. Light flooded in the window, illuminating dozens of potted plants set throughout the room.

"You were not joking about having a lot of plants."

"They're my friends," Soviel said with a twinkle in her eye. She said it like she was being absurd but there was a kernel of truth there.

"How do you care for them all? I once tried to grow a tea-tree and it was perpetually scraggly and ill."

"Oh, I'm suited to it. Plants and life and all that, it's all connected. They make me more powerful," she wiggled her fingers at Ferrin, again only half-joking.

"No wonder your skin always looks so good. Have you *ever* had a pimple?" Ferrin asked.

"Not in recent memory," Soviel said with a hint of pride.

"Must be nice," Ferrin nodded, noticing the various other plants hanging from the ceiling. She hadn't seen those at first.

Soviel shuffled some papers off the small writing desk and shoved them into a drawer a little too quickly. "Well then, have a seat. Which one are you less attached to?" she asked, gesturing to Ferrin's arms.

"Hmmm…" Ferrin made a show of looking back and forth between the two nearly-identical thieves' brands. "This one has worse memories attached to it," she said, propping up her elbow on the desk.

"Calomba?" Soviel asked, arching a brow as she tied on a smudged, white apron.

"Yeah," Ferrin said, frowning. Had she mentioned that? The story was a violent one, traumatic. Hours of her life completely at the mercy of that terrifying woman, waiting on Zare to bust her out after he'd promised her there was no way she'd be taken.

"This might hurt a little," Soviel warned, turning to one of the herbs growing in a puddle of sunlight. She plucked a few leaves and grabbed the tiny mortar and pestle from the desk. She set to grinding the leaves to a paste before turning back to Ferrin. "Arm," she ordered.

Ferrin obliged. The paste was cold, thick and green as Soviel slathered it over the old burn.

"Right. This scar looks pretty old, so it will only fade slightly. If you really wanted it gone, it would take a few goes. When is this from?"

"Oh, I was sixteen, maybe? I hadn't even really gotten involved with Zare yet at that point," she shared.

"Sixteen. And you were interrogated by Calomba Herotis."

Ferrin nodded. "Only for a few hours. I thought I was going to die, though."

"I would be terrified," Soviel said, setting down the bowl. "Ready? This is the worst part."

"Go ahead."

The sensation was warm, at first, and then it grew itchy, she *needed* to scratch it but Soviel's hand and all that green gook was in the way. Then Soviel did something and it started to burn, like she'd fallen asleep in the sun and scorched her skin to the point of peeling.

"Doing alright?" Soviel asked, her voice ever-gentle.

"Uncomfortable, for sure," Ferrin said, gritting her teeth.

"It's almost done, look," said Soviel without removing her hand, which was now faintly *glowing*.

At last, Soviel took her hand away. Sure enough, the brand had faded — it was paler, less red and less raised.

"*Storm-steeds trample me*," Ferrin sucked in a breath, examining her arm. The green paste had dried and gone brown and crusty, almost like the life had been sucked from it and put into her. "Sov, that's some power you've got there."

"Thanks," she said lightly.

"You know, you being from Njorske and all, wouldn't you have some affinity for flame in your family?"

Soviel let out a short laugh, "Well, Ferrin I don't think *anyone* really has affinity for flame anymore." She passed a wet cloth to Ferrin to clean off the paste. "Even so, my mother's side of the family is Veiran and a little bit Efelian if you go back a few generations. That's where my gift comes from."

Nodding with appreciation, Ferrin pulled her sleeve back down. "Well, thank you."

"Thank you for being my test subject," Soviel smiled, removing her apron.

"Hey, I wonder if you might give me a hand with some research on something, actually."

"Research? On what, how to lose a suitor in less than a week?" Soviel teased.

Ferrin smacked a hand over her chest in mock-offense. "He's still here! There's still time."

"Right, I'm sure he's still enchanted with your womanly wiles," smirked Soviel, her devilish streak showing through.

"No, but in all seriousness, it's about Taroch Forest, actually. My father wants to chop it down and burn half of it for a new garrison."

The grasses and shrubs in the forest seemed to lean towards Soviel. Ferrin couldn't explain it, but it was like the greens grew *greener* in her presence, which seemed outlandish. Perhaps she was woozy from the healing.

"Right, well, here," Soviel crouched by a little family of toadstools, "these are edible. They also work wonders for belly pain on your monthlies," she added, drawing a palm across her abdomen.

"What are they called?"

"Talea mushrooms."

Ferrin scribbled it down, adding an ugly little sketch beside her notes. Those things seemed to be everywhere in here.

They continued through the forest, Soviel pointing out different plants and herbs that were used in the kitchen and the infirmary. She also pointed out the presence of wild boar tracks that looked a little too fresh for Ferrin's comfort. Those beasts were nasty.

"It just doesn't make sense," she muttered aloud after an hour or two of learning how to identify plants of importance.

"What doesn't make sense?" Soviel asked.

"The whole plan. Why a garrison in the south? If Bourjony did attack, it would be by sea, right?"

"I don't know much about military strategy," Soviel said, her voice even as she looked up at the branches of the trees, where the sun was filtering in slanting beams and columns. "But that sounds logical."

Ferrin picked her nails. "It seems like a lot of effort and destruction for something pointless."

"Maybe there's something else going on, some secret reason for it," Soviel suggested casually.

"Maybe," Ferrin nodded slowly, squinting at Soviel. She needed to find a way into her father's office. Maybe there was an ulterior motive to building that garrison, to destroying the forest.

"Did you hear anything else while you were in there?" asked Soviel. "What kind of soldiers they're housing? Maybe it's for officers."

"No, they threw me out rather quickly," she sighed. "Bastards."

"Well anyway, we should start heading back. I don't want to be caught out here after dusk with the boars." She shivered. "Tell me, what did you get up to after that, uh, incident?"

"I ran some errands with Lukas," Ferrin said casually as they turned to head back up to the castle.

"Oh?" Soviel raised her eyebrows expectantly.

"He's an interesting sort."

"Do tell."

"Tell *what*?" Ferrin laughed nervously.

"Oh, come *on*. You can't tell me you didn't drool just a little when you saw him remove his shirt at the Pit."

Ferrin felt blood rush to her cheeks at the memory of his carved, muscled body. At the memory of his fingers light as feathers on her back as he'd helped her lace her stays yesterday.

"Fine, he's very handsome," she conceded.

Soviel squinted at her skeptically.

"As I was saying, we ran some errands. I saw the village. The slums looked…" she paused, trying to express how she'd felt. "It was an awakening. I knew things were bad, but I never realized how horrible the conditions were." She shivered at the memory of what she had seen, barely a mile from the palace she was so keen to escape. "Now I feel like a spoiled brat for thinking only of how to run away again."

Soviel nodded, a strand of white-blond hair falling into her face. "My parents were lucky they had their estate to fall back on. After their property here was seized, they had to flee the country. I haven't seen them since last time I visited home."

Ferrin fidgeted with her nails again. "I'm sorry, Sov. I've been so wrapped up in my own problems, you must think me a selfish idiot."

"Everyone is selfish, Ferrin," Soviel said, stopping her with a hand on her shoulder. "It's how often you act on it, how often you let it impact those around you, that matters."

"You're very wise," Ferrin blinked in recognition. "I'm really glad they stuck you with being my lady-in-waiting. I really don't know what I would do if you weren't here."

"I'm glad, too," Soviel said kindly. "I consider you a friend, still, you know that? Not just my duty."

Ferrin felt her heart swell. "Remember when we were kids and we used to follow Rhi around all the time, and try to play Field Sticks with him and his friends?"

Soviel laughed, and it lit up her whole face, crinkling her deep-earth eyes. "I remember *you* getting nearly trampled to death by one of those boys as you followed him around the field the entire game."

"In my defense, I had taken a massive fancy to him," Ferrin grinned.

"What was his name again?"

"Coran. Coran Chenowith," Ferrin said, reaching deep into her memories, as if they were from a past life.

"Yes, I remember now. He felt *quite* guilty as I remember. I think he thought Rhi was going to kill him."

Rhi had always been so kind-natured for an older brother. He never told her to leave him and his friends alone, and always made space for her to join their hijinks.

"I am famished," Ferrin suddenly said, linking her arm through Soviel's as they passed through the palace gates. "What do you suppose is for dinner? And more importantly, do you think we can have it brought to my chambers again?"

"Nimhe's half in love with one of the kitchen boys. I think she mentioned it was crew hens tonight. She's down at the kitchen every day asking what the meals are to be, supposedly on *your* behalf."

Ferrin chuckled. "I hope her effort is rewarded — tumbling a kitchen boy probably means extra helpings every day."

CHAPTER THIRTEEN

No matter how weary she was from her long day, Ferrin couldn't seem to fall asleep. Her mind wandered in and out of memories and plans and problems she didn't know how to solve. She couldn't shake the nagging feeling in her gut about the forest, nor the images of hunched, hungry bodies of the children and beggars she'd seen the day before.

Spending the afternoon in Soviel's companionable presence had been a balm, one Ferrin hadn't realized she'd been missing so much. Her heart sank as she thought of Asha, her best friend aboard The Gravedigger.

What had Zare promised Ash to get her to agree to the plan? How much had her betrayal cost? Or had he simply cut her throat and dumped her overboard when she resisted?

She wanted to believe that some of the crew would have been against selling her out, but she also remembered how easily swayed they'd been by Zare in the initial mutiny against Captain McGidrew. She herself had been no exception. Zare could have fed them any number of lies about her. That she was a colonial spy, rooting out pirates, that she was wanted for a gruesome murder in her home country, that she was stealing from them.

She wanted to believe just a few of her friends would have seen through it. Ash, Pierre, maybe Tabka. It stung.

With a sigh, she swept her covers back, swinging her legs over the side of her bed. She pulled her dressing robe around her shoulders, over the white linen shift she slept in, and opened her shutters. No luck, the clouds and the half-bright moon concealed all stars from view, and there was nothing to look at in the blue-black haze. She drew her robe around her tighter and stalked out of her room to gaze out the big window at the end of the hall, overlooking the courtyard.

Something rounded the corner and slammed into her.

"You have to help me! Please!" The girl's pleas came in heaving sobs, hands clutching at Ferrin's arms, tears streaming down her face, her brown hair a mess and the rouge on her cheeks smudged.

"Alright, alright," Ferrin said reassuringly, concern rising in her as she steadied the frantic girl. "What has happened?"

"S-something - something bad—" the girl stammered, her breathing fast and deep. She was panicking. "I don't know!"

Her fingers wrapped around Ferrin's wrist like a vise and she dragged her around the corner to Rhi's room, where the door was half-open already.

"Shit," Ferrin cursed under her breath. Her stomach plummeted to her knees as she anticipated what she was about to find.

They burst into the central room. It was in utter disarray — a few articles of clothing strewn about, glasses of varied fullness scattered around, whisky soaking into the rug, and Rhi—

Rhi was on the floor, pale and shaking. His eyes had rolled back in his head, spittle foamed at the edge of his mouth.

"Shit, shit, shit!" Ferrin repeated, scrambling towards him. She dropped to her knees beside him, unsure of what to do. His shirt was open at the top, and a thin sheen of sweat covered his chest and face.

"He-he just suddenly stopped talking and then h-his eyes rolled back in his head and he fell, th-then Toumas and Julian left, and-and-" the girl faltered. Her pupils were pools of night-time black against the shrinking rim of her golden irises.

"Fetch me water and a blanket," commanded Ferrin as calmly as she could. The girl stood frozen. "Now!" she yelled, her voice so stern, she surprised herself.

The startled girl fetched the pitcher of water from Rhi's side table and a fat blue quilt from his bed.

"Were you taking popava?"

"What?" the girl's lower lip trembled.

"Popava!" Ferrin bellowed, "Did he take any?"

"Oh," the girl sniffed, still on the verge of hysterics. "We all did."

Had they left him as soon as he got sick? She was going to find out who had been here and ruin their lives.

She tried to get him to swallow water. After three futile attempts, she gave up, opting to simply shove her fingers down his throat.

"Damn it, Rhi!" she roared when nothing came up. "How much did he take? Did he swallow it?"

"We were-we were drinking whiskey and he mixed some in," she cried.

"How much popava?"

"I'm not sure."

"Bleeding Gods," Ferrin spat, sitting back.

"What is it?" the girl squeaked, wringing her hands.

"I can't fix this!" She looked around until her eyes landed on a pillow discarded on the floor, which she pulled behind his neck. "Wait here with him. Keep him on his side, see if you can make him throw up."

"What if someone finds us?"

"Tell them they can take it up with me," Ferrin called over her shoulder as she sprinted down the hallway, bare feet slapping against the cold, hard, stone floor. She ran barefoot through the halls, barely dressed and by some grace of pure luck, managed not to come across another soul. At last, she reached the door she was looking for. She slammed her fist against it repeatedly.

"Lukas! Wake up!" she hollered, praying this was the right room.

She kept knocking, furiously bruising her fist against the wood until she heard footsteps approaching and a latch sliding out of place.

Lukas opened the door, his hair unbound, wearing nothing but a pair of very soft-looking trousers.

"What is it?" He rubbed his face, eyes half open.

"It's Rhi," she gasped.

His eyes went wide and he retreated back into the room, springing into action. He grabbed a canvas bag by the door and shrugged on a shirt before stepping into the hallway.

"Where is he?"

"In his room — something is wrong," she said, pulling her dressing gown closed over her shift, suddenly a little cold, and a lot aware of her state of undress.

"Get a healer. Meet me there," he ordered before he took off running in the direction of the royal wing.

Ferrin turned to the south wing of the castle to rouse Soviel.

Lukas sprinted up the royal wing, nearly eating stone as he skidded around the corner and into Rhi's rooms. A pretty, dark-haired girl in a bright yellow dress was sitting on the floor beside Rhi.

"Move," he ordered as he slid down next to Rhi, dropping the bag beside him. He pulled back one of Rhi's eyelids. His pupils had gone wide, and he was burning up.

"Shit. He took too much. Shit," Lukas swore, putting his fingers under Rhi's jaw to feel a pulse. "Hand me the tin at the top of that bag, please," Lukas commanded the girl as he maneuvered Rhi's jaw open. "Damnit, where is that healer?"

The girl handed him the tin, and he popped it open, pulling out three waxy red berries. He popped them into Rhi's mouth and cracked them between his teeth. The powdery insides poured out of the berries, dissolving in Rhi's mouth.

"Come on, Rhi, swallow it," Lukas shook his head, cursing.

"Is he-is he going to be alright?" the girl asked in a timid voice.

Lukas looked back down at Rhi. "Hand me that paper cartridge," he said.

The door burst open and Soviel flew to Rhi, Ferrin on her heels.

Ferrin and Soviel had run through the halls back to the royal wing, not caring who saw two ladies sprinting about the castle in their nightgowns in the wee hours of the night. They blew into Rhi's chambers, Soviel rushing immediately to the floor where Rhi lay, taking a cartridge from Lukas's hands as she sunk to her knees beside him.

Ferrin watched, nerves abuzz as she stood still, not sure what to do or how to help.

"Tell me your name," she said to the girl.

"Meria. Meria Catalara."

"Who else was here?"

Meria listed a few names Ferrin wasn't familiar with.

"And they just left? When this happened?"

Meria nodded, seeming terrified.

"Meria. Thank you for not leaving my brother, and thank you for getting help," she said, her heart still racing as she leaned in close to the girl. "But if you let word of what you saw here slip, I will make sure everyone across the kingdoms knows you were here and you will be ruined."

"I wasn't — with—" she hiccuped.

"Not. A. Word."

Meria nodded, her eyes going wide. Ferrin couldn't help but feel bad for her, whatever late night paramour she'd been with had fled and left her with a poisoned royal.

"You will leave now."

Meria bobbed her head once more and ran out the door.

Ferrin returned her attention to where Lukas and Soviel tended Rhi.

"What can I—" she stopped mid-sentence, seeing that Soviel looked like she had gone into some kind of trance, her eyes wide and locked on Rhi. Torchlight flickered in the sconces.

Something green glowed in her palm as she raised her hand, as if in some choreographed dance. Little blue flecks rose out of Rhi's skin — the drug, Ferrin realized. It was being forced through his tissue and out of his body, a purging.

Lukas stuck the paper cartridge under Rhi's nose at Soviel's instruction. Two very long moments later, Rhi's body relaxed and his chest rose and fell in deep, labored breaths.

Soviel continued to hover her hands over his chest and abdomen, searching for more toxin. Lukas stood and backed up, rubbing his jaw worriedly.

"Gods… I warned him about this."

"So did I," Ferrin crossed her arms. Her terror was slowly ebbing out of her, making room for her unbridled anger.

"I told him never to take more than a pinch. He looks like he took a cup of the stuff."

"He needs to not take any!" Ferrin shouted, whirling on Lukas.

"He'll be fine. My guess is he'll stop taking—"

"If you hadn't gotten it for him, in such huge quantities…" she trailed off. "What the hell is wrong with you? You could have killed him!"

"I didn't force it down his throat, Ferrin!"

"You're enabling his dangerous habits! You're bringing him enough to incapacitate a damn elephant!"

"Now hang on a minute, Princess. You've heard him. He shares it around at his revels, and frankly, it's not my business! He knew the risks, he's a grown man! It's not as if he couldn't get it from someone else if I stopped bringing it to him!" Lukas exclaimed defensively. They were both yelling now.

"Oh, sure, tell yourself that, Lukas," she spat. "Look at him!" She threw a hand out at where Rhi now slumbered under Soviel's watch. "He's a mess! He's taking it every day and you just keep bringing him more!"

"Ferrin," Lukas said her name softly.

"Thank you for your help," she clenched her jaw. "Now get out."

"Fine," he shrugged, plucking the tin of red berries out of his bag and setting it on the table. "If you're too stubborn to listen, then that's just fine. At least give him two more of those when he wakes up. It'll help."

"Fine."

"Good night." He turned and walked out the door. It slammed behind him.

Ferrin turned back to where Rhi and Soviel were nestled on the floor. Soviel stood, a little shakily, catching herself on the arm of the couch.

"He'll be alright, we should get him into his bed," she said a little woozily.

When they'd managed to pull him up off the floor and deposit him into his bed, Soviel staggered back, bracing a hand on the wall.

"Are you alright?"

"Yes, that was just—" she was swaying. "I need to sit down."

Ferrin helped her to the couch where she passed out cold.

*   *   *

After Ferrin had managed to tuck Soviel onto the couch in a manner where she wouldn't roll off, she stalked over to her brother's giant sea of a bed and flopped onto the opposite side, which was where she woke up to the dawn streaming in through the windows.

Soviel was gone from the couch, the throw blanket neatly folded over the cushion where she'd slept.

Ferrin was going to be late for stable duties, there was just no avoiding it.

"Rhi?" she whispered, giving his shoulder a shove. "Rhi, are you alive?"

No response. She picked up her foot and gave him a gentle, but firm kick to the side. His eyes flew open and he sucked in a gasp like a drowning man released from the depths.

"I'll take that as a yes," she grumbled as she sat up and rubbed her eyes.

"Oh, Gods," he groaned, slapping his hands over his face. "What happened?"

"You're an idiot, is what happened!" Ferrin growled. "You went too far and you fell off the edge." She got off the bed. "Lukas and Soviel pulled you back from near death."

"You mean I died? Sounds like our dear healer friend is somewhat proficient in witchcraft."

"No, Rhi, you didn't die," she rolled her eyes. "But you almost did. Don't ever do that again."

"What do you mean?"

"You took so much popava you were on the ground, shaking and drooling with your eyes rolling back in your head. That poor girl who actually bothered to stay here came to get me, unlike the rest of... whoever was here. If she hadn't, you would have been poisoned."

"Oh, Ferr, it can't have been all that serious," he said with a strained yet boyish grin.

"It was serious. I swear to the gods I am going to kill Lukas when I see him next," she cursed under her breath.

Rhi said nothing.

"Where is the rest of your stash?"

"What do you mean?"

"Drink this," she ordered, refilling his cup of water from the pitcher. Then she set the tin of berries down. "Take three of these. It'll help with the headaches. You're not going to feel very good for a few days."

"What? Days? I'm hungover, not plagued."

"When you stop taking a substance like popava after your body is used to it, it can cause sickness."

"It was a one-time accident, Ferr, it isn't going to happen again," he said defensively.

"If you think you have a choice here, Rhi, you're wrong." She pushed the glass of water towards him.

"Ferr," he pleaded in his sweetest voice.

"Rhiach, if you continue to whine about it, I am going to smack you upside the head like when we were kids. Don't think I won't do it just because you nearly died."

"Fine," he sighed. "I'll stop."

"Where is your stash?" she repeated.

"I'll get rid of it later."

She leveled a stony glare at him.

"Fine, there's one in my night stand, and the box from the sitting room. There's also some inside my old boots in the closet," he gestured to the big, mahogany armoire.

"Anywhere else?" She tapped her foot expectantly.

"No." He didn't sound sure.

"I will rip apart your room," she promised.

"Under my mattress," he finally admitted begrudgingly as he sat up.

"Is that all?" she asked as she went around gathering it all up inside of a pillowcase she'd stripped from the bed.

"Yes, oh pitiless warden, I swear it," he said, staring at the ceiling.

"Great, I'll call in your servants to bathe you. You're covered in your own drool," she grimaced.

"Ferrin?" Rhi said, his voice stopping her as she was halfway out the door.

"Yes?" She turned in the doorway.

"Thank you," he swallowed.

She nodded slowly, "Before I go… there's something else we should discuss later, in detail."

"What is it?" Rhi asked between sips of water.

"Father and some other men… from some companies or something. They want to log and burn Taroch Forest."

"Really? For what?"

"A new garrison and a wall to the south."

Rhi frowned. "Really?"

She nodded.

"That's odd. I didn't think anyone would want to touch the forest."

"Well, apparently there's some reason they do. I'll come back later after stable duties to check on you. Get some rest." She pulled the door shut behind her and set a brisk pace to go and check in on Soviel before arriving painfully late to the stables. She only hoped Alick wouldn't be mad at her tardiness.

CHAPTER FOURTEEN

Lukas swung his axe in a furious arc, cutting through the wood with a satisfying *splunk* as it cleaved in two.

She was so damn *stubborn*.

He was itching to seek her out, clear the air. That would have been a mistake. She needed to cool off. *He* needed to cool off. Maybe then he would talk to her.

The thought of her hating him for almost killing her brother was more than he could stand. He should have paid better attention to the signs, should have realized how bad Rhi's state had become. Of course she was furious at him; he'd been turning a profit on something that was now obviously a great cost to Rhi's health.

He cursed inwardly, moving another piece of wood to the block. Maybe he should go down to the Pit and blow off some steam. Ryder was sure to be around, though of course the big man would probably clean the floor with him again. Besides, summer was coming and he didn't need all this wood to burn in the cabin.

With a deep sigh, he shrugged his shirt back on and embedded the axe into the chopping block. He'd head to his rooms, grab fresh clothes and make his way down to the Pit and go a few rounds in the practice ring with whoever was around. That would clear his head.

He was just coming out of the little wooded area surrounding the cottage when he heard her.

"Really working off some tension there, weren't you?" the voice was equal parts sharp and cool, clear and crisp. Queen Nerena was seated on a fallen log at the tree line, looking fully out of place with her finery and crown. In a bright cerulean dress, bedecked in gold and jewels, she looked like the kidnapped bride of a faerie king, come to live amongst the woodland realm.

"Your Majesty," Lukas bowed. "I must apologize for my appearance."

"Hm," she dismissed the idea with that smile that never reached her eyes.

"Is there, ah, something I can do for you, Majesty?" Lukas asked.

"As a matter of fact, there is." She stood from the stump, running her fingers over the trunk of the felled tree. "I know the sort of… work you do around these parts. Anything for a price, isn't that right?"

"I'm not sure to what you're referring," he said tentatively. *Shit.*

"I was hoping to recruit you to form a brute squad."

Lukas cocked his head. That was unexpected. "A brute squad, Majesty?" he puzzled. "For what purpose?"

"Ah, that is an important detail, now, isn't it, Mr. Mazrihn," she mused. "Things in the town have grown restless. Lawless, even. With the visiting royals here, and some important improvements coming in to play soon," she paused, "well, things need to be smoothed over before they begin to crack."

"I understand, but," he shook his head, "I was in the village not two days ago. All seemed peaceful. Quiet, even."

"Well, I'm sure it would seem that way on the outside. But the rebels are power hungry beasts, and the masses are just a few angry words away from becoming a mob," she claimed, stepping a little closer. "We don't want another incident like the mill riots a few years ago. Stop it before it gets out of hand."

He stared at her a moment, then said, "I'll look into it, Your Majesty."

"Alert me when it is done." Her voice was polished steel.

"When what, exactly, is done, Your Majesty?"

"I want anyone found inciting violence and unrest sent to labor in Danvery Prison. Up north."

He swallowed, watching the ice flicker in her eyes. It wasn't lost on him that Nerena shared traits with both Ferrin and the late queen, Arabella. Pale skin, wavy black hair, sharp features. From the portrait he'd seen of Ferrin's mother, it was clear the king had a distinct taste.

She left quickly and without ceremony, without so much as a nod. He was left thinking again of Ferrin's sharp features. The rage that had churned and roiled in her eyes had haunted him all day. He couldn't get it out of his head, hadn't bothered to even try going back to sleep after last night's events.

Out of the corner of his eye, he spotted something glinting on the pine-needle carpet. Where Nerena had been sitting on the stump, something had fallen, perhaps from her pockets. When he stooped to pick it up, he immediately recognized the little type of metal capsule he'd packed up many a time with various powders, pigments, salts and the like. Often, such things would be filled with finely-ground *popava*.

What on earth was the Queen doing with this? He made sure it was screwed shut and tucked it into his pocket to deal with later, continuing to his rooms to change clothes.

On his way back out of the castle, Lukas nearly bumped into Taran, one of the guards he had an in with. They greeted and passed each other, but then Lukas stopped and wheeled around, falling in stride with him. "Hey, did anyone ever get eyes on that ship?" he asked.

"What ship?" Taran asked.

"The one I reported to your commander yesterday. I have that stuff you asked after, by the way."

"This is the first I've heard of it," Taran said, shaking his head. "And thanks, I'll come by the Pit later to pick it up."

"Wait, no one's mentioned it? A Bourjon warship, this far off course? It seems like something that should have caused some concern. No one's been dispatched to look into it?"

"Not that I've seen," Taran shook his head before glancing around and dropping his voice to a low whisper. "Though, I did see Captain Greely send a rider north with an important message late yesterday. But I didn't tell you that."

"I won't say a word," Lukas nodded. "Alright, well, thanks Taran."

He found the Pit relatively empty, as it typically was in the middle of the day. Without the crowds to bet on blood and knockouts, the place was transformed. Lukas liked the quiet that came with being in a place during the day that existed for the nighttime. It felt like stepping out of time. It was liminal, surreal.

Ryder, who kept the Pit clean in exchange for the room above the office, always seemed to be there. He lifted a non-committal palm in greeting at Lukas and returned to sweeping up from last night's fight.

"Rough morning?"

"Long night," Lukas grunted back as he dropped his bag on one of the seats and pulled out his hand wraps. He really needed to wash those.

"Do you ever sleep?" Ryder asked. They'd been up late the previous night after their day of selling the cover-up fish and moving the smuggled goods into a secure location. He'd given Ryder a solid cut from both profits for his help, and they'd both promptly found themselves elbows deep in keg and card at the alehouse. He'd returned to his room and slept only a few hours when Ferrin had come knocking.

He chewed his cheek and tried to wrench his thoughts away from how she had looked, cheeks flushed from running through the palace, eyes wide and wild.

"Not nearly enough, Ryder. Not nearly enough."

"Lady troubles?" Ryder asked with a smirk.

"Something along those lines," Lukas admitted, unsure how to categorize it. He shook his head as if he could dislodge the thought repeating itself over and over. "I need to clear my head, are you game?" he asked as he began winding the linen strips around his wrists and through his fingers.

"You really like the taste of sand, huh?" Ryder quipped.

"It's good practice," Lukas retorted.

"For what, getting run over by a carriage?" Ryder cracked his knuckles.

"For fighting giants," Lukas deadpanned. "Besides, in back alleys and under docks, there's no guarantee. It's good practice to lose."

"You're a strange one, Lukas," Ryder said, stretching his neck as he stepped into the ring. "Mufflers?"

"Thanks," Lukas nodded, catching the big, padded leather gloves.

"For your sake," Ryder conceded.

"You keep talkin' shit and eventually you'll end up in it," Lukas scoffed as he strapped on a muffler. "I could still beat you. One of these days."

"Tell yourself whatever lets you sleep at night." Ryder squared up.

"Just remember who gives you a solid deal on that *arimopo* chew you like so much," said Lukas as he stepped into the ring.

*   *   *

Ferrin lay in bed later that day, still dressed in her dusty stable clothes, turning her mother's ring over and over in her hand.

She wasn't a fool; she knew there were only two ways it had ended up on that shelf in the library. One, her mother had left it for her to find and H.G. Serengath was some sort of clue, or two, her mother was dead and the ring had been taken off her body and left in the library for gods knew what other reason.

She rolled through the message in her head. Was it a residential address? A ship? A person?

She sighed and slipped the ring on. It fit perfectly on her ring finger. A sudden rush of breathlessness went through her, like she'd taken a jump on horseback, or she'd caught a gust aboard a racing skiff. It felt like she'd sprinted up a hill but without the resulting strain or tiredness.

She rolled out of bed and slipped into her boots. Maybe the library would have answers.

The day was starting to wane, and the light was coming sideways through the ceiling-height windows of the library in gold shafts that picked up the flecks of dust and debris in the air. At the front desk, the bookkeeper was bent over a thick tome, wire-rimmed glasses pushed up his nose. In the corner, a few young nobles were being tutored by scholars.

Ferrin returned to the book stack where she'd found the ring shoved behind her favorite novel series. It had been in stack eight, where most of the adventure novels were.

Eighteen, seventeen, sixteen…

She halted, the realization slamming into her like a hurricane wind. It wasn't a code or a message or an address, it was a stack number, and an author.

Halting mid-stride, she turned and stalked back up the row towards stack twenty-four, halting before the great bronze plaque inscribed with the numeral.

And there it was.

It was an old volume, and now she realized why the name had sounded so familiar. Zare had a copy of one of H.G. Serengath's compilations aboard *The Gravedigger*: *The Tales of the*

Old World. She slid out the tome, brick-colored cover stamped in fading gold, pages yellow and soft at the edges. Curling gold lettering surrounded a slightly raised golden embossing of a key.

Legends and Truths, by H.G. Serengath.

She turned it over in her hands, searching for another message. She bent to peer into the slot she'd pulled it from. Nothing. With a frown, she began to thumb through the pages, searching for something. Anything. She held it by the spine and shook the pages, waiting for a note to fall out. Again, nothing.

"Oh, for fuck's sake," she huffed, turning the book back to the front and swiping a hand over its cover.

A cool wind blew through the air.

"The ring... is that you, Arabella?" The voice floated on the draft. Ferrin wasn't sure she hadn't imagined it. She whirled around, but there was no one nearby.

"Who said that?" she hissed. Had the sleep deprivation finally gotten to her? Perhaps Zare's poison had long-lasting effects.

"Take the key, Arabella." The voice was coming from the book!

"You know my mother?" she whispered at the book, feeling both frustrated and mystified. Then, realizing she was standing in the middle of the library having a conversation with an inanimate object, she spun around to make sure no one had noticed.

"Take the key, daughter of Arabella."

"What key?" she demanded.

She turned the book over. "*This* key? What does that mean?" She glanced over her shoulder again.

"Use your gift," said the voice as it seemed to fade away.

"What does that mean?" she repeated, desperate and *sure* she'd gone mad.

With one final glance over her shoulder to make sure no one had come to investigate the ravings of the girl in the corner, she hid the book under her shirt and stalked out of the library. When she returned to her room, she collapsed on her bed and cracked it open. It was time for some answers.

By mid-afternoon, Ferrin's eyes were practically crossing from scouring the pages of *Legends and Truths*. She slammed the book shut and set it down on her desk, needing to get up and move before she went insane.

She strolled down to the kitchens and had a couple of sandwiches made up from honey-encrusted pheasant and roast vegetables. The overly-polite cook named Patra packed them into a basket for her and sent her on the way with a smile.

Soviel, looking far better than she had the previous night, was seated at her desk in her room, tiny watering can in hand as she hydrated a line of little succulents and potted plants.

"How are you feeling?" Ferrin asked. "I stopped by this morning after you weren't on Rhi's couch when I woke up but you must have been asleep."

"Yes," she grimaced. "That really knocked the energy right out of me."

"Thank you," Ferrin said earnestly. "You saved his life. I don't know what I would've done if—" she broke off, feeling a lump rising in her throat.

"Of course." Soviel nodded, eyes wide. "How is he doing?"

"He's managing," Ferrin explained. "He's not going to enjoy the next few days, that is for sure."

"If he needs any help," Soviel said, "Let me know."

"I will," Ferrin nodded, her chest aching with gratitude. If anything happened to Rhi, after she'd abandoned him all those years ago, she'd never forgive herself.

"Did you need anything else?" Soviel asked. "I was about to rest a little before readying you for dinner…"

"Oh, no. Sorry, I'll leave you to it. And, I will not be attending dinner tonight, I still don't know where I stand with Havian, and my father and all. So, rest all you need."

"Alright, just send word if you change your mind," Soviel said, standing from the desk.

"I shall. Enjoy your nap."

*   *   *

When the evening rolled around, Ferrin was happy to have Rhi as an excuse to poach some food from the kitchens and skip dinner in the Great Hall. She was just closing the ancient tome when Nimhe arrived to help her dress for dinner, with an abundance of enthusiasm and a simple turquoise gown in hand.

"Sorry, Nimhe, I'm not going to dinner tonight. I meant to send you a note, but I lost track of time."

"But won't you want to go down and smooth things over with…"

"No, I really don't, Nimhe," Ferrin said matter-of-factly. "I hardly slept last night, and I will likely only make things worse."

"That can't be so, I'm sure if you just speak with him all will be well."

Ferrin shook her head. "I'm sorry you came all the way up here for no reason."

"It's no trouble," Nimhe said pleasantly as she set the gown down on the vanity chair and grabbed Ferrin by the hand, squeezing gently. "Really."

"Thanks," Ferrin said, surprised by Nimhe's sudden display of affection.

"That's a pretty ring, is it new?"

Ferrin drew her hand back, glancing down at the rubies in the ring. "Just something I brought back from the Meddemara. I'm sure it's a fake," she lied.

"Really? It looks so genuine," Nimhe said enthusiastically, peering closer. "If you'd like, I can bring it to the jeweler in the morning to be cleaned and examined," she offered.

"There's no need. It has more sentimental value than any-thing."

"Oh," Nimhe responded, seeming dejected.

"I'm sorry, I don't mean to be cross. I've had an exhausting day. Go enjoy dinner. Really. I'll see you later," Ferrin said, feeling a pang of guilt at having snapped at Nimhe.

"All is well," she nodded. "I hope you're feeling better to-morrow." With that, she turned and left the room, her bright curls bobbing with each step.

Ferrin let out a breath. Nimhe had seemed distracted lately, as if something else was bothering her. Perhaps she had taken a fancy to someone in the Efelian delegation and didn't want them leaving prematurely.

After washing her face, Ferrin headed down to the kitchen, her stomach growling like a pack of wolves. With a tray piled full of seasoned chicken and some kind of squash, she strode to Rhi's room, where her brother was still in bed, a book propped on his knee.

"How are you feeling?" she asked, setting the tray down in the sitting area. Someone had clearly been in to clean up last night's mess, and fresh pillows had been thrown onto the couch.

"Just tired, really," Rhi answered, setting down his book and swinging his legs out of bed.

"I brought you some food, and a cup of broth in case you can't stomach the rest."

"Thanks," he said, settling into the armchair beside the couch. A fire was crackling cheerily in the fireplace.

Ferrin reached for the nearest plate on the tray, pulling it towards her on the table.

"Have you ever read *Legends and Truths*?" she asked her brother.

Rhi frowned in thought for a moment. "Who's it by? It sounds familiar."

"Some H.G. Serengath," she answered.

"Not sure, maybe. Is it any good?"

She shrugged. "I was hoping you would know."

She subtly turned the ring over on her finger so that the stones faced down, hidden from view. She didn't want to trouble him with this just yet.

"Right, so, this business with Taroch Forest."

"Wait," Rhi blinked. "Have you seen Lukas today?"

"No, not since last night. About this thing with the Forest—"

"I forgot I was supposed to meet him for an ale."

"He probably knows you aren't feeling well after last night," she crossed her arms angrily.

"He didn't know, Ferrin."

"What?"

"You're cross at him because you think he's been funneling deadly amounts of *popava* down my throat."

"He clearly has been," she waved a hand at him.

"That's not *exactly* true."

She waited, willing to listen.

"A few weeks ago, he asked why I was buying so much and told me it could be dangerous if I over-indulged."

"Well," she scoffed. "I suppose it would hurt his business if his best customer dropped dead."

"Ferrin," reprimanded Rhi.

"He's a selfish prick." Even as she said it, she felt a trickle of doubt. She had been harsh with him, and maybe what Rhi was saying *was* true.

"I told him I was giving it out to parties of... like thirty or so people. In small doses."

"Don't defend him, he was using you to turn a profit," she snapped. Zare flashed in her mind.

"If that were so, don't you think he would have cleared out at the first sign of danger? He'd have been in a lot of trouble if I'd died from *popava* poisoning. He's my friend, Ferr. And he isn't a bad person."

She frowned.

"Well," Rhi finished. "If you run into him, tell him I'm sorry to have bailed on our drink."

"Alright, I will. Now can we *please* discuss the matter at hand?"

"Right, right, sorry." Rhi cleared his throat. "What, exactly, is happening with Taroch Forest?"

"Well, after Father finished reprimanding me over the," she paused, searching for the words, "*Havian situation*, a few of his business advisors, I think, came in to present their proposal for the building of a new garrison and defense south of the palace."

"Alright, what exactly is the issue?"

"As I was saying, they want to chop down acres of the forest to do so, claiming it is in the name of defense. But—"

"But the forest itself is a natural defense…" Rhi finished her sentence, nodding thoughtfully.

"Precisely. And when I tried to reason with Father on the matter he slapped me and threw me out."

"He *what*?" Rhi gasped. "I know the two of you have long been at odds, but…"

"I'm fine, it's beside the point."

"I can't believe he'd do that." He shook his head. "I mean: I believe you, I'm only surprised."

"Well, there's to be some official meeting about it in a few weeks. Will you help me prepare and present a counter proposal? Or at least a rebuttal?"

"Yeah, of course," Rhi said nodding. "Where do we start?"

"I'm not sure, there's loads of reasons why it's a bad idea, but the thing is, none of those reasons are terribly lucrative in the short-term."

"We have time. We'll figure out a way."

Still clad in her stable clothes, which were bordering on nasty after the day she'd had, Ferrin wound her way down to the Pit. The crowds were filtering out and stumbling in the direction of various pubs, or going home with their winnings.

Fighting the current, she made her way down to the bottom of the arena, where Lukas was leaning on the ropes across from a giant of a man whose light beige skin was covered in inky blue-black tattoos. They were chatting as the big man counted a stack of paper bills.

Standing awkwardly in the doorway, she knocked on the wooden frame.

Both men looked up. Surprise flickered across Lukas's face. The big man looked back and forth between the two of them, clapped Lukas on the shoulder and disappeared into the back office.

"Care for an ale?" she asked, jerking a thumb back towards the outside world.

"What, so you can throw it in my face?" he said warily.

"No," she muttered as she crossed her arms.

"What are you doing here, Ferrin?" His voice was tired.

"Rhi can't meet you for an ale—" she began.

"Does he know you're here telling me to stay away?" he said.

"That's *not* what — look, he's just not feeling well. He could barely stomach his dinner, and he didn't want to be rude. Anyway, that's not why I'm here."

He arched an eyebrow and waited.

"Oh, don't give me that look," she said, uncrossing her arms. "I'm here to apologize."

"*Really*?" He drew the word out lazily, picking up a rag to dust off his hands.

She exhaled, "I said a lot of accusatory things last night. This morning." She blinked, shaking her head. "You were in a difficult position, and didn't know the extent of Rhi's *personal* use. He told me. I'm sorry for accusing you of endangering him on purpose for a profit."

"Well, I suppose you make mistakes when you jump to conclusions," he said, tossing the rag back onto the ropes.

"That's rich coming from you, Mister stab-first-ask-questions-later," she snorted. "Are you coming?"

"First of all, I did not *stab* you," he frowned, falling into step behind her as they ascended the steps of the arena. "And second, I thought you were a thief! How was I supposed to know you were a wayward royal?" he mocked, throwing up his arms. "Look, I apologized when I realized my mistake," he said. "Thank you for doing the same."

She halted suddenly, causing him to nearly run into her. Turning on the steps, she placed a hand on his shoulder. Standing on different steps, they were at eye level. Face to face.

"Can you promise me something?" she asked.

"What?"

"You'll stop bringing *popava* to Rhi. Into the castle *at all*."

"Done," he raised his hands in submission.

"Even if Rhi bribes you."

"Even if he offers to pay me triple," he nodded. "Listen, I don't want that to happen to him again, either. He's my friend, you know."

"I know," she said quietly as she turned around and continued up the stairs, Lukas following.

They found their way to the same pub they'd gone to a week earlier with Rhi and Soviel.

"Two ales," Ferrin ordered, tossing a few coins down on the bar as Lukas slid into the seat beside her. The barkeep filled two tin flagons and set them in front of her.

"Thanks," Lukas said when she passed him a mug.

"Don't mention it," she smiled, sipping the foam.

She watched him as he took a long drink, her eyes catching on the sharp line of his jaw, the swell of his shoulders under his coat as he lifted his mug.

"Any fallout from your Efelian problem?"

She snorted. "Not exactly. Not yet, anyway." She set her mug down and looked at him.

He nodded, his eyes fixed on nothing in particular on the bar surface. He seemed tense.

"What?" he said, feeling her watching him. His usual smug, self-satisfied exterior was less present than usual.

"What's bothering you?" she asked before she could think better of it.

He laughed to himself, turning his attention back to the bar-top. "Not sure you're the person I can bring my troubles to in this particular predicament, Princess."

Ferrin said nothing, but continued to stare him down. When he realized she wasn't going to let it go, he inhaled deeply and let it out. "Fine. The queen has asked something of me."

Ferrin tilted her head and furrowed her brow with curiosity.

"Something I can't… I mean I shouldn't do, don't *want* to do," he explained, shaking his head.

"Oooh," Ferrin breathed, then said, half-joking, "Does she want you to share her bed?" Queens took lovers, it wasn't un-heard of. She wouldn't put it past Nerena to use her influence to bring younger men to her bed. "If it's that, you can buy this powder and you mix it with ground up elderberry and—"

"What? No!" he fought a laugh. "She asked me to form a brute squad."

"A brute squad? For what?"

"She says there're rebels causing trouble, riling up villagers." He took a sip of his ale. "She says the unrest could turn into a mob. Which, from what you and I have *both* seen, is the least of the problems anyone should be taking with what's going on in that village."

"I don't think half of them could lift a sword, much less storm a castle," Ferrin agreed. Little did Lukas know there *was* a rebel hideout in the town. Not that their goal seemed to be riling up villagers. Nerena was playing at something else here. "What would you have to do? Kill townspeople?" she asked, quietly aghast and not wanting any of the said townsfolk to hear their conversation.

"They'd be arrested and taken to Danvery Prison. They'd be interrogated. Maybe executed, I don't know," he said glumly.

Inhale.

Exhale.

"She wants to make an example, deter what little spark may or may not be there," Ferrin murmured.

"And she wants it done in the worst of ways," Lukas agreed, staring morosely into his drink.

Ferrin found herself without words, as she rubbed her finger along the rim of her glass.

"I don't know what to do," he sighed heavily.

"Well," she pondered a moment, "what do you think is right?"

"You know what I th— I can't outright disobey an order from the queen, Ferrin. I'd have to—"

"Shh. No, no, no," she said, cutting him off. "I mean all consequences aside, no repercussions, what would you *choose* to do?"

"I obviously don't want to throw dozens of impoverished townsfolk into a jail to die of consumption and dysentery," he said angrily, then added, "I spent two years fighting almost this exact thing back home, and now I'm to be on the opposite side of it? I can't do that."

She nodded. Ash had grown up in Khalim too, and she'd told Ferrin plenty of stories of being forced to dive on wrecks in the harbor as a kid, salvaging goods for the Veiran army.

"So don't do it."

"Shit, Ferr, how strong is this ale? Have you heard a word I've said? I was given a direct order."

She nodded, then stared at him and widened her eyes as if clueing him in on some inside joke, "So don't disobey her."

"What are you saying?"

"Listen," she straightened in her chair, turning to face him. Their knees touched. "Form a brute squad. Be ineffective. Don't arrest anyone. Better yet? Arrest people who *are* causing actual harm to the rest of the town. Gods know, someone should be."

He turned back to the bar where the barkeep had just set down a second round, unprompted. He picked up his glass and downed half before twisting to face her again. "You think that'll work?"

"I think," she laid a hand on his forearm as she assured him, "that it will buy you time."

He nodded as she picked up her ale and drank.

"Then that's what I'll do. For now." He braced a hand on the edge of the bar and stood.

A they were walking out of the pub, Ferrin said quietly, "I wonder if you could help me with something, as well."

He noticed her worried expression. "What is it?"

"You're good at finding things."

"I am," he replied with slow caution.

"I want to find my mother."

"Ferrin," he said sympathetically. "The queen is long gone. Whether she's hiding out on the continent or drinking rum and fruit juice on a beach in Corsovena, or *wherever*, I don't think she's findable."

"I disagree. I think she's alive. And I believe she's closer than we think."

"Why do you say that?"

"Because she left me a note in one of my favorite books."

He considered her sincere expression and thought a moment before asking, "but couldn't anyone have left it?"

"She left it rolled up inside a family heirloom ring." She held up her hand to show him the ring glittering on her finger. "I think she wants to tell me something."

Lukas arched his eyebrows dramatically, nodding as he considered the possibilities.

When Ferrin returned home that evening, she found her copy of *Legends & Truths* lying open on her writing desk.

*   *   *

Rhi was sitting up in bed trying to focus on the military history chronicle of some Finnio the Elder propped up on his knee when a someone knocked on the door. It was just as well, considering how dull the first half of Finnio the Elder's life had been.

"Come in," he called.

The door opened and Ferrin strode around the corner from the atrium into his bedroom, dressed in dirty work clothes.

"How are you feeling?" she asked, perching at the foot of his bed.

"I've had better days," he said. "Please tell me you didn't skin Lukas alive."

"No," she said sheepishly. "We discussed last nights events. Like mature adults."

Rhi raised one eyebrow and she rolled her eyes at him.

"Did you happen to hear or see anyone go into my room in the last few hours? A few things are… not how I left them."

He shook his head. "I haven't left my bed since this afternoon. What's missing?"

"Well, nothing is *missing* that I could tell. It just looked like someone had perhaps gone through my things."

"Could it have been one of the maids, straightening up?" He moved the book from his knee and set it aside on his nightstand.

"Maybe," she said ponderously, though she didn't sound convinced. "Well," she set her hands on her thighs and made to stand, "I just wanted to check in on you again before I go to bed —"

"Wait! I did some thinking about this Forest business," Rhi began.

"You did?" She hesitated, halfway off the bed.

"Yes. I'm on board, but we need to be careful. Father's already asked me to sit in on the council meeting in a few weeks, I assume it's in regard to this."

"It must be."

"But, Ferrin… we need to be cautious in handling this. Father may give you a slap on the wrist for your rebelliousness, but this will be different. Both his children *openly* defying him on a matter of state is serious. He will not take it well, and it may land us in a world of trouble."

"I know." She bit her lip nervously.

"I'm willing to risk it, it's the right thing to do, but I want to make sure we're prepared," he said, swallowing. "Our argument must be ironclad and objective. We can't let it seem like an attack on him."

"I agree— I think you should be the one to present it."

Rhi nodded, "You're right."

"Do you think I should be there? Or if it's even possible?"

Rhi considered for a moment. Ferrin had an inflammatory presence when it came to their father. The two of them had rarely gotten along, even years ago before her stunt with running away. But, she was his sister and she had brought this issue to light. "Yes, I think you should be there, but only to observe. I know it's unfair but—"

"—But anything that comes from me is going to be taken as an attack in his point of view," she finished.

"Right," Rhi nodded tightly.

"Any idea of the angle we might take?"

"I'll think on it," Rhi said, trying to think of how his open defiance of his father was going to look to everyone in the court.

"Alright," she said, patting his knee. "Try to get some rest. And drink some water. I'll see you tomorrow."

"Night, Ferr."

"Night, Rhi."

*   *   *

"Well, what do you have to say for yourself?" Ferrin's father was in the calmest mood she'd see him in since her return. She'd been summoned to see the king upon waking, again being excused from her morning stable duties. For something that was supposed to be a punishment, she seemed to be excused from it fairly often.

"I'm very sorry for putting a strain on our alliance and our trade agreement with the Efelians," Ferrin muttered through tight lips and clenched teeth.

"And?" her father looked down at her expectantly. His tone was almost... pleasant?

Ferrin racked her brain. Surely, she must be forgetting something. What else did she have to apologize for? Had he learned of Rhi's episode? Was he blaming her for it?

"Well, do you want to be of use or not?" he asked.

"Oh. Yes, sir?" she answered.

"Very well, then. The infirmary is overwhelmed. In the afternoons you will help out with whatever they need."

"I'd be happy to help, but I'm not sure what this has to do with the Efelians? Or how much use I'll be, for that matter," she admitted frankly.

"The convalescence hospital that was added to the infirmary is full of Efelian soldiers recovering from grave wounds suffered at the front. We had the space for them, and here they are. Not that those stingy bastards have given us a break on their damn tariffs for our troubles," he added aside to himself.

"Right, then," Ferrin nodded. "I understand."

"You will report there after lunch three days a week, in addition to your stable duties. In fact, it's time for you to go now. Speak with Madame Leone, she'll put you to work."

"And… is there anything else you wanted me to do?" She bit her cheek, bracing herself for more screaming or at least a demand for her to apologize publicly.

"I am handling the rest of it," he said curtly.

For that moment, he seemed almost as he had years ago, before the disappearance of the Queen: reasonable, diplomatic. But Ferrin knew better than to trust his good temper would last.

The hospital building was a new, but mostly temporary structure. It was comprised largely of wood scaffolding and paraffin-coated canvas. The top was vented for smoke to waft out from the various braziers, leaving the air inside clear but warm.

The convalescent wing had been thrown together hastily a few years ago, Soviel had told her. They'd quickly put together the facility in response to the slew of disfigured and injured Efelian soldiers. Just a boat trip across the channel, and the Efelian soldiers had a relatively safe place to heal and recover.

Ferrin pulled back the entry flap, the bottom six inches of which were stained with mud from the last rain. As she stepped in, her senses of sound, sight and smell were assaulted all at once.

Nurses and healers rushed back and forth, all clad in thick, linen coveralls and habits to keep their hair back. The stench of blood and decay was driven away only by the hint of sweet smoke. Orders were barked over the many cots, and grunts of pain and idle chatter echoed throughout.

It was overcrowded. Sick and injured people from the castle were strewn about on cots and chairs, soldiers and guards and civilians alike. The convalescing soldiers were in varying states of health. Some were heavily bandaged, some missing limbs, some blinded, with wrappings over their eyes. Some wore their arms in slings, others had injuries Ferrin couldn't see.

"Pardon me," Ferrin said to a woman who was dropping some soiled linens in the bin near the door. The woman's eyes widened and she began to curtsy.

"Oh, no, please," said Ferrin, raising her hand. "There's really no need to—" she stopped as the woman curtsied anyway. "I'm here to work. Where can I find Madame Leone?"

The young nurse pointed to an older woman leaning over a man with a puncture wound, spidery purple veins spreading under his skin from the site.

"Thank you," Ferrin smiled to the nurse. Now *really* did not look like the time to interrupt Madame Leone. She looked to be fifty years of age, her expression stern and focused. The bright white of her coverall dress contrasted her warm-toned, medium-brown skin. Peeking out from beneath her habit were tendrils of reddish brown curly hair, so deep a shade, it resembled wine. Her eyebrows furrowed in focus as she examined the man's wound.

Suddenly, the man on the cot began shaking, his whole body locking up and trembling, nearly falling off the bed like he'd been taken ahold of by some foul spirit.

"Get me an herb chest!" Leone called over her shoulder.

One of the apprentices ran up, small wooden chest in hand. Leone snatched the box from the nurse's hands and pried it open with shocking efficiency before rooting around inside. It took her a moment before she found what she was looking for.

In a mortar, she dropped a few herbs, grinding them before scooping them into the man's mouth. After a moment, his seizing relaxed. His eyes drifted shut, and his chest rose and fell in an even rhythm.

"Get me some whiskey," Leone said to the apprentice, wiping her hands on her bloodstained apron. "We'll not want that wound festering further."

Now that the immediate urgency had faded, Ferrin slowly approached Madame Leone, who was scrawling notes into a little leather-bound notebook she'd taken from her skirt pockets.

"Madame Leone?" Ferrin asked gingerly.

"Yes, girl?" Leone said. Her accent was hard to place, but something in it sounded vaguely Bourjon. She didn't look up from her notes as she continued scrawling.

"I've been sent down from the castle to help, I was instructed to find you."

Leone snapped the notebook closed and looked up. Her dark eyes were sharp as she looked Ferrin up and down. "Aren't you the princess?"

"Yes, Madame." Ferrin shifted uncertainly on her feet.

"Very well then," said Madame Leone. "Put these on over your clothes," she instructed as she reached into a cabinet, pulling forth a folded gray cover-dress and habit. "Branick will show you around," she said as she jerked her chin and whistled a sharp note at the red-haired boy who appeared to be washing bandages in a big white basin. At Madame Leone's whistle, he snapped to attention and ran towards them.

"Hello, 'mam," he said in a thick, West-Barrian accent.

"Branick, show Ferrin around after she gets changed. Have her help you with washing the bandages, show her how to dress a wound."

"I have some experience dressing wounds—" Ferrin began.

Madame Leone gave her an all-knowing once-over before making an unimpressed *hmph.* "Branick will show you an *efficient* and *clean* way to stop infection and bleeding that doesn't involve backwashed whiskey and rags of an old shirt. Then you can make some rounds with me." With that, she turned on her heel and went off to tend to her next patient.

At Leone's instructions, Ferrin tugged the cover-dress over her head. It was made of thick fabric, designed to protect the skin and underclothing from spills and sharps. She slipped the habit on over her hair, not convinced she had done it right.

"Follow me, Your Highness," Branick turned and walked down the row of cots, pointing out where various medicines and implements were stored, where to dispose of different types of waste, where to put dirty bandage laundry. He pointed out Madame Leone's office at the end of the structure; it was closed off by tent flaps.

"Got it," she nodded, taking note of each thing as he pointed out.

"Come now, let's go bandage up some flesh wounds," he said cheerily.

Ferrin followed after Branick, who couldn't have been any older than fifteen. He showed her how to disinfect a cut, and had her watch him do a few basic stitches, which he did *not* let her try. About an hour into her shift, a new patient came in, and she watched as Branick did the intake. The patient was a boy in his teens. He was oily, pale, and dressed in a blood-covered kitchen uniform. Beside him sat one of the kitchen maids.

"He's nearly cut off his fingers," she moaned. "His name is Neddy."

"Here, onto the cot, Neddy," Branick said.

Neddy obliged but said nothing, a vacant and panicked look in his eyes.

"Hold pressure on the wound to stop the bleeding," Branick said to Ferrin, handing her a clean rag. "There, like that. I'll be right back."

"What? Where are you going?" Ferrin called after him. When he didn't reply, she shook her head and turned her attention to the wound, pressing down as hard as she could to squeeze the edges shut. "What's happened?"

The kitchen maid shook her head, "It was strange, he's never done this."

"What, chopped into his hand?"

"He had some sort of… fit." The maid shifted uncomfortably.

"What do you mean?" Ferrin asked. She could feel the boy's pulse in the wound.

"One minute he was fine. He came back from his break, started chopping vegetables for the dinner, not shutting up about some upstairs maid he's been mooning over, the next he goes quiet. Then he gets this terrified look on his face and starts mumbling something about his parents being there. Next thing you know he's nearly diced his fingers instead of the carrots."

Ferrin frowned.

"His parents are dead," the maid clarified.

At that moment, Branick emerged from the din, carrying a bottle of clear liquid, a jar of dried-up leaves and more fresh cotton bandages.

"Right then, let's clean that up."

"Branick, it sounds like he had some kind of fit that made this happen. Should we—?" she stopped. She didn't know the protocols.

"What happened?" Branick turned his attention to the young maid, her blue eyes wide. She repeated what she'd told Ferrin.

"He was seeing ghosts, you say?"

"Well, that's what he seemed to be saying. It was difficult to tell. But he was *terrified*. I thought for a moment he'd pick up the knife and come at me!"

Branick inhaled and nodded, frowning. He peeled back the compress to check the wound. "Hm. That bleeding isn't slowing down as much as I'd like." He handed Ferrin the jar of leaves. "Here, grind these up and rub them on the edges, they'll make the blood start to clot."

"Alright," she responded before Branick ran off again. She turned back to the maid. "What's your name?"

"Brina."

"Brina, has he said anything since this happened?" Ferrin asked, grinding up the leaves.

"No. He came back from his break completely fine, chatted as usual and then went all panicked. Then when he cut his hand, it seemed to shock him into silence."

"Do you know if he ate anything strange?"

"I didn't see what he ate, he left the kitchen to go see someone."

Ferrin nodded.

"I don't think he was doing that *stuff*, if that's your meaning," Brina added.

"Stuff?" Ferrin asked.

"Pop. Popava."

"Oh, that isn't what I was saying," Ferrin was quick to clarify.

"It's what I'd think if I didn't know him," Brina huffed.

"Is that a common effect of *popava*? Hallucinations and terror?" Ferrin asked. She'd always heard it had more of a relaxing-yet-stimulating effect, like strong whiskey, but with a kick that kept you awake. That was how Ash and Pierre had described it, anyway.

"I don't know," Brina shook her head. "But I've heard a few people say they got a bad batch of the stuff, and that they started seeing things."

Ferrin chewed the inside of her cheek in contemplation. She'd have to ask Lukas if he'd heard anything like this.

Branick returned with Leone, and the two of them spoke in hushed tones while Branick gestured at Neddy, who still seemed to be in a state of shock.

"I'll take it from here, thanks," Madame Leone said, moving to the bedside and dismissing Ferrin and Branick.

"Let's wash up the rest of the bandages," Branick said, striding to the center aisle.

"Right," she obeyed. "But what was all that about?" she asked, looking back curiously.

"That's the third person this month who's been reported as behaving like that. The last two were found dead in the streets, and when Madame contacted their families, it turned out they had been hallucinating and had run out of the house and into the cold. She's been up all hours trying to figure out what killed them."

"You think they were poisoned?"

"More like dosed intentionally," Branick said, throwing a glance over his shoulder. "I don't think whatever is in his system is deadly, per se, but if left on his own, who knows what would have become of him?"

Ferrin nodded slowly. "Why would someone do that? And why these people, are they connected?"

Branick shook his head. "It doesn't seem like it."

"And you think it's *popava*?"

"Maybe. Some strain of it."

"I've never seen anyone act like that, like what she described," Ferrin said.

"I asked around — one of the people found dead was known to use *popava* often. Where he got it from, we don't know. It must be laced with something, or the plant itself was engineered differently," Branick shrugged.

"Branick, would you tell me if anything else like this happens again?"

"Sure, why?"

"A friend of mine used to take *popava* a lot, and on the off chance he starts up again, I want to make sure this doesn't happen to him," she explained. She hoped Rhi would be able to resist consuming *popava* again, especially if someone was putting this deadly version out into the world.

Ferrin left the infirmary tired but energized, and though much of her day had been consumed with gore and injury and menial tasks, she felt good. It was nice to feel useful, to be busy. The buzz she had from her full day seemed to be steering her right to Lukas's rooms.

I just want to ask him about the popava *thing,* she reasoned. *Sure you do,* sniped a deeper part. She shook both voices from her head and knocked on his door.

Moments later, the door opened, and Lukas poked his head around it, only half his body visible to Ferrin. He wasn't wearing a shirt.

"Oh, it's you," he said, looking significantly relieved.

"Gods, who did you think I was?" she asked when he opened the door the rest of the way, revealing the dagger in his hand.

"*That* list is a lengthy one." He sheathed the knife and set it back on the hook where it usually hung.

"Noted, lots of enemies." She forced her eyes to fix on *anywhere* but his lean, broad chest. Anywhere but those defined lines running down and across his abdomen and disappearing under the low-hanging waist of his breeches —

"So. What can I do for you?"

She opened her mouth to reply, but nothing came out.

He quirked an eyebrow at her.

"I wanted to see if you were doing anything interesting I could tag along for."

He bit his lip and said, "Not particularly. I was planning on staying in the rest of the night. But if you want to distract me from the pile of inventory papers calling my name," he gestured toward the back table, which was indeed covered in piles of disheveled booklets.

"Sounds, uh, fun?"

He laughed. "You can stay a while if you'd like." He gestured to the couch adjacent the small coffee table. He plucked a discarded linen shirt from the back of one of the mismatched chairs and slung it on over his head.

"Alright." She plopped onto the couch, instantly putting her feet up on the table. After a moment, she thought better of it, and removed them.

"Do you want anything? I have some figs, bread, wine," he offered.

"Yeah, I could drink some wine," she blinked, "I suppose I wouldn't mind a bite, either."

"Here," he grinned, tossing her a fig.

"Thanks," she said, catching it.

"So, what were you hoping I'd be doing?" He flashed her a wicked smirk.

"Oh, I don't know. Something. Anything. Maybe a Pit fight, some gambling. Roughing someone up by the docks." She made a one-two punch gesture that she immediately regretted.

"You are ridiculous," he laughed. "It's not as if I spend all my time beating people up and losing money at cards."

"Only half your time, then?" she teased.

He snorted and popped the cork out of the wine bottle.

"So, what illegally imported wine do I have the privilege of trying?" she asked, shifting on the couch to face him as he settled next to her.

"Ha. It's Bourjon," he said, pouring two glasses.

"You must be talented at this smuggling indeed, if you managed to fetch anything out of Bourjony."

"Told you I was, Princess." He raised his cup.

"I admit it: I'm impressed," Ferrin smiled.

"Was that a compliment?" Lukas asked, sounding dumbfounded.

"You tell me," she countered, heat flushing her face at his gaze and their proximity. "I've always been able to appreciate a smart move of items across borders."

"Tell me," he lolled his head to the side and back, stretching his neck. "Where in Bourjony, in your opinion, do they have the best wine?"

"Hmmm," she breathed, thinking a moment. "Further south. Close to the coast on the Meddemara side. A vineyard outside Cavarelle, a little family has owned it for generations."

"South side vineyards run a little sweeter on the whites, but the reds, I'm told, are more full-bodied."

"That's sound," she agreed, reaching across the table for another fig.

"Hey, is that a—" he squinted at the skin beneath her elbow. "*Brand*?"

"Oh, this?" She pushed up her shirtsleeve, revealing the ugly "T" character in a double circle. Red, puffy, and permanent. Or maybe not, given how Soviel's magic had successfully faded the one on her other arm.

He reached out and caught her arm, running his thumb over the red mark. "That's a thieves' brand from the Khalim police, I'd know it anywhere."

"Would you now?" she raised her eyebrows.

"Yeah, they slapped one on me when I was thirteen and I flayed it off before it could heal."

She blanched. "That's quite violent."

"Better than never being able to get a job in the city again and starving my family," he explained. "How'd you get it?"

"Got caught cutting purse-strings in a wealthier neighborhood. They did this and threw me in a cell." She shrugged one shoulder, moving her eyes from where he touched her skin to meet his impressed gaze.

He whistled. "How did you get out?"

"My… the captain. Zare," she grumbled, "fished me out two nights later."

"He let you rot in a Khalim jail cell? For two nights?" Lukas asked, incredulous.

"Wasn't the only time," she bit her cheek and took a swig of her wine at the memory. She had more than a few scars that were a result of Zare taking his sweet time getting her out of whatever trouble he'd landed her in in the first place.

"Where else?"

"You ever hear of Calomba Herotis?" Most people had. Her work enforcing for the darker side of the olive-trade along Kalassa's coast and throughout the Meddemara was legendary, as was her beauty. She'd been mentioned in a scandalous exposé pamphlet about international crime published throughout the continent a few years back.

"Shit," Lukas breathed.

"I got caught on the wrong man's estate with a number of stolen items in my pockets. Zare swore up and down he had a contingency plan in place if I was taken."

"And?"

"She interrogated me," she shared, shuddering at the memory of it. Not of the pain or the scars, but of the fear, the not knowing when it would stop. "For two and a half hours, before he decided to show up." She shook her head. "I was barely sixteen. She gave me these." She reached up and pulled the collar of her shirt to the side, revealing the white slashes and chunks of skin where she'd been cut and split by brass knuckles and knives alike on her shoulders and chest. They had grown fainter over the years, but any time they were exposed to sunlight, they seemed to jump out, a ghoulish white against her skin.

"Not many have lived to tell the tale of one of her interrogations," Lukas said, running his eyes over her collarbone, the curve of her shoulder. "He just *let* you get taken in?"

She shrugged, wishing she could forget the memory. "I know it was stupid to keep trusting him time after time. *I* was stupid."

"That's not what I meant."

"It's the truth, though." She took another drink of the Bourjon wine, pulling her shirt back over her shoulder. "Over and over, I watched him lie and manipulate everyone else around us, but I thought because we—" she stopped and shook her head again. "I thought I was exempt from his schemes."

Lukas bit his lip, as if he was teetering between saying something and not.

She set her wine down, determined to change the subject. If he started pitying her, she wasn't sure she could handle it. "There was something I wanted to ask you about, actually."

"What is it?"

"Ah, well, I was helping out at the infirmary today and I stumbled on some interesting information."

"I see. About what?"

"Some kid came into the infirmary. Almost cut off his own fingers."

"And as tragic as that is, why should I find it interesting?"

"Seemed like he'd been drugged."

"How do you know?" Lukas asked, frowning.

"He came in with one of the maids from the kitchen. She said he had some kind of fit. "Then when I asked the kid who was showing me the ropes at the infirmary about it, he said this isn't the first time this has happened."

"People having fits?" asked Lukas.

"No," she clarified. "They found two bodies. People who disappeared after behaving like this boy who almost cut his fingers off. Their families reported that they were seeing things after smoking or ingesting *popava*."

Lukas sat back, his expression worried. "My friend Ryder said his wife got some *popava* from a guard she knows and that they both had strange reactions to it."

"Do you think it came from your source?"

"I sure hope not," Lukas said. "There are other people who find ways to get it over here undetected and sell it."

"It just seems odd. Seeing ghosts? Panic?" she pondered. "I thought *popava* was supposed to be more like strong drink."

"Any mind-altering substance can affect different people differently. But, generally, yes." He stroked his chin with his thumb. "And ghosts? Are you sure?"

She nodded. "That's what the maid said he was raving about."

"That seems oddly specific."

"Branick, the boy who works at the infirmary, told me the other families reported the same thing."

"Maybe someone's messing with the supply, lacing the doses and letting it trickle into the market to discredit sources and drive all buyers to one place," Lukas theorized.

"You think it's about money?" she asked, skeptical.

"Most things are, Princess."

"But who would have the knowledge, let alone the resources, to even *do* that?"

Lukas said nothing, his lips pursed as he shook his head. "I'm not completely sure it was her who dropped it," he shared, "but when Nerena came to talk to me the other day, I found a little concealment vial where she'd been sitting. Didn't want to open it before I turned it in to her guards. But, it was the kind of container people generally tuck powdered substances into."

"What?"

"Dosing servants seems a little below her list of priorities. She's the *queen*, after all."

"No, no, you're right about that. But still, she doesn't strike me as one who likes to numb the mind." Ferrin added Lukas' story to her growing list of little mysteries that she could only hope breaking into her father's office would solve.

CHAPTER FIFTEEN

The days passed in much the same fashion for a time. Ferrin would wake up, go to her stable duties and muck stalls, trade jokes with Alick. Then she'd eat a small lunch before rushing off to the infirmary, where she cleaned bandages till her hands were pruned, and wrapped wounds till her fingers bled. On her second day there, Soviel had greeted her and explained she'd requested Ferrin shadow her. She'd trail Soviel through the infirmary, ready to hand her bandages, herbs or fetch water on command.

They'd break for snacks together and walk around the grounds laughing about whatever bizarre occurrence the infirmary had brought forth that day. ('Lord Brochlands got *what* stuck *where?'* and 'Serene Bollinton broke out in hives and looked like a leopard because she used corn-paste as skin cream' and 'Mr. and Mrs. Jorgen from the coffeehouse on Main Street both came in with oophenpox but both swear up and down that they've been faithful').

For a second time, she'd come home one day exhausted from stable duties and work at the infirmary to find her desk in disarray. *Legends & Truths* was sprawled open face down on the desk, her drawers were halfway open, and someone had pried up the floorboard beneath her bed.

Definitely not the work of the maids.

Nothing was missing, and the nook beneath her bed had been empty, thankfully, since she'd dropped off her dagger to be sharpened that morning. But twice now someone had come into her room, looking for something.

She'd spent some time with Rhi drafting what they'd say when they attended the council meeting about the garrison and the Taroch Forest. He'd been doing better, but still wasn't sleeping well since throwing out all of his *popava*. She was thankful he had stopped, especially when there'd been two more cases of bad reactions to the drug.

Lukas had been keeping his ear to the ground, but he hadn't stumbled upon anything useful regarding the drug or the possibility that someone was lacing it. Ferrin and Lukas had journeyed to the black market a few more times, hoping for answers, and come up short.

When she wasn't falling into bed exhausted, she was scouring the pages of *Legends and Truths* for answers. So far, all it had revealed were stories she already knew. Tales of Strata and her chariot of storm-steeds. Gwelie, rumored to be the first queen of Caelbarrow, the storm maiden who had driven out the vampires from the cloud-stricken lands. Tales of the twin sea gods, Merras and Merriye, and how they'd banished the beasts that their nameless father had set into the sea to the Old Deep, where they could not hunt ships and locked it tight. There was the tale of Lalana and Isila, who pulled all the trees and plants and green things from the rocks, creating fertile soil, soft earth out of unforgiving crags and stone.

That night, she shut the tome with a sigh. There was no hidden message between the pages, no dog-eared page marking a location, no notes scrolled in the margins, no underlined phrase hinting at an explanation.

She had nothing to go on. She had been thus far unsuccessful in figuring out what her mother was trying to tell her. She had been unsuccessful in breaking into her father's office. The door was always locked, and almost always guarded, and she certainly wasn't going to go in while he was *there*.

The answers weren't going to fall out of the sky. She would have to seek them out. It was time to do some digging.

*   *   *

The day was growing late, and the mid-spring sun was starting to roll down its slope towards the horizon. Ferrin's feet were leaden after standing all day, since the infirmary had been busy as usual. She'd shadowed Branick for an hour, then assisted Soviel, who had been on edge all day, before being turned loose to treat the most minor injuries on her own.

Soviel worked a few rows over, and Ferrin found herself envious of her skills with the craft, as well as the healing magic she wielded. Her hands fluttered effortlessly over a man's wounded leg, surveying the damage that was slow to heal.

Without magic, he'd have been lucky to keep the limb, Branick had explained. Ferrin was still in awe of what she'd seen only days earlier when Leone had healed the soldier on the brink of death, his mouth frothing and his head twitching back and forth like an enraged demon.

As the hectic pace slowed to a trickle, she felt her nerves return. She took a deep breath, trying to shake her anxiety in approaching Madame Leone with her particular questions as she finished tending to the scraped elbow of a messenger girl.

Dusting off her hands, Ferrin pushed back the canvas flap that served as the door to Madame's office. Madame Leone sat at her desk, papers and ledgers illuminated by lantern light, wire-framed glasses balanced on her nose as she studied her work.

"Yes, girl?" Madame Leone said without looking up from the notes she was revising. Ferrin couldn't understand how she wrote so fast without making a mess of her letters.

"I have a question."

"Sit," Leone commanded. Her eyes were still focused on the paper before her.

Taking a seat in the worn wooden chair by the desk, Ferrin began, "I've been doing some… reading. And I wanted to ask you how much you know about magic. In general."

Leone set her pen down evenly, straightening her back as she leveled her gaze at Ferrin. "And exactly what kind of books were you reading?"

"Old, dusty books, from the back of the library," Ferrin explained. "Really old. Things about magic in the old times."

Almost imperceptibly, Leone tilted her head to one side, sliding her fingers together in front of her as she exhaled. "Well, it didn't just vanish, you know."

"Right."

"Around two hundred years ago, magic began to fade. It was gradual; fewer and fewer people were born with it, as if it was diluting over the generations. And people forgot how to use it, stopped teaching their children to wield it. Slowly, it just faded. Almost like it went to sleep. You could blame it on lack of necessity or curiosity." She looked squarely at Ferrin.

"But then what about now? Could it come back? What about people like you, like Soviel?" asked Ferrin slowly.

"Healers never quite lost their touch. I personally believe it's because the necessity for them was so great. Even in times of peace, people injure themselves or become ill and require our gifts. And the power of earth and plant magic, of *life* magic has always been worshipped devoutly; Lalana and Isila have massive followings. Especially in any land where the Tyggoths once roamed. You know of them, I presume?"

Ferrin nodded uncertainly. Her history books claimed the Tyggoths were the ancient tribes of people who ranged the land that was now Efel to Kalassa.

"I'll lend you this book on it, if you're interested," said Madame Leone as she reached for one of her books and handed it to Ferrin.

"I have no Tyggoth blood. I won't be able to use the magic," said Ferrin, examining the cover.

"No, perhaps not, but that doesn't mean you won't find the information useful, and perhaps applicable elsewhere." Madame Leone arched an eyebrow in a way that seemed almost like she was implying something but didn't want to speak it aloud.

Ferrin frowned at the book, biting her lip.

"Say what else it is you want to say, girl. I have little time or interest in beating around the bush."

"There's been other things, too… rumors."

"Yes, I've heard talk of strange occurrences. A woman making it rain in the middle of dry season, saving her village from drought. The boy stopping the fire from scorching his home in the tundra with a mere wave of his hand. I suspect you are coming to me because you've *also* seen something?" Leone asked, her tone expectant.

"Well, no. Not exactly. I was reading more on the regions of magic, and both those instances occurred where that type of magic was once prevalent. The rain in Dromata sounds like the water magic of the south. And the fire? Couldn't he have been controlling the blaze like a flame wielder of the north?" she asked.

Leone blinked slowly, removed her glasses and folded them neatly in her elegant brown hands. "Like I said, magic was largely linked to necessity. Affinity for fire in a land of cold and ice where one might easily freeze to death, control over water in the desert, where the drought might kill you? It is necessity that brings such things about. In the vast fields and plains of the Tyggoth land, there was need to farm and heal constantly."

"And on the island, here?" Ferrin asked, already knowing the answer.

"Storms, air, wind," Leone said. "The ability to control the air current and stop the hurricane from destroying one's village, to stop the wind from smashing one's ship on the rocks. To traverse the high cliffs and mountainous scape of the islands. Perhaps to channel the lightning away from the livestock and crops," Leone explained.

"So Strata blessed our land."

"I know very little of Barrian lore, I'm afraid. You'd be better off asking that Caelish man I've heard runs the stables. I hear he has some knowledge on the matter."

Alick? Ferrin hadn't thought to ask him. "I read something in a very old book. Some legend or myth that Strata had blessed a Caelish queen with the gift of flight long ago. If that were true — in theory— she'd be my great-great-great-times-a-hundred grandmother, right?" Ferrin repeated, "In theory."

"I do know that myth," Leone smiled. "In theory, yes, she would be."

"And do you—" Ferrin couldn't believe how ridiculous she sounded, "Ah… do you believe it?"

"It's not what I believe that matters, now, is it?" Leone leaned forward and winked. "The Gods smile on those who have faith in their power."

Ferrin swallowed. "And what about the other rumors? The Dromatan woman, the boy from Njorske?"

Leone sat back and sighed, "Perhaps twenty years ago, sparks of magic began appearing in every region. Still few and incredibly far inbetween. But it was there, trickling back." She closed the notebook she'd been writing in, the ink now dry. "But I have to wonder, magic faded because there was no longer as much need for it. Now it swells and grows once more. Why now? The question we should be asking is, what's to come?"

"Do you know anything else?" Ferrin asked brazenly, Leone's ominous question setting her spine prickling.

"I'm not a walking library, girl. You'd best ask the horse-master. Perhaps he has the answers you seek about these stories."

"I will," Ferrin agreed, nodding sharply as she stood.

"Good."

She thanked Madame Leone and turned to leave, but paused with her hand on the tent flap.

"Out with it," Leone said sternly.

"What is the *Dionas*?" Ferrin asked, clutching the book and her jacket to her chest.

"They no longer exist," Leone said darkly. "They were an order of magic-practitioners, trained and sworn to protect, and if necessary, restore the balance of nature at any cost. They faded from existence years ago."

"I see," Ferrin nodded, swallowing. "Thank you for your wisdom, Madame." She curtsied and dipped through the tent, heading home.

Lukas and the two men he'd enlisted strode through the village with a wooden club in his fist. So far, the prison wagon had only two townsfolk in it — one who had raped the butcher's daughter, and another who'd been caught breaking into homes and stealing jewelry and flatware.

He had not arrested any of the people the queen had insinuated were rebels, but was still not *quite* disobeying her instructions. He'd just have to hope she wouldn't look too closely at the results.

"Come on, let's check down this street, I heard reports of loud noises and cries coming from a house by the tannery," Lukas said to the guards flanking him.

"Aren't we supposed to be looking for the rebel hideout?" asked Jones, an ex-guard.

Lukas scoffed, "The rebels operate out of the north. Everyone knows that."

"The queen said there're more than that," Jones spat a wad
of *arimopo* onto the cobblestone street. "And I saw a Caelish
rebellion symbol painted in sheep's blood on the side of an alley
down in the slums!"

"'Caelish rebellion symbol'? What does that even look like?
It was probably just kids trying to scare the neighbors," smirked
the other man, a guard named Adair. He was an easy-mannered
son of a lesser lord. He seemed most interested in going to the
tavern and searching for rebels at the bottom of a glass or in the
cleavage of the barmaid.

"Well," Jones looked back and forth between Lukas and
Adair, realizing he was outnumbered. "Well, I saw a woman go
into that house there wearing a bright new patterned shawl. The
kind *specifically* outlawed after the mill riots." He spat another
wad of *arimopo* on the ground.

"I think we can find something a little more substantial than
a lady's shawl, don't you, Jones?" Lukas rolled his eyes.

Jones whirled on him, getting right in his face. "What are
you, some kind of sympathizer?" He reeked of whiskey and
arimopo. "You think you can just let all these pieces of shit get
away with it because you're half Cael? You weren't there two
years ago when that mob of miscreants killed two guards at the
mill," he snarled.

Lukas sighed angrily. "I'm also half Akhatan. I take no side
in this," he hedged. "As I said, there are bigger things to worry
about than some people bending a few rules."

"You're going soft on them for your own purposes. Her
Majesty never should have hired a criminal to—"

Lukas had Jones pinned against the wall of the alley they'd
turned down, club pressing against his throat, before Jones
could even finish his sentence.

"You are a pathetic excuse of a guard. Oh, I mean *ex-*guard," Lukas mocked, getting in close. "And I think you know that. Is that why you're so desperate to run after schoolchildren, and women wearing patterned shawls? So you can feel like a big, strong soldier? Do not mistake people's wishes for a more prosperous life for some bloodthirsty intent for rebellion."

Jones narrowed his eyes, but the fear was still there.

"Do you understand me?" Lukas asked, pulling back the club a fraction of an inch so he could answer.

"Yes," Jones croaked through tight lips.

"Good." Lukas bared his teeth and slammed the man into the wall once more for good measure before releasing him. "Now, get out of my sight."

Jones backed down the alley before turning and breaking into a run.

Lukas stalked out of the alley. "You coming, Adair?"

"Yes, sir," Adair answered a little nervously, scrambling after him.

"This is the house the complaints were made against," Lukas said as they approached the building.

"What kind of complaints?" Adair asked.

"A few things. Kid's been showing up to his apprenticeship beaten halfway to hell, the mother never leaves the house," he said, then added, "And the man *is* known to spout borderline-seditious Cael sentiments when he's had a few at the tavern. It'll please the queen."

"Ah," Adair nodded. Lukas had the sense that the soldier had no interest in arresting peasants who clung to their now-outlawed roots. He'd likely only signed on for the pay and the hours it would take off his normal duties. "We have a name?"

"Macray," Lukas replied. "Leather tanner."

Adair nodded briskly. "So, what now, do we just bust in there?"

Lukas frowned, thinking a moment. "In case there's been a mistake we should probably knock."

"Right, then."

"Here, you're the one wearing a uniform. Go on," Lukas gestured, pointing to the door.

Adair glanced at Lukas, then tentatively raised a fist to knock.

"It's open!" a female voice called out, muffled through the door.

Adair raised his eyebrows at Lukas and turned the handle.

There were two women: a blonde with her hair messy and unbound, and a brunette, who was comforting her. There was a faint, bruised swelling under one eye of the blonde woman and her forearms were marked with bruises varying from dark purple to faded yellow. She looked to be holding back tears. In her arms was a young boy. No more than ten. Similarly bruised. He stared straight ahead, silent and unblinking. Lukas's stomach turned and he remembered marks like that on his own mother and sister when the soldiers had come to collect after a bad week.

"He's in there," the brunette pointed fearfully to the back room. It was she who had called for them to come in.

"Please don't hurt him, he just—" the blonde woman shook her head, breaking off mid-sentence.

Lukas and Adair marched into the office, where the man sat at his desk.

"Have you come to get that meddling bitch out of my house?" the man growled. There was a half-empty bottle of whiskey in his grip. His muddy-brown hair hung tangled and greasy to his shoulders. He looked to be in his mid-forties, but he could have been younger and simply aging poorly due to his personal-care habits. After all, a rotten soul tended to rot the outsides too.

"Allister Macray?" Lukas said. "There's been a lot of talk about you in the rumor mill."

"Look, a letter from Port Galan, it's even got a Caelish seal on it," Adair held up a document he'd snagged off the desk.

"Rip off the seal for proof, give me the letter," Lukas ordered before lunging at Macray. He grabbed him by the shirt collar. The man struggled back, his movements slowed by the liquor oozing from his pores.

"Got it," Adair said, then joined Lukas to tie Macray's hands.

"That letter's not mine! It was sent here by mistake. I've nothing to do with the rebels!" he hissed defensively.

"Save your stories," Lukas hissed in Macray's face. Then, to Adair, he said, "Let's go. Bring the child and mother up to the infirmary."

"Yes, sir," Adair nodded. "What about the other woman?"

"Carine!" Macray seethed like a wild animal as they entered the front room where the women were sitting. "You bitch, you think you're better than us?"

The brunette — perhaps the sister of Mrs. Macray — stood, paling at the violent expression on Macray's face. "Get out of here, Allister. I hope they *never* let you out, I hope you *rot*!" she screamed.

The blonde woman fought a sob, covering her mouth with her hand.

"What power do you have to do this?" Macray sneered at Lukas, straining against the ropes at his wrists. "I see no uniform."

"I'm under strict orders from the queen to clear the rabble out of the village. And by your smell, I'd say that includes you."

CHAPTER SIXTEEN

In her spare time, Ferrin had sussed out a few more entrances to the hidden servants' passages. She could enter just beyond her rooms and cut over through the old, stone hallways to pop out right in her father's rooms, if her estimations were right. She'd found it by mistake when exploring nearly a week ago. It had seemed too easy, so she'd come back several times to re-check the route.

When she left her rooms, clad in fine but plain men's clothes as to not attract attention, she passed only one chambermaid and a messenger boy before ducking behind the potted plant that concealed the entrance to the servants' halls. Armed with only large pockets, a pencil, paper, her wits and a singular knife, she slid open the hidden door and ducked inside. When she rounded the corner nearest the panel she was looking for, she drew a cloth up and across the lower half of her face. It was time for some light treason.

As she'd gleaned from what she'd learned of her father's schedule, his office was empty at this hour. The maids would have just left for the day, and her father wouldn't return for another hour.

She held her breath as she pushed on the door and it swung open into the office. From the other side, it was just another peach-colored wall panel. She left it cracked, just in case it only opened from within.

The large, flamboyant desk was beautifully polished in the most stunning red-gold stained wood. Atop it, the king's things were in pristine order. The drawers were an entirely different story.

Broken pen tips, empty ink wells, crumpled papers and two elegant, deadly knives were among the disorder in the drawers. Among all that, she found a few different ledgers, all bound in leather and embossed with different labels. *Shipping, Staff, Machines, Fueling.*

Hmph, she grumbled inwardly, moving on to the next drawer. More of the same: a disconcerting amount of clutter. She tried the next drawer. It was empty, save for a few baubles shaped like little goblins and wolves, and a discarded golden chain. The next drawer was locked.

"Oh, for *Saolath*'s sake," she cursed to the trickster-god. She snatched a brass letter opener from on top of the desk, making careful note of where she'd found it so she could put it back in its proper place. Crouching down again to the bottom drawer, she slid the letter opener across the top of the drawer, trying to find the latch that held it shut. *Just find the right,* she thought to herself… *spot!* The latch clicked open.

The drawer was organized, tidy, uncannily full. Not a paper was out of line, and the files were labeled in a numerical order. Each had a code scrawled at the top, along with key words. At the front, there was a contract with Corsovena, the Efelian colony in the Meddemara, for *arimopo* trade.

Cautiously, she leafed through each document, scanning the page until she found what she was looking for.

It was there— a demo-order for Taroch Forest. It had every argument they planned to use in the proposal. Some of the listed reasons were sound, and some were far-fetched and ridiculous. Weed out vagrants living in the woods, clear space for farming, take timber for the new garrison and wall, rid the land of the wild-men and beasts inhabiting it.

Ferrin was certain the only wild-men in the forest were the ones who wandered in looking for a faerie wife after having a few too many whiskeys at the tavern.

None of it was unexpected, but at least they could prepare for each individual argument with some kind of rebuttal. She read through the list of benefits. Some could be negated tenfold. Most were only beneficial in the short term. The arguments were all thinly veiled excuses for the king to do what he pleased, and the council would doubtless do exactly as he decreed. But Rhi had a shot at changing their views. He had to.

She pulled it out and made quick work copying it onto a slip of paper, setting it down on the floor next to her knee to dry. What she stumbled upon next was strange. Below the elegant script, numbered *382.00*, were some observational notes.

Popava strains.

She gasped.

Subject eight-five has shown side effects similar to those before. Terror, panic and hallucinations immediately following exposure. The after-effects, when not deadly, have proven successful. We will move forward with Strain-D in all future experiments, though the dosage may need to be scaled back. All surviving subjects found to be compatible.

It was dated two weeks ago.

Who's writing was this? Ferrin wondered with horror. *The queen's?*

Sloppily, she copied down as much as she could, waving the paper around in the air to dry the ink faster. She then set to replacing everything she'd moved. She slid the door closed, and used the letter opener to pop the latch back into place. Folding the now-dry paper, she stood and slid it into her pocket.

The sound of voices by the main door caught her attention. "Shit," she breathed, moving quickly towards the secret door. She was steps away from the wall panel when it swung open and a slender brown-haired girl holding a tray of tea froze as she caught sight of Ferrin. The girl screamed and dropped the tray with a clatter.

The main door burst open and three guards poured in, each with a sword ready and one with a musket trained on her.

"Assassin!" one of them shouted, calling for backup. "Assassin in the king's chamber!"

Their red and gold jackets swept behind them as they advanced on her. She had to act fast. She dodged to the side just in time to avoid the musket ball that would surely have killed her, and ducked the mean end of the bayonet slashing towards her. She fell into an old rhythm, her muscles remembering what it was to fight and dodge. She grabbed the end of the musket and forced it back, clocking the guard in the jaw with it as the other two advanced. He went down and she stopped thinking, drawing her knife.

The other two came at her at the same time, one swinging his cutlass. She dropped to sweep his leg, and his head hit the floor with a *whack*!

The third guard was on her in a second, slashing for her with his sword. She leaned out of the way in her signature fighting style of avoiding and evading, waiting for an opportunity to strike. His blade embedded in the wooden post of the daybed, and she stumbled back onto the piece of furniture, scrambling away. He drew a knife from his belt, the sharp of its steel glinting as she backed away on her hands and feet. He slashed for her chest, just as she rolled, and caught her in the upper arm.

Ferrin let out a bark of pain as red spread across her sleeve and onto the bed. She rolled onto the floor and landed on her feet, eyeing the window that the guard was now blocking. The covering on her face was the only thing keeping him from identifying her.

Without giving herself a chance to second-guess, she feinted low, to his right. It drew his attention as planned, and when he leapt to intercept her, she tucked and dove low past his legs, sliding across the marble floor. She slammed into the side of one of the book cases, her body skidding to a sudden halt. Her ribs creaked with the impact. She was up and scrambling to the window when his hand closed around her ankle, yanking her back by the boot. Grunting, she kicked and pulled, but his grip held firm. His other hand closed around her foot.

"In here!" he shouted to others through gritted teeth.

She could make out the words of the guards outside, and her kicks became more desperate. Those guards would flood in by the dozen and she'd be done for.

Her eyes fixed on the bronze statue of Heleion that had fallen from the bookshelf, it was about the size of her forearm. She let go of the book case and let him pull her back, scrunching her body into a tight curl as he did. Her fingers closed around the statue and she swung. It connected with his temple in a sickening crunch, and his fingers uncurled from her boot like the legs of a dying beast.

Once she was up, she threw the balcony doors open and burst onto the stone deck. Her arm was bleeding badly. It was too high to jump safely, and there was nothing to climb, but she had little choice. Hopping over the railing, she lowered herself as far as her injured arm would let her and dropped to the ground, biting back a howl of pain.

Something twisted and snapped in her ankle when she landed. She bit back a string of curses and forced herself up off the ground. There was no time to waste. Shucking off her coat, she let the conveniently tucked skirts fall from their folds around her waist. She dropped the coat, bloody mess that it was, into the unkempt topiary, along with her face covering and hat. The rush of the fight was leaving her, making space to feel the heightening pain in her ankle, ribs and arm. She had to get to Soviel before it was too late to repair all of it, and before those guards came to and disclosed the injuries that the would-be assassin would have.

The infirmary at the foot of the castle's hill wasn't a far walk, but in that moment, it seemed to Ferrin like it stretched on for miles. Every footfall hurt, and she was limping badly by the time she reached the tent. She pressed her hand to the bleeding wound throbbing in the meat of her upper arm and sent a silent prayer out to Haz and his Luck-Sprites that Soviel was working as scheduled.

Finally, she reached the tent flaps and poked her head in. Branick was at the bedside of a young woman with curly black hair, bandaging her forehead.

"Branick!" she called under her breath.

His head snapped up.

"Could you fetch Soviel, it's urgent." She gritted her teeth.

"You're not on the schedule today," he said, rising slowly.

"*Please*, Branick. It's important."

"What's wrong?"

"Just get her!" she hissed, stepping inside the tent and grabbing a discarded cover-dress. She shrugged it halfway on, pulling only her uninjured arm through the sleeve.

Branick scurried off and returned a few moments later with Soviel in tow.

"What's going on?" she asked in a hushed tone, stepping closer as Branick reluctantly returned to his work.

"I need some help," Ferrin clenched her jaw. Now that she'd slowed down, everything was starting to ache. "I'll explain later."

Soviel nodded, giving Ferrin a once-over. "Follow me."

She led her back to Madame Leone's main office.

"Madame won't mind we're in here?"

"She's off eating lunch in the woods and looking for berries," Soviel said dismissively. "Sit." She pointed to the narrow couch, before sweeping back out to the main room. She returned a few minutes later carrying a box of supplies.

"What, in the name of *Lalana*, happened?" she asked, setting down the supplies.

"It's a long story," Ferrin winced, slipping the coverall over her head.

"Well, considering I'm about to stitch you up, and by the looks of your walk, set your ankle, too, I'd say we have time."

Soviel's voice was commanding, her soft, polite edges non-existent.

"I was looking through my father's things and I got caught," Ferrin confessed outright.

Soviel stared at her a moment. "Do they always brutalize royal children for being nosy?" she asked, drawing Ferrin's inured foot into her lap.

"I was in disguise," Ferrin winced. "I snuck in through the servant's entrance, so no one saw me go in. They thought me an assassin."

"Did you find the files? Did you make copies?" Soviel asked, yanking at Ferrin's bootlaces.

"What?" Ferrin snapped her gaze to Soviel's pinched face. "What files?"

"I suppose now is a good time as any to let you know," Soviel said, tongue in cheek as she slid off Ferrin's boot. Her ankle had swollen triple its size. Soviel braced her hands on either side of her foot. "Ready, one, two—"

Something crunched. Ferrin covered her mouth with the back of her hand to keep from yowling like a cat as the joint was cranked back into place. Soviel leaned over to the table, plucked up a few green stalks of some plant.

"Let me know *what*?" Ferrin demanded as Soviel clutched the stalks in one hand. They began to wither as she held her other hand over Ferrin's ankle. "Soviel, what?" she repeated.

The burning sensation in her ankle intensified and she groaned.

"Helene," Soviel stated simply, offering no further explanation as she moved on to her arm. Whatever she did, it stopped the bleeding but didn't seem to fully repair the wound. There wasn't time for that.

Ferrin just stared at her, dumbfounded and waiting for more.

"We'll discuss it at length another time. For now, we need you patched up. Make sure people see you working out there. You've been here all day, got it? Now, please tell me you didn't leave anything incriminating behind."

"Soviel, *what* are you saying?" Ferrin urged, not trusting herself to put it all together.

"You know exactly what I'm saying, Ferrin. Now trust me on this," she said, her eyes flickering to Ferrin's for a brief moment. The sharp, focused look Ferrin had seen there only a handful of times was completely unveiled. It hit Ferrin with the force of a brick wall.

Soviel was among the masked members of the Rebellion. She was the mole in the castle. She'd likely been the one to orchestrate Ferrin's involvement, verifying that she would be an asset to the Resistance.

"You were there when they brought me in," Ferrin whispered. "Was it you who went through my desk the other night?"

"Your desk? No. That wasn't me," Soviel said as she examined Ferrin's ankle. "This swelling is going to be painful. We'll have to fix the rest later. How's the cut? Can you get out there and be on your feet for a few hours?"

Ferrin nodded, speechless. Who, then, had been rifling through her things?

"Here, clean coverall," Soviel tossed her a fresh canvas garment.

Ferrin pulled it on, sure she must be in some kind of hallucinatory state.

"Did anyone recognize you?"

"No, my face was covered," Ferrin assured her.

"Good," Soviel nodded once, definitively. "Anywhere else injured?" She jerked her chin around the rest of Ferrin's body.

"I don't think so — I slammed my side into a book case but it feels alright."

"Let me check it."

Soviel laid her palm over Ferrin's ribcage on the side she'd hit. The feel of the magic was a thrumming pulse. Alive. Seismic.

"Just a bit bruised," Soviel informed her. "Now, get out there."

Ferrin emerged into the main corridor, plastering what she hoped was a calm, disinterested smile on her face. Her heart was pounding. Branick eyed her skeptically and pointed to the row of empty cots at the back wall. The prep station. Being ordered around by Branick was a bit like taking orders from an apple-cheeked woodland sprite.

She set to mixing the herbs used for anti-inflammation, and then the ones for disinfectant. She'd been at it for only five minutes when guards burst through the flaps. Thankfully, the one she'd fought was not amongst them.

Ezabila, an older Efelian woman who was closest to the entrance, was the first one they approached. She looked up from her work.

"Ma'am, there's been a break-in at the castle, in the royal chambers," said the guard, though he didn't mention an assassination attempt, or even that it had occurred in the *king's* chambers. "He took off in this direction. Skinny fellow. Dark hair. Wounded. You see anything like that?" he asked, stepping closer to her.

Ezabila shrank back as he invaded her space but met his eye, "No, sir. The only new patients we've had in today were some servants with headaches and a few children with scrapes."

"Hmph," he sniffed. "We're going to take a look around."

Ferrin's heart hammered in her chest. *Breathe*. They thought it was a male assassin, that boded well for her. At least, until the guards who'd seen her up close awoke.

The guards fanned out. There were six of them in all, and the one who'd spoken to Ezabila was making his way up the corridor towards where Ferrin worked. Her hands trembled as she ground up more herbs. There were people everywhere, surely someone had seen her stumble in, wounded, not ten minutes ago.

The guard was making his assessment of each empty cot, each space beneath every bed, the inside of every laundry bin, coming closer and closer. Her heart pounded in her ears and her fingers shook. She noticed a spot of blood on the back of her hand and scrubbed it off. Had her breathing always been this loud?

"You," he stood in front of her, narrowing his eyes.

"Excuse you?" she asked, forcing herself to sound offended, as she stood up straighter to look down her nose at him.

"Your Highness," he nodded as he backed off, realizing who she was. His tone was mistrustful, though, as he eyed the herbs she was mixing. "I was told to keep an eye on you."

"I *beg* your pardon?" she said indignantly.

"Captain Greely, Your Highness," he introduced himself as he offered a small bow.

"Captain Greely," she repeated, "is there something I can assist you with today? Or have you merely come to insult me?"

"Where were you thirty minutes ago?" he asked hesitantly, leaning towards her.

"I was here, captain." She refused to shrink back from his bulk, no matter how badly she wanted to. "You may ask anyone," she declared, though she prayed he wouldn't, and jerked her head to Soviel. "She's my supervisor."

"You, girl," he waved a hand at Soviel, beckoning her over. "I'm told you head the shifts here when Madame is out. How long has Her Highness been here?"

"Her Highness has been here since before noon, sir," Soviel bowed her head, her voice once again soft and non-threatening.

"You'd better not be covering for someone," he warned, his voice a low growl. "We will find out." He narrowed his eyes again, brushing past them without apology.

The two girls exchanged a relieved look as the men finished sweeping through the infirmary. They left without another word, heading off to search the surrounding area.

"Thank you," Ferrin released the breath she'd been holding.

"Don't mention it," Soviel smiled, taking up the station next to Ferrin, folding bandages. "I just hope what you found was worth it."

"Me too," Ferrin agreed. "I'm hoping you can make sense of it. There was something odd — it looked like testing was being done. Of *popava*."

"We'll visit our friends tonight, after dinner," Soviel whispered and returned to her work.

*   *   *

Helene's brow furrowed as she ran her eyes over the messy pages Ferrin had brought back from the palace. Soviel slumped in the chair next to her, arms crossed.

"This is quite odd indeed," Helene tilted her head at the page. "And this log was in an entirely different handwriting than the rest?"

"Yes, it wasn't my father's."

"Any idea who's it might have been?"

"I didn't recognize it. Maybe one of his advisors? Maybe Nerena? The queen, I mean," Ferrin surmised.

"Right," Helene said simply. "I'll have a few of my other agents look into it. In the meantime, let's shift our focus to the business of the Taroch Forest. What do you have to show me?"

"These. It's nothing we hadn't already guessed at, Captain Wilcoe," Soviel said, addressing Helene with her official title.

Helene sat back in her chair, skimming the documents. "The loss of the forest *and* a brand new garrison are not in our best interests, obviously." She scratched her head. "I just can't figure out what the ulterior motive is here. It has to be more than an idiotic scramble for extra protection."

"People will eat anything if it's served the right way," Ferrin reminded her.

"Then it's going to be up to you and your brother to do away with the garnishes," Helene said, looking pointedly at Ferrin.

"You need to find something to appeal to their purses," Soviel chimed in. "They won't ignore monetary benefits."

"Easier said than done. Look at these figures," Helene said, gesturing to the page. "The plan is lucrative; all that lumber, all that brush to burn? And, it'll give work to a lot of people, builders and loggers and all."

"Only for the short-term."

Helene sighed with exasperation, her red hair tumbling over one shoulder as she set down the page. "It is a tragic symptom of old, rich men that they can see only so far into the future. Even less so when there's money to be made."

"Then we show them the danger in it, the effect it could have on the neighboring farmland, the destabilizing of the soil," Ferrin suggested.

"No, no," Helene muttered, drumming her fingers absently on her desk. "Too intangible."

"Well, what about the readily available resources? I know they won't care about the peasants who use the forest to forage for berries, but they'll certainly care for the wild boars and the deer they love to hunt so much. And herbs that are used in the kitchen, not to mention the hospital."

Soviel slammed a hand down on the table, jumping up from her chair. "Dinner!"

"Are we keeping you from something?" Helene drawled.

"No, Captain. The boar? Berries, herbs? Take it a step further. *Show* them the things the forest provides. Make sure a dinner is served and have it be centered around things harvested from the forest," Soviel said, pacing. "Men with full bellies are far more agreeable than hungry ones, no?"

Helene listened thoughtfully and looked pleased with the idea. She said to Soviel, "Have a word with our man in the kitchens. You know what to do."

Soviel bowed her head and took her leave.

"Now let's go over what you're going to say at the council meeting."

"I had actually thought to let Rhiach do most of the talking, since he's favored by my father and more familiar with the rest of the nobility."

"Hm, I see your point," Helene agreed, pressing her palms together and leaning her chin onto her fingers. "And you're sure your brother sees eye to eye with you on these issues?"

"He — yes," Ferrin nodded with certainty. "He's had a bit of trouble the last few weeks, but he's clear-headed now."

"Clear-headed?" Helene sounded concerned.

"He's been ill," Ferrin explained.

"I see."

"He's much better now," she repeated, hoping she sounded reassuring.

"And you think he'll be able to do this? Not back down when questioned?" Helene asked, seeming skeptical.

"I'd say I know him better than you do," Ferrin countered, not bothering to dull the edge in her voice. "Rhi is the diplomat between the two of us. He can do it."

"Very well," Helene said. "His arguments will need to be firm. Now write this down…"

PART THREE

CHAPTER SEVENTEEN

Soviel headed down to the kitchens with a sweet, benign smile plastered on her face. The pretty blue linen frock she wore was lightweight, pastel and soft against her skin. She smiled blandly at every servant and nobleman she passed in the hallway, nodding at them passively. She was just the right amount of pleasant to not stand out. Before she opened the door to the kitchens, she pulled an ugly rough-spun cloak around her shoulders, letting its drab fabric cover the fine make of her gown.

The kitchens were busy with the after-dinner rush of cleaning dishes and throwing scraps to the hounds. Soviel slipped in unnoticed and headed to the counter where Adan, a junior cook and informant of hers, was dicing stalks of celery.

"Hello, there," she said quietly, slipping in next to him.

"Soviel!" he flinched. Perhaps she'd been a little too invisible. "You shouldn't be down here."

"Relax, no one saw me come in," she said, laying a hand coyly on his shoulder. "Do you have any sweet cakes?"

"For you? Always," he grinned, jerking his chin at a large platter of desserts that had only been half finished by those feasting in the Great Hall.

She picked one up and bit into it. "Mmmm," she moaned. "Thanks," she said as sweetly as she could, expressing a little more gratitude than was necessary for table scraps. "What's the celery for?"

"Vegetable broth," Adan answered, using the knife to slide the chopped stalks into the pot next to his cutting board.

She looked at him questioningly.

"Apparently there's been an increase of people sniffing around the kitchen looking for a cure for their hangover," he said drily.

"Ah, probably from all the festivities from the visiting royalty, right?" Soviel asked, popping the last of the sweet cake into her mouth.

Adan shrugged. "Maybe. It's been mostly servants though."

"Hmm, odd." She made a show of licking her fingers clean of frosting before looking up at him with big, doe eyes. "I wanted to ask you something."

"What is it?" his caramel brown eyes lit up.

Oh, you poor soul, she thought to herself.

"It's a favor, actually."

"What kind of favor?"

"I need you to make sure that wild boar from Taroch Forest is served at the council meeting in two days," she said. "If you can manage it, berries and herbs from the forest would be good as well." She flicked her eyelashes at him ever so subtly.

His expression crumpled. "So, this is a business visit, then."

"Nonsense," she patted his forearm. "I came for sweet cakes," she joked.

"Look, I'll see what I can do, but it won't be easy. These things are planned months in advance—"

"I know you can make it happen, Adan," she winked, plucking another dessert from the tray. "I'll see you soon." She smiled suggestively and slipped out the door she'd come in, making her way towards the royal wing where Ferrin and Rhi's chambers were.

So, the jig was finally up with Ferrin. Playing a role with someone she considered a friend had been considerably harder than flirting with kitchen boys and simpering to noblewomen. She'd nearly slipped up once or twice, early on. While she was glad to be through with hiding such a secret, she wasn't sure it was going to make things much easier. If someone had been sneaking into Ferrin's rooms and going through her things, that could only spell trouble for Soviel's own part in the operation.

She'd spent many winters in this palace with no friends, no one to comfort her and no one to stand up for her. From a young age, she'd learned to manage people's perceptions of her. Spending much of her time in a foreign court where her parents were exiled and she was small, lonely and shy, she'd learned quickly not just how to tell people what they wanted to hear, but show them what they wanted to see. By the time she was thirteen she'd mastered the art of being anything to anyone. She let them see what they wanted to see — a shy, docile girl, sweet and kind once you got to know her. Easy to like and easier to trust. She was pretty, but not enough to provoke jealousy. Pretty, but forgettable.

It wasn't long before all the other young ladies were confiding in her, before young lords were letting slip secrets of their families' financial states. Who would think twice about forgettable, unassuming, sweet-faced Soviel? She'd turned what had been a weakness, her general nervousness around strangers, into a weapon.

Sometimes it worked a little too well, and she found herself clawing at the back of the mask she always wore, searching for some shred of what was actually real about her. After all, what was the difference between being everything and being nothing?

Her power helped soothe that ache. Healing, learning, tending her plants; it all kept her grounded. It anchored her to herself when she felt she might be swept away by the carefully crafted perceptions she wielded.

Back in her room, Soviel took to watering her dozens of potted plants. The energy that rolled off of them and into her was bracing, revitalizing. It was life magic, and it filled her soul. She could drink five strong cups of coffee and never get the same dose of vibrant energy as this.

She sat, slumping in her desk chair, a copy of Ferrin's notes from the king's office folded in her hands. There wasn't much to go on, but it read like an observational log, and sure enough, some of the notes matched descriptions of behaviors of the popava poisonings that had come into the hospital. Paranoia, hallucinations, terror.

But to what end? What was the purpose of slipping hallucinogens into someone's pipe or tea? Several logs were detailing behavior and mood, not physical effects like vomiting or trouble breathing. Perhaps most disturbing was the little black X by the subjects who had died. What could it mean in the 382.00 log, that the after-effects had been a success?

She needed a better look at those files, she needed to break into the office herself. Someone was up to something much bigger than simply trying to poison unsuspecting people, like the poor kitchen boy who'd nearly chopped through his fingers.

As for Rhi's near-poisoning, that had simply been a typical response to taking too much of the substance. He hadn't gone into a fit of terror, or seen ghosts.

So where was this new strain coming from?

CHAPTER EIGHTEEN

Rhi awoke that morning with the dying remnants of a thudding headache. The pounding in his head really hadn't stopped since his bout of *popava* poisoning, but in the last few days it had dulled into a low thrum in the front of his skull.

Ferrin and Lukas had both checked in on him and periodically doted upon his health. Yes, *doted*. It had passed strange, moved into the territory of endearing, and finally come full circle to being annoying.

The nausea had mostly stopped within the first week. It had been a miserable thing, he'd emptied his stomach onto the floor next to his bed, splattering it everywhere. He'd been prepared the next time by having a bucket left at his bedside. The fevers and chills had begun to wane as well, and he'd finally managed to sleep through the night.

He swung out of bed with a grunt, scrubbing at his face. The memories of his first time trying *popava* had been circling in his mind like hungry sharks waiting to strike their prey. He'd been sixteen. His mother had vanished into thin air, his sister was set to leave for school. It had all started around a blazing fire at Midspring.

Imogin, the daughter of some wealthy merchant, had been pining after him for weeks, and he'd at last resolved himself to give her a chance. Her eyes were big and blue as oceans when she'd offered him a drop from a tincture. It had tasted like dirt and felt like sugar water on his tongue. The rest of the night had faded into a beautiful blur of the warm fire and the stars above, with no moon out to hide their light. He'd forgotten all about Imogin's longing stares and expectantly fluttering lashes, and danced around the fire, content to cherish the feel of spring grass beneath his bare feet until the sun came up to melt away the dew.

From there he'd tried it a few more times — smoked in a pipe, inhaled as a powder, even rubbed it on his gums once or twice. By the time he was seventeen and had grown out of his awkward years, he'd begun to seek it out to share at parties of his own. That had turned out to be a very popular decision, elevating his revels to legendary status. No one wanted to miss out.

So how had it all gone so wrong? he wondered.

He poured himself a cup of cool, clean water and nursed it slowly, still not sure if he was going to be sick again. His stomach grumbled.

Good, he thought. If he was hungry, that meant he was getting better, right? With minimal stumbling and only a little sweating, he managed to dress himself and get out the door to find some food. He'd need his strength for the council meeting later that day.

Halfway down the hall on his way to the kitchen he ran into Lukas, who seemed to have popped straight out of the wall. Rhi wondered briefly if he was delirious, but Lukas seemed to know every shortcut and secret passage in the castle, so it made sense that he'd use them.

"*Strata*, you scared me!" Rhi braced a hand on the wall.

"Rhi, you look like hell," Lukas put out a hand to steady him.

Rhi snorted. "Do I?"

"What are you doing wandering around in this state?"

"I'm starving."

"Can't you ring a little bell and have your every need taken care of without leaving your bed?" Lukas cocked an eyebrow.

"Yes," Rhi answered flatly. "I wanted to get some air."

"Alright, let's get you some soup."

"Yes. Soup," he agreed with a pained cough.

"Then we'll get you cleaned up. You smell like the inside of a forgotten pair of boots. Pretty sure your sister would have my head if I let you wander around like this."

Rhi stopped himself from grumbling about wanting to rip out Ferrin's hair and let Lukas help him to a rickety wooden bench just outside the servants' entrance to the kitchen.

"Be right back. Stay here," ordered Lukas.

Leaning back against the cool, hard, brick wall felt good. Lukas returned a moment later with a mug of steaming soup that smelled of garlic and chicken. The top layer was slick with olive oil the color of burnished gold.

"Go on," gestured Lukas. "If you keep that down I'll give you something for the headache."

Rhi shot him a suspicious look.

"It's an herbal tea," he clarified.

"I'll take what I can get," groaned Rhi.

Once his mother had been gone for months, and his father had started changing, the pull of the drug had intensified. He'd done his best to remain dutiful, bright, pleasant. He'd been shattered inside, his own dark thoughts just as angry as the feelings Ferrin had made no effort to hide. Although, her anger had been directed solely at their father, and not their mother.

He remembered her lashing out for weeks, as if her fury could protect her from the same suffocating quick-sand that was dragging at him. And then she had left to go to school across the sea, where she, too, had vanished, leaving him well and truly alone.

The walk from the kitchen to Lukas's room was a painful blur, but as he sipped at the broth, he found his headache receding, and his mind clearing. Perhaps the salt was exactly what he needed.

Soon enough, he was sitting in a little wooden chair that wasn't quite balanced, one leg always hovering off the floor, shifting based on how he sat. Lukas pressed a steaming ceramic mug into his hand that smelled of peppermint and bitter berries.

"Thanks," he nodded, raising the mug to his lips.

"It'll get better in a few days," Lukas promised. "I'd reckon you're about out of the worst of it."

"How do *you* know that?" Rhi looked up.

"I know everything."

"Bloody jackass."

"Don't you have some kind of princely duties to attend to today?"

"Just an all-important meeting where I'm to publicly oppose my father," Rhi coughed once more.

"Oh. Shit." Lukas leaned back against the cabinet. "Are you going to make it there?"

"It's not until dinner, thank the gods," Rhi grimaced. "Lately, I've been feeling better by evening."

"Are both of you going?" Lukas asked hesitantly.

"Yes, my sister will be there," Rhi nearly rolled his eyes at Lukas's veiled attempt to ask about Ferrin.

"Be careful, both of you. Tensions have been growing over the last few weeks, people are getting more and more agitated out there." Lukas rubbed his hands together.

"I know, that's why we have to do it." Rhi brought the tea to his lips and took another gulp, the liquid still so hot he could feel it in his chest.

Lukas took out that little pocket watch that Rhi was sure was a fake, meant to conceal small goods, and checked the time, which Rhi also knew it never seemed to tell.

"Why do you *really* keep that thing?" Rhi asked, not expecting a straight answer.

Lukas closed the watch and weighed it in his hand, gazing at it almost lovingly. He took a deep breath. "I'm not sure. I just like having it. Every time I've tried to gamble it away or have it fixed, it winds up returned to me in the same condition. I gave up trying to hock it months ago. Besides, I like the way it looks." He flashed the bright brass back at Rhi.

Rhi arched an eyebrow. "Very strange."

CHAPTER NINETEEN

Ferrin's hands shook as she sat down next to Rhi in the High Council room. They'd never been allowed in here as children, even when it wasn't in session.

There was a great, oblong table of glossy, varnished wood, with a gilt inlay mimicking the concentric circles of the inside of a huge tree. The edges were left artfully raw, the thick bark glazed over with a glossy resin. It was surrounded by two dozen chairs. At the edge of the room were additional chairs for observers. Seats for Rhi and Ferrin had been added as a courtesy, and the rest were filled by members of the High Council: lords, wealthy merchants, and big land-owners in the surrounding area.

The room was floor-to-ceiling luxury. The walls were pale green panels separated by golden framework and hanging velvet dividers that could be used for smaller meetings. The ceiling was coffered and gilded; the floor, marble and covered in a huge, beautifully woven rug that must have taken dozens of hands many weeks to complete.

Rhi drummed his fingers on the table next to her. He had a stony look on his face, and he was pale, either from the illness that had been plaguing him, or from plain old nerves.

They'd spent the afternoon hours perfecting their case, scratching out notes and points about what the Taroch Forest provided. It had been a long day, after her stable duties, and Ferrin had made several treks back and forth between the library and Rhi's rooms with stacks of books on botany, zoology, *Culi-*

nary Craft of the Barrian Isle, and one particularly old, dusty and withering copy of *A History of The Castle at Everness*. Both Soviel and Nimhe had stopped in periodically, offering fresh perspectives, snacks, and tea.

They were hoping the inclusion of the Festival of the Hunt that took place every fall as part of both Cael *and* Lundi tradition would at the very least make the council stop and think.

The rest of the councilmen were trickling in and taking their seats, laughing and chatting like they were about to attend a Field Sticks match. Would any of them take the side of sourcing the lumber elsewhere? Would any of them dare disagree with the king?

Once they were all seated, Ferrin looked around. She knew some of the council members. They were all older, and most of them were Lundi-born nobility. At last, Ferrin's father entered the room, flanked by a contingent of his guards, and they all stood and bowed. He sat, and everyone else followed suit.

The members of the council murmured amongst themselves and to their assistants, and servants swept in with platters of food and began serving it up: roasted boar, pheasants rubbed in herbs, berry-jellies and wine.

"Very well, gentlemen, shall we?" said the king.

The first man stood, addressed the king formally, and rattled off the proposed benefits that the space cleared from the forest would add. More room for businesses to grow at the edge of town, the underbrush and scrub that could be stored and burned periodically.

Ferrin's eyes almost bulged out of their sockets. Did they really think that made it worth it? Half the town's main source of food came from that forest. How could they sit there and act like it would benefit the town? She moved to say something to Rhi, but he shook his head, the action almost imperceptible.

She settled back into her chair, knowing Rhi was probably right to wait.

The next man stood and presented the plans for the new garrison, and explained that the forest was the most readily available option for lumber, as well as the least expensive.

The garrison to the south, the wall; the plan made no sense. It wasn't as if Bourjony would go through the trouble of invading from the south, where there was no convenient harbor, and then march up only to be stopped by a wall. The harbor sat just east of Everness.

A man to Ferrin's left was busy digging into the ham on his plate and mumbling something about how delicious it was.

Her blood boiled at the willful ignorance in the room. The avarice. Maybe pirates were greedy thieves too, but it was never like this. The cost was almost always out of the coffer of a man who could afford to lose.

When the last council member had presented his section of the plan, Rhi pushed back his chair and stood up, notes in hand. Ferrin, as planned, remained seated. Both of them knew the council would not respond well to her, given her history and reputation for trouble.

"Father, Councilmen," Rhiach began, his easy charm infusing his words as he smiled pleasantly, "Thank you for allowing me to join you today."

A few of them nodded and mumbled greetings, but the king was glaring at Rhi in a fashion that only Ferrin was accustomed to.

"It is my belief that we should *not* move forward with the plans to remove the southernmost section of Taroch Forest at this time." He turned over the first page.

Their father's face began to broil.

Rhi swallowed and continued, "Taroch Forest is home to many important plants used for medicine, and for food." He listed some specific herbs and berries. "Without ready access to the plants they come from, we would have to import them. Likely, at a far greater cost."

Some of the councilmen began chattering quietly amongst themselves.

Good, Ferrin thought, use your heads. Don't let the crown cow you into a bad decision.

Rhi turned the page. "Not only does the forest offer a natural defense to anyone looking to invade the town and castle from the west, but it keeps the farmland to the southwest stable with its roots."

A man Ferrin recognized as one of her father's advisors stood. "All due respect, *Your Highness*," he said, not trying all that hard to keep the condescension from his tone, "but what do princes know of farming?"

Rhi glanced at the man quickly, but ignored him and continued. "The trees also offer shelter and food to the people living beyond the village." He extended an arm, gesturing to the feast, "And, of course, every morsel of food you've all just enjoyed for dinner came from directly from Taroch Forest."

A murmur broke out across the room and a tiny, victorious smile tugged at the corner of Rhi's mouth.

Ferrin would have missed the small movement had she not been turned her attention from Rhi to her father at that very second. The king jerked his chin, the motion almost imperceptible. Two guards moved from where they stood behind him, fixing their eyes upon Ferrin and Rhi.

"Sit down, son," the king said in a booming voice.

Rhi turned to face their father, his face draining of color.

"I let you come here so you could observe the way things are done, not so you and your rebellious sister could play contrarian and deter my plans."

"Father—" Rhi began, trying to deescalate the building tension in the room.

"That forest will burn, and we will move forward with our plans. The garrison will go up, as will the wall. War is coming to our shores, and I will not allow your half-cocked notions of the world to interfere," snarled the king.

"He is *right*." Ferrin stood, fists clenched at her sides. "Burning that forest will harm *all* of us, regardless of whether you are rich or poor, a new garrison and a wall won't protect—"

"Please escort my children out," ordered the king, waving a hand at the guards. "They know not what they speak of."

Two guards marched Ferrin out into the hallway as she struggled. Two more guards escorted Rhi out as well, which surprised her.

She fought against their grip as they dragged her to her room, clawing and elbowing and grunting, probably making things worse, but she didn't care. One of the guards lost patience and slapped her. She hissed, getting one arm free, and managed to land a punch somewhere on his chest before she was shoved through the door. She stumbled and lost her breath as she took an elbow to the gut, hitting her face on a chair as she fell to the floor.

She hadn't taken a beating in years, but this took her back all the same.

She was sixteen, just barely. The smell of olives and figs filled the room — no, the cellar, she realized — as the woman circled her. An enforcer for one of the biggest bosses in the Kalassan olive trade. She had fallen out of a tree in one of the groves directly into the path of some guards. With a stolen seal and forged papers in her pocket, no less.

Zare had some boys watching her back, so why hadn't they intervened? They'd have outnumbered the pair of guards in the grove. Why had they let her be taken?

"How did you get past the guards?" the woman asked. It wasn't common for someone of her size, of her build to be an enforcer, a bruiser. It wasn't common for someone who looked like her, soft angles, a small frame and a warm face, to be so feared. None of that was common, but the rumors surrounding Calomba Herotis were.

Notorious for her ruthless interrogations and vile messages, usually sent using infliction of pain or loss of limb on the part of the 'messenger', Calomba was one of the most feared enforcers this side of Khalim.

Dressed in a simple, unadorned cotton shirt with the sleeves cut to fend off the heat, and wide-legged brown pants, she didn't look like much. And yet, there was no mistaking her wicked intent.

Ferrin was breathing hard, praying to every god she could think of that Zare would be smart enough to figure out where they'd taken her, where to find her. Any minute, he'd come busting in with Tabka and Pierre, guns blazing. Right?

Calomba leaned in close to where she sat, tied to the chair in the center of the cellar.

"We're going to have a rather difficult chat, aren't we?" said Calomba in a deceptively gentle voice.

"Piss off," Ferrin spat back. Her tone was bold, but the veneer was thin. A varnish of defiance to keep her true terror from spilling out and drowning her.

"Rather impolite way to start off an acquaintance, don't you think?" Calomba said as she tied back her honey-gold hair.

"They'll come for me," Ferrin said, sounding more confident than she felt as she glared at Calomba. The woman couldn't have been much older than forty.

"Oh, darling. Don't be silly." Her voice was soft as butter, sweet as cream. It was unnerving. "You're so very far from where we found you, and so very well hidden." Her smile widened, her teeth were white and gleaming and her tone was venomous.

"Eat dirt," Ferrin said through her own clenched teeth.

"Hm," Calomba snorted, the sound delicate as she examined Ferrin's face.

Ferrin did her best to stare back, fighting the urge to back down.

Then the first blow came. It was a half-pulled jab to the throat, just hard enough to make her choke on her own breath and gasp for air. Immediately after, she felt the hit to her gut, full force. She lurched forward, doubling over her binds.

"Now," Calomba bent down to eye level, her voice soft as ever. "When you catch your breath, you can tell me who it is you're working for," she said quietly as she tucked a piece of Ferrin's then-short hair out of her face and behind her ear, the gesture almost motherly. "And how you got past the guards."

Still wheezing from the blow, her mouth agape as she tried to suck down air, Ferrin lifted her eyes to Herotis's again. "I said…" she gasped. "Fuck… off." The words came out in more a pathetic rasp than actual speech.

Herotis rose, letting out an exasperated sigh. "I really don't have time for these antics, child."

Ferrin was too busy fighting for breath to answer. She glared back at Calomba as she rose.

This wasn't the plan, this wasn't supposed to happen, *she thought,* Where is Zare?

"If you think someone's going to find you, you're sorely mistaken."

"He will." Her faith in Zare was far too strong for her own good. "He always does."

"Very well then, I suppose while we wait for this mystery hero, you and I will get better acquainted." She slid her fingers into an apparatus of bronze rings, fit with blunt spikes across the back of her hand.

Knowing what was coming, Ferrin had braced herself, tried to send her mind far, far away. It took Zare hours to find her.

It turned out pain was all the worse when you didn't know when it was going to end.

After they were both locked in their respective rooms, Ferrin wondered if the guards had hit Rhi at all, if he'd gone quietly or if he'd fought them. Though she'd never been in her father's favor, she was surprised at how openly he'd allowed the guards to manhandle her, and especially Rhi. He was a man who valued reputation. Perhaps certain rumors long since put to rest about her mother's faithfulness had arisen once more. Perhaps Nerena was with child, and Henrik was hoping for the crown to pass to *her* offspring.

She lay in bed sore, defeated. The forest would burn, the wall would go up, and the garrison too. There was no doubt of that now. The king's word was final, and for all their cleverness and maneuvering, it hadn't changed a damn thing. All they had done was anger him. It wouldn't matter if they could convince the council. Those men would never risk falling from his favor when he controlled their wealth.

The place she'd picked wildflowers with her mother, the place where children played hide and seek, the place where the poor gathered food from when they had nowhere else to turn, the place all the little creatures lived… No matter how badly she wanted to cling to it, to those memories, it would all be gone.

Her lip had stopped bleeding by the time the old clock struck eleven. The castle had gone quiet an hour ago. Sore and numb at the same time, Ferrin paced in her room, unable to sleep, unable to stay still.

Sometime in the hours after dinner, Nell had come in to draw her a bath and help her out of her clothes. Soviel and Nimhe had been elsewhere, apparently. In undressing, she'd found her ribs purple and bruised. One eye was black, and her split lip stung when she submerged in the bath. She'd dressed in her night shift and thrown her dressing gown over it. Nell had left her a plate of food, which she hadn't touched. She hadn't eaten much at dinner, and she had no appetite now.

It didn't sound like anyone had locked her room after Nell hurried out, and when she pushed the door open later that night, she didn't see any guards posted. The hallway was utterly empty.

She ducked back inside and grabbed an ancient rust-and-green tartan blanket that had been her mother's, and shrugged it around her shoulders. She ducked out the door, letting it shut gently behind her as she stepped gingerly into the hallway. Her chest was heavy as she wandered mindlessly, numb from the events of the evening. She needed to go somewhere, to *do* something, If she didn't, the air in that room would crush the life out of her.

She couldn't bring herself to go and see Rhi, yet. She'd dragged him into a horrible mess when he was still recovering from his brush with death. Guilt gnawed at her, she needed to be alone, clear her head.

She wandered for a while until she found herself in the old fort, deeper within the castle. It was different there, though the floors were marbled and the walls were adorned in plaster and gilt and porcelain, the bones of the ancient stone fortress showed through. The air felt colder, almost as if it was full of memories, frozen in time.

She ran her hand along the wall panels, letting her fingers bump over the texture absentmindedly, realizing she was by one of the offshoots of the servants' tunnels she'd been exploring in her spare time. It wasn't the same door she'd used to break into her father's office, but it was probably connected.

She had no end-goal in mind when she figured out which panel was the one that opened. She had no destination when she pulled one of the sconce-lanterns off the outside wall and slipped inside.

She wandered through the passage. It was different from the other one, older. Its floors were stone instead of wood, and its walls were damp with condensation. A small noise echoed behind her, and she whipped around to find that it was only a rat scurrying across the floor.

She turned a corner, the walls growing coarser, narrower, as the stones grew wider and rougher. Thickly cut and more like rubble than cobblestone, its purpose clearly to defend against things far worse than swords and arrows. This stone was perhaps a thousand years old. It was a dead end.

Only, it *wasn't* a dead end.

Beneath the age-old grime was a wide, rectangular door. Perhaps a secret exit from the castle's days as an ancient fort. The handle was centered, the nob cold and metallic to the touch.

Rhi had spoken of hidden veins and passages within the castle, so deep they'd been forgotten and lost for generations. Was that what this was? He'd told her how they led down to caves, deep inside the cliffs, full of pits of monsters that would love to gobble up annoying little girls who stole their brother's toy horses.

That had been fraternal teasing, of course. But how much of it was true?

She shivered as a draft blew through the cavern. This hallway looked like it hadn't been used in years. Maybe decades. The slippery, cold touch of fear slid down the back of her neck. If she lost her way, if something happened down here, no one would ever find her bones.

Shaking the eery thought from her head, she reached out and tried the handle. It was locked, of course. The big old-fashioned keyhole should have told her that. She sighed, resigned to not knowing the mystery of what was behind the door, since she certainly didn't have a key.

Take my key, daughter of Arabella. The perplexing words of the book floated through her memory. Was this the place where this 'key' was to be used? She hadn't found any such a key, nor a reference to one, anywhere in the pages of that blasted book.

A draft blew through the cavern from gods-knew-where again, chilling her to the bone. She needed to get the hell out of there before she went mad, before she lost her way.

She turned from the door and strode back towards her own hallway, resolving to swallow her shame and check on Rhi before going to sleep.

CHAPTER TWENTY

Ferrin awoke the next morning after an abysmal amount of
dreamless sleep. But although she felt awful, there was a blissful moment just before she was fully conscious, when she had
yet to recall the events of the day before. She blinked her eyes
open and it all came tumbling back to her. She groaned out
loud.

The sky was starting to lighten, and she was going to have
to haul her ass to the stables to make it on time.

Rolling out of bed, she stalked over to the washbasin. The
cool water stung the cut on her lip and a pained hiss escaped her
mouth. The swollen bruise around her eye hurt too much to bear
touching, so all she could do was splash some water on it and
let it dry on its own.

There was a knock on the door, and Nell entered bearing a
tray with a light breakfast, and her folded, cleaned clothes. She
thanked Nell and began to dress, munching on a piece of toast
as she did. The breeches snagged against her goosebumps as she
tugged them on, and her ribs throbbed when she brushed past
the big, ugly bruise forming there. She threw on her boots and
jacket and headed out.

"Morning," she mumbled to Alick when she stalked past the
barn office's open door.

"Whoa, whoa, whoa! Get back here," he called after her.
She heard him get up from his seat and come to the doorway.

She stopped and turned around slowly.

"What in harrow-hall happened to you?"

"I don't want to talk about it," she leaned her shoulder on the doorframe, eyes down.

"What happened?" he asked again.

"I really don't want to talk about it," she repeated, swallowing. Gods, her throat was dry.

"Well, that's fine but I'm not letting you work like this," he shook his head. "Did they hit you anywhere else? Other than your face?"

"Yeah," she nodded glumly. "I've got some bruises. Nothing broken, though."

"Who hit you? Was it the suitor? Is he still here?"

"No, no, it was guards. And… a chair."

"Guards? As in palace guards?"

"My father's finest," she said, wincing when her lip cracked. "Really, the chair is responsible for the worst of it."

"Why on earth?"

"Rhi and I publicly opposed him in a business matter."

"And for that he had you beaten?"

"It isn't as bad as it looks, really," she protested. If he sent her home, she didn't know what she would do with herself. Go mad in her room, most likely. "I got in a few hits."

"It looks bad, kid," he observed. "You're not working. You can stay, but you're not working."

"Fine," she conceded.

"Keep me company while I clean out a few stalls and we can call it a day's work, alright?"

She gave a tepid nod and followed him down the hallway. "I did actually want to ask you something," she said hesitantly as she hopped up on the top of a grain barrel outside Dandy's stall, careful to stay out of the path of the muck.

"Ask," Alick said as he carted over a wheelbarrow.

"How much do you know about the history of old Cael magic?" She fidgeted, picking the line of dirt from under her nails.

"About as much as anyone can know nowadays," he shrugged. "Which isn't much."

"Oh," she said, disappointed.

"But there's some information that was tucked into old stories, if you know where to look."

She sat up straighter. Dandy munched some hay in his feedbag against the wall, quietly observing them with his big, brown eyes.

"Gwelie, one of the oldest Cael queens — from when the Caels were made up of smaller bands of people across the island — was said to have been gifted by Strata herself, blessed with flight."

"I know the story."

"You know the myth, the nursery rhyme. Three magic eggs, a prince and all the rest." Alick sniffed and paused. "But according to much older writings, it was different. Strata rode her chariot through the sky, her storm-steeds thundering over the clouds on the wind, lightning whip cracking through the storm. She was passing over our island, as usual, when she heard the desperate prayers of a young queen.

"It was said that Gwelie, the young queen, was the most beautiful in all the land. Of course, every story of old seems to center around the most beautiful maiden or the most hideous witch, no one was ever just average," he rolled his eyes. "Anyway, Gwelie was being held captive by a Northern Vampire prince who wanted to Change her and take her to be his wife."

"Northern Vampires, on Lindbarrow?"

"Caelbarrow, then. And yes, this legend predates the wrath of the sun." He began shoveling the side furthest from Dandy. "As I was saying. She was being held captive, up in the cliffs, and Strata heard her desperate prayers."

Ferrin listened, pulling one foot up, and propping her chin on her knee.

"So, it's said that Strata took a strand of silver hair from her storm-steed's mane. Next, she gathered a few raindrops that had just fallen through the sunrise-red morning sky, and they turned to rubies in her palm. Finally, she cracked her whip, calling lightning down, and turned it into diamonds. She pressed these into the silver hair, crafting it all into a ring."

Ferrin straightened, now in rapt attention.

"She whispered a gust of each of the four winds into Gwelie's ear, and slipped the ring onto Gwelie's finger, telling her to keep the wildness of the storm in her heart always. Then Gwelie flew away, escaping the clutches of the Vampire prince."

Ferrin swallowed. "And, Gwelie, she would have passed this magic down to her children?" she asked as casually as she could.

"While magic was still prevalent, I would think so. Who knows what's become of it now, the ring or the wind's whisper," he raised his eyebrows dramatically. "It was most likely lost some time during the warring years. Maybe even melted down."

"You don't think it was ever passed down to say… my mother?" she suggested.

"That," Alick let out a heavy sigh, "is not a question I can answer for you, I'm afraid."

"Well, you were childhood friends, right? Did she ever talk about that sort of thing? Those stories, I mean." Ferrin shifted on the grain barrel, crossing and uncrossing her arms.

"Of course she did," said Alick, approaching the stall door, pitchfork in hand. "She loved sneaking up to the rooftops in Avaree, looking out at the horizon. She told me the wind whispered secrets to her when she was alone," he shared, looking down at his feet.

"She used to tell me the story about Gwelie. She told it differently every time, you know," Ferrin offered.

"Stories are always changing," he shrugged as he pushed the wheelbarrow towards the barn door. He squinted up at the sky through the door, the morning light bright against his skin. "Going to be a beautiful, clear day. Was there something you needed to go do?" he asked peculiarly. "Maybe something you wanted to do before the castle is crawling with people?"

Ferrin's head snapped up, a moment of confusion before she understood.

"Yes. Yes, there is. I'll — uh — I'll be back," she said, nearly knocking over the grain barrel and tripping on her own feet as she scrambled down the hall, running out of the barn and hurtling towards the castle with renewed fervor.

*   *   *

She stepped out onto the roof. It was the highest tower in the castle that she had access to, and the wind was so strong up there, it ripped her hair out of its braid. Her stomach dropped. Hundreds of feet below, she could see the courtyard. By now, people were up and about, readying for their days and heading to work.

She'd spent a half hour down there trying to convince the wind to obey her, to lift her from the ground. She'd tried a running start, leaping from the ground. Maybe this was one more thing she was going to fail at.

She'd returned to her room and flipped back to one of the stories in Legends & Truths that had mentioned the gift of flight. Strata requires trust. Most of Legends & Truths had turned out to be spectacularly useless, so her odds of ending up splattered on the stone patio of the courtyard were higher than the very tower she stood on.

So there she was: balancing on the edge of the roof, many stories off the ground, hoping that that was more truth than legend. If she died, she planned on harassing H.G. Serengath for eternity in the afterlife.

With a deep breath, she squeezed her hands into fists, palms sweaty against the metal of the ring on her finger. She took a step…

and fell.

The breath rushed out of her, and for a second she panicked. She'd taken this stupid, stupid leap of faith, and now Strata surely sped by with her storm-horses, cackling at the idiocy of Gwelie's descendant.

But then she felt it — like the main sheet on a small craft going taut in her hand when a gust catches the sail. The lift of the wind, obeying her and carrying her up, up, up. Every nerve in her body was aware of its own gravity, something shifting within her to respond to the wind.

She pushed her arms back as the pressure of the air around her flattened her clothes to her body, drove the tears from her eyes and down the sides of her face, and she soared.

This was it. The wind screaming around her, the earth falling away, the clouds within arm's reach. This was what she'd sought, what that restlessness inside her had been missing. That untamable restlessness that seemed it would hound her into perpetuity. It was what she'd been searching for galloping through the moors on the fastest horse she could find, what she'd been looking for cutting across the waves on The Gravedigger, cleaving sea from sky. It was a gift and a blessing. It was freedom.

She soared west, away from the busying paths between the castle and village. She turned a somersault over the little patch of woods where Lukas's cabin stood, then caught the smell of smoke and realized she'd ventured too close to Taroch's southern edge. Her heart caught in her throat from the smoke and the jarring sight of it — how much forest had already been cut, how the brush had already been burned from its acres.

She looped around, heading back to the castle. She could probably pop right in her own bedroom window. Her mother had to have known of this power. With all her stories of Gwelie and her adventures, she had to have known. So why would she leave it behind?

CHAPTER TWENTY-ONE

Something odd was going on with the king.

Of that much, Soviel was sure. As a royal woman's lady-in-waiting, she had access to the fancier salons within the castle, where men and women might gather to discuss, well, anything, really. It typically amounted to the elite class simply sharing cigars and aged whiskey while the king held a much less formal version of court.

Soviel was perched in a corner seat, nursing a glass of white wine and cooling herself with a delicate lace fan. She'd styled her hair into the latest fashion, curled and piled into a bouffant of volume that her thin, fine-stranded hair had no business achieving on its own (Nimhe had helped her wrangle a wad of cushion-stuffing beneath the poof, then slathered it with pomade and powder). She wore her finest day dress of pale blue silk, trimmed in cream lace. Around her neck, she'd donned a strand of pearls Ferrin had lent her to complete the outfit.

Something odd was definitely going on with the king. Since Ferrin had brought back those notes from his office regarding the popava test trials, Soviel had begun casually trailing him almost everywhere. Between the strange occurrences linked to the drug that she'd encountered in the hospital, and now this… Someone had bigger plans for popava, and they were using the general populace as their test-subject.

Captain Wilcoe had agreed that Soviel's presence in the salon would draw significantly less attention than Ferrin's, so here she was; playing eligible, coy, marriage material. People might think her an upstart, trying to use her looks and flirtation to catch herself a husband of higher station than she. It was good to give them something to find buried shallow, it kept prying eyes from digging deeper and asking why she was really there.

The queen was nowhere to be seen. The king was surrounded by courtiers and was chatting loosely about the plans for the new garrison. She was just within earshot to hear it all, but the information was nothing new. Today, Soviel was watching for his moods.

The far door opened and a noblewoman strode in with Nimhe on her heels. Soviel squinted. She had told Nimhe she was meeting up with a potential suitor, but hadn't mentioned she would be coming to the salon.

Nimhe's eyes widened in surprise and she lifted a hand in greeting. Soviel half-heartedly returned the gesture, before subtly shifted her gaze back to the king, hoping the girl wouldn't draw attention to her.

Ferrin had offhandedly mentioned odd shifts in her father's mood, the way he could become furious at nothing, his blood practically pounding to get out of his skin, provoked by little, or at other times, remain perfectly calm when faced with something far worse.

Someone was clearly using a popava strain on him that was known to imbue docility. In the notes Soviel managed to glimpse, it mentioned that an unfortunate side effect was extreme irritability when the tranquility wore off. Maybe he was taking it knowingly, but maybe someone was dosing him for their own gains.

But why? Who stood to gain from altering the king's moods? Especially with a method that seemed so unreliable.

Soviel could feel Nimhe's gaze on her from across the room and prayed she wouldn't come over. She liked the girl well enough, but she could be somewhat clueless. Soviel felt sorry for her. Nimhe's position at the castle was fragile, and one slip-up could land her in a far lower position than lady-in-waiting.

A young man sat down across from Soviel at her table, pulling her out of her thoughts.

"Is this seat taken?" he asked with a slight smile.

"Oh, no. Go right ahead," she fanned herself delicately, smiling with her eyes. The gentleman sat, adjusting his dark blue coat.

"Dane Grant, at your service." He dipped his head in a slight bow.

She returned the gesture, "Soviel Larksen."

"A pleasure to meet you, Madam."

They sat quietly, taking in the goings-on of the salon. With his pale fingers wrapped around a crystal whisky tumbler, he reached out his glass to clink hers.

"Have you been in the castle long?" Dane asked.

"For a few years," she answered. "Before that, I was back and forth between here and Njorske."

"Ah, the tundra," he nodded knowingly. Only the northern-most part of her homeland was permafrost, but he seemed un-aware of his blunder.

"I will say the weather is far more temperate here," she said blandly. She was about to resign herself to the game of keeping him interested just enough so that he wouldn't ruin her cover, when a commotion stirred up. Plates and glasses shattered on the floor and a young woman burst out of her chair. It was Lady Denison.

"No, No!" She scrambled away from the table. "Get away from me!" She started to furiously brush off her arms and her chest, as if she was covered in something ghastly.

She stumbled back and tripped, her dainty slipper catching on one of the discarded napkins, and fell to the floor. Her hand connected with one of the shards of glass, and blood flowed.

But she didn't seem to notice as she clambered backwards, away from nothing.

Soviel was up in a flash, rushing towards the Lady.

At this point, several other patrons had risen and were hovering a safe distance away from the agitated girl. Soviel dropped to her knees next to Denison and glanced up just in time to watch Nimhe slip out the servant's door.

"Lady Denison, can you hear me?" Soviel knelt beside her where she'd drawn up against the wall, still panicked.

Her breaths came fast and shallow, her chest hitching with terror as she beheld some invisible threat. Her eyes were wide and her lips moved in some silent rhythm, repeating the same inaudible word over and over.

"Lady Denison," Soviel repeated softly. "Can you hear me?"

"Don't let him take me, please," she wheezed, tears beginning to roll down her face.

"Who?" Soviel asked as she took hold of Denison's injured hand, gently turning it over. There was an ugly gash across the meaty pad below her fingers, extending up onto her wrist. She was bleeding badly, and the cut was deep enough to have severed her tendons. "Get me some whiskey, please," Soviel said to no one in particular.

The queen, whom she was sure hadn't been there before, handed her a glass.

Soviel had to do a double take. "Thank you, Your Majesty."

She tore the handkerchief from her pocket and doused it with the whiskey, pressing it to Denison's wound. The young woman should have howled in pain or at least winced, but whatever trance she'd fallen into was holding her attention still.

Soviel didn't have her stash of healing herbs on her, but it wouldn't take much on her part to simply close the wound, fresh as it was. Denison's fingers twitched pitifully, blood dripping onto the marble floor. She'd lose her dexterity if it wasn't fixed soon.

Drawing a breath and squeezing her eyes shut, Soviel called on the green, light energy that lived somewhere deep inside her. Her pulse quickened. She felt the flesh, the hundreds of tiny vessels, each alive and beating, knit back together. The blood stopped flowing. Soviel was panting now. Denison was still shaking, eyes fixed on something that wasn't there.

"Lady Denison," Soviel said again, gasping. "Look at me." Lady Denison merely slumped over and curled into a fetal position. Soviel bent and felt the pulse at her wrist— her heart was a galloping horse.

"Someone—" Soviel stood, bracing herself with a hand on the wall. "Someone needs to go fetch Madame Leone from the infirmary. This woman needs help."

She shouldn't have healed the wound without a power source. Gods, she was exhausted. Not to mention the attention she might have drawn to herself. Idiot, she chided herself internally.

She wrapped the bloody kerchief around Denison's hand, hoping no one would notice that she'd healed the wound out of thin air. Lady Denison remained that way, shuddering, eyes now squeezed shut against whatever evils she was seeing, hugging her knees. Soviel adjusted her skirts to make sure the lady was fully covered.

"Give her some space," Soviel ordered, waving a hand at the gathered crowd of curious onlookers. Falling back against the wall, she caught her breath. A sheen of sweat had broken across her brow and her chest.

"She's sick too!" she heard someone shout.

"It's catching!" another voice warned. "We must go!"

Soviel squeezed her eyes shut. Leone would be there soon, and she could…

Soviel awoke to stern hands gripping her shoulders. "Soviel!" Madame's voice was harsh in her face. "Good, you're awake."

"Madame," Soviel breathed. "Lady Denison, is she —?"

Leone glanced around for eavesdroppers. "What were you thinking healing that cut here? It wouldn't have killed her to leave it open a few more minutes until I arrived with supplies, you foolish girl!"

Soviel grimaced, sitting up. "I'm sorry, I know. But, in her state—"

"She was dosed, the same as the others, I'm afraid."

"Will she survive?" Soviel asked, her chest feeling tight.

"The others were killed by circumstances secondary to the dosing, she should be fine if she doesn't let the hallucinations drive her to jump from a cliff or freeze to death in a river." Leone's voice was gruff as she handed Soviel a glass of water. "This is nasty business, this altered strain. Be wary. Do not drink or eat anything someone hands to you."

"I will not."

"Good, I must go and see to the lady. Get some rest, for Lalana's sake," she instructed, clucking her tongue as she rose.

Soviel sighed, straining to rise from the floor. The salon was now empty, save for a few servants attending to the mess. She swallowed as she looked around, the creeping sense that someone was watching her had become impossible to shake.

One thing stood out in her mind from just before she had passed out: Nimhe slipping out the side door of the salon, just as Lady Denison had fallen ill.

CHAPTER TWENTY-TWO

When Ferrin arrived at dinner, she made a point to take account of anyone behaving strangely, anyone who might be falling victim to the mysterious *popava* experiments.

Soviel had done her best to fade some of the bruising on her face before dinner. She'd been thoroughly exhausted and appeared almost sickly, though, so Ferrin had stopped her after she tried to close the cut on her lip and had nearly passed out. She'd ended up directing Soviel to lay down while Nimhe helped her dress in the unnecessarily complicated gown. This one was a teal-and-grey striped silk confection with a fashionable puff in the back.

"Do you want to wear a sapphire ring instead? The rubies don't complement that gown at *all*," Nimhe said, reaching for Ferrin's jewelry box.

"No, I'll keep this one," Ferrin shook her head.

Nimhe shrugged apprehensively.

Now, sitting next to Rhi in the Great Hall, Ferrin had no appetite. Neither did her brother, judging from the way he poked at his plate with his fork. They sat in a glum silence, the rumble of the dining hall dulled around them by their shared gloom.

Rhi appeared to be clear of bruising, but he seemed tense, stiff. She'd never imagined their father would have Rhiach, his —everyone's—Golden Prince, physically reprimanded.

Nerena was nowhere to be seen at dinner, and all was relatively quiet, with the suitorial processions having been abruptly sent home over a week ago. Ferrin didn't know how Rhi and her father had managed to smooth things over with the Efelians, but between Rhi's easy charm and her father's will to preserve his reputation, the Efelian king and prince had left on good enough terms. It felt like she was letting Rhi fight her battles for her, but the fact was that she'd have only made it worse if she tried to ease tensions with Havian.

And now they'd both paid dearly for their father's greed and their own act of defiance. As Ferrin stared down at her mess of a plate, her eyes slid to the lower tables. She'd seen a few pitying glances for the fading bruise around her eye. Most of the talk had wondered not only *who* had lain hands on the princess, but *what* she'd done to deserve such a beating.

She was tired. Her soul was itchy, and the urge to run again nipped and nagged at her edges like she was fraying fabric. She wanted to run again, and *gods* it would be easy this time. She could wait until nightfall and pack a light bag, tie it around her back. Then she could simply slip out her own bedroom window and never be seen again. She could go anywhere.

But the problem did not lie in her ability to leave. All the freedom in the world, and still she had no destination.

She eyed Rhi. She wouldn't leave him here again, no matter how suffocating things became. Before, she'd been selfish, foolish. She hadn't given a single thought to the people around her when she had taken off. Rhi, Soviel, Alick, Lukas… they were her ties here.

Still, she could daydream. There was a beautiful freedom in the act of disappearing, even just into her own thoughts, even just for a few moments.

She had finally found her appetite and was about to take a bite of her potatoes when it happened.

"My gods, they'll let anyone be a valet these days. I thought His Majesty had the good sense to keep those Caelish rats in the scullery where they can't be seen," scoffed a woman a few steps away at a neighboring table as the young red-headed server walked by. He couldn't have been older than twelve. The woman sloshed back more of her wine.

"Well, it's no surprise. At least the royal children don't have that dreadful hair," sneered the noblewoman's companion who sat beside her.

Ferrin tensed.

"I can't believe Lindbarrow is going to fall into the hands of some half-breed children when His Majesty passes, *long live the king*," said the first woman as she made a praying gesture, "It'll be a bloody miracle if we aren't overrun by savage folk."

These opinions weren't uncommon, but to be blasting them about in the open? In the middle of the Great Hall, in all sorts of company? The woman was drunk, she had to be. Ferrin set down her fork, listening intently to the rest of the conversation.

The red-haired servant boy returned with a platter of roasted vegetables. Ferrin watched him as he tried to ignore what the ladies were saying.

"And all the exiled rebel-*scum* will come back like an infestation," the first woman added. The boy's hand trembled.

Ferrin scooted her chair back and rose.

"Gods help us, maybe the ships will all sink on the way back from Njorske—" the woman continued. She stopped abruptly as three stalks of asparagus rolled onto her dress.

"I'm sorry, I beg your pardon!" the boy stammered, scrambling for a napkin.

"You clumsy little wretch! You did that on purpose!" In an instant, the woman had grabbed the boy's arm and twisted it over his head, the platter of vegetables scattering on the floor.

Ferrin rushed over.

"It was an accident!" the boy cried.

"Don't you talk back to me, learn your place!" yelled the woman, as she delivered a slap to his ear.

"What the hell are you doing? It was an accident!" Ferrin shouted at the woman, who had a tight grip on the boy's arm and was marching him to the side door.

The hall went quiet, all eyes on the trio.

"This doesn't concern you," spat the noblewoman. "Your Highness."

Ferrin was taken aback. She may not have been favored among the nobility, but basic respect was still expected.

"Let go of him," she demanded, following them to the door.

"He's a servant who is careless, he will be *punished*," the woman said, turning.

"He's just a boy," Ferrin said, following them out the door.

They were in the hall now, with only the two sentry guards witness to the altercation.

"Shut your filthy mouth, you Caelish brat. You think you're above me? My husband *died* defending us from your mother's bloodthirsty people. Barbarians!"

Ferrin reached out and grabbed the woman's arm that was holding onto the boy. "Let go of him. Now," she said.

The woman reeled on her, letting go of the boy's arm. He fell to the floor as the woman slapped Ferrin *right* on the side where her bruise from the night before was. It hurt like hell.

"Oh, you *bitch!*" Ferrin clapped a hand to her own face, which only made it worse. She dropped her hand. The boy had the good sense to retreat into the servants' passage entrance by the potted plant. The guards did nothing.

"Serves you right!" the woman slurred, spittle flying. "You and your brother won't get *near* that crown with your filthy Caelish *bastard* blood, you—"

"What seems to be the problem?"

Nerena had appeared out of nowhere, her rich plum-colored gown trailing on the ground in a soft whisper.

The woman clammed up. "Nothing, Your Majesty." She bowed.

"Ferrin?" Nerena turned her attention to her.

"Nothing." She still didn't know how she was supposed to address Nerena. By name? Her Majesty? Stepmother?

"Well, shall we return to dinner?" Nerena suggested sweetly.

"I must confess I've lost my appetite," Ferrin said, swallowing.

"Hey, is everything alright out here?" Rhi said, stepping out of the double doors.

"Rhiach, let us return to the feast," Nerena said coolly.

"Ferr?" Rhi asked, fixing his attention on her and the noblewoman.

"Yeah, I'm alright, Rhi," she said. "You go on, I'm not hungry."

Nerena and Rhi returned to the Great Hall, followed closely by the drunk and belligerent noblewoman. Ferrin pressed the back of her fist to her mouth to stave off the sob that was coming.

"Lot of help you are," she spat over her shoulder at the guards who hadn't so much as blinked when the woman had slapped the king's daughter.

She moved quickly down the hallway, doing everything she could not to break into a run. Why did one bigoted, drunk Lady's opinion matter? How had everything become such a mess here? She knew she and Rhi had work to do, to fix this place before it rotted completely from the inside out.

Another fear had trickled into her mind and taken root. If she had stayed, if she had done what was expected of her, would things be different? How much of this divide was her fault for running off?

The tears were burning the back of her eyes. She'd gone weeks without crying after Zare dumped her into the waiting arms of the Lindbarrian Navy, but now, twice in twenty-four hours, she was losing it.

The thought of Zare sent her over the edge completely—the shame of his betrayal, the guilt of leaving here, of leaving Rhi to fend for himself, of leaving her country behind without a thought. It was all too much, and she was suddenly in an alcove, sinking to the ledge, in the quiet of the castle, nothing but the burbling of the fountain to cover up the sound of her fighting the building sob in her throat as she fought for breath.

"Ferrin?" There was a rustle and the leaves in the decorative potted fern outside the alcove were moved out of the way. "Rough evening, Princess? What are you doing—"

"Oh, gods, Lukas, what are you doing here?" she sniffed, scrambling to her feet.

"This is one of the doors I use to get to the servants' passages… Are you alright?" His voice was gentler than she'd ever heard it. It made her want to crumple in on herself.

"I'm fine," she said, dabbing the corner of her eyes with her sleeve. "I'm fine."

He looked her over, seeing her split lip, the bruise on her face, the one peaking out from the neckline of her dress. "No you're not," he said, worry creasing his brow as he stepped into the alcove with her, "What the hell happened?" He lifted a hand to her face, hovering over the bruise on her cheek, her eye.

"It's fine, it's old news," she said, turning her face away.

"Who did this?" he asked angrily.

"Guards."

"Guards?"

"Why is everyone so surprised at that?" she sniffed again.

"Ferrin, you look…" he pursed his lips, shaking his head. "What happened?"

She tried to steady her breathing, to inhale and let it out slow, but the muscles in her chest would not obey, would not let her slow down and she didn't know where to start and the deep, cracking sob she'd been fighting to suppress suddenly tore out of her throat, the sound of it barely registering in her own ears as it shook her. She stumbled face first into Lukas's chest, his arms enfolding her.

"Hey, hey," his voice was again uncharacteristically gentle as he held her, his chin grazing the top of her ear.

She felt his hands on her back, one snaking up to cup the back of her head as she sobbed into his shirt, shaking her head as if she could dispel the events of the last weeks and months. Then his hands found the sides of her face, calloused and rough fingertips startlingly gentle as he tipped her head back.

"Hey, look at me, Princess. Look at me," he said. "*Breathe.*"

She sucked in a wobbly breath as she locked eyes with him, their faces only inches apart. His brow furrowed as he swept back a lock of her hair that had come loose, though it was damp and she knew she must look a wreck.

"Do you want to go somewhere else?"

She bit her lip, nodding.

"Alright, come on."

Lukas set a cup of water on the coffee table before her. The walk to his rooms had steadied her, something about being on the move settling her constantly buzzing nerves.

"Thanks," she said, taking a sip. He settled onto the other end of the couch, close enough to touch, but enough space between them for her to breathe, relax.

"Which guards did this?" he asked.

"I don't know." She shifted self-consciously. "It was at the council meeting. Last night."

"At the council meeting? For what?"

"The Forest. The new garrison…" she trailed off. "You don't know."

"No, what happened?"

"A few weeks ago, I learned about a proposal to destroy the southern part of Taroch Forest, to build a new garrison and wall south of the castle grounds, Rhi and I went to the council meeting and presented an argument and… it was going well. So well, I think, that my father had us dragged out of the room by his guards."

"And they beat you for it?" Lukas asked, eyeing her brutalized face.

"Well… they dragged me out kicking. I fought against it and that made it worse. When they shoved me into my room, I fell and smacked my face on a chair," she admitted.

He raised his eyebrows in surprise. "If you need help getting out of the castle, getting away from here, I can help," he said earnestly. "I know a man. He does papers, they're not perfect, but they're passable, and there's a boat—"

"No. No. I won't do that again," she said defiantly. "I can't keep running away when things get hard."

"I only meant if you think your father might take steps to… remove you." Lukas's voice was careful, somber.

She shook her head, swallowing. "No. I have to stay here and fight to make things better."

He nodded, quietly giving her room to add more.

"I can't help feeling that if I… if I had stuck around before, maybe things wouldn't have gotten this bad. If I had been here, maybe Rhi wouldn't have fallen so hard, and maybe my father would have been kinder." Her voice was hoarse.

"There's no way of knowing that. For all you know, it would have made things even worse."

"But I could have tried. I could have tried instead of wasting years of my life on something that wasn't even real." Her voice threatened to break again as she admitted it out loud for the first time. "I keep seeing it over and over again in my mind how *stupid* I was. Like I thought just because he and I were—that I was immune to his games, safe from them because we—" she broke off again, swallowing a sob.

He reached across the space between them and laid a hand on her upper arm. "Listen, Ferrin," Lukas sighed. "I've only known you a short time, but I've known you long enough to know it's extremely unfair, not to mention, unimaginative to call yourself *stupid* for a mistake you made. Especially one you made so young." A wistful glint sparked in his eye and she wondered if he was thinking of a particular mistake *he'd* made.

She dropped her head into her hand.

"Stubborn? Rash? Quick to draw conclusions? Maybe. But not stupid."

She let slip a laugh that was almost a hiccup. "Hush *up*."

"All I'm saying is… it *is* stupid to sit around making yourself miserable over what might have happened and what you *should* have known. All you can do is learn and not make the same mistake again."

"Why does that sound like such sage wisdom?"

"I told you. I have many talents."

Lukas was readying for bed when he heard a knock at his door. His first thought was that Ferrin had come back for the delicate lace shawl she'd left on his couch. How such a flimsy garment was supposed to keep a woman warm, he didn't know.

"It isn't locked," he called out, hand resting on the hilt of his dagger, just in case.

"Good evening, sir." The royal page stepped into the room. "I come with a summons from the queen."

"Oh?" Lukas raised his brow in puzzlement. "And what might the queen need at this hour?"

The page looked as if he were going to chide Lukas, but then thought better of it. "She requested your presence in her private office."

"Right now?" Lukas squinted. It was nearly midnight. "Well, let me dress."

The page stepped outside and Lukas shucked off the shirt he'd worn all day. It was rumpled and damp from Ferrin's tears in the hallway. He wondered what had set off everything she'd been holding back tonight.

He shrugged on a clean shirt and coat and pulled his hair back with a ribbon before striding out the door. He looked presentable enough. The page led him to the queen's suite, where she kept her living quarters and a big, sprawling atrium that acted as her office.

As the servant opened the door, Lukas had a creeping feeling he was in some sort of trouble. He entered the room and glanced around. It was simple: marble floor, whitewashed walls, gold leaf, a few artfully-placed potted ferns.

The queen sat at the head of a long, lacquered, walnut table. Her expression read calculated patience, her posture erect, nearly rigid in its stillness; a panther crouched on a limb, awaiting prey.

"You summoned me, Your Majesty?" Lukas bowed.

"Yes. Have a seat."

Lukas sat, trying to shake his hesitation as he pulled one of the baroque chairs out from the table, two seats down from the queen. He watched as she poured herself a glass of wine from a crystal carafe, the red liquid swirling a little like blood. He kept his features neutral, but the building feeling of unease that had taken root in his gut refused to budge.

"It has come to my attention, Lukas, that you've been rather… lackadaisical in your quelling of the village uprising." She set the glass down in front of him with the slow precision of a lioness biding her time in the tall grass.

"I haven't found much to be amiss, Majesty," he explained, eyeing the glass.

"Perhaps you don't think so, but I've had men investigating for weeks now." She poured a second glass of wine and stood with it. "It may be time to look a little harder or simply remove yourself from the task."

The queen walked to a little cabinet beneath the dark window, where a vase of roses sat. She picked one up, cupping it in her palm.

"I'm not sure I understand your meaning," Lukas said, the hairs on the back of his neck standing on end. He knew this was a scare tactic. The wine, the quiet calm that could only mean a great and terrible storm was coming.

"If you do not take care of what needs to be taken care of," she turned the blossom in her hand, and Lukas could swear he saw its color drain, its petals crumple, before she tucked it back into the vase among its brethren. "I will appoint someone else."

"That may be for the best, Your Majesty," he said evenly. "I may not be the man for the job."

"A miscalculation on my part." She turned back to him. "I assure you, they are a rarity."

"I have no doubt."

"Allow me to make one thing clear," she said as she circled back to her seat. "If you interfere with the investigation, with the subsequent raids, there will be consequences. I'd hate for some of my guards to snap under the pressure and take it out on the businesses beneath the town. It would only take a few well-placed sparks to make it a very poor day indeed for those gathering beneath the old warehouse."

Lukas was taken aback, and was about to dismiss it as a bluff, thinking that she couldn't possibly know the location of the Pit, of the market. But she *did*. His heart thudded, tightly wound in his chest.

"There is important work going on here, Mr. Mazrihn, even if you can't see it yet. Important work that must not be impeded." Her voice was cold and sly and curdling. "Make no mistake, that damn rebellion you're so insistent doesn't exist is causing stress in all corners. Don't make me reconsider allowing you to walk away from this."

He bit down on his lip, hands fisted at his sides. "I under-stand your meaning, Majesty."

"Wonderful," she blinked. "The traitors will be transported north to the prison before the festival at week's end. They will be under guard, so do not take up any foolish ideals. You are dismissed."

Ferrin lay in bed unable to sleep. Again.

The cut on her lip had reopened, probably because she kept biting it out of stress. Her eyes were raw from crying. She sighed and pushed up out of bed, stalking to the mirror. The blood was tangy and metallic on her tongue, and she brought a fingertip up to her mouth. It came away smudged with red.

The last twenty-four hours had taken a toll on her—mentally and physically. She'd broken down in a damn hallway alcove, and if that wasn't bad enough, she'd probably snotted all over Lukas's shirt.

Something had shifted between them. Somewhere along the way, their bickering had given way to flirtation, and maybe even to something more. It scared her, more than a little. Zare had made her gun-shy and she was in no way looking to enter a romantic entanglement in the near future.

But still… something about him warmed her. His teasing nature, his willingness to listen. Beneath his rough-and-tumble exterior, there was something deeper. Something she'd caught a glimpse of when he'd let her sob into his chest behind a potted fern.

She thumbed open the old copy of *Legends & Truths*, not noticing the little smudge of half-dried blood she'd dabbed onto the front cover. Maybe reading through some more of the legends would offer her some distraction from the storm inside her.

As she turned another page, she nearly missed the distinct sound of metal hitting wood, muffled by the pages of the book.

With a frown, she closed the cover. Had she unknowingly knocked over an inkwell again? *That* would be annoying.

She had to blink to make sure she wasn't going mad.

There was a key.

A bronze key, an *old* bronze key. It was just sitting there, on the table, where the dusty front cover had been laid open. She shook her head and picked up the book. It looked an awful lot like the…

the key from the cover! It was gone, or rather, it was no longer upon the cover, but sitting on her coffee table, real, and metal, and heavy.

She set the book down, frowning with wonder. She *had* hit her head two nights ago… But when she reached out to let her fingers brush the key, it was cold, and metallic, and definitely real.

She sucked in a breath.

The secrets of the old castle awaited her.

CHAPTER TWENTY-THREE

Once dinner had finished for the night, Soviel set out to follow Nimhe. She clung to the shadows of the hallway, clad in a plain, brown linen dress. With a bit of grease smudged on her hands and chin, and her hair tied up messily, she could easily pass for a scullery maid to anyone who might throw her a cursory glance.

Nimhe wove through the west hallway of the castle perhaps thirty paces ahead of her, seemingly unaware that she'd picked up a tail nearly an hour earlier.

Since that day in the salon, Soviel had begun to see Nimhe in a different light. Perhaps she was not as simple as she wanted everyone to think she was. Perhaps she was playing the very same game that Soviel herself was playing.

She ducked down a side hallway and Soviel followed. By all accounts, it seemed she was headed towards the kitchens. She could be on her way to flirt with the kitchen boy she'd been keen on all spring; that would be the simplest explanation. But given how often little things had been going wrong, Soviel doubted it.

Bending down and pretending to scrub at the wainscoting with her rag and bucket, Soviel hid her face as Nimhe cast a quick glance behind her before opening the kitchen door and slipping in. Soviel waited ten seconds and followed after her.

"I'm here to request refreshments for Duchess Langley…" Nimhe was saying to one of the cooks, a stout brunette woman with frown lines etched in her aging, sallow face.

Soviel moved further into the kitchen, doing her best to look busy as she strained to hear over the post-supper din.

"You're not our usual runner, aren't you an upstairs-girl?" The cook looked Nimhe up and down, taking note of her out-of-place finery.

"I'm here on special request of Her Majesty, the queen," Nimhe said primly.

"Well," the cook scratched her head through her cap. "What sort of refreshment has Her Majesty requested?"

"These, please," Nimhe said, reaching into her skirt pockets to pull out a rolled-up paper with a list written on it.

The cook gave the list a once-over, brow furrowing. "At this hour?"

"Her Majesty was very specific," Nimhe said.

"Very well," the cook sighed.

Ferrin wandered the castle after dinner that evening, waiting for the blanket of night to lull everything into sleep. When the bell struck ten, she pried up the floorboards under her bed, and took up her knife, which she'd since had sharpened and bought a new sheath for, and belted it around her waist beneath the knitted cardigan she'd shrugged over her dress. In her pocket-bags, she tucked a spool of twine and the big, bronze key. Beneath the folds of her skirt, they were well-hidden.

She pulled on her boots and headed out the door, tracing her steps to the particular servants' passage she'd ducked into on the night she'd found the door.

A chill gust wafted through the stagnant air of the castle halls. There was a cold front blowing in off the sea, and it would probably rain by morning. Ferrin quickly surveyed the hallway to make sure no one was around before cracking open the wall panel and silently slipping in.

The floor was even damper than it had been the last time, as if the entire castle was sweating in anticipation. From vague memory, she wandered down the hallway, careful to note any turns or forks. The lantern she'd taken from the sconce, just like she'd done last time, would burn for no more than four hours, and only illuminated a few feet into the darkness ahead.

At last, she came to the door. Just as before, it was locked. She retrieved the key from within her dress and slid it into the lock, turning it. The bolt clicked open with a loud, echoing boom, and she pulled the door open.

The knob on the other side had the same keyhole; so she left it unlocked, but tucked the key back into her skirt before closing the door behind her.

Next, she removed the ball of twine from her skirt and tied one end securely around the knob, setting down the lantern to do so. She looped the lantern handle over one arm, and took up the spool in the other, stepping gingerly into the darkness.

It was late, two hours until midnight, when Soviel crept from the castle and followed Nimhe with her basket of goods down to the village. She'd lost her for about ten minutes, as Nimhe had returned to her own room, presumably to fetch a cloak. What else had occurred in that time remained a mystery.

Wreathed in the dark, Nimhe had pulled her deep plum-colored cloak over her red curls, and was walking at a breakneck pace towards town. Soviel bit her lip against the teeth-chattering cold and wished she had a more substantial coat with her as she followed behind Nimhe. The edge of the village was a mess: broken windows, soldiers patrolling the streets, dragging people out of their beds. Small fires burned on street corners and a few carriages lay overturned in the road. Soviel darted down an alley to avoid being seen.

Nimhe took a left towards the border of the merchant's quarter, cloak swishing behind her as she passed under the last street-lamp on the block. The more affluent street was quiet and dark for the night, unlike the fringe neighborhood in chaos only a few blocks back.

Then something strange happened.

She knocked on a door, and a man answered. Nimhe handed him a loaf of bread and one of the jars of tea. Soviel squinted. The old man took the bread and tea from Nimhe and thanked her before returning inside.

She did the same at several other houses on the street.

When Nimhe had finished her work, and headed into the pub closer to the town's center with her final items, Soviel slumped against a tree. Maybe she was being paranoid. What cause would Nimhe have to poison people, people who shared in her plight? This could all be completely unrelated to what had happened to Lady Denison in the salon.

She was just about to turn and head to the safe house across town to spend the night there, when the screaming began.

She whipped around, expecting to see soldiers breaking windows, people being shoved out of their houses by force, and fires erupting on rooftops.

What she saw was something entirely different.

A young woman had run out of the first house, the one where Nimhe had delivered bread to the old man no more than a half-hour earlier. She collapsed to her knees on the steps, clutching at her face and neck as she emitted a haunting wail.

Soviel pushed off the tree she'd been leaning against and ran to the woman. Just as she arrived, more screaming erupted out of the house's open door.

The old man's voice was raw and sharp as he backed out of the house, running from something. She'd barely managed to stand up and stop him from falling down the steps. He whipped around, eyes wide with terror, and looked her up and down.

"Who are you? What have you done with them?" he cried.

"Sir, calm down! I'm not going to hurt you," she said gently as he scrambled back from her hands.

"Demon! Demon!"

The young woman still knelt on the steps, mournful shrieks tearing from her throat as she patted the ground, searching for something that wasn't there.

Soviel let her power drift into the woman, searching, analyzing, "I'm trying to help—"

She was cut off as more screams broke out up and down the street. A few houses down, someone threw themselves from a second story window, a sickening thud sounding as they hit the ground. Someone took off down the street as if the beasts of harrow-hall were hungry on their heels. A child of no more than five cried from the center of the street, abandoned.

It was the same as those who had been dosed with tainted *popava*, the same as Lady Denison, as Neddy the kitchen boy, the townsfolk who had ended up dead. Of that, there was no mistake.

Nimhe had done this. Nimhe had *been* doing this, for months now, Soviel suspected.

The question was, for what purpose?

She stood and made a mental note of which houses had been dosed—at least eight on this street. And Nimhe had headed into the pub…

Soviel turned and sprinted back towards the pub. If she was right, if Nimhe was poisoning people, she had to get to that tavern and stop her from dosing the keg of ale. The scope of damage she could do from there was unthinkable.

She pumped her arms, breath coming hard as she raced towards the little pub on the corner. Her lungs ached, and her knees throbbed. She still wasn't at full strength after helping Lady Denison, and she choked down air as fast as her body allowed.

She skidded to a stop across the street, watching through the windows. Nimhe had settled into a seat by the bar, her cloak still drawn over her head. She set the basket down beside her, one small flask still inside.

Soviel gulped as she tried to make a plan.

"This way, men! Round them up! If they give you trouble, you've got full authority to use force!"

She jumped out of the way just in time as a flood of soldiers rounded the corner, heading towards the street she'd just come from. Soviel stood there, torn. What could she do? Running to the safe house for help would take too long. She glanced back in the pub window. Nimhe and her basket were gone.

"Shit," she swore under her breath, turning to follow the soldiers.

The condition on the street had worsened. Chaos reigned, and they were rounding up men, women and even children. Half of the people being shoved into the prison wagons were obviously sick with the effects of the dusted *popava*. Some were clawing at the inside of the prison wagon so violently, their fingers bled. Her gut wrenched at the sight.

She stepped to the edge of the alley she was hiding in, intending to find out what was going on, when galloping hoofbeats sounded behind her. Something connected with the back of her skull, and everything went black.

The night air was thick with spring humidity and the cloudless, moonless sky was pitch black and studded with stars, though the cloud cover rolling in from the east was soon to hide them.

Lukas lay on his belly in the reedy grass outside the village, listening, waiting. The prison wagon would take one of two routes north to reach its destination, and if he could figure out which, and loop ahead, he could thwart this whole thing without blatantly disobeying the queen's orders.

They'd rounded up people of all ages—he'd seen them shove a child of only seven years into the barred wagon, crying and kicking. The image had been too familiar. For a second, he was back home in Khalim again, watching the Veiran soldiers take away people to dive and labor against their will, watching a soldier backhand his mother and wreck half her store, watching Damijan cough up blood and dust in the desert.

He shook his head to clear it. Lukas was many things, a smuggler and even a criminal, but he could not let this stand.

The carriage waited under heavy guard, but as soon as it left the city, it would be vulnerable, because they knew they weren't transporting anything appealing to thieves and highwaymen.

They were still loading up the wagons when Lukas overheard the conversation between two of the guards outside. "There's still two more neighborhoods to comb through," said one. "At this rate we won't be able to leave before tomorrow evening."

These guards were not ordinary palace guards, they were marked with Nerena's own sigil, a blue rose. The Queensguard.

"No, we're on the road at midnight. Dawn at the absolute latest. You heard the orders," said the second guard, before hocking a wad of *arimopo* onto the ground.

Lukas had what he needed, he could go wait out the few hours at the pub and grab a bite to steady his nerves. Then he'd act.

The secret hallway was unremarkable. Stones, cobwebs, planks of wood across the ceiling and floor, like a mine. There'd only been about *four* times where she thought she was going to die. Each terrifying sound had turned out to be vermin or wind.

She walked down the hall, cautious not to make too much noise or turn a corner too quickly. By her estimation, she was almost across the castle, at the opposite end from her rooms, when she came upon two doors. Neither was latched or locked, just two doors with a little hand-hold to swing them open.

Behind the first was a hallway that veered hard to the left. Behind the second was a spiral staircase that led far up into the gloom, and down a short ways into another sloping, dirt-floor hallway. She took two steps into the first hallway before being blasted by warm, wet air, ripe with the smell of decay.

"*Absolutely not,*" Ferrin muttered to herself before turning back to the atrium.

Down the stairs she went, switching the twine roll into the hand that held the lantern, so she could grip the iron railing with her free hand. It, too, was warm and damp and wholly unsettling.

She looked up, unable to shake the feeling that someone or something loomed above, watching. She quickened her pace and descended. The iron creaked, either from her own weight or from something far above. Terror gripped her. What had she been thinking, coming down here alone?

Her fear launched its full assault when the string went taut in her hand and she nearly dropped it. She hadn't run out yet, but she was close. She scurried down the remaining stairs, through the low stone arch and into the dirt path. She needed to get out, she needed air.

The twine ran out—it fell from her hands and sprang back at an alarming rate that had nothing to do with its elasticity. Something or someone had grabbed hold of it. She broke into a run. The metal on the stairs behind her creaked again. All pretense of calm was dropped as she sprinted down the hallway, hand on the hilt of her knife. Her heart was in her throat, her blood roaring in her ears. She had to get *out*.

Was that light ahead? She couldn't tell and she wouldn't risk dropping her lantern to find out. She barreled down the dirt tunnel, barely taking note of how it seemed to narrow around her. If she was lost, she no longer had the security of the twine to lead her back the way she had come.

There *was* light ahead… the dimmest streaks of it coming through the ceiling. She didn't care what it was, she just needed to get out, above ground, to breathe fresh air before the tunnel swallowed her with its grave-dirt maw. She dropped her lantern and it shattered before going out.

The sound of her breath was drowned out by the blood pounding in her ears. Was that the sound of her own footsteps echoing, or was something racing after her?

Beneath her, the ground sloped up until she was forced to slow her run to a scramble, the ceiling closing in. There were suddenly roots in her face and dirt falling around her and she was choking on it, being buried alive as she crawled through the tight space, reaching, clawing, and spitting out the dirt as it fell on top of her, in her mouth until—

Fresh air!

Her chest heaved as she gasped down the cool, night breeze, still tangled waist-deep in the clutches of the earth, roots and dirt entwined around her as she came up through the half-covered hole in the ground. The exit was concealed by the tangled, gnarled roots of a big oak tree, not far from the patch of woods and the cabin. She hoisted herself the rest of the way out, panting as she dragged her legs from the hole. What *was* that place?

Something had been in those tunnels with her. Something hungry.

Lukas dropped into a window seat at the pub, view of the wagon in his periphery.

"Whiskey?" the barmaid asked, holding up the bottle.

"Just one," he gestured. "And some bread, too, if you please."

"Right." She turned and headed into the back, leaving the filled glass and the bottle. She returned quickly with a heel of bread and a tiny dish of butter, and Lukas passed her some coins.

He settled back into his seat, resting one ankle on the opposite seat, and took stock—he had two pistols at his hip, hidden beneath his coat, a dagger in his boot. Only his sword was not concealed. Sheathed at his belt was a simple claymore he'd bought when he'd first arrived on this cold, wet island two years ago, with the last of the money he'd saved back home.

He tore at the bread, popping a piece into his mouth. It was beyond dry, but he supposed that was to be expected, considering it had likely been sitting out since dawn. He slathered some butter on the next piece and picked up the whiskey glass. Glancing out the window again, he noticed another guard had been posted.

He was nursing his glass of whiskey when a couple staggered in off the street, setting off the bell over the door. He looked back at his glass and it was full again. Had the barmaid topped it off?

Shaking his head in confusion, he took another sip. There was no way he'd finish it with the night he had ahead of him.

He found his fingers wrapping around the little pocket watch, useless thing, and pulling it out. He flipped it open as he'd done time and time again. The hand was whirring forward at triple the speed it should have been, winding and winding and winding in a circle, drawing hours into minutes, minutes into seconds.

It was unsettling, as if it was reminding him he was running out of time. He snapped it shut with an abrupt click, returning it to his coat pocket. He glanced back outside. All was the same, there was time. He turned back to his whiskey to see it was full again. *Who* was filling it? The barmaid had taken the bottle when she'd …

He turned his head, craning his neck to get a look at the bar.

The room started spinning. "Shit," he swore, bracing a hand on the table.

He'd barely taken three sips of that damn whiskey, what was wrong with him? There was still time, he just needed to eat a bite.

Francine, the barmaid, emerged from the back again and he waved her over. "Can I get some water?" he asked.

She nodded and appeared a second later carrying it. He hadn't even seen her walk away. What was happening?

"You look like you've had a rough day," she said. She pressed the cup into his hands and pushed it to his face. The room was starting to blur.

He grumbled in protest as she all but poured the water down his throat. It burned.

He gulped it down and everything swayed. He glanced back out to the carriage—

It was gone.

He stood, nearly falling as he did. "I have to go, thanks."

"Get yourself home."

He leaned into the door as it opened, and made his way onto the street. His head spun like he'd guzzled a gallon of whiskey. Where had the prison wagon gone?

He turned in a circle. Nothing.

Maybe they were taking their prisoners to the castle for holding before transporting them in the morning. He could buy time, find out what was happening and then get Ryder and some boys from the Pit to help orchestrate…

His vision went black for a second and he blinked. The ground was spinning beneath him as he staggered towards the castle, his sight blurring in and out of focus. The scene from earlier that day played in his mind, mixing and mingling with old memories from back home.

The queen had quadrupled the number of her personal guards on the raids. They'd gone down and rounded up men, women and children alike, shattering windows, wrecking shopfronts. The Caelish quarter of town had been smoking rubble by the end of the day, and some of the Merchant's Square too. Lukas had chanced the queen's threat and gone to warn as many houses as would listen to a stranger knocking on their doors before dawn.

The arrest papers had detailed specific acts that were now, by 'emergency decree', considered treason against the Crown. It was a blatant and complete crushing of the Caelish people who were making a living in the Capital, one that had been a long time in the making.

At Danvery Prison, they'd be forced into labor, interrogated or left to die in the damp, moldy air.

Lukas nearly collided with a lost child in the road. He slammed to a halt, about to ask if the small boy needed help, but then he flickered out of view.

He sucked in a breath. "What the hell?" he mumbled to himself.

The child appeared again. "You let them take us," the boy said accusingly. A slight woman with black hair and kohl-rimmed eyes appeared next to him, her face hollow and her dress ragged. She looked like she was made of dust.

Lukas squinted, leaning closer.

"You're a coward, a coward who lets people *die*." Another figure appeared, this one far louder, yet far more spectral in appearance. It was a man clutching a bonnet. His clothing was of Akhatan fashion; lightweight tunic and loose trousers. His skin was gray and ashy and sunken, a bullet hole festering in the side of his head.

Lukas's heart was hammering in his chest. This wasn't real.

This wasn't real.

He must have had some moldy bread, some bad liquor.

"You are a murderer." The chilling voice that slithered out of the fog next was all too familiar. Damijan.

His friend's eyes were bloodshot and flat as he stepped from the throng of ghosts. His white shirt was stained with blood that had dried years ago. His eyes were sunken and fresh blood dripped from the corner of his mouth. His skin had soured and spoiled in death.

This isn't real.

Lukas gasped, his breath catching in his throat as panic seized him. The ghosts all around him were closing in. "This is *not* real," he tried to reassure himself. He ran, straight through the crowd of incorporeal bodies. As if trying to prove to himself that it was a trick. It didn't stop their voices, their stares.

He ran and stumbled, catching himself on a tree and shoving off it to get away. A shape appeared before him, but he couldn't stop in time and nearly sent the both of them tumbling to the ground. It was Ferrin.

"Lukas? What the— oh, my—your *eyes*. Are you...?"

"Someone... drugged me," he breathed, just before his knees gave out and he keeled over.

Ferrin froze momentarily as Lukas collapsed on top of her. He was so heavy, all she could do was ease him to his knees, where he seemed to regain consciousness.

"Lukas?" she gripped his shoulders, steadying him. His head lolled back as he opened his eyes. "Lukas?"

She grabbed his chin, gently forcing him to look her in the eye.

His sea-green irises were fogged over, and the whites of his eyes were bloodshot.

"Ferrin," he mumbled, his eyelids tipping closed. He smelled faintly of alcohol and something else, something sharper.

"What happened?" she demanded.

"I'm sorry," he snorted, blinking.

Why was he laughing?

"What do you mean?" she asked, trying to pull him into the relative shelter of a tree.

"Your hair is so…" He picked up a lock of her hair almost dreamily, only then noticing the layer of dirt covering her. "Dirty?"

"Lukas, *answer* me. What's happened?"

"What?" He leaned his head back against the tree, eyes drifting shut.

"What happened?"

"Not sure."

"Please look at me." Something was wrong.

He opened his eyes and she saw terror in them as they fixed on something in the distance.

"Hey." She gripped his chin again. "Eyes on me. What happened?"

"Go home, Ferrin," he slurred, his eyes now locked on hers.

"What is going on with you?" she demanded.

"Had some whiskey in the pub and then…" He closed his eyes again, shaking his head.

"Lukas, stay awake!" she yelled. "Did you drink the whole damn bottle?" she asked, more to herself.

"Something… bad in the food. Or the water. Tasted off."

"Come on, we need to get you inside."

"Go *home*," he repeated.

"I'm not leaving you out here like this." She didn't quite know *what* to do with him, but she wasn't about to leave him passed out under a tree to be robbed, or worse. "Come *on*," she prodded as she stood, tugging on his hand. "Please, Lukas."

His eyes opened and cleared as he focused on her. "I'll be fine. What do you care anyway?" There was an edge in his voice.

"You're not fine, you're wasted off of gods know what," she snarled, refusing to let go of his hand.

He sighed, shaking his head again. With a labored breath, he stood, back against the tree. "I couldn't stop it."

"Stop what?" she asked, offering her other hand to steady him. He looked a wreck. "Lukas, for *Saolath's* sake, tell me what *happened*. Let me help you."

His eyes fixed on something in the distance again, and he went rigid as he sucked in a breath. "They're here."

She spun to see what he was looking at. "There's no one there."

He shook his head, that fog creeping back into his eyes. Some terror has seized him. He squeezed his eyes shut and exhaled a word. Perhaps a name, one she couldn't make out.

"No! Do *not* pass out here!" she shouted, trying to keep the panic out of her voice. She'd never be able to drag him back to his room if he was unconscious.

"Ferrin," he whispered.

"Yes, that's me. Now, come on," she ordered, pulling him forward. He swayed once, then seemed to remember his legs and took a step. She looped his arm over her shoulder, letting him lean on her as she snuck a glance at his face. His eyes were fluttering closed again.

"You need to keep your eyes open," she instructed as they ambled back towards the castle.

Somehow, she managed to get him to his room without being seen. The hour was late —far past midnight—but servants might still be called to duty at odd hours. She opened the door and they stumbled in. As she pulled the door closed behind them, a surge of relief washed over her.

Lukas turned his face into the side of her hair. "Thank you," he breathed.

It sounded like he was coming back to himself. She had an inkling of what was in his system.

"Come on, let's put you to bed."

She half-expected him to make a cheeky remark about that, but instead he flopped down backwards on top of his covers, his feet still on the ground.

"Stay here. I'll be right back," she said. She left his bedside but quickly returned to his bedchamber with a bucket and a cup of water, and placed both on the little end table beside him.

He was not faring well; he'd gone pale and his breathing was uneven and shallow. She tried to heave him onto his side, but he wouldn't stay. She tried again, and he rolled right back onto his over onto his back.

"Luk!" she cried in frustration. She couldn't leave him like this to sleep it off. If he got up and started hallucinating whatever it was he'd been seeing, who knew what he'd do. She sighed and climbed onto the bed beside him. With a pang, she realized she was still filthy from crawling through the dirt in the tunnels. Wedging him onto his side, she cautiously lay down beside him, and wrapped an arm around his waist. She tucked the tail of his tied-back hair under his head so it wasn't in her face. Finally, when her terror wore off, Ferrin's eyes began rolling back in her head from the exhaustion of the night.

For hours she stayed like that, half-awake, listening to the sound of his breathing to make sure he was alive. Sometime before dawn, she had the thought to seek out Soviel for help, but she didn't want to leave him by himself until he woke up.

By the time dawn arrived, his breathing had quickened, and a cold sweat had broken across his skin. After a few minutes of his shivering, she squeezed his shoulder, "Lukas?"

He grumbled something unintelligible.

Ferrin sat up. "Lukas," she repeated. "Are you awake?"

"Mhmm," he moaned.

Ferrin looked out the window and saw the pale light tinging the edge of the sky as if it had been dipped in a pool of silver. Day was coming. "I got you a bucket if you need to be sick," she said quietly. "And I'm going to borrow some of your clothes for a bit," she told him. Dozing off in her stays had not been terribly comfortable. She sighed deeply and climbed off the bed.

Lukas grumbled something that she didn't quite catch.

Ferrin strode to the other side of the room and stripped off her clothes. Her dress pooled in a sea of muddy, dusty linen at her feet. She stepped out of it and began to try and wriggle out of her stays. She really needed to get herself a set that laced up the front. At last, she undid the cord and shimmied them off. She exhaled as the pressure on her ribs fell away.

Oh, the scandal! she thought to herself wryly as she dropped her undergarments on the floor. Standing in only her thin, linen shift, she plucked a rust-colored tunic from Lukas's armoire and shrugged it over her head. It fell past her hips, offering a little cover over the translucency of her finely made shift. She returned to the bed and climbed on, enjoying the feel of the sheets and blankets on her bare legs.

"Are you alright?" she whispered.

Lukas groaned, "no."

Finally, a coherent answer. She felt like that was progress, at least.

"Are you going to be sick?"

"Yeah."

"Alright, you'll have to sit up."

Another groan.

"Lukas. Sit. Up." She grabbed him under the shoulders and tried to haul him upright, grunting against his bulk.

He grumbled his protest, his skin almost waxy under the sheen of sweat all over his body. He braced his elbows on his knees.

"Oh, gods," he grimaced.

Ferrin placed a hand on his back and gathered his messy hair behind him. It had come undone in his sleep, so she gently swept it back behind his head, doing her best to soothe. He tensed, leaned forward, and emptied his guts into the bucket. He heaved once, twice, and finally, it stopped.

She patted his back gently, grimacing at the smell and sight. "Here, drink this." She handed him the glass of water. "Little sips."

He took one swig, swished it around in his mouth and spat it into the bucket, then drained the entire glass.

"How do you feel?" she asked as he stripped off his shirt and flopped back onto the bed, one arm thrown across his eyes, putting his entire glorious chest on display.

"Dead," he answered flatly.

"Are you going to be sick again?" she asked.

"Maybe," he nodded, rubbing his forehead.

"I'll stay," she said. It couldn't be far past five in the morning, and after what she'd witnessed last night, she was worried. Lukas's behavior was so similar to the descriptions of the people who'd been dosed. And two of them had wound up dead.

"You don't have to do that."

"It's not up for debate."

"I'll be fine," he said flatly.

"Let's hope so." Ferrin peeled back the covers and climbed under them, laying down beside him. Only the sides of their arms touched, and she listened as his breathing evened out. Unable to fight sleep any longer, she let her eyes close, and drifted off.

Hours later, Ferrin awoke to hushed voices coming from the doorway. At first, she forgot where she was, but quickly remembered that she was half-naked in bed with a brawling smuggler. Just as quickly, she realized he was no longer in the bed, and that someone was at the door who might see her. She carefully moved the second pillow over her face, to block it from the view of whoever was at the door, but allowed her ear to remain uncovered so she could listen in.

When she realized who's voice it was, her eyes flew open and she turned over, preparing to join them at the door.

"What in the pits of hell happened to you last night?" came Rhi's voice. He must have seen her dirty, rumpled dress on the floor because he then asked, "Ah, better question; who'd you bed last night?"

The words made Ferrin freeze just as she'd hopped out of bed.

"Wait a second… is my *sister* in there?" Rhi winced, catching sight of her.

"Mind your own damn business, princeling," Lukas's voice was dry and unamused.

"You *seduced my sister?*" Rhi started towards him.

"Hey!" Ferrin was between them in one swift move.

"What exactly, pray tell, are you doing here?" Rhi demanded, his tone more exasperated than angry.

"Breathe, Highness. I assure you I was *not* the seducer," Lukas said.

Ferrin glared at him, eyes narrowed. Did I not just hold your hair back while you hurled up the contents of your stomach? she telepathically communicated to him.

He raised an eyebrow, almost in a challenge.

"Not. Helping." She set her jaw.

"Nothing happened, I swear," Lukas finally admitted, palms raised.

Ferrin frowned. "Not that it would be any of your concern."

Rhi rubbed his face with his palm, looking exhausted. "Right then." He paced to the pile of Ferrin's dress and underthings on the floor and gestured expectantly at it. "Do either of you care to explain this to me?"

Ferrin shared a look with Lukas and knew instantly that he didn't want to tell Rhi what had happened the night before. She wasn't even sure how much of it *he* remembered.

"None of your bloody business," Ferrin crossed her arms, glaring at her brother.

Rhi looked like he was deciding whether or not to say anything, but must have realized it would be futile because he threw his hands up in concession. "Fine, fine. You're right! I'll just go," he said, his voice a touch sour. "Enjoy your morning."

As soon as the door closed, Lukas collapsed again, catching himself half on the table and half on Ferrin.

"Oh—let's get you back into bed."

"Thank you," he gasped. "That hit me really fast." He toppled onto the mattress.

"You're feeling… better?" She eyed the sick bucket, which was now empty. Clearly, he'd gotten up earlier to wash it out.

"For a little bit." He shifted onto an elbow to face her. It looked like he had washed his face too, and maybe even run a comb through his hair before tying it back. "I'm not opposed to waking up to a lady in my bed, especially one wearing my shirt, but somehow I think the circumstances that led us here were not of the enjoyable kind."

"I see you're feeling more yourself," Ferrin responded wryly. "How much do you remember?"

"Bits and pieces…" He shook his head. "Thank you for bringing me back here."

"What happened out there last night, Lukas?" she asked.

He sighed. "I don't know."

She fixed her attention on him. "You're not getting out of it that easily."

He groaned and sat up. "I was sitting in the pub waiting for the damn prison wagon to leave so I could track it and ambush it, and then suddenly I lost time and started seeing…" He shook his head, eyes distant. "…things."

"Wait, hold on. What prison wagon?"

He leaned forward and put his elbows on his knees. "The queen figured out what I was doing and took me off the squad. She replaced me with about two dozen of her personal guards."

Ferrin inhaled sharply.

"I warned a few houses, but not enough."

"So someone must have known you planned to thwart them when they left, and drugged you to put you out of commission."

"Maybe, but who could know?" He shook his head, bewildered.

"I've got a guess." Ferrin said. "Nerena tried to force your hand, then she made sure you couldn't remedy it." She bit her lip, and cursed. "She could be puppeteering this whole damn kingdom."

"Well, whoever it is, it doesn't matter anymore. Dozens of innocent villagers were sent into what is essentially slavery. They'll die up there, Ferrin."

"It's that awful?" Ferrin asked, raising a hand to her mouth. She'd never seen Danvery Prison.

"It's bad," Lukas nodded. "It's a death sentence, drawn out over weeks or years."

"Maybe…. maybe not. Not if we do something about it." She raised her gaze to meet his.

"What are you saying?"

"I'm saying, if you still want to prevent all of those deaths, it's not too late," she postured. "Get some rest, Lukas. I'll be back by sundown."

CHAPTER TWENTY-FOUR

There was no way she was getting caught this time.

Ferrin sighed, and blinked the tiredness from her eyes as she wrapped the black cloth over the lower half of her face, knotted it, and yanked it down around her neck. The early morning rush was in full swing, and after last time, she couldn't have anyone placing her near the king's chambers. Not when some important documents were about to go missing.

The old faded-black coat was another hand-me-down from Rhi, and though it had been made for him when he was thirteen, it fit her splendidly at nineteen. She strapped onto her belt two knives that she'd acquired from the blacksmith's shop in town, and slid a third into the sheath she'd sewn into her boot. With her hair tied back with a ribbon and her hat lowered, she was almost unrecognizable as the princess.

No one seemed to pay her much mind as she strode boldly through the castle; she walked tall past chambermaids and sentries alike. When she reached the section of hallway with the servant's quarters she intended to use, she surveyed the entire area. When no one was nearby, she opened the door and popped inside.

The walk down to town was startlingly mundane, given everything that had transpired in the last two days alone.

There she was, on her way to commit treason, stolen documents on her person, innocent townsfolk being imprisoned, and yet the sun was shining dully through the sparse clouds, wind moving the tree branches gently to-and-fro in some forgotten dance of old, and to top it off, wildflowers had begun to spring out of the ground everywhere she looked. It made her want to fall off the side of the road and take a little doze among the blossoms, and let the mid-afternoon light wash over her with its buttery gold warmth.

The old brick house on the corner street was shuttered as usual, the heavy wooden door locked and barred. If only she'd been let in on the secret knock. Stupid Grey.

"Um…" she puzzled a moment, her brow crinkling. She hadn't thought this part through. She knew the door and lock were reinforced, so there was no way she could bust it open, she didn't know of any spare keys, and there was no time to figure out if it was a lock she could pick (she'd never had the patience for that skill, truthfully), so she settled for knocking. "Hello!" She rapped on the door. "It's Ferrin!"

No answer.

"I need your help with something!" she hissed through the door.

After trying and failing several times to get the attention of whomever was in there, she backed away from the door. She saw no first-floor windows that weren't boarded and shuttered. She paced up the block, then back, glancing for some opening, but there was nothing.

She let out a sigh and peered up. There were a few windows on the third floor that looked open, or at least not boarded up. She grunted and double-checked no one was out on the street before she began trying to climb the brick wall.

She barely made it four feet before she slipped, nearly re-injuring her ankle. Her fingers burned and stung, stripped raw from the abrasive brick she'd clawed at. A tiny river of blood ran down her hand, pooling with the sweat in her palm and staining the metal of her ring.

She let out another groan, this time at her own stupidity, and backed away from the building ten, twenty, thirty paces, glancing around to see if there were any onlookers. Shaking her head, she broke out into a sprint straight at the building and leapt into the air, letting the wind catch her as she bent it to her will. She was master of the air currents around her, and her heart leapt into her throat as she shot into the sky.

She didn't think she'd ever get used to that rush.

Flitting up to the window on the third floor, she took a deep breath. Of course it was locked. She would have been completely screwed if she had managed to climb up there. She drew backwards and launched herself at it, feet first, shattering the window panes as she tumbled through. When she landed inside, surrounded by broken glass, she was face to face with the barrel of a pistol.

Hands raised, she stood slowly in surrender. "I'm here to talk to Helene. I don't know the secret knock but I've been here before. To help," she explained in an even tone.

The man was masked, tall, and solid. "Someone should have told you about the drop spot." He inched closer. His voice sounded augmented, like he was trying to disguise it to sound more intimidating.

"I-I don't know about that."

"We have orders to shoot anyone who breeches security, at our own discretion," he said menacingly.

"No, please don't do that," Ferrin said, swallowing. "I'm not here to cause trouble, I swear."

"Maybe we should interrogate you."

"You can bind my hands and bring me to Helene," she suggested, though the idea did not sit well with her.

"Find out who you're working for, what you're after, how in the name of Strata you got in through the third floor window…" he listed.

"Listen, please, I'll tell you whatever you'd like to know. Honest." She gulped, eyes fixed on the gun.

"Find out what weapons you have, any other information…" he continued. "Oh, and maybe find out why you haven't been coming to stable duties for the last two days."

"Please I swear, I'm not—wait, what?"

The gun was lowered, and a scarred, calloused hand reached up and pulled off the mask concealing his face. Ferrin was greeted by Alick's familiar grin, salt and pepper hair and trimmed beard.

"Alick!" Ferrin gasped, clapping her hands over her mouth. "What are you doing here?"

"What do you think?"

"Gods, I really thought you were about to shoot me," she laughed with relief as he pulled her into a hug.

"Nah, I just wanted to scare you a bit," he said in his own voice.

"Is Helene here? I really do need to talk to her."

"Follow me," Alick chuckled, clapping her on the shoulder.

"So, do you live here?"

"No, no. I live up in the grounds-cabin by the stables," he said.

"Ah," Ferrin nodded. "I take it you've been here for a few of my visits, then?"

"Aye," he nodded. "It was hard not to just go on and welcome you, but we have to be careful, especially those of us who work in the castle."

"I can't believe this—well, I can, but I'm a little taken aback."

"I take it you learned what you needed about your ring? Given your entrance back there," he smirked.

"I did," Ferrin admitted. "How did you know about it?"

"How do you think? Your mother was my—one of my best friends. She told me all about it. She discovered it when she was younger."

"How?"

"Her, Lenore and I were on the palace wall one night, and of course we'd snuck some really horrid cinnamon-whiskey out there, and she stumbled off the wall. Stopped mid-air, just, floating."

"Huh." They continued down the stairs to the office. "Why on earth would she leave it behind?"

A flicker of sadness crossed Alick's face. "Your mother was a woman of many mysteries, Ferrin."

Helene's office door flew open. The captain stood, surprised. "Ferrin, I didn't expect to see you back here so soon."

"Yeah," she raised her eyebrows. "There's something happening you need to know about, and I'm wondering if you will lend me a few people to stop it before it gets worse. If you don't already have a plan to stop it—"

"I don't make a habit of sending off people and resources with civilians as their leader." She raised her chin. "But go on."

"The queen has rounded up most of the poor in the Caelish quarter and ransacked the village." Ferrin dropped into the chair.

"Yes, I know this. I pass through there nearly every day."

"Right, well, I know where they're taking them." She leaned forward in her seat.

"Yes, to Danvery Prison, up north," Helene said, still scrawling away in her notes.

"To be labored to death and interrogated," Ferrin emphasized.

Helene shut the book, saying nothing.

"So, I assume you have a plan to rescue them? Let me help."

"At the risk of sounding truly heartless, it can't be our top priority. I've sent a message to Port Galan and if they see fit, they will do something about it. They're closer."

"But we could get them out, add some of them to our numbers," Ferrin said, straightening in her chair.

Helene sighed with exhaustion, sliding the book back into its drawer. "Ferrin, if we rush that prison, guns blazing, and manage to get all of those people out, we are risking exposure, we risk leaving the safe house inadequately guarded, and we risk losing our agents in the castle. That's a lot more lives at risk for a rescue that's not even sure to work. I already have four agents who were compromised and have to flee the city tonight. Besides, even if we could accomplish it, without all of those things happening, then what?"

Ferrin's stomach dropped. Helene usually had such… such will to triumph. Zest, even.

"I have a plan, I have maps and I have the layout of the prison." Ferrin stood from her chair. "Hear me out."

"We are on the brink," Helene blew out a long breath, "of a great shift in power. Now, it could go one of three ways, and I worry our grasp is slipping. I cannot spare the men for this, I cannot spare the resources and energy. I wish that wasn't the case. But this is what happens. I am responsible for those under my command here, and this is a hard choice I must make."

"I'd only need a few," Ferrin said, almost pleading.

"I'm sorry, I can't." Helene put her head in her hands for a moment. She really did look exhausted.

"Alright," Ferrin nodded, resigned that this was not the way. She stood and left to find Alick.

Alick didn't have the information she needed, but he walked her up to the castle and told her a story about when he and her mother were young and had picked all the beach plums that had rotted in the dunes of Avaree and stuffed them into the Lundi delegation's boots. Ferrin was starting to wonder if her mother and Alick had perhaps been childhood sweethearts.

When they reached the grounds, she stopped him. "Wait. I won't be at stable duties for a while. A few days, maybe."

"I see. Everything alright?" he asked, giving her fading bruises a once-over.

"Hopefully. Also, don't drink anything that you didn't pour yourself."

He frowned. "I won't."

"Right, thanks," she said, then lurched forward and tackled him in a bear hug before turning to go and search for Soviel. "I'll see you soon!"

She ducked into the castle and ran to Soviel's room. The stolen documents were still burning a hole in her pocket, and she wondered how long it would be until someone discovered they were missing. Time was of the essence.

"Soviel!" She knocked on the door repeatedly until her fist hurt.

The door flew open. "Good gods, Ferrin."

Soviel looked worn out. Her skin had dulled, her eyes had dark circles under them, and even her hair was a mess.

"Whoa, are you alright?" asked Ferrin, her eyes widening. "You look exhausted." Soviel usually managed to look put together, glowing even when she was covered in blood or vomit.

"Thanks," Soviel pursed her lips drily. "It's been a rough week."

"Sorry," Ferrin winced. "You just looked tired. What's going on?"

"The infirmary has been a hellhouse, among other things." She stepped aside, silently inviting Ferrin in.

Even her room was messy. Books and papers littered the desk, a few empty mugs were strewn about. Ferrin could swear even her collection of potted plants looked tired, drooping as if they were giving her their all.

"Do you need anything?"

"No, I probably just need to eat. Dinner is soon," she said. "What can I do for you? Seemed urgent when you were trying to batter through my door."

"Sorry about that," Ferrin smirked. "I need to know which agents were compromised, which ones are set to flee the castle tonight."

"Anything else?" asked Soviel.

"Yes, what kind of bribery might suit them."

PART
FOUR

CHAPTER TWENTY-FIVE

Soviel was having an awful week. In the wee hours of the morning, she'd woken in the alley surrounded by rubble and ash and the smoking remains of last night's raid on the town. A lump had formed on the back of her head.

She'd crawled to a nearby tree and clung to it as she healed herself, but the headache had not fully disappeared. Maybe it had something to do with exerting herself a few days prior. Maybe it had something to do with whatever was sapping the energy of every little plant in her room.

She wasn't sure what exactly Nimhe's involvement was, as she hadn't *seen* her dose the food. It was still possible she was merely a pawn, blind to the fact that she was instrumental in the destruction of so many lives.

Soviel doubted it, though.

"I'll have the names for you in a few hours," Soviel had agreed to Ferrin's request.

Gods knew what those people were destined for at that prison up north.

"Before you go, though," she'd said, "when you asked if it was me who'd gone through your desk, can you remember what was missing? What was out of place?"

Ferrin had puzzled. "Well… nothing was missing, actually. Things were just torn apart. My jewelry box was open and a mess, and an important book had clearly been rifled through."

"Your jewelry box?"

"Yes."

"All those expensive jewels, and not one thing was missing?"

"Well… no."

Soviel paced, pondering this conversation. A thief would have snatched a handful of gems and been a rich fellow. The motive had to be something else.

"Does Nimhe know you won't be here for a few days?" Soviel had asked.

"I sent her a note."

Soviel now lay in wait in Ferrin's rooms. The curtains were closed, the lanterns were doused. She sat on the stool across the room from the vanity, tucked in the corner in the dark, waiting.

It was only an hour before the door slowly creaked open, a ray of light piercing the dark as Nimhe slinked in.

*　　*　　*

The two of them were settled across the kitchen table from each other in Lukas's woodland cottage. Coarse rain had begun to fall in sheets outside, and had made apparent a leak in the roof. The silence was punctuated by the periodic *drip, drip, drip* of water falling into a soup pan.

Ferrin shifted nervously. She'd gone against Helene's orders, bribing three agents into delaying their journeys to the continent in order to help with the mission. Lukas had recruited Ryder, and Ferrin had found three of the four agents who were leaving anyway. Soviel had helped her track them down and set up a meeting point. All she knew was that they were Caelish Resistance soldiers with experience in clandestine operations.

She had a plan. She just hoped it would work. And she'd deal with Helene's wrath when she returned.

It was a two-day ride to the Northern Prison, and she'd only been able to smuggle so much food out of the kitchen. The loaves of bread and blocks of cheese would have to be enough for the six of them until they found a place to stop.

The road would be mud-slick from the rain, and chilly too, and she hoped the extra pair of wool socks she'd tucked into her pack would suffice.

"The rain, at least, should give us some cover getting out of the castle tonight," she said to Lukas.

The color had returned to his face, but the ghost of grimness from last night still clung to his edges.

"How are you feeling?" she asked carefully. Whatever had happened, he'd seen something that had left him shaken. And he probably had somewhat of a hangover, too.

"I'm fine," he shrugged, laying out various weaponry on the table.

"That's a shit answer and you know it," she crossed her arms.

"Listen, Ferrin. Things got out of hand. I'll be alright, it was the *popava* making me see things."

"What kind of things, Lukas?" she asked gently.

"Things better off left buried."

"Lukas."

"Thank you," he exhaled deeply, "for making sure I didn't hallucinate myself off a cliff."

"I wasn't—" she shook her head. Did he think she was fishing for gratitude? "I just wanted you to know you could talk to me about it. If you want to."

"There isn't much to say, and in truth I don't remember a lot of it. All I have now are flashes." He shook his head and stepped around the table to her side. "Now, let's see," he said, picking up a set of pistols and turning to her. "What sort of experience do you have?"

She looked from the guns up to his face, arching an eyebrow playfully.

Clearing his throat nervously, he clarified, "with weapons."

"I'm alright with these," she said, taking one of the pistols from him, "and I'm a great shot with a rifle, but my swordplay isn't the strongest." She took the other pistol from his hand and the belt holster with it, and began strapping them on, lifting her eyes to his when she was finished.

"Take your pick, Princess," he offered, sweeping a hand over the table.

"Quite the collection you've got here," she complimented, as she walked the length of the table.

"I can't say no to good steel."

She smirked over her shoulder at him. "I see that. Dethos craftsmanship?" she asked, holding up a cutlass.

"Let me guess. You pilfered something of similar make once?"

"Something like that." Zare's favored sword had been of the same style—hammered metal grip guard, enamel work on the hilt and carved silver on the pommel. She set it back down and finished her circuit around the table, plucking up a few things: a long knife far superior to the one she kept beneath her bed, a short sword, and a rifle for her back.

Lukas had already begun buckling and strapping various weaponry to his person, and halted when he saw she was done.

"Oh. Here." He reached into the inner pocket of his coat.

"What is it?" She stepped closer, frowning.

"Boot-knife," he said with a grunt as he dropped to a knee in front of her.

She was surprised, and leaned back into the table on her palms when she felt his hand wrap around the back of her calf and nudge it towards him.

"You'll be glad to have this," he said, his hand on the back of her knee where her boot ended, tucking the sheathed knife into the space between her wool stocking and the stiff leather, "should we be caught." He stood.

They were inches apart, the table at her back, warmth radiating from where he stood in front of her.

"Thanks," she breathed.

"Don't mention it."

She swallowed, nodding.

His gaze dipped downwards to her bandaged knuckles. "What happened here?" he asked, frowning as he took her hand. Her knuckles had been skinned raw when she'd clawed her way out of the ground the night before.

His touch was at once rough and gentle as he turned her hand over, his thumb against her palm. When she looked up at him, his eyes were fixed on where their hands met. Slowly, he raised his head, his sea-green eyes burning into her own from beneath his thick, dark lashes.

Her breath hitched as his hand moved up her wrist, his thumb running over her thieve's brand. She let her attention drop to his mouth for a fraction of a second, something low in her belly heating and curling like a hungry, lazy dragon. She could see the hesitation in his darkening gaze, could feel him warring with himself as she drew a shaky breath.

The door banged open. "I brought jerky!" Ryder, presumably.

He dropped her hand.

The big man she'd seen that day in the Pit strode into the room. He looked between them, clearly picking up that he'd interrupted something, and sheepishly tossed a sack of dried, smoked meats onto the table. "That'll last us a while."

"Thanks," Ferrin said a little too cheerfully.

"So," Lukas cleared his throat, "where are we meeting the others?"

"Out past the gates. We're to pin these on our coats to identify ourselves; they'll have the same." She took three green, felted leaves from her pocket.

"Great, proof of treason," Lukas joked.

"You sure you know what you're doing?" Ryder asked Ferrin.

"Yes," she lied.

"Great, well we'd better pack up the horses."

Soviel let Nimhe rifle around in Ferrin's vanity table for a few minutes before she spoke.

"Looking for something, Nimhe?"

Nimhe started violently, jumping back.

"Soviel, I..."

"I know what you're doing."

"I was only looking to straighten up Her High—"

"Save your lies." Soviel stood, slowly drawing back the curtain to let the light flood in. "What are you looking for, and for what purpose?"

"I'm not looking for anything," the girl gulped nervously.

"I saw you, last night. Poisoning all of those people. Why, Nimhe? Why would you help them drive your own people out like that?"

"You don't understand, Sov."

"Don't I?"

"Please," Nimhe bit her lip. "I had no choice. I had to do it. For my family."

"Your family is banished! By the very people seeking to imprison all those villagers!"

"My family has nothing! They are forced to reside in a foreign country with no help, with no prospects!"

"How can you use that as an excuse to do the same to other people, to other *families*?" Soviel gritted her teeth, stepping towards Nimhe.

"Soviel, please," Nimhe pleaded, backing away. Terror had crept into her eyes and voice.

"The one thing I don't understand is the *popava*. Why? Why dose people with a strain that drives them mad, only to throw them into a prison?"

Nimhe shook her head, choking down what might have been a sob. "I can't—I can't say."

"You're coming with me," Soviel stated, stepping closer, keeping her tone as even as she could manage. "You have done such *unspeakable* harm, I don't imagine my colleagues are going to be terribly understanding of your plight."

"I'm not going anywhere," Nimhe declared, backing towards the curtains.

"You don't have a choice," Soviel let a steel edge slip into her voice as she reached for Nimhe's wrist.

The girl jerked back, faster than Soviel expected her to. In an instant, she'd pulled a pistol from beneath her cloak and pointed it at Soviel's head.

"I don't want to hurt you. In fact, I rather like you, but if you don't let me leave, I *will* shoot you," Nimhe promised, her voice steady even as her hands shook.

Soviel stilled, her eyes wide and fixed on Nimhe and her weapon. Nimhe backed one step towards the window, and used one hand to push it open. "I'm sorry it has to be this way, Soviel," Nimhe whispered, backing towards the window, weapon still trained on Soviel. "But I will do *anything* to bring my family home. Even if it means ruining myself. Now back up, against the wall, and turn around."

"You're *despicable*," Soviel seethed, backing towards the far wall. "Your parents would be disgusted if they knew what you'd done."

"Turn." Nimhe cocked the gun.

Fury swirled and eddied beneath Soviel's skin as she obeyed the command. "You're going to rot for this, Nimhe. You're a traitor."

"Goodbye, Soviel. I don't expect I'll be seeing you again."

In one swift movement, Nimhe was out the window. Soviel rushed to the balcony, but she was nowhere to be seen.

CHAPTER TWENTY-SIX

Rhi had nearly sawed his plate in half trying to cut through the tough steak that had been prepared for the evening. Whether it was because the meat was so overcooked or because he had buried an odd resentment at his sister and friend for whatever it was he'd stumbled into that morning, he wasn't sure. He didn't covet Lukas, nor did he think Ferrin too good for him, but the idea of them entangling set him on edge.

He had a vague, unrelenting sense of plummeting through a chasm with nothing to catch him and nothing to grab onto. The seed of fear that had been planted since Ferrin had returned was beginning to sprout. She'd leave again, he was sure of it. It was what happened with everyone in his life.

"Well, boy," said his father, who sat beside him. "What say you about the new servants?"

He was in his father's private dining chambers with a few businessmen. Despite his recent disruption, it seemed Rhi had fallen back into his father's good graces. For now.

"What about them?" Rhi asked.

"I was just explaining to Duke Edding here that we have acquired several dozen new indentures from the Veira. Conflicts in the Sunda region have been increasing." He paused to sip from his wine. "And at half the usual rate."

"Conflicts?"

"Oh, a little farmer's rebellion that's turned into quite the destabilizing skirmish," Duke Edding chuckled. Rhi wondered if his toupé was from a horse or if it was indeed human hair.

"I didn't know about that," he admitted.

"Well, it's certainly continued to work in our favor," his father wiped his mouth with a napkin as he spoke. "Which is why we are in no rush to have our stationed troops take further action just yet."

"We have troops in Veira still?" Rhi asked with surprise.

"Why wouldn't we?"

"I thought we recalled them when the trade line was severed."

"We recalled most of them. But some important officials of commissary have remained, along with some backup. They remain to keep the production flow of arimopo steady. In time, perhaps we won't need those stingy Efelian bastards as middlemen."

Rhi paused, fork halfway to his mouth. "How so?"

"Incentive protection, one might say," Duke Edding interjected.

Rhi set down his fork. "That sounds a bit like forced labor, which, if I am not mistaken," he looked directly at the king, "you have explicitly expressed disgust for, Father."

"Don't be ridiculous, Rhiach."

"Then explain it to me. Are our soldiers there protecting farmers? Intervening when skirmishes break out? It doesn't sound like it. How is that any different than exploiting poor Barrian farmers to work for free?"

"Have your bruises faded too quickly? You are here to learn, and if you can't do that, then you are to keep your mouth shut," the king snapped.

Nerena arrived, sweeping through the door and settling into the seat across from Rhi with calculated grace.

"Well, Father?" Rhi clenched his fists. "I'm trying my best to learn." It felt good to be defiant. The bruises hadn't faded but he wondered if this feeling of heart-pattering boldness was what kept Ferrin sane in the face of all this.

"You were a much better heir when you were addled and high," his father muttered.

The words stung, wrapping tendrils around Rhi's chest, sinking in like barbs. He fought to formulate a reply, but his mouth had gone dry. He hadn't thought that his father even knew about the popava incident. A lump was growing in his throat like a demon growing in his body.

"Nimhe, dear, why don't you pour some more wine for the prince?" Nerena nodded to the red-haired girl who had followed her in. With no effort to conceal her actions, Nimhe poured red wine into Rhi's cup and then emptied some reddish powder into it. It dissolved instantly.

It was a substance he was all too familiar with. "What the hell is this?" he demanded, beginning to stand. Suddenly, strong hands were on his shoulders, forcing him back down into his seat.

"Ah-ah-ah," Nerena scolded, her voice icy as her manservant clapped his hand over Rhi's shoulder.

"Father?"

The king shrugged. He'd turned back to his conversation with the Duke. What was happening?

"Drink up."

"You won't kill me, you can't." Rhi shook his head, more to convince himself than Nerena.

"Oh, but I can certainly have Mister Drake here ruin your arm permanently. How would it feel to be crippled for the remainder of your life?"

A blade pressed against his shoulder, the cold steel of the flat side chilling his skin even through the layers of his clothing.

"Why?" he pleaded, knowing full well what he was going to choose.

"All in good time," she said, pushing the glass toward him.

His hands trembled as he reached for the glass and lifted it to his lips.

"Please," he breathed faintly with his last shred of dignity.

"Empty the glass," Nerena ordered calmly.

He closed his eyes and obeyed, downing the cup and letting the sweet poison seep into his veins. When he opened his eyes, everything was fine.

It came on fast. First, the beautiful calm, the content feeling that all was well and always would be. He tried to remember why he'd been so against this, but couldn't seem to care. The steel at his shoulder was relinquished and he stared in a daze as the man sheathed the knife.

His food was still wholly unappetizing, and he felt himself growing tired as the conversation carried on without him. His chair felt strange.

The tired phase hit him like a ton of bricks and he heaved a deep breath, trying to fight the call of sleep. Then, as if he had dozed off for a moment, and snapped awake, the room instantly changed, moving like mercury on a summer day. It was silver and swelling and changing before his eyes. Time slipped like sand through his fingers.

The king's crown was made of bones.

He looked across the table at Nerena to see if she noticed it too, but he couldn't quite make out her face, as if a fog had descended into the room. One moment she was cool and beautiful and the next, half her face was being picked clean by maggots and worms.

Rhi started, blinking the fog from his eyes. Her skin was ancient like a crone's, but the maggots were gone. He blinked again and she was back to her polished, youthful self. His pulse quickened, or at least tried to. He could hear it drumming in his ears. Could they not hear it?

Nerena smiled and blood poured through her teeth like juice.

Rhi scrambling backward out of his seat, the chair falling over.

"Sit down, you wreck," the sheep-headed man in the crown said. His eyes were yellowed, his golden-ringed hands covered in dust.

"I h-have to get out of here," Rhi gasped. He stumbled, nearly falling over a chair as he sprinted from the room. His heart raced as he staggered through the hallway. Servants ignored him, a portrait glared at him with glowing, red eyes full of inherited sins. He ran.

He found himself passing Ferrin's room and stopped. She could help him. She'd be furious he'd risked the drug again, but she'd help him. He burst through her unlocked door, and found the room empty. That's when he remembered she had mentioned leaving for a few days. He let out a guttural sigh of defeat.

At least the room was empty and cool. No dead queens to drip blood down his throat. Rhi leaned back against the closed door and sank to the carpet, panting to catch his breath.

"Silly little Rhi," said a voice. A voice he'd longed to hear for so many years. "I see you're still here, unmoving, feeble and ineffective. Pathetic." His mother's voice was harsh and abrasive as he pressed the heels of his hands to his ears. "You may truly never amount to anything. You just sit idly by and let things happen." Her spectral voice floated through the room.

"No, no, no." He squeezed his eyes shut, trying to blink away the bad trip. This was some new pocket of hell that had swallowed him whole.

"It's no wonder everyone leaves you, when you're so desperate for attention, clinging to them like a needy little child." This was Lukas's voice. He'd appeared on the bed, daring to take up all the space he could with his easy, intimidating form.

"Even I had the guts to run away from here, and I was barely more than a child," Ferrin snarked as she lounged at the foot of the bed, idly picking her nails. "Mother always knew I was the strong one."

"No, no," Rhi's breathing was becoming more and more shallow.

"You couldn't even keep me around," laughed the lanky blond man who had materialized. He was just as Rhi remembered him. His face sweet and handsome. "I was a poor, titleless nobody, and you couldn't even get me to stick around with all you had to offer. You're useless. Worthless."

"*Please*," Rhi begged, praying some god would take pity on him and render him unconscious.

"Please *what* Rhiach?" the voices blended together.

"Leave me alone," he cried.

"Isn't that what you're so afraid of?"

"Please, not you. Not you. Not you," he squeezed his eyes shut again, shrinking towards the wall.

"You were not worthy of me, and everyone knew it," continued the blond man. His first love, the one that had ended in bloodshed. "Even your own mother."

"I wouldn't wish the burden of being married to you on anyone," Arabella said, sitting beside her daughter at the foot of the bed.

Ferrin flipped her hair over her shoulder. "He can barely stand up for himself, let alone others. What a dreadful king he'll be. Spineless and whining. Worse than his father."

"Useless."

"Unworthy."

"Pitiful."

"A waste of space."

"Pathetic."

"Child."

"Weak."

The voices came faster and faster, more and more ghosts of his past appearing until the words became jumbled and inhuman.

Stop, stop, stop, he pleaded silently. It was no use, they kept coming, throwing every awful thing he'd ever thought or said about himself back in his face, chanting his shortcomings until he curled his fists around his head and sunk into the wall, covering his ears and begging for it to end.

CHAPTER TWENTY-SEVEN

The band of six had been riding for a few hours when the rain started coming down in sheets. The gentle summer shower that had been comforting and almost pleasant, if a little cold, had transformed instantaneously into a violent dousing.

Ferrin was wet down to her toes, her hair sticking to her face through the hood of her soaking cloak. On top of that, her several sleepless nights were beginning to weigh on her. She could feel in her throat that she was going to fall ill soon if she didn't get warm.

The three rebel agents had met them beyond the gates, safely out of sight and just before dawn. Ferrin had paid them up front, since regardless of how things went, they would not be returning south.

Hatra was a linguist of Akhatan descent, and she spoke at least seven languages, from what Ferrin had gathered. She was in her late twenties with long dark hair and maple-brown skin. She and Lukas had been chatting back and forth in their native tongue for a while.

Petir was a rosy-cheeked man with a clear and pleasing tenor voice. His light blond hair and pale complexion reminded Ferrin of Soviel's. Though he was in his thirties, he couldn't grow a beard. But in spite of his baby-facedness, he was broad-shouldered and nearly as bulky as Lukas's friend, Ryder.

Akachi, the third agent Soviel had been able to contact, was known for his stealth. He could slyfoot and walk silent as a ghost with preternatural grace, despite the fact that he was as tall as a tree. He had a peaceful face, dark brown skin and short-cropped black hair. His parents were from western Dromata, but had emigrated to northern Lindbarrow just before he was born thirty-something years ago. He spoke in an even tone about the mission as he rode next to Ferrin.

"And how many prisoners are we expecting to extract?" he asked.

"Lukas thinks they took in around twenty or thirty," Ferrin said. "But it could be more."

He nodded contemplatively. "Captain Wilcoe really has no idea about this mission?"

"Not if I can help it," Ferrin winced. "She wasn't exactly amenable to the idea of spending resources on a prison break."

"Lucky you had Soviel to track us down. She is quite wise for her age," he stated.

"She is, and full of surprises, too."

"You really think we can pull off this plan of yours with only six of us?" he asked.

"Yes, I do think so," she nodded, not feeling nearly as certain as she sounded. "I'll lay it all out in detail when we stop for the night."

"Think we ought to be doing that soon?" Akachi suggested, squinting up into the gloom. "Dry our clothes before it's too late and we all catch sickness from the damn cold?"

"I couldn't agree more," Ferrin nodded, pulling her cloak more tightly around her shoulders.

"If we're stopping soon," Petir rode up beside them and offered, "I grew up a few towns over and I know a little inn. We should reach it about a mile up the road."

"That works for me," Ferrin said, wiggling her numb toes.

"Ferrin was just saying how she'll be going over the plan in detail when we stop," Akachi explained to Petir.

"I think we'll be needing hot soup and a blazing fire to dry out our socks first," Petir said.

"I think you're right. Soup sounds good," Ferrin agreed, her eyes unintentionally drifting to where Lukas and Hatra rode ahead, deep in conversation in a language she barely understood.

"Don't fret, she's married," Petir leaned in, his voice low and conspiratorial.

"I wasn't—never mind."

"I'd be envious too, if he were mine," Petir winked.

Ferrin's cheeks heated. "He's not mine," she frowned. "He's…"

Petir waited expectantly.

She let out a frustrated sigh. "You can't own someone emotionally." Then she shook her head dismissively. "And we're not together, if that's what you're suggesting."

"Why not?"

"You're serious?"

He nodded.

"I only recently got out of a prior, uh, engagement, I guess you'd call it," she shared awkwardly.

"Captain Zare?" Petir tilted his head.

"Storm-steeds," she cursed. "How does everyone know about it?"

Petir smiled at Ferrin's discomfort. "Wilcoe is head of intelligence for the southern half of the isle. There's not much she doesn't know. She started looking into Gillian and Zare a while back as potential allies. You confirmed yourself to be Gillian, so the jump isn't that difficult to make."

Ferrin shuddered. Whether or not the cause was just, her life and secrets had been pried open and poked at. She felt stripped bare, studied like a dissected specimen.

The rain seemed to become heavier and heavier as they continued north, and all conversation fizzled out with each crack of thunder in the distance. Finally, they reached the inn. To say the tavern was at the center of a town would be an overstatement, but the building was surrounded by a few others. A settlement, really. The tavern was the largest of the buildings, with a small stable attached to it, and a big, peeling sign that read: TAVERN AND ROOMS in fading red letters.

Petir led the way to the hitching post. It was only a little after dusk, but the thick clouds and rainstorm had caused the dark to fall early. "Used to stay here on intel runs between Avaree and the capital. The old bar keep was," he trailed off with a small smile. "I hope he still tends the tavern here."

"How are you faring?" Lukas said as Ferrin pulled up next to him. "You look—"

"Like a wet rat?"

"I was going to say cold, but now that you say it…" he teased.

"I'm alright. How's your head?"

He'd told her earlier that it was pounding, some remnant of the dusted popava in his system giving him a headache.

"It's faded to a dull ache," he reassured her. "Hatra and I have been discussing the homeland. She lived in Khalim for a while too."

"Oh, really? Did you ever cross paths?"

He shook his head, "Nah. It's a big city. She was nearer to where my sister's husband's estate is, further south along the Naz. I grew up in the slums, downstream. Besides, she only lived there a short while."

"Even so, Khalim sounds very warm, very dry, and very appealing right now," Ferrin said, imagining the golden sands, hot sun and dry air as she tied her horse to the post. Her fingers trembled, her gloves soaked through with rainwater.

Lukas grabbed her hand in his, peeling off her glove. "You're freezing," he said, feeling her fingers.

"Yeah," she admitted, looking up at him, a little surprised. "We'll be inside soon though."

"Here, you go in and pay for the room and get everyone some food. I'll take care of your horse."

She clutched the reins in her stubborn, shivering fingers.

"You're going to get sick if you don't warm up, Ferrin," he insisted "Go on. The faster we get hot meals, the faster we all warm up."

"Fine," she nodded, her teeth now chattering. Reluctantly, she passed him the reins and retrieved her coin purse before heading inside.

The tavern was a dull rumble compared to the exhilarating chaos of the underground Caelish Witch back in Everness. Lanterns cast a warm glow on weary travelers camped around the oblong bar in the center of the vast room. A fire crackled in the big hearth, and more than a few wet coats hung along hooks to dry by the fire. Smoke rolled out of pipes in slow, lazy curls, like beasts awakening from deep slumber in dark caves.

A handsome man tended the bar. His arms were tattooed with organic, vine-like scrolling lines and blooming flowers, revealed by the elegantly folded-up sleeves of his pale green shirt, which he wore underneath an off-black waistcoat. His dark hair was cropped shorter than was in fashion, and was nearly shorn on the sides, revealing a row of silver earrings running up the curve of his ear. He had tan skin and thick lashes, accented by a neat line of black over the edge of each eyelid, and the sculpted bone structure of a sun-god.

He looked up from the glass he was polishing to meet Ferrin's eye as she approached the bar. "And what can I do for you, love?" He raised a brow, eyeing her unkempt appearance.

"Hi," she greeted, pushing a strand of wet hair out of her face. "How many rooms are available?"

"Only one left with that storm raging," he said. "Soup?"

"How did you guess?" she said wryly, sliding onto the bar stool. "I'll need six bowls and I'd like to book the room."

"Of course, anything else?"

"Not presently. My traveling companions are just tying up the horses."

"Right then," he said, setting out a big tray. He quickly, yet artfully arranged six ceramic bowls in a circle on the tray. Hefting over the big soup pot from where it warmed atop a blue wood stove, he ladled golden broth full of vegetables and shredded poultry into each bowl.

"Mind if I take it to a table?" she asked, taking out the coin purse.

"Anything s'open is just fine. Anything that's not, well that's none of my business if you want to rough someone up for a spot nearer the hearth." He glanced around at some of the rougher looking travelers, then cast her a wink.

"I'll keep that in mind. How much do I owe you?" she asked.

He grabbed a thin sheet of paper, totaled up the bill and slid it towards her. She handed him the coins, then picked up the tray, doing her best to hold it level and not spill the steaming soup all over herself as she walked to the nearest table.

Soon, the heavy door swung open, bringing with it a blustery gust of cold air as Lukas stepped in. His broad shoulders and tall form filled the doorway and attracted a few glances from the other patrons. Behind him were Hatra, then Akachi, and then Petir and Ryder, who both had to duck under the doorway because of their ridiculous heights.

Lukas dropped into the seat next to Ferrin, casting his hood off to reveal rain-slick hair that had come out of its ties, sticking to his forehead as he glanced at Ferrin.

"Soup's good," she said, as she shoveled the hot broth into her mouth. "Room's all paid for, but there was only one available."

"That'll work fine enough," Lukas said, pulling one bowl towards him. "All warmed up?"

The others had made a stop at the bar to order a round of ales and Petir was chatting up the handsome bartender.

"I'm warm," she nodded. The radiant heat from the hearth was nothing compared to the rush of fire through her as Lukas pulled her hand into his. "We should find you some dry clothes."

"We all need to dry off," she reminded him. "Here's to hoping there's a hearth in the room." She raised the bowl of soup in her free hand like it was a fine toast.

"And enough bed space," Lukas chuckled. "Something tells me Petir is a starfish sleeper."

"Something tells me Petir won't be sleeping in the room tonight," Ferrin gestured with her soup bowl. Lukas hadn't let go of her hand.

He looked toward the bar and raised his eyebrows. "I was about to get an ale, but now I don't want to interrupt them." His thumb brushed absentmindedly over her knuckles.

"He better get back over here so we can go over the plan." She took a sip from her soup.

Hatra, Ryder and Akachi joined them, each carrying an ale. Lukas released Ferrin's hand and stood, leaving her acutely aware of the cold air on her hand where their skin had touched.

"So, what's their story?" Ferrin asked the group, flicking her chin toward Petir and the bartender. She wrapped both hands around her soup bowl, relishing its warmth.

"Ah," Hatra sighed. "That is the infamous Andran. Petir's old flame, I suppose."

"Not so much an old flame as a constantly recurring flame," Akachi said through gulps of ale. "Petir talks of him often. I suspect that's why he agreed to this mission."

"He mentioned something about the two of them moving to Avaree and opening a printer's shop," Ryder added.

"That's sweet," Ferrin said.

"The man's obsessed," Akachi chuckled. "I'll swim the length of the Naz when Petir finally settles down, though."

She watched as Lukas approached the two men, ordered an ale, and said something to Petir. The two of them came back to the table, drinks in hand.

"Right, let's talk."

CHAPTER TWENTY-EIGHT

The room was cold. It was dark, and he was shivering.

His bones ached as he sat up hazily off the floor. They were gone.

They were *gone*.

"Hey, wake up!" a voice commanded. Soft white-gold hair fell around a delicate-boned face.

"Willeem?" Rhi said, eyes swimming and unfocused as he tried to take in the vague, ethereal blur above him.

"What? No, it's me. Soviel. Ferrin's lady-in-waiting. What are you doing here, Your Highness?"

"Oh, *gods*," he moaned.

"Hey!" she patted his face. "Don't pass out again. I need to know what you took."

"I didn't *take* it, it was forced down my throat at knifepoint."

"Alright," Soviel sighed, exasperated. "You'll thank me for this later. Help me out here, Your Highness." She bent to scoop under his arm, helping him to his feet.

He staggered up, standing with Soviel's help, and she dragged him to the washroom, where she dumped him unceremoniously into the tub with all of his clothes on. Seconds later, a bucket of freezing water crashed over him.

"Hey!" he cried in protest.

"Wake *up!*" she commanded.

"Why are you doing this?" Rhi asked, holding his hands up to block the next stream of water.

"I found you on the floor trembling, as if you were being haunted. What did you take?" she repeated. "What did they give you?"

"*Popava.* But it was different. I've never… never had hallucinations or… seen things like *that* before."

"It's a new strain. Or it's been dusted. I'm not sure, I have yet to get my hands on a sample. Who gave it to you?"

"The queen and my father."

Surprise passed over her face as she passed him a glass of water. "Drink up. Who else was there?"

"A Duke and Nerena's manservant. And a lady's-maid. She's the one who poured the wine and added the *popava.*"

"Which Duke?"

"Edding. He and my father were discussing how they'd schemed cheap indentures out of Veira. Exploiting instability to get free labor."

"Of course." She bit her nails, pondering. "What maid?"

"Red hair. Maeve? Nave?"

Soviel looked him in the eye. "Nimhe?"

"Maybe."

"Of *course*," she said again, as if this was some incredible revelation. "That sly little waif."

"Care to enlighten me, or were you simply planning on dousing me with more frigid bathwater?" Rhi asked, bracing his hands on the side of the tub.

She launched a towel at him, along with Ferrin's dressing robe. "Get dressed, Your Highness. We have work to do."

Ferrin explained the plan, or as much of it as she was willing to share while they were in the very public tavern. She'd shown them the rest of the floor plan once they were in the privacy of the room, the big drafting sheets laid out on the wide bed.

Parts of it were far-fetched, and part of it involved her flying up to the roof and dropping into the building's administrative section, but she hadn't explained that she wouldn't be climbing. That was the only way they could get the keys undetected. She'd had to guess at where the village prisoners were being held, and it was possible that they were spread out across multiple blocks.

She hated to admit that she'd thought through most of it as if she were Zare.

The room was small but clean enough, and had one bed that could just fit two, a dusty divan and a chest full of old wool blankets at the foot of the bed. The floor had a washroom at the end of the hall, where Hatra had gone to wash up. Akachi had gone back downstairs for a second bowl of stew, Petir had vanished with the bartender after a quick nod goodnight, and Ryder had apparently read the room and gone to 'check on the horses'.

That left Ferrin and Lukas alone with merely the sound of the crackling fire.

She sat cross-legged on the bed, fidgeting with the edge of the quilt, an anxious feeling creeping through her that had been building since she started talking through the plan out loud. A few feet away, Lukas leaned against the blanket chest, tin cup of water in hand, his hair unbound and curling from the heat of the fire as it dried.

"So, the escape route," he began. "You're sure that will work?"

Ferrin chewed her bottom lip before meeting his eyes. "I'm not *sure* about anything. But I studied those maps for hours yesterday and I think that's the best option."

Lukas set down his cup and turned to face her. "It's a good plan. It's smart."

Her cheeks flushed. In the light of the fire, he looked gilded, like an old god. "I hope so, I had to commit several crimes to get to this point and we haven't even broken into the damn place yet."

The rest of the gold she'd raided from the treasury, upon which a significant part of their plan was contingent, was heavy in her pocket. "Do you think we can trust them? With the gold, I mean."

"I think you'd know better than I, since you're the one who hired them."

She'd given Lukas the barest explanation about the spy network. He knew of its existence, but not of the safe-house, or the extent of its reach. She hadn't mentioned Soviel's involvement; it wasn't her secret to tell.

"I know. The possibility of betrayal is unnerving, though."

"I don't like it either, but I think we have to put a little faith in humanity on this one."

Ferrin's stomach tied in knots and she continued to chew her lip. Zare's betrayal still stung, and the idea of simply putting her trust in others was not something she could do lightly.

"I know," Lukas said, sitting down on the bed next to her, bumping her shoulder with his. "It's never easy."

She turned to look at him. The light in his eyes had returned since whatever harrowing vision had gripped him the night before, but he still looked weary. "Are you doing alright, after last night? I mean besides the headache," she clarified.

He frowned briefly. "It's all blurred together, the bits and pieces I remember are… well, they're not good memories, Ferrin. This stuff, whoever is engineering it, they aren't making party favors. They're making a weapon."

She nodded, pulling the blanket tighter around her shoulders. Her shirt was drying by the fire, along with her socks, breeches and boots. She wore very little beneath the blanket.

He stood, and she reached out her hand, wrapping her fingers around his wrist.

"Wait."

What are you doing?

He turned, slowly, eyes pinning her to the spot as she scoured her mind for the words. "I was… really worried for you last night, and I," she exhaled deeply. "I want—"

He tilted his head, listening expectantly.

She swallowed. "I want to make sure you're careful tomorrow."

Oh, that's brilliant.

An easy smile spread across his face. "Worried for my safety, highness?"

That familiar flirtatious game between them slid back into place. "I don't relish riding back to the capital all by my lonesome." She suddenly became very interested in smoothing every wrinkle from the quilt in front of her.

"Nonsense. You'd have Ryder. I'm sure you could discuss your shared affinity for embarrassing misspellings. Though his was on a sign for a Pit match and not a royal embroid—hey!" He ducked the pillow she chucked at him. "I would truly love to see that finished piece."

"I should have thrown it in a fire years ago." She narrowed her eyes.

His grin was impish.

"Right, what are we going to do about this sleeping situation?"

Lukas paced to the fire and picked up her shirt, rubbing the fabric between his fingers before tossing the dry garment to her. "You and Hatra should take the bed, since I don't think any other combination of our little band of giants will fit. I'll take first watch, Ryder and Akachi can spoon on the divan, or draw straws for it."

"I think either you or I should be awake at all times. Take turns, just in case." She shrugged the shirt over her head, holding the blanket around her waist like a big, drapey skirt.

"Agreed."

"Toss me my breeches?"

He gave her a scalding once over, his green eyes wildfire-bright in the hearth's glow as he reached slowly for the garment.

Ferrin was no blushing schoolgirl. She made a point of marching right up to him, blanket-skirt in hand as she took the wool pants from him. Her face was hot from the fire's proximity as she returned his look.

This was the game they played, had been playing for weeks now. Teasing, nudging towards *something* inch by inch, and waiting for the other one to yank on the reins. She stood, nearly chest to chest with him, smirk plastered on her face as she leaned in close, close enough to share breath. She tilted her head up, eyes lidded.

"Thanks for your assistance," she said with a light pat to his chest. Without another word, she brushed past him, pants slung over her shoulder as she made her way to the washroom, her blanket-dress trailing behind her like a regal, moth-bitten train.

CHAPTER TWENTY-NINE

"Let me get this straight," the prince said as he hurried along beside Soviel down the long hall. "Someone has been engineering popava, not to make it more fun, but to make it horrible. Why?"

"That's what I'm hoping to figure out—I really need to get a sample of it." Soviel's mind was racing.

"I fail to see how causing people to hallucinate all sorts of nasty things can further anyone's political agenda."

"As do I, but there's got to be more to it. Someone has most definitely been observing the outcomes of people taking this strain. Now we know who, thanks to you, but why? What is Nerena after?"

"It sounds like we actually know nothing," Rhi grumbled. "And where are you taking me?"

"The infirmary. Madame Leone may be able to help us, somehow," she said.

"Alright, alright. Must we charge down there at this insufferable pace? I'm still recovering from my harrowing experience, in case you hadn't noticed."

"Sorry," Soviel said, slowing her pace. She was wrapped up in her thoughts.

Nimhe had been working against her this whole time. Suddenly it made sense. All the little things that had gone wrong from the kitchen boy winding up dosed to her strange absences from her duty.

The infirmary wasn't busy. The gentle spring breeze lazily blew the flaps of the tent back and forth behind them as they stepped in.

"Is Madame in?" Soviel asked, spotting Branick.

"Office," he jerked his chin towards the back. "Can you come take a look at something for me first, though?"

"Of course," she agreed.

"Should I just wait here, or—" Rhi trailed off.

"Come along," she waved a hand at him.

"She came in a few hours ago," said Branick.

"Who?"

The question was answered as Branick flipped aside a privacy divider to reveal none other than Lady Denison Fairbora sitting cross-legged on a cot. Her golden curls were brushed out and un-styled, her face was clean of her usual rouge and powders, and she wore no jewelry, no fancy dress. Clad in a loose shirt and a plain blue skirt, she was almost unrecognizable from her usual, fashionable self. Soviel might not have recognized her if she hadn't known her since childhood.

"Lady Denison. Are you feeling alright after your poisoning?" She wasn't sure if anyone had told Denison exactly what had happened in the salon, or if she even remembered it clearly.

"Soviel," Denison said. "That is your name, right?"

"Yes."

"I need to get out of here."

"Out of where, Lady?"

"The castle. Everness. I can't go through with it."

"Go through with…"

"The marriage."

Soviel nodded, taking her hand and silently checking for the presence of any substances in her system.

"The things I saw, in the parlor… I know now. I have to leave. I tried standing up to my father, but he says," her voice hitched, "I must marry Lord Candris."

"Do you remember what you drank, or ate, just before?" Soviel asked gently.

Denison started to shake her head, then froze. "A cup of sherry. A servant sent it over, said it was compliments of the Lord, but—" she shook her head. "He wasn't even there that day. I have no idea where it came from."

"I see."

"Soviel, a word?" Madame Leone's voice came from the divider.

"Stay here," Soviel said to Denison. "You can hide out as long as you need. Just be careful. Keep your wits about you."

The girl nodded, biting her lip.

"Yes, Madame?"

"Come, both of you, into my office."

Soviel and Rhi followed.

"In, quickly," Leone ordered, holding the flap aside for them.

"We wanted to ask you—"

"I know why you're here, dear." Leone settled into the chair behind her desk. "And you, Your Highness, are you feeling alright?"

Rhi blanched. "I'm—"

"Give me your hand," she commanded, pulling the little potted tree on her desk towards her. "I can ease that headache for you."

"How did you—"

"Experience," she huffed.

"We're looking for—"

"Answers about this damn popava strain running rampant through the castle? As am I."

"Oh."

"Whoa," Rhi gasped, bringing a hand to his temple. "How did you—"

"Drawing the toxin out of your blood stream," Leone said, holding up the now-withered handful of jade-tree leaves. "These are good for absorbing all sorts of nasty, malevolent bits."

"Thank you."

"As I was saying. A huge shipment came in off the docks last night, according to Branick. He said something about barrels coming off a ship with a Veiran name. And a heavy bribe to the customs officials."

"Did he say anything else?" Soviel asked, making a mental note to recruit Branick into the intelligence operation when he got a little older.

"No, just that they loaded them onto a cart and brought them up towards the castle."

Soviel nodded. "Then that's where we'll start." She got up and started to follow Rhi to the door.

"Wait, Soviel."

"Madame?" she asked, turning.

"You used your power without a source again, didn't you?"

"No, Madame, I swear."

"Then what is weighing on you? I can see your exhaustion plain as day. You've been drained. Come here," she beckoned.

Madame gripped her by the wrist in her usual, efficient manner, and Soviel felt the probing, sweeping sensation of Leone's experienced magic coursing into her.

"You tend plants in your room, yes?"

"Of course."

"How are they faring?"

"Not well, Madame," she admitted.

"Hmph. I suspected as much. Don't spend another night in that room. Something nearby is affecting you and I suspect you'd be far worse off if they weren't absorbing most of that poisonous energy."

"I- I won't," stammered Soviel.

"Pack up what you need and find somewhere else to sleep. Far, far away from that part of the castle."

Soviel swallowed. She wasn't sure how, but she knew Madame Leone was right. Something despicable was seeping through the walls of her room, something awake and hungry.

CHAPTER THIRTY

Everything was in place. Thanks to a gossipy guard they'd run into at the town nearest the prison, Hatra was able to confirm that the new prisoners were indeed being kept in the east cellblock, before being spread throughout the prison.

Ferrin would enter the warden's office via the roof, while he was on his nightly rounds, and snatch his keys. She would then sneak down the hallway of the administrative level and pass off the keys to Akachi, who she'd let in one of the side doors. Akachi would then bring the keys down to Lukas, Petir and Ryder, who would have gotten in via the guard's entrance.

Ferrin would cover the ground between the laundry room and the east cellblock, where she would administer the sleeping spores that Soviel had given her, and clear the path to their exit. She would then make haste to the north cellblock, which held the largest population of prisoners, and start a ruckus. That would raise the alarm, drawing more guards towards the northern part of the prison, leaving the southeast relatively clear while the guards were distracted. The only issue was that eventually, one of the prisoners in the north block was bound to snitch that some girl was running amok in the middle of the night, when all prisoners should have been under lock and key.

Afterwards, they'd all meet in the east cellblock, where they'd begin freeing prisoners and fleeing through the laundry, then make their way to Avaree with the three agents to a ship called *The Green Bottle*. Hatra would ride ahead to bribe the captain in advance. The freed people would be taken to Njorske, where they'd be recruited into the Caelish base, or be given a small sum of money to get back on their feet.

Ferrin hoped there was enough gold. She hoped whoever ended up distributing it didn't decide to keep it all for themselves. There was a lot riding on other people's follow-through, which perhaps unnerved her even more than breaking into the secure prison facility.

"Right. I'll meet you at that door in ten minutes," Ferrin confirmed with Akachi, pointing to the side door, part of the administrative wing. No prisoners, just access to the guard kitchens and offices.

"I'll wait in that tree," he said.

"Alright, be careful."

"You as well, it's a long way down."

With a curt nod, she rounded the corner of the building, out of sight. She hadn't told anyone other than Alick about the flight ring yet. She wanted to tell Rhi first, and hadn't yet had the chance.

The night was dark enough to conceal her ascent. The others had questioned her climbing abilities (rightfully so, she was no master), whether she needed rope or tar or a spotter to assist her. Since explaining that she could take flight in the wind was likely to raise more questions than they had time for, she'd assured them she was a fast climber from all the time spent in riggings.

With a deep breath, she leapt skyward, the thrill of the flight overtaking her in a pure, wild rush. She whisked through the damp air, her braid pulling free from where she'd tucked it into her coat.

The warden's office was on the third floor, with its own stairwell to the outside so that he could exit and enter without going through the main body of the prison. Perfect in case of a riot.

The window was locked, of course. That was fine, she had a backup plan.

She circled the gable and pulled up short. The small balcony was not empty. She hadn't heard the chatter over the wind, but two men sat in rockers on the balcony, smoking pipes and enjoying what looked like an expensive bottle of brandy.

Shit.

One of the men was a soldier, an officer. A high-ranking one, based on his shiny epaulets. She didn't recognize his face, dimmed by the fog and the dark as it was. He looked like he was in his forties, golden hair neatly tied back in a black ribbon.

The other man must have been the warden. He wore no uniform, only a finely made brown coat and matching breeches. He was older, maybe in his fifties or sixties, face lined and ruddy as he laughed with the officer as if they were old friends.

Well, that entrance is off the table.

She crept closer, landing silently on the roof. Did he have the keys on him? It didn't look like it, but it was hard to tell. If he did, she was going to be in a world of trouble. She could drop down behind them both quietly, slit one's throat and fight the other, but which was the bigger threat? She couldn't shoot them without alerting everyone of intruders.

Maybe the keys were inside.

Silently, she pushed off the roof and circled back to the window, peering in at the desk. Was that a key ring? It was hard to make out. The dying remains of a fire crackled in the hearth. She returned to the roof and searched her mind for a plan.

She could make out some of their conversation from her perch above.

"The Duke thinks by month's end, all will be in place. He's been hard at work to secure us all positions once the power changes hands." The golden-haired officer took a drag off his pipe. "Bramblehall will become the temporary base of operations while the other cities are… rehabilitated."

"And what of the other cities?" the warden asked.

"Galan has been a problem, as always, but with the right strategy, it will bend."

She wanted to wait and listen to more, but she was running out of time. Akachi was waiting on her, and they needed those keys.

Her eyes roved the rooftop and landed on the chimney.

Oh, no. This was going to be nasty.

She flitted to the ridge of the roof, laying a hand on the brick chimney. It wasn't smoking anymore, but the air rising from it was warm, and it would only get worse the further down she went.

What if someone in the lower levels decided to start a fire while she was still shimmying her way down? Would she be cooked to a crisp? Was there some sort of grate that would prevent her from entering the room? It was hard to make out through the dark—only a slight aura radiated from the embers below.

She could always fly out, if she met an unbeatable obstacle, right?

There was only one way to find out.

She swung her legs over the side and braced the toes of her boots on the soot-blackened bricks before lowering herself into the chimney. A gust of hot air choked her and she pulled the linen scarf she wore over her face. It rushed under the back of her jacket, under her shirt, braising her skin ever-so-slightly. She wriggled down faster. If she was in here too long, she'd burn.

The sides of the chimney slickened as she descended, the remnants of whatever had been boiled up for dinner forming a greasy condensate on the walls. She tried not to gag at the out-of-place bacon smell.

The air heated further and she bit her lip to keep from crying out as impossibly hot air singed the skin around her wrist.

She had to be halfway down by now.

"Oh, here, this is a good one!" She halted at the sound of a voice. The officer had come inside.

The scorching air blasted her skin again as she waited to hear a sign that they were still inside, and she bit down on her lip as the skin on her back burned. Nothing. Perhaps they merely came back to fetch another cigar.

She couldn't stay in here any longer. If she had to fight one of them, so be it. She had two loaded guns strapped to her chest, and knives enough for each limb of her body. It wasn't ideal, and it left a trail, but it was better than roasting to death in a chimney.

She shimmied the rest of the way down, her back chafing and her skin drying like tanned hide when she at last reached the bottom. The opening in the flue was a squeeze, and the hot metal singed the end of her braid, releasing a truly horrid smell as she passed through.

She tried to miss the coals with her feet, but wound up scattering a few onto the hearth as she ducked out of the chimney.

Shit, shit, shit. She stomped them out and kicked them back into the fireplace. As she came into the light, she could see she was covered in soot, the mottled gray-black covering her reddened skin. She was going to leave footprints.

Better to leave some questionable smudges on the hearthrug than a trail of sooty breadcrumbs. After wiping the soles of her boots on the carpet as quietly as she could, she made her way to the desk, snatching the keyring.

"Well, I should get back to the west block and check in on that interrogation." The officer stood and set his glass down on the railing.

Time to go.

She tiptoed her way to the door and undid the latch; their voices were just the outside the balcony door.

She slipped out, closing the door behind her just as they entered the office.

With no time for a sigh of relief, she sprinted down the stairs to hand off the keys to Akachi. She was already late and things had *not* gone to plan. She could only hope everything else went smoothly.

Lukas and Ryder were perched behind a rather large bush full of blueberries, several of which Ryder had crammed into his face, the tips of his fingers turning purple.

Lukas stared at him.

"What? I eat when I'm nervous," Ryder shrugged his huge shoulders.

Across the path, Hatra and Petir were crouched behind a similar bush. They would wait for a small group of guards to come in for their shift change, and Hatra would approach them, begging for assistance. Then, they would make their move and steal the uniforms off the guards so they could enter the prison while Hatra rode hard to Avaree with the bribe for Captain Pearce of *The Green Bottle*.

Guard shift changed at midnight. It was a little after eleven, as far as Lukas could tell. From what he'd gathered in the little tavern a few miles back, the guards spent their breaks drinking ale and enjoying the by-the-hour rooms at the inn, before making their way back for the night shift.

When the sound of the hooves echoed in the distance, Hatra stood out of the bushes and into the path. She nervously rang her hands in front of her and pulled her shawl close, her face pinched in worry as she made herself shiver.

Hatra resembled Lukas's older sister, Eman, in a lot of ways, from her long, curly brown hair to the way she seemed to put those around her at ease. He wondered how she was doing, how her children were growing. It had been over a year since he'd seen her.

Three guards came on horseback. They saw the distressed woman and one of them signaled the others to stop as he swung off his horse. "Madam, you shouldn't be out here at night. Are you lost?" he asked, approaching her.

"Yes," she said with a groan. "My carriage was set upon by thieves, I have no idea where my servants are, or my husband, or my things!" she cried, her voice wavering as if it might break.

Lukas was about to give the signal, but he paused when he heard it.

Horses. A carriage.

"Ah, that'll be Duke Hadringston. Madam, which road were you traveling on? He is coming from the south, he may have come across your companions," the soldier said.

That's when it hit Lukas—that wasn't a guard's uniform. He must have been infantry. The carriage rounded a bend, and with it came a contingent of soldiers. They couldn't ambush a group this large, not without a colossal amount of unnecessary deaths.

The carriage pulled to a stop behind the mounted soldiers, and a footman hopped off the back.

"What is the hold up? We shouldn't be stopping on the road like this, there are thieves," called out one of the soldiers.

"Surely you would not object to helping lady who has been accosted and has lost her people," countered the dismounted one.

The carriage door opened and a tall man with a handsome face stepped out. "The lady may travel in my carriage," he said in a smooth voice.

Hatra swiveled to look at him and gave a light curtsy. "Your Grace, I would not want to intrude. If it is no trouble, might you just point me in the direction of the nearest town?"

"There's not a town for miles, we're outside a prison, ma'am. It would be improper and unchivalrous to leave you out here alone with all sorts of dangerous criminals nearby," he said, extending a hand.

Hatra looked back and forth between his outstretched hand and the carriage. There were over a dozen soldiers in the entourage. All of them armed to the teeth and wary of their surroundings.

Hatra swallowed. "Very well, your Grace. I thank you." She took his hand. "I will find passage to Avaree in the morning, perhaps," she added loudly.

"Right this way, Madame."

The footman helped her into the carriage and the duke climbed in after. With a jolt, the entourage was on its way down the path.

When they were out of earshot, Petir shot up out of the bushes. "What the hell was that?"

Lukas stood. "He must be visiting to do an inspection. Or an execution."

"Just what kind of prison is this?" Ryder asked, his whole mouth stained purple.

"It's low security, just debtors and thieves and the like," Lukas threw his hands up, shaking his head. "Something is off, here."

"You don't say! Who is going to take the gold ahead to Avaree now?" Petir asked with alarm. "Hatra was our fastest rider."

"I'll go," Ryder said, standing.

"Really?"

He shrugged. "It's not as if we were going to find a guard uniform that would fit me anyway."

Lukas huffed a nervous laugh. "True. You know the ship?"

"I do indeed."

"Right, help us ambush the next group. Then haul it to the coast. Make sure you talk right to Captain Pearce. Meet back in the capital after, if you can."

Ryder nodded.

The next group of guards had to be close behind, the shift change was soon.

With the little container of sleeping spores clutched tightly in her fist, Ferrin crept down the hallway towards the laundry. Soviel had cautioned her about making sure the top chamber was facing the right way, so she didn't accidentally dose herself.

One breath of the little spores would knock a person out cold. For how long depended on the dosage. She hoped she would have enough. Each hallway was said to be guarded by a pair of soldiers, but judging on how the events of this night had gone thus far, she braced herself for trouble.

The burns on her back and wrists were painfully chafing against her clothing, and the soot covering her skin made her a ghastly sight to behold. She was sure there was bacon fat in her hair. With a shake of her head, she ignored how badly she needed a warm bath and some soothing lotion.

She rounded the corner on light feet and came to the first set of guards.

"Hey! State your business!" one of them commanded.

"Oh, goodness, I'm so sorry!" she exclaimed, flipping open the device of spores. Soviel had shown her the mechanism that scooped a little into a chamber on top of the box and could be easily blown at someone. With a puff of breath, the spores knocked both guards unconscious.

She tucked the box back into her pocket and began dragging the guards into one of the empty cells as quietly as she could.

The next hallway was much the same—a pair of guards, a quick job of tying and gagging them in case they woke up, then moving on to the next. There was one more hallway between her and the laundry, but when she passed through it, there were no guards standing sentry, and the cellblock branching off the hallway was empty too.

She looked around quickly, the dim torchlight glancing off the walls revealing nothing. Cautiously, she continued into the laundry room. It was dark, and there were big canvas hampers full of linen, huge barrels of water, stacks and stacks of lye soap wrapped in waxy paper and tied with twine. The door to the outside was barred by one big, iron bolt, which she slid out and hid beneath a pile of linens. Slowly, she pulled the latch and edged the door open, testing it.

As planned, it opened out onto a moor, lit dimly beneath the moon. There were two guard towers that faced out over that moor, which brought her to her next task: the distraction.

She closed the door and made her way out of the laundry, tracking back through the three hallways, where the guards were, thankfully, still unconscious. She skirted the edge of the southern cellblock, staying out of sight, then passed the entrance to the guards' mess hall. It was a small room with a few tables and a roaring fire. Half a dozen guards were scattered across various methods of seating, eating bowls of what smelled like rabbit stew by the hearth.

She passed them unseen, and finally made it to the north cellblock, where the largest population of thieves, murderers and criminals waited to be executed.

It was empty.

Ferrin gasped and staggered, catching herself on the doorframe. There wasn't a soul in the sprawling room.

They *really* must have come at a bad time. Where the hell were all the prisoners? A few small changes in layout were to be expected, but an empty cellblock implied at least a hundred missing souls.

Something else is going on here.

Just to be sure, she stepped further into the cellblock, scouring each row for evidence of people. She looked under cots, in corners, in the deepest shadows, but found nothing. No one.

She reached the opposite end of the cellblock and traced its edges. She needed to raise that alarm somehow. There was a closed door in the corner, one that she hadn't recalled from the floorplan. Of course, those plans had only proved to be halfway accurate so far, but the door looked new. She wiggled the handle as quietly as possible and opened it.

She stared into a darkness thick as oil and deep as a grave. There was no floor, only a straight drop into a deep pit of gods-knew-what. Something exhaled a breeze of warm air up from below like a great, big breath, fraying her nerves. She clapped a hand over her mouth in horror and slammed the door.

"Where is Ryder?" Akachi asked as soon as they were in a side hallway. "Did Hatra get on the road with the money?"

Lukas and Petir, clad in their stolen guard uniforms, shook their heads.

"What the hell happened?"

"Some important duke is visiting. Brought a ton of soldiers, decided to play chivalrous and we had to bail on ambushing that group. Hatra is with him now," Petir ran a hand through his hair in distress.

"This is not good," Akachi frowned, voicing what they were all thinking. "Something went wrong on Ferrin's end too, she got the keys but she appeared out of the office covered in soot and burns."

Lukas balked. "Burns? Is she alright?"

"Apparently the balcony was occupied, the warden and an officer. She said something about shimmying down the chimney."

"This plan is turning out to be a lot more complicated than advertised," Petir said, exasperated.

"It's like we came at the worst possible time," Lukas blew out a breath.

"Think it's a coincidence?" Akachi frowned.

Lukas shook his head. "I don't believe in those."

"We've come this far, the sooner we're out of here, the better. What are we going to do about Hatra?" Akachi asked.

"She knows the plan, she knows the signals, if she can break away, she'll come find us, and if not, we'll go find her."

With that, they made their way towards the east cellblock. Lukas clapped an unlocked manacle around Akachi's wrist as Petir took his place on Akachi's other side.

In this formation, they could easily navigate the prison without raising alarm or question. Just two guards escorting a prisoner to a different block. By the time they got there, Ferrin would have raised the alarm and the bulk of the eastern guards would be pulled to deal with whatever was happening in the north end of the prison. From there, it would be quick work of unlocking cells and ushering the prisoners to the laundry to make their escape.

Petir checked his watch. "Any minute now," he muttered.

They passed the last empty hallway before the entryway to the east cellblock.

"Where's the damn alarm, Ferrin?" Lukas cursed under his breath.

"Oi!"

Oh, shit, Lukas thought.

"What are you doing with a prisoner out here after hours? You know the rules."

"We were just bringing him in to do an interrogation," Petir said smoothly, as if they were all in on a big secret. Well, a different big secret.

"Make it quick," the guard said, spitting a wad of *arimopo* on the ground.

"Will do," Lukas answered, "sir."

When the guard didn't immediately leave, Lukas's stomach dropped. Did he want them to actively *beat* Akachi in front of him?

"Wait a minute…" the guard stepped closer, peering at Akachi's face, his linen shirt. "He's one of the new ones they brought in? You're not supposed to be damaging them before they're cleared for the research lab."

"Right, of course. We'll return him immediately," Petir gave a curt nod.

The guard narrowed his eyes. "I know most of the guards who work this shift, I don't recognize either of you."

"I'm new," Lukas said, at the same time Petir said, "I just have one of those faces."

This was all going sideways so, *so* fast. Where was the damn signal?

"I need to verify your credentials. We've already had a lady come in on the road under suspicious circumstances tonight. Something doesn't seem right—"

Petir punched the guard, hard enough that he should have gone down. Somehow he remained conscious enough to scream for help as he staggered back, clutching his busted nose.

"Time to go!" Akachi said, shaking off the manacle and gripping the heavy chain in his hand. A weapon. He swung it at the guard's head, and the man went down in a heap.

The trio dashed back to the empty hallway and around a corner, just missing the guards rushing past with their muskets drawn.

"Can we get them out without the alarm?" Petir asked.

"I think we might have a problem getting *ourselves* out at this point," Lukas observed. "We need to wait out the alarm, the east cellblock is going to be crawling with guards until they figure out what's going on."

"Maybe we shouldn't have left the guard with the caved-in head lying out in the hallway," Akachi gritted his teeth.

"Have they found him yet?" Lukas asked Petir, who was peering around the corner.

"It looks like they went into the cellblock… I'll drag him out of the hallway." Petir stepped out of the alcove they were in and stalked to the body of the guard. He was midway to one of the unoccupied holding cells that lined the hall when a musket cocked.

"Stop. Right. There." Two guards stood between Petir and the alcove where Lukas and Akachi were hidden, guns pointed squarely at Petir's head only a few feet away.

Petir dropped the guard's legs and raised his hands in surrender. Lukas stepped from the shadows and pointed his gun at the second guard's head.

The guard stiffened. "You won't shoot, it'll have every guard in this place flooding the hallway in minutes."

"You wanna bet?" Lukas asked, cocking the gun.

The guard didn't move. Akachi stepped from the alcove and began shackling him.

Footfalls echoed in the hallway and six more guards filtered in.

"Fuck," Lukas breathed.

"You there! Drop your weapons!"

With seven muskets now trained on the three of them, they had no choice but to slowly lower their own and set them on the ground.

Where was that alarm? Had Ferrin been captured?

"What do we have here?" One of the guards advanced as the first one retreated to block their other exit. They were truly and royally screwed.

Lukas felt a bayonet prod the side of his face, poking into his cheek, nearly hard enough to draw blood.

"Three imposters, it looks like."

"We should shoot them and be done with it, we can't have such discord with the duke visiting."

"No," said one of the guards, shouldering his musket. His coat had a single silver epaulet against the red and blue, indicating status. "These men are in fine fighting shape. We'll have three new subjects for the research venture."

Lukas did *not* like the sound of that.

"Tie them up."

Two more guards came forward to help the first one with the restraints. Four guns were still pointed at them. One wrong move and they'd be done for.

"What research venture?" Lukas asked nervously, eyeing the guard who approached him with a set of shackles.

"Oh, you'll wish you'd taken the musket ball," laughed the lead guard. "Come on boys, let's tie them up all proper-like."

Lukas struggled as the guard attempted to shackle him, and heard a gun cock. Then something inky moved in the darkness beyond the guards.

Please let us have just one stroke of luck.

A shot rang out. He tensed and waited for the searing pain, for his own blood to spread over his clothes. Instead, one of the guards crumpled and chaos erupted. He didn't waste the chance, slamming his shoulder into the nearest guard and picking up his dropped pistol.

A loud crack of metal on bone sounded and Ferrin materialized out of the dark, eyes blazing with some kind of frenzied panic, covered in soot, Hatra on her heels with a smoking gun in her hands.

Ferrin swung what looked like a heavy iron cross-bolt at the next guard, missing his head, but catching him in the throat, crushing his windpipe and sending him gasping to the ground.

Lukas whacked the next guard in the head with his gun, and shot another. It misfired, so he cracked him in the temple. Petir and Akachi were making quick work of their own opponents. The hallway had erupted into absolute bedlam, and it wouldn't be long before many more guards poured in.

"Boys," Ferrin said, breathing hard as she mimicked the man's words from minutes before as she gestured to the guards who'd been knocked unconscious. "Let's tie them up all proper-like."

Once the seven guards were secured, the group made their way towards the east cellblock.

As soon as they reached the next hallway, Lukas crushed Ferrin to his chest, wrapping his arms around her tight.

"Ow," she said into his jacket as her sore skin throbbed.

"I thought you'd been caught. When the alarm didn't go up," he pulled back, holding her at arm's length. "What happened?"

"Let's start unlocking chambers before more guards come pouring in," Petir said before she could answer. "Chances are they've all heard those shots." He glanced at each wall of the cellblock as they stepped through the huge doorway.

As the five of them moved further into the room, it became evident that there was *still* more at play than they knew about.

"There should be more people in here," Lukas said anxiously.

Indeed, there were far fewer than Ferrin had assumed there would be. Most looked quite young, or quite old.

"Well, let's get on with it and figure the rest out as we go. This is already a mess as it is," Akachi said, scratching his head.

People in the cells who were awake were watching them warily as they discussed what to do.

Ferrin said, "I'll walk the length and see if I can find out anything useful, you all start unlocking the doors and leading them to the exit. Remember, there are still guards in the tower since the alarm wasn't raised. Be careful."

Petir and Hatra nodded.

Ferrin walked quietly up the main artery of the cellblock, stopping whenever she saw someone awake so she could talk to them. She mostly offered assurance that help was coming, that they were getting out, but finally she found a middle-aged woman who looked alert enough to answer her questions.

"Can you tell me where the rest of the villagers are? From Everness?" It was so dark she could barely see the woman's face as she answered.

"When we got here, they took the young, healthy ones," answered the woman, her accent thick and her voice hoarse.

"Where to?" Ferrin urged.

The woman shook her head. "We couldn't see, something about a lab. Maybe to work? They took my son," she added weakly.

Ferrin's heart lurched at the pain in the woman's voice. She sounded so tired.

"Help is on the way, we're going to find the rest of them, just hold on."

The hallway in the east cellblock seemed to extend into eternity. The image of that awful dark pit and the smell, the breath that had come out of it, was still stuck at the front of her mind, and every time she closed her eyes, she saw that empty gaping maw behind the door in the empty north cellblock. She didn't want to think about it. Was that where the healthy prisoners had been taken, or was this laboratory part of something else?

She continued down the hallway, asking the people where they'd been brought in from. Gods forbid they accidentally sprang a murderer or a rapist along with the rest of the refugees.

"Everness."

"Lochdale."

"Your mother's room."

She rolled her eyes at the last one.

How could they know? How could they pick and choose who to release?

A place like this was evil. No one deserved to languish here, waiting to disappear. She hadn't had time to ask exactly what had happened with the other group while she was snatching the keys. Hatra was supposed to be halfway to Avaree by now, but apparently Ryder had gone instead.

The answer for a lot of it seemed to be that some important noble was visiting from the South. But what business could a wealthy duke have here?

Ferrin had the sinking feeling that they had stumbled into something much worse than a simple prison, and that there was a certain demand for more bodies here. She shivered at the thought. She didn't want to end up in that pit, or in whatever the 'laboratory' was.

She heard a commotion behind her. Lukas had stopped one of the prisoners.

"What's going on?" she asked, the need to get out growing and growing and causing her fingers and toes to buzz with anxiety.

"Allister Macray," Lukas said. "I arrested him for beating his wife and son. He stays."

"Look at this," Macray rumbled through his crooked, yellow teeth, "The jailor breaking out the prisoners."

"Well, we can't leave him, he could talk. He obviously knows who you are," Ferrin whispered harshly.

"She's right, I could. Then you'd be my cellmate," Macray jeered. "Wonder how that will work out for you."

Lukas glared at the man.

"I don't think you want to be stuck here. So if you don't want me talking, you'd better take me with you."

Meeting Lukas's stare, Ferrin widened her eyes and tossed her arms up into an exaggerated shrug. "We're running out of time, we can't just leave him here to blab."

"Oh, I like you," Macray said with a disgusting grin.

"Don't get too comfortable," Ferrin bit back at him.

"I don't—" Lukas started, then sighed and shook his head. "We don't have another choice, do we?"

"Get him out, I'll check up ahead to see if there's anyone else."

Lukas nodded and Ferrin jogged back down the hall, resuming her search for the missing prisoners. She was nearing the end of the hallway, the sporadic torchlight doing little to show her the inhabitants of the cells. The very last cell was dark and damp, and she almost passed it, but a lump in the corner moved, and coughed. Pulling the lantern off the wall, she could see there was a figure lying on their side with a threadbare blanket thrown over their body. She began to turn back to let Akachi know there was someone sick in the last cell, when a familiar voice came out of the dark corner.

"Gill?"

Ferrin stopped in her tracks, her hand still holding the lantern.

"Gillian? Is that you? Are—are you real?" Another shuddering cough.

She whipped around and stared into the dark cell, eyes wide, unable to move or speak as she processed exactly who the voice belonged to.

As she stepped closer to the bars, the dim light from her lantern seeped into the cell. She could make out the familiar face, honey-brown skin, choppy, shoulder length burnt-umber hair. The girl's amber eyes were wide as they stared up at Ferrin from where she lay huddled in a burlap blanket on the far wall of the cell.

Asha did not look well.

Snapping out of her shock, Ferrin set her jaw, fist clenched around one of the bars so hard it stung. "What the hell are you doing here?"

"Navy patrol picked me up outside of Port Galan," explained Ash, her voice weak. "You're breaking people out— why? What are you here for?"

"The innocent ones," Ferrin fired back. The rage she'd been carefully shoving down for weeks now was bubbling back up. "Give me one good reason I shouldn't leave you here to rot, you backstabbing—"

"Zare," Ash coughed, and it was a wet and rattling sound. "He knocked me out after I heard what he was going to do," she said, fighting another coughing fit. "I was eavesdropping. He said you were a valuable prisoner that the Barrian Navy was willing to pay for, and that he was going to split the pay with Danske and Mitch—" she broke off. "Gill, how did you escape?"

Ferrin just glared at her. "Keep going."

"Zare found me listening outside his cabin and I went off on him about how you loved him and trusted him and he was supposed to do the same, but then someone hit me over the head with a *fucking* wine bottle, or so I assume. He dropped me off on the beach with my pockets full of stolen jewels and documents he needed to be rid of. I woke up in a prison wagon. I've been here for weeks, I swear."

"How am I supposed to believe that? After all of Zare's lies?"

"Gill… I never lied to you. Most of us didn't even know what he was doing—" she resumed that awful, rattling cough. "Please, bring me with you. If I stay another night here, I think I'll die."

Ferrin sighed. Whether or not Asha had been part of the betrayal, Ferrin could not leave behind the girl who'd been her closest friend aboard *The Gravedigger* for two years. "Fine, but I want a real explanation when we get out," she said as Lukas jogged up behind her with the keys.

"Hey, is this the last one?" he asked, unlocking and opening the door. He stepped into the cell and froze as his eyes landed on Ash's shivering form. "Ash?"

Ferrin had never heard him sound that stunned.

"Lukas!" Asha sat bolt upright.

Ferrin didn't think it was possible to be more shocked than she already was. One more unplanned surprise that day and she just might keel over.

"Oh, gods. What are you *doing* here? And what—" She broke off in another fit of coughs.

Ferrin looked back and forth between the two of them. "How do you two know each other?" she asked, warily eyeing Lukas's horrified expression.

Asha managed to croak out an answer despite her choking laughter, "should I tell her, brother, or will you?"

CHAPTER THIRTY-ONE

Hatra and Petir went ahead with the first group of prisoners. They'd all agreed that going in small groups was less likely to draw the eye of the guards in the towers. Akachi was working on opening the rest of the cell doors while Lukas and Ferrin helped Asha out of her cell.

She'd lost some weight from her usually muscular yet compact frame, and her skin had paled. Her eyes looked sunken in the light from the lantern, and her legs were shaky as she stood.

She started shivering, and Lukas shucked his coat off and gave it to her. His *sister*. Ferrin had to ignore that bit of information until they got out of this mess, or she was going to slip up.

Just then, the alarm began to ring out.

"Someone must have found the dead guards. *Shit*," Lukas cursed.

"Let's go, maybe we can get to the laundry before they get here," Ferrin said, hastening her stride.

"Alright… climb on," Lukas said to Asha, bending down so she could jump on his back, like they were kids playing piggyback. They broke into a jog just as the guards burst through the doors, separating them from the hallway leading to the laundry room, and from Akachi and the rest of the prisoners.

A dozen soldiers flooded in, wearing uniforms wholly different from those of the standard prison guards. Their coats were deep violet and embroidered with a circle of gold thorns,

Bramblehall. They must have been personal guards of the visiting noble Hatra had mentioned.

Whoever they were, their muskets were trained on Ferrin, Ash and Lukas.

"Who goes there?" one of them called in a booming voice as the three of them froze.

There was no talking their way out of this, but their odds of winning the fight against twelve armed soldiers who'd already cocked their muskets were even worse.

"Stand down, by order of the crown," Ferrin said, drawing herself up tall as she strode forward.

"Stay back! Halt!" the guard ordered.

"I don't take orders from foot soldiers," she said coolly.

"Who are you to have authority of the crown?"

"I am Ferrin Valcara Kasing, daughter of King Henrik Elvon Kasing and Queen Arabella Calowair Valcara. The princess of Lindbarrow," she declared.

"Right, and I'm Lady Lalana of the meadow," one of the soldiers snorted.

"If you fire on me, you are committing high treason."

"Ain't Old Henrik planning on carting her off to the Cliff Hallows?" one soldier asked.

"That can't be her, she looks like she crawled out of the scullery," another said.

"Tie them up," the leader ordered.

"But what if she's telling the truth?"

"Do you not see the empty cells and open doors?"

She took another step. A shot fired past her head.

"That one was a warning. Now you can move again and get one between the eyes, or you can come with us *quietly* until we can get this sorted out," the leader spat.

Ash groaned something unintelligible. Lukas was perfectly still at Ferrin's side.

"Alright, alright, I'm sure you gentlemen will be reasonable," Ferrin said evenly.

Half of the soldiers shouldered their muskets and approached to secure the three of them. Her hands shook as they were forced behind her back at an uncomfortable angle.

"Put this one down."

"She's sick," Lukas argued.

"You want a musket ball in your brain, *boy*?"

"She can barely stand!" he exclaimed.

Ferrin could see the tip of the soldier's bayonet cut into Lukas's cheek.

"She won't be any trouble, please, just let him carry her," Ferrin said.

"Set the girl down, or I blow *both* your heads off."

Reluctantly, Lukas set Asha down. She clutched his arm as she adjusted, shivering.

A shrieking, piercing howl suddenly sounded from the north. It was a sound no creature of the living realm could *ever* make.

"What was that?" asked one of the soldiers nervously as he confiscated the remaining pistols and knives from Ferrin's waist.

"It must be feeding time, how fortunate for you lot," said the one tying Ferrin's hands. "Over much quicker than the laboratory."

Ferrin gulped. What in the name of all that is holy is going on in this place?

"All secured, Captain."

"Excellent, let's move."

They were escorted by six of the guards down the hallway that led back to the horrifyingly empty north cellblock.

Ferrin's head reeled with questions. Had they followed Akachi and the others? Did they realize how many prisoners had been let out? Or were they feeding so many of them to whatever had made that sound that they didn't bother keeping track anymore? Most importantly, what exactly were they being led to?

"This one's not fully grown yet, but it'll suck you dry all the same," laughed one of the guards.

Think.

"I thought we were only to be detained until my identity could be verified? Surely, you don't want to risk treason on account of some pitiful hungry creature. Isn't there a stray cow you could feed it?" Ferrin asked.

"Even if you are who you say you are, we aren't too worried," the soldier replied.

Ferrin blinked. Surely there had to be at least some fear of retribution for harming her.

"Keep it moving," spat the blond soldier who was practically carrying Ash.

Ash moaned once and stumbled forward. She crumpled to the ground, her breathing shaky and wheezing.

"Ash!" Lukas started forward before being yanked back by two soldiers.

"Up you get," grunted the soldier as he stepped to her side and hauled her up by the shoulders. She staggered up, catching herself on his waist. She coughed twice, pulling the burlap blanket around her shoulders tighter with her bound hands. She shook and shuddered, her eyes slitted in exhaustion.

They were escorted to the north cellblock. Lukas shot Ferrin a questioning look when he saw it was empty. The door on the far wall, the one that wasn't on any of the plans or maps, was emanating a foul and fell energy. She did not want to see what lived in that darkness. She did not want to go near that door again.

"Should we wait for His Grace?" one of the guards asked.

"No, he won't want to be disturbed while he's inspecting the laboratory. He'll be present for the later feedings," the leader explained.

Ferrin's heart raced jackrabbit-fast in her chest and her eyes caught on the lists on the wall indicating how many people had been *fed* to whatever was in that pit.

"You're lucky, you know. The creature eats you fast, sucks the very life right out of you. And when it's strong enough, it'll be able to drain the life out of land. You're part of an *important* plan now," the leader mocked. "Rowlins, the door please."

The blond guard unlatched the door and swung it open. It truly seemed like the sort of door that should be kept bolted and locked, the key thrown away.

"The weak one first," ordered the captain.

The two soldiers each braced an arm under Asha's shoulders. She staggered again, and as she tripped, she spun, sweeping out with her arms and the long dagger that she had swiped from the blond soldier's belt when she'd fainted in the hallway.

Blood sprayed in an arc as she slit both their throats. Even ill and fatigued, Ash was a skilled fighter. Her compact frame made her faster than lightning, and the muscle she had from her days aboard *The Gravedigger* had not yet wasted away.

Ferrin and Lukas didn't hesitate to take advantage of the chaos that erupted. Dropping swiftly to a crouch, Ferrin swept the legs of her guards. One went down sprawling, the other stumbled back and turned, drawing his sword. One of Lukas's guards flew into him after being shouldered hard, and they both stumbled, almost falling into the pit.

Another piercing, shrieking rumble erupted out of the pit, one that curdled Ferrin's blood like bad milk.

"Ash!" Ferrin shouted, gesturing for her to cut her ropes.

With one swift motion, Ash sliced through the ropes tying Ferrin's wrists as the other three soldiers faced them down. One of the two who had been guarding Lukas was gone, presumably fallen into the pit. The other three were bearing down on them, weapons raised.

Ash raised her stolen dagger, a feral glint in her eye. Ferrin popped the knife out of her boot. It was short, but sharp. The guard in the middle came at her and she swiped with her blade, but had to block the blow from his sword at the last second. The impact rattled every bone in her arm as she kept him from slicing her in half. She shoved off and feinted to her right before dropping low and diving left around him.

He moved at the last minute and she wound up tackling him around the waist, taking them both to the floor. Not to lose her advantage, she stabbed her knee into the meat of the inside of his upper arm, causing his grip on the sword to relax. When it clattered to the ground, she kicked it towards Lukas, hoping he'd pick it up. She didn't have time to see as she drove her fist into the man's face.

He reached for her throat, and she pulled back, but too fast, losing her balance. She was under him now, her arms pinned.

"You fucking bitch," he spat blood on her face as he sat back, wrapping his hands around her throat.

A wave of panic lapped at her heels, rising like the tide. *Keep it together*, she told herself as her throat closed. She blinked once and wrapped her hands over his wrists, squeezing them towards each other at the same time she bucked her hips. It was enough to send him off balance. Just enough for her to gulp a breath and find the knife that had landed somewhere near her head and slam it up, in between his ribs.

He inhaled sharply and she pulled it out, the wound sucking. She rolled out from under him as he fell, clutching his side.

The second soldier was dead on the floor next to Ash, and the third, apparently fed to the creature as well. She had been too distracted to hear it roar again.

"Come on, let's go!" Lukas yelled, helping Ash up as she grabbed for another weapon. "There's always more guards."

They scrambled down the hall towards the laundry, but stumbled to a halt as they heard voices echoing down the hall.

"We have to find another way out, they must have seen the others go out through the laundry," Ferrin panted.

"This way," Ash said with a tired jerk of her chin towards the west.

"The west side? That's where the offices are."

"And the lab," Ash said ruefully.

"*Why* would we go towards that?"

"Before I was too sick to leave my cell, they had me on the cleaning crew. They dump the bodies out a chute in the hallway."

Ferrin blanched, but they were out of options. They fled to the west, waiting for some new batch of soldiers or guards to crawl forth from the shadows. Twice they had to duck into the dark corners of open cells when guards ran past them, called to the north cellblock to see what the commotion was.

Finally, they reached the hallways of the west end of the prison. There was no big block of cells, only a few holding areas, and three white metal doors with huge, heavy deadbolts on the outside.

What were they *making* here?

"This way," Ash croaked as she led them to the end of the hallway. There was a trap door, the smell of decay growing worse and worse as they neared it. Ash was grimacing when she pointed at the door. "Open it."

The smell wafted out in a sickening wave. It was sharp and invasive and almost sweet. Ferrin fought the urge to gag.

Voices sounded in the distance.

"Alright, in you go," Ferrin said to Ash. The last thing they needed was for her to pass out before they could escape.

Ash nodded, held her breath and stepped in, falling with a thud on the pile of rotting flesh below.

Once she was clear, Lukas dropped down after her and scooted out of the way. Ferrin let herself be buoyed by the magic of the ring as she dropped through and pulled the trap door closed behind her before falling with a sickening slap.

It was the most gruesome thing she had ever experienced. The bodies were in various stages of decay, some hours fresh, some stiff with rigor mortis, some bloating and rotting as if they'd been down there for days. They all shared the same dark blue spidery veins, visible beneath their pallor.

She scrambled away as quickly as possible, trying not to think about what she was touching, what each slap and snap and crack was as she clambered off the body pile.

At long last they were outside.

"Come on, we just have to make it to the tree line," Lukas said to Asha.

"I can make it," she nodded weakly.

The trio broke out in a run across the bare expanse of grass between them and the woods, completely exposed. A shot rang out, missing them by mere feet, then another.

They were almost there, they were *so* close.

Ash tripped. Lukas hefted her over his shoulders and kept running.

They made it to the woods and didn't stop until they'd reached the thick cover of a huge rhododendron bush.

"Horses?" Ash asked hopefully.

"They're on the other side, assuming anyone waited for us," Ferrin explained.

Ash nodded, gasping for breath.

"Come on, let's circle around. We won't last long out here," Lukas said.

Two horses had been left for them. Thank the gods, that meant the others had gotten away. The compromised agents and the remaining refugees, of which there'd been only sixteen, would flee to Njorske.

Ash was propped weakly against Lukas on his horse, and Ferrin wasn't sure what would happen from here. They could flee back to the capital, but by now the missing maps would have been discovered, and once word spread, someone might very easily figure out it had been her who had orchestrated the break-in.

Whatever they decided, Ash needed a healer's touch— and soon.

CHAPTER THIRTY-TWO

After riding through dawn and most of the day, barely speaking a word to each other out of sheer exhaustion, the trio finally stopped to rest.

Lukas boiled up a cup of water for Ash to sip on while Ferrin went off to try and snare a rabbit. When she returned, the silence was tense. They'd made camp, or as close to it as possible with their limited supplies. There was a tiny tin of salt and a few pieces of jerky left in their packs on the horses, and two bedrolls.

Ferrin sat down by the fire with the rabbit, handing it to Lukas. He looked like he needed something to do with his hands. He'd boiled some of the beef jerky into a makeshift broth for Ash. It seemed to be helping; some of the color had returned to her face, and she was coughing less.

Seeing Lukas and Ash side by side, she could easily see their resemblance. How many times had she mentally compared the two of them? She had thought they only looked alike in the way that people from the same region might have similar features, but now she could tell it was a familial resemblance.

They had the same warm-toned brown skin, wavy hair that seemed to muss easily, the same elegantly planed faces and dark lashes, though Asha's eyes were the molten gold-brown of a honeycomb in the hottest part of summer and Lukas's were the blue-green of the sea on a calm and clear day.

The tension hung thick in the air as Ferrin looked back and forth between them.

"Well, shit," Ash coughed. "Someone say something."

Lukas stabbed the knife he'd been skinning the rabbit with into the log he sat on. "Fine," he said, sighing deeply. "Where the hell have you been for the last three years?"

Ash fixed her stare on him, hurt flashing in her wide eyes. "A lot of places, Lukas—"

"You just ran off. Our mother grew so ill with worry she had to leave the city. She lives on Eman's husband's farming estate with them now. She had to sell her shop."

Asha looked stricken. "I didn't mean—"

"You just vanish into the streets, a fifteen-year-old girl. We thought you had been killed, or worse!" His voice rose.

"I didn't mean to!" she shouted back.

He recoiled visibly, as if that were an answer he hadn't prepared a response for.

"I didn't mean to," she repeated quietly. "It was an accident."

"Explain to me how you run away by accident."

"Lukas, it's different when you're a girl! You wouldn't understand. Gill gets it."

"That's not the same thing!"

Ferrin was becoming increasingly uncomfortable, and she hadn't even begun to explain her portion of the story yet.

"Well, clearly you're too pigheaded to listen to me!" Ash flung a hand wide in frustration. "Like I said, I didn't mean to run away!"

"Do I at least get to know where you've been the last three years?" Lukas asked, voice dripping with barely-bridled frustration as he rubbed his temples in tired circles.

"Fine. But I'm going to sleep first," Ash grumbled as she curled up on the bedroll, pulling her blanket around her.

Ferrin shivered as the fire died down to embers. She had only her coat and cloak to warm her, as they'd piled the extra blanket on top of Ash once she'd fallen into a feverish sleep.

Lukas had given Ferrin a questioning look, as if he planned to ask her to explain why she knew his sister. She simply shook her head. The two of them needed to work out their own issues before she barged in with witty tales of her and Ash having the time of their lives in the Meddemara.

She pulled the cloak tighter around her shoulders and dreamed of a hot bath. She was still covered in soot, and more than anything, she needed to scrub the feeling of corpse-flesh from her skin. Every time she closed her eyes she saw that dark pit, or those ruined bodies shot through with dark, distended blue veins. Fortunately, the burns on her back and wrists weren't severe, only as painful as if she'd fallen asleep in the summer sun all day and blistered from it. Nonetheless, she'd had chills since the sun set, and it was only getting worse.

The wind was relentless as it rustled through the underbrush, rousing her into a state of half-sleep. Seeking warmth, she rolled over, right into Lukas's solid form. As she was about to scoot away, he wrapped an arm around her in his half-awake state, pulling her into the warmth of his body. He grabbed the edge of her cloak and pulled it over so that it covered both of them, trapping their heat.

"You're awake?" Ferrin whispered.

"Can't sleep with you shaking like a leaf right next to me," he said with a sleepy half-smile, eyes still closed. She settled into the heat of his chest, letting him hold her close as she breathed in his warmth. And so they slept.

Morning crept in cool and misty, the dew settling over everything like a blanket of limpid gems as the sun broke over the horizon, Heleion stretching lazy arms up as she began the day.

When they woke, it became clear that Asha's condition had deteriorated in the night. Her breathing was short and high-pitched, and she could barely get out two words as she squinted up at them. All of Lukas's resentment from the night before had vanished, and he gently scooped her up and mounted his horse.

"Madame Leone can help her," Ferrin assured him as she swung up on her horse. "We can make it back to the castle before nightfall, but we'll have to ride hard."

"We don't have much of a choice," Lukas said, spurring his horse into a gallop.

CHAPTER THIRTY-THREE

Soviel and Rhi ended up in the servant's hallway somewhere near the kitchens, thanks to Branick's not-so-specific specifications. They'd mostly avoided any awkward run-ins, save for one chamber maid carrying a meal tray who'd turned back three times, squinting at the back of Rhi's head as if trying to discern whether or not she'd imagined the Crown Prince taking a stroll through the concealed servants' hallways.

Muffled voices could be a heard from each of the rooms they passed.

"No, no, I have to get this to Edding immediately," said a clear, male voice as light spilled into the corridor ahead. "It just came in from up north. He'll want to see this, I can't linger."

Soviel threw out an arm, stopping Rhi in his tracks.

"But, you swore you'd stay for tea. It's our anniversary!" a second voice cajoled from the other side of the door.

"Dedrich, I know, but if I don't deliver this response in a timely fashion, Hadringston will have my head when he returns from inspecting the prison. Do you want to spend your next anniversary with a headless corpse?" The speaker backed into the corridor, shrugging his jacket on.

"Fine, but if you aren't home for dinner, you can sleep out in the barn," Dedrich grumbled.

"I know, love. I know," said the first one, who Soviel realized was a messenger. They were near the aerie. "I'll see you later."

Soviel remained frozen, several yards back from the open door. It wasn't all that dark in the corridor, since lanterns hung every few dozen feet.

The messenger began to whistle a tune as he headed off in the opposite direction. She exchanged a look with Rhi.

He nodded and they followed the messenger.

Staying as far back as they could, Soviel and Rhi traced his steps through the dim hallway, careful not to draw attention to their presence. He made a few turns, passing the kitchen entrance, until he finally reached his destination. By Soviel's estimation, they were somewhere east of the kitchens.

Soviel looked at Rhi and raised a finger to her lips as they approached the door. She began to move towards the door, but Rhi clamped a hand onto her wrist.

She shot him a questioning look.

"Duke Edding. He was there when I was poisoned," whispered Rhi.

"Alright, well, we need to find out what's in that letter."

"How?"

"Wait."

They listened at the door, only half-hearing what was being said on the other side of the wall.

"This came just now? From the prison?"

"Yes, Your Grace. Just now."

"This isn't good. Isn't good at all."

Soviel's heart hammered in her throat. Their friends were up there.

"What is it, Your Grace?"

"A break-in… dozens of prisoners… here. Wait a moment and I shall draft my response."

Rhi's grip tightened on her arm, his face white. A few minutes passed in silence.

"Hide," Soviel breathed. She wrenched her arm free and grabbed Rhi by the wrist, dragging him into an offshoot of the hallway just as the door opened.

"Stall the messenger," Soviel whispered to Rhi. "I'll get the letter from the duke. Rendezvous at th—"

Rhi stepped out and clocked the messenger in the forehead just as the door swung shut. He went down with a thud.

"Rhi!" Soviel hissed.

"That letter can't leave this palace," Rhi explained, his tone dead serious. She'd never heard him sound like that. "Right?" He looked back at her.

Soviel swallowed, nodding in agreement as Rhi fished through the messenger's bag and pulled out the letter Duke Edding had just written. He tucked it into his coat pocket and stood.

"So how do we get that letter from Edding?"

She chewed her bottom lip, thinking. "Drag him out of the way first," she said, pointing to the messenger sprawled on the floor. "Poor man has plans for dinner, the last thing we want is someone stepping on him."

Rhi dragged him to the side of the hallway and propped him up as Soviel crouched beside him, drawing out the pouch of fresh ivy leaves she kept in her pocket. She healed the bruising he was sure to have on his face from Rhi's well-placed punch, and did her best to prevent any lingering headache he'd have upon waking.

"Oh, *shit*."

"What is it?" she grunted, standing from the unconscious messenger.

Rhi began to read in a hushed voice.

"Cal,

I have received your missive via eagle regarding the breach in security at the prison. I will need a more precise count on the number of souls remaining, as feedings for the creature will need to remain consistent, and sourcing new prisoners can take time. There is a plan in place that should reap several dozen new prisoners, going forward.

Please respond in haste to say whether the laboratory was breached. Our work there must be accomplished under total secrecy, until it is time to reveal our success. If there has been a breach, you must take action by whatever means necessary to prevent the information from being disseminated.

Best,
Maxun Edding

"Do you know what any of that means?" Rhi asked Soviel.

"Not exactly…" Soviel said, her mind racing.

"Not exactly?"

"The bit about the beast…" she mused, dreading saying it aloud in this dark, damp place.

"What is it?"

"I've had my suspicions for a while. About something living beneath the castle. It sounds like there is one of those… things… in the prison. They're only taking so many prisoners because it has to be fed so frequently."

"*What?*" Rhi's eyes widened.

"I'll explain it all later, we need to—"

"Oi, you can't linger out here!" a nasal, male voice called from the opposite end of the hallway, light spilling from the door he'd just come through.

"Sorry!" Soviel called, channeling embarrassment into her voice. She moved to block the unconscious messenger with her skirts.

"We got a little distracted," Rhi drawled in a lazy, embarrassed tone, turning his body towards hers, blocking the messenger and creating a very specific image.

He knew how to play the game, she realized.

"So sorry," Soviel said, her tone flustered and breathless as Rhi trailed a finger up her arm.

"Well, get moving," the man grunted. "There's perfectly good alleyways and bedrooms all over the damn place. Gods damned rabbits, you lot."

The door slammed shut and he made his way towards them, an empty tea service on a tray in front of him.

"Hey, what is—" he halted steps from them.

"It's nothing, just—"

Rhi reached out and grabbed the tea tray so fast she almost missed it, then he slammed the metal into the man's head.

"Rhiach!" Soviel scolded. "You cannot just knock everyone unconscious!"

"He was about ten seconds from raising an alarm. We need to go."

Soviel and Rhi hustled back the way they'd come, only to be turned around several times by the sound of approaching footsteps. Finally, they ended up in the wine cellar. The huge, long room was cool and dry. Hundreds of bottles lay on their sides on wooden racks, labeled by the year and grape type.

"Sweet Strata, this is a lot of wine," Soviel said under her breath. "How can anyone possibly finish all this in one lifetime?"

"Oh, you can't." Rhi shook his head. "There're bottles down here that are over a hundred years old. I'm not even sure they're still safe to drink."

Soviel grimaced.

"I found a worm in one of the bottles once. Almost gave it to Ferrin in a glass."

"That's disgusting."

"Sure, guts hanging out and blood and gore are fine but you think a little worm is disgusting?"

"I don't *eat* the blood and guts."

Rhi shrugged. "True. Come on, the quickest way back to the main hallway is this way. And *yes,* it is discreet."

"You come down here a lot?" she asked wryly.

"Yes, though usually with much different company."

"Ah, so we're hiding out in your smooch spot, is that it?" she asked with a smirk.

"Well, yes. But it quenches the allure when you refer to it as a 'smooch spot', so thanks for that."

"My apologies, Your Highness. What should I be calling it, 'romance rendezvous' ?'Tryst tunnel' ?'F—"

"Alright!" he cut her off. "Your way with alliteration has been noted. And your point, taken."

Despite the serious nature of their mission, Soviel stifled a laugh.

"Anyway," Rhi cleared his throat. "Now that you mention it, I want to show you something."

"What is it?"

"A few weeks ago, I found something down here. A trap door."

"And?"

"It was empty," he said. "Just a hole in the ground. But the temperature and humidity control down here is perfect for storing dried *popava* leaves before they're powdered for use."

"Branick did say he saw those barrels being transported back to the castle…"

"Exactly."

"You think—"

"Only one way to find out, my dear Soviel."

She frowned skeptically.

"It's right over here," he said, tracking over to a rack of reds.

Sure enough, there, on the ground, was a trap door, partially covered by a fading woven rug. She dropped into a crouch across from Rhi and they rolled the rug back between them. She wrapped her fingers around the little iron O-ring and pulled up.

There they were, two huge, round-bellied barrels. They were big enough to fit a person inside.

"Oh," she said with a sigh. She was just about to reach for the lid of the barrel when Rhi grabbed her hand.

"No. Wait. I don't," he hesitated and shook his head. "I don't want to be here when you open it."

"Ah," she nodded. "Alright, I understand. I'll come back later, with something to put a sample in. Then, we destroy it."

The pained expression on Rhi's face seemed to ease at that.

"Come on, let's get out of here. There's one more thing I need to do."

CHAPTER THIRTY-FOUR

Asha was tired. Everything was foggy as she drifted in and out of consciousness. She didn't open her eyes into the brightness of the world, not yet. The sheets of the bed she slept on felt different. Not the smooth, soft linen that she so often woke on in Old Orini with Brigitte, and certainly not the rough canvas hammock she dozed in aboard the ship. Where was she? Something was missing.

Perhaps Brigitte had sent all of the bedding to be cleaned? Had there been rats recently? And why was it so damned cold? What day was it?

She couldn't remember, something was missing, something was wrong…

Her face was swollen and her joints ached as she woke up. *Blink. Blink.* Her eyes opened and adjusted to the too-white surroundings, with two blurry head-shapes looming over her.

Blink. Her eyes flew open and focused. The head-shaped blobs became an older, more rugged version of her brother and a paler, more tired version of Gillian. Her breaths came shorter and faster as the room became brighter and brighter, blinding her.

Where am I?

"Relax," Gill said, her face pinched with concern. She was covered in dirt and what looked like soot.

"Where am I?" she slowly turned her head to meet Gill's eye, then Lukas's. "What are you doing here?"

"Her head will clear within the day, she's had a high fever. Sometimes it can cause the mind to scramble a bit, but she'll be alright," a voice said from her periphery. She squinted and turned her head, seeing a dark-skinned older woman scrawling in a notebook.

"Gill," Asha bolted up, "Gillian, you have to listen!" She gripped her friend's hand. "Don't trust Zare, he's going to—" her chest heaved as a rattling cough seized her. "He's going to sell you out for whatever he knows about you! H-He's—" She dissolved into a coughing fit, unable to gulp down a breath.

"I know, Ash, it's already happened," Gill said, smiling sadly. She sounded different. Older. She gave Ash's hand a gentle squeeze. "You have to rest."

"You need to watch out!" *Why won't she listen?* "He could kill you, you're in danger!" The woman in the white coverall came to the side of the bed and pressed a hand gently to the center of Asha's chest, calming her lungs and sending her into blissful unconsciousness.

Once Ash was settled and resting, Ferrin took off towards the castle, leaving Lukas to watch over Ash in case she came to. They still hadn't discussed exactly how she and Ash —his *sister!*— had known each other.

She cursed herself for not grabbing for a vial of salve from the infirmary as the fabric of her shirt chafed against her raw back. She was covered in soot, grime and the haunting memory of dead flesh.

Passing by guards on the road, she was glad for the hood of her cloak and the grime on her face to hide her. She had no idea what she was about to walk into, but she needed to see Rhi and make sure he was alright. A sinking sense in her stomach had her feet quickening. If Rhi had faced the consequences of her rash actions again, she would never forgive herself.

Ferrin made her way quickly to her rooms to wash up and change, but nearly collided with Soviel, who was lurking just outside her bedroom door.

"*Strata,* you scared me!" Soviel pressed a hand to her chest. She winced as she took in Ferrin's appearance. "What happened to *you*?"

"Things did not go as planned up north," Ferrin shared. "Have you seen Rhi?"

Soviel gave a dry laugh, "Yes, come with me."

Ferrin tilted her head quizzically.

"A lot has happened in the last few days," Soviel warned her.

Ferrin followed Soviel into her own chambers, past the little atrium into the bedroom. The door swung open to reveal Rhi reclining on her couch, intently examining a little potted succulent. He scrambled to set it back down on the shelf next to the others. Dozens of Soviel's potted plants now lined Ferrin's desk, vanity, and bookshelf.

Rhi's shirt was rumpled and there was a blanket slung over the back of the couch. His black hair hung loose to shoulders.

"Did you sleep here?" Ferrin asked.

"Yes," Soviel and Rhi said in unison.

"Like I said, a lot has happened since you left on your mission."

"Don't worry, Soviel is a perfect gentle-lady," Rhi snorted as he stood. "Anyway, I think Father is trying to have me killed. How was your trip? Has Lukas returned as well? I need to trouble him for some more of that tea," Rhi said casually.

"Hold on. You think Father is trying to kill you?"

Rhi exhaled, his chest deflating. "Indeed, if the guards sniffing around outside my room at all hours are any indication. I barely made it down the rose trellis before they burst into my room last night."

"Rhi! Why are you still in the castle? We have to leave."

"There's more—Soviel, tell her about Nimhe."

"What about Nimhe?"

"She's the one who's been slipping about the castle dosing people with the bad *popava* strain."

"How do you know?"

Rhi raised a hand with a pained grin. "I got a taste of it, safe to say it has *fully* dulled any temptation I had to touch even the good stuff again. Soviel went to confront her and found her room completely vacated."

"*Gods*, Rhi, are you alright? What happened?"

"Well, Nerena's manservant held a knife on me while our dearest Nimhe poured it directly into my wine, so I drank it. Then I saw a bunch of horrible things, and I woke up to Soviel dumping freezing buckets of water all over me, gem that she is."

"You're welcome," she retorted.

Rhi inclined his head with a wink.

"Nimhe was the one going through your things, as well. I caught her in the act." Soviel crossed the room. "She was looking through your jewelry box, again. She wouldn't say what she was looking for."

Ferrin swallowed. Someone else must have known about the ring. "Right then, why can't we at least go stay somewhere *not* crawling with guards? We're both going to be in a world of trouble if they get their hands on us."

"We're working on that," Rhi said. "Soldiers have been arriving by the boatload every day. The guard has doubled. I don't know if they're anticipating an attack or what. Maybe Bourjony has finally made its move against our navy and they're worried King Avent will sail here next. Maybe the Efelians have abandoned us."

Ferrin chewed her lip. This was bad.

"Ferrin, Helene knows about the prison break." Soviel absently picked up the potted succulent from its shelf, running her ring finger over its rubbery leaves.

Shit. "How mad is she?"

"She was mad. But it's been a few days. You should go down there and talk to her."

"Great," Ferrin groaned. "Wait. Why did *you* sleep here? If Nimhe is gone, who else is after you?"

"Madame suggested that I stay somewhere far from my own rooms, since their proximity to something… bad is draining my energy."

"Oh. You did look exhausted before I left," Ferrin observed.

"Yes."

Ferrin nodded. "Right, well, I have a few things to take care of before I see Helene. Someone I knew from before was in that prison, and it's all gotten very complicated. Meet me at Lukas's cabin tonight, both of you."

CHAPTER THIRTY-FIVE

Asha was stirring slightly in the cot. It had been a few hours since she'd last woken up, but Madame Leone had explained that the fever was coming down and her pulse was level.

Ferrin crossed and uncrossed her arms as Ash's heavy-lashed lids fluttered open. She'd been there all day, as had Lukas, other than when they took turns to go and bathe. Ferrin didn't think all the scented soap in the world would get rid of the feeling of all those corpses under her. She shivered just thinking of it. All of those senseless deaths in that place, and in service of what? Whatever consequences she faced in the wake of the prison break, she only hoped they'd managed to halt or at least disrupt whatever evil was being done there.

Lukas was due back any minute, so she was glad to have a moment to talk to Ash alone first.

There was clarity in Ash's dark maple eyes as she squinted and propped up on her elbows.

"Good," Ferrin sighed with relief, "you're awake."

"How… how did we get here?" asked Ash, looking around at the infirmary tent.

"You were delirious and fevered, so we pushed the rest of the way here so Madame could heal you. We were on the road all day, which probably didn't help things."

"Right, right," Ash swallowed drily. "And… where is here?"

Ferrin laughed lightly for the first time in many days. "You're in Everness, Lindbarrow's capital. My home."

"Lindbarrow, huh? Thought it felt cold and wet."

"You remember everything?" Ferrin arched an eyebrow.

Asha closed her eyes and nodded. "I was in that *place* for weeks, or maybe months, you guys stumbled in, you yelled at me, then we were all equally shocked when you came to the realization that your new beau was my *brother*," she smiled wickedly as she ticked each event off on her fingers. "Then we escaped, Lukas yelled at me, I went to bed, and now we're in this fine establishment." She tucked her hands behind her head in a gesture of leisure for effect.

"First of all, Lukas is *not* my—" Ferrin waved her hands, sighing exasperatedly. "Never mind. Anyway, how do you feel?"

"Thirsty and tired," Ash pouted as she sat upright.

Ferrin picked up the glass of water perched on the bedside table and handed it to Asha. "Slowly," she directed as she let go. Ash, of course, did no such thing and gulped down the entire glassful. Ferrin rolled her eyes.

"Where's Lukas?" asked Ash.

"He went to wash up. And also to check on my brother and one of the other men who helped us bust out of the prison."

"Right," she nodded, shuddering. "I could use a bath."

"Ash, what were they doing in that place?"

Ash shuddered and drew her knees up to her chest.

"That place isn't a prison, it's a weapons factory. The thing they're growing in the pit and the things they're making in the lab… they're weapons, Gill. Horrible, horrible weapons." She blew out a long, shaky breath. "I only saw bits and pieces when they brought us out to clean. I scrubbed blood off the floors in that lab more than a few times."

"What are they making?"

Ash shook her head. "I never got a good look. I just know they took prisoners in there, healthy, young ones, and they didn't come out the same."

"Are you alright?" Ferrin asked. "I'm sorry I yelled at you."

"I get why you would assume that I knew what Zare was going to do. He had us all fooled, Gill," Ash shook her head. "I think," she frowned and sighed deeply. "I think he killed Pierre."

Ferrin's heart lurched. Pierre was one of the younger crew and when she wasn't with Zare, she, Ash and he were thick as thieves.

"Why?" Ferrin asked, her voice hollow.

"Same reason he dumped me on that beach. We questioned him about what he had done to you."

"I hate him. I hate him so much." Hot tears burned at the back of her eyes.

"He tried to tell us you were going to sell *us* out so he was doing it first. The second he brought the damn navy into it, I knew that prick was playing something."

Ferrin dropped her head into her hands.

"So," Ash said, trying to change the subject and stretching out one leg. "You have a brother?"

"Yes. And it seems he and your brother have become good friends. Funny, isn't it?"

"Huh," Ash nodded absently. "So, uh, what is it you do here?"

"Oh. Um," Ferrin picked at her nails. "Don't laugh, but, I'm sort of a princess."

"*Mafatehama*," Asha blurted in Akhatan. "No. There's no way!"

Ferrin cringed, pursing her lips. "It's true."

"So you're telling me that you left behind not only three meals a day and a roof over your head, but a fucking *palace*?"

Ferrin nodded sheepishly as she chewed her bottom lip. "Ash, I was fourteen, my mother had just disappeared, I was a mess." She laid her hands in her lap. "It was brash. I was a little dramatic."

"*A little*! You ran away from a life of royalty!"

"Don't you start in on that, too!" Ferrin frowned, standing up to walk to the tent flap. She pulled it aside to get a look at the sky. It was bright and gray and hurt her eyes to look at. The damp wind that had howled through the night hadn't settled down, and the storm roiling in her itched to take to the skies.

"I'm just teasing," Ash said, setting down the empty glass. "Mostly."

"Also my real name is Ferrin," she added with an apologetic wince. "Leone is going to want to check on you again," she warned as she spotted Madame walking down the aisle at a stately gate, causing nurses and healers to jump out of her way.

Ash groaned.

"Ferrin," Madame Leone offered a curt nod. "Would you go and check in on Lieutenant McGaily's bandages? They'll need changing, soon, if not now. We want everyone feeling their best before that storm rolls in."

She wasn't talking about the weather, and Ferrin could feel it too.

Lukas returned to the hospital after washing the nasty feeling of death and decay off his body to find Ferrin perched on the end of Ash's bed, the two of them animatedly chatting about something.

He cleared his throat as he approached. Ash looked up with a nervous smile and wide eyes. Ferrin stood from the cot. "I'd better go check on McGaily and give him his next dose of anti-inflammation tonic." She gave his arm a gentle squeeze as she strode past.

"So," Ash said. "I guess you probably want an explanation."

Lukas pulled a rickety stool up to the edge of the cot. "Yes, I do."

Ash let out a deep sigh. "I never meant to disappear like that."

He watched as she shifted on the cot, turning to face him. She had grown in the last three years, she was taller, more broad-shouldered, her face less round and her once-long hair now hung barely to her collar in choppy brown and gold layers.

"I ran off that day because I overheard Mamma making an arrangement with our awful neighbor to marry him because she couldn't afford to pay the fees and taxes for her spice shop, and didn't want to ask Eman for help. And you were drowning yourself trying to help put food on the table, so I thought I would go out for the day and come back with some money." She took a deep breath. "But I got lost. And I kept getting turned around, and suddenly I was miles away in a part of the city I didn't know, and there was nothing for me, nowhere to sleep and no one to look out for me. So I kept stealing things to get by. And I got really good at it."

"Well, that doesn't surprise me," he said, raising a wry eyebrow.

She flashed him an impish grin, "Until I started hitting more dangerous marks. I stole from the wrong person and I got grabbed by these two huge guys, one Bourjon and one Kalassan, I think. Part of the *popava* trade. They tossed me in a chest, sailed out of the harbor and threw me over the side of a ship."

Lukas flinched hearing this.

"Somehow I got out of the chest before I drowned, and I held onto the top of it for a day or so before a ship picked me up in the middle of the sea. And that's how I met Gillian, '*Ferrin*'," she said Ferrin's name in an affected voice, as if it were a massive joke.

Lukas fidgeted with the empty cup on the end table for a moment, and then looked up. "I'm sorry for blowing up at you. It's been a very strange and eventful few days, and I thought you were dead. Or worse." He blew out a long breath, something tight in his chest finally easing. "Gods, I'm so glad you're not dead. You have no idea."

"Me too. I prefer being not-dead," she grinned.

"Are you feeling better? Your lungs? The intimidating healer said you'd probably inhaled some sort of chemical they were using in that facility, and that in combination with the cold, damp air, your lungs were full of gunk."

"'Gunk'?" Ash raised an incredulous eyebrow. "Is that the technical term?"

"She put it more eloquently than that," Lukas admitted.

"You're not still irrationally angry?" Ash asked.

"I was being perfectly rational," Lukas responded as she wrapped her arms around him.

"Sure you were. About as rational as that time you and Damijan tried to sled down the dunes on a spare windowpane."

He masked the pang of sorrow that shot through him. "How do you even remember that? You were five."

"I have my sources."

"Sand-sledding on a sheet of glass? Remind me how you've survived this long," Ferrin asked, coming through the tent flap.

"Our mother stopped him before he and Damijan could shred themselves apart *and* ruin a perfectly good, expensive windowpane."

"I really can't wait to hear more about this, how old was he?" Ferrin asked, plopping onto the end of Asha's cot.

"Oh, about ten?"

"So the two of you are… what, five years apart?"

"Four and a half. I have a summer birthday," Ash shared. "So, I'll be nineteen soon."

"Yeah, you're still the baby though," Lukas snorted.

"Ash, what will you do now?" Ferrin asked.

Lukas glanced at Ferrin and then his sister. He could tell they shared the same wild spirit.

"Well, I can't go back to Zare." She squeezed her eyes shut. "And I know I should at least write a letter to Mamma and Eman."

Eman, their eldest sister, was two years older than Lukas and shared the same father. She had married a merchant farmer five years ago and had two beautiful children. His mother had moved to their farm a little after Ash had disappeared.

"I can send it for you," Lukas offered.

"But aside from that, I'm a fugitive in a country I've never even *been* to before now."

"If you want," Ferrin said, laying a hand on Ash's knee, "you can stay here with us. In hiding, if need be."

"Oh, right, you're *royalty*," Asha drawled with a mischievous grin.

"Barely," Ferrin huffed. "I was this close to being disowned *before* breaking dozens of people out of prison."

Lukas froze. He had forgotten how she had announced herself to those guards. Word could have gotten back to the capital by now, and with the maps still missing from wherever she'd stolen them, Ferrin could be in big trouble.

"Ferrin, you should probably be the one going into hiding," he said.

"Yeah, where would I do that? I pissed off the one group of people who might take me in."

He didn't know much about the rebel intelligence base, but he did know that Ferrin had intentionally gone around their leader's wishes to orchestrate the prison break. "You can stay in the cabin for now, I guess. Both of you."

"Oh, thanks. So we can start figuring out exactly what's going on in that hellhole prison while dodging raindrops from the leaky roof."

Lukas shot Ferrin a glare for her comment and she met it with a grin.

"Well, I guess we'll head down there as soon as everything is sorted here," she said.

That evening, Ferrin and Ash settled into Lukas's odd little cabin. After much argument, Madame Leone allowed Ash to leave the hospital *only* if she promised to be gentle with herself. Ash had begrudgingly agreed. Ferrin had wondered aloud what had happened to Ryder, to which Lukas answered with a tense, dismissive shake of his head. He had not returned to the capital yet.

When they left the hospital, Leone had pulled Ferrin into an uncharacteristically warm embrace.

"Something is coming, dear. Be on your guard and keep your friends close," she'd whispered before drawing back. Ferrin had shaken off the warning as superstition, but still, an uneasiness loomed over her.

She managed to scrounge up some breeches and a clean shirt for Ash, and the two of them were brewing up some stew in the hearth. Before Lukas had left to take care of some business in the castle, Ferrin had asked him to send Soviel to the cabin. She'd been so distracted by the surprising relationship between Ash and Lukas that she hadn't gotten to tell Soviel everything about the prison break. She paced as she waited for her to show up at the cabin.

Her two worlds were beginning to collide in a way she had never expected.

"Oh, shit. The soup!" Ash's expletives drew Ferrin out of her thoughts.

"Shit, shit," Ferrin gasped, rushing over with a dish rag. "Here."

After carefully rotating the hearth rug, all evidence of the boil-over was hidden by the small woodpile. Lukas would never have to know that they'd spilled soup on his rug. And burned a hole in it in their scramble to move the pot from the fire.

"It'll be fine," Ferrin nodded confidently.

There was a knock on the door. The wind was still whipping the trees against the side of the house, and the door swung wide as it caught a gust when Ferrin opened it.

"*Strata* above, it is howling out there!" Soviel exclaimed, entering with Rhi right behind her. Her pale, wet hair was stuck to her face, which was white as a sheet. "You've got stew?"

After introducing Soviel and Rhi to Ash, and burning her tongue on the first sip of stew, Ferrin set down her bowl.

"So, you're Lukas's *sister*," Rhi said, squinting at Asha.

"Well," she clarified, swallowing a mouthful of broth, "half, technically. Different dads."

Rhi nodded. "You do look alike. And you sailed with ah, *Gillian* here?"

"Sure did," Ash chirped.

"Speaking of Lukas, will he be joining us?" Ferrin asked Rhi.

"Haven't seen him since this afternoon, I think he had some business to attend to."

"Alright, then," Ferrin stood, pacing in front of the fire. "Soviel. Rhi. I probably should wait till all involved parties are present, but frankly, I'm way too afraid to see Helene after directly disobeying her wishes." Ferrin took a deep breath. "Danvery Prison is more than a labor and holding facility."

"What happened up there?" Soviel asked.

Ferrin pursed her lips. "There was some important duke visiting, too important to care about checking in on some backwater jailing facility. And there was—"

"They're growing something in the basement. A creature," Ash interjected.

"Something that had to be fed people," Ferrin said, shuddering as she remembered the feeling of the darkness exhaling in the chasm. "A lot of people."

"Like what? An animal?" Rhi chewed his thumbnail.

"Something else," Ash answered. "Something that drains the life out of you. The ones they didn't bring to the laboratory were eventually fed to the pit."

"I think they might be growing something like that here, too," Soviel said quietly, her brow pinched.

"Where?"

"Beneath the older part of the castle. There's a lot of walled off hallways. My room is on that side and sometimes I can hear things through the wall." She swallowed. "And that would explain some of the missing people around the town."

"For what purpose, though?"

"That guard said something about it sucking the life out of land," Ash said, blowing on her soup.

Seeing Soviel frown, Ferrin asked, "What is it?"

"I forget what the name for it is in the common tongue. The word in Old Njorski is *razr'kato*. Ravager."

Ferrin froze. "Is that the same as the Bourjon *rasernemaud*?"

Soviel nodded somberly.

"What does it do?" Rhi said.

"It's been so long since anyone's seen one full grown. If cultivated, it can grow strong enough to cause the destruction of everything around it for miles. Landslides, earthquakes, fires, floods, windstorms," Soviel explained. "If they're feeding it people every day, it won't take long till it grows strong enough to begin destroying the land."

"But why use something like that to fight over land if it's just going to destroy it?" Ash asked the question they were all thinking.

Soviel shook her head. "I don't know. We have to go and talk to Wilcoe in the morning."

Ferrin groaned. She was not looking forward to that.

"If she's still angry, she hasn't said anything about it. I haven't been down in a few days."

"Well, I suppose I might as well get it over with. We'll go in the morning?"

The early morning air was cool and prickly as Ferrin and Soviel meandered down to the village from the cabin, where they'd all slept the night before. Town should have been bustling by now, with people out buying their bread and eggs for the day and heading off to work, but the streets were nearly desolate, still in ruins from the recent raid.

A wayward gust of wind blew a single sheet of newspaper across the alley as they approached the safe house. Windows were shuttered against the coming storm, awnings were furled, the various peddlers who had once lurked on the street corners were nowhere to be seen.

Ferrin was anxious, perturbed by this unnatural silence. The weather had cooled off and she wished she'd had the sense to grab one of Lukas's coats before heading out.

"Has it been this quiet all week?" she asked Soviel.

"No," Soviel answered, sounding uneasy. "After the raid, people were cautious, but it hasn't been so empty like this."

They strolled down the side street to the main door. Ferrin was unsurprised to find it locked, and turned to Soviel. "You do the honors," she said, stepping aside.

"Ach. I can't believe Grey wouldn't just teach you the damned knock," Soviel huffed, rolling her eyes.

"I'd say it's because he doesn't like me, but I think he's just crotchety to everyone."

Soviel snorted as she rapped a series of short and long knocks on the wood of the door. "He's like a grouchy old man sometimes. But you'd be surprised at how kind he can be. Under the right circumstances."

"Really?"

Soviel nodded. "We used to… court, if you must know." She squinted at the word.

"*Really*?" Ferrin asked, eyes wide.

"Oh, don't look so shocked," Soviel grimaced as she repeated the knock. "He's very different one-on-one. And you can't deny his beauty."

"That's fair," Ferrin laughed. "I'd think romance amongst operatives was forbidden."

"Oh, Helene has tried. But truly, her decree that it was against the rules had the opposite effect. Besides, who else are we going to meet? People we're spying on?"

Ferrin could barely stop herself from chuckling. "All good points."

"Alright, why is no one answering this door?" Soviel spewed a storm of curses uncharacteristic of her.

"Do you have a key?"

Soviel shook her head, chewing the inside of her cheek.

"Maybe everyone is out and about?"

"No, no, there're protocols. There's *always* someone to watch the door, at least a few sentinels."

"Alright, I'm going to go in that window up there, please don't panic."

"Good luck, the walls were built with anti-climbing masonry. The gaps between the—Oh my gods, *what* are you doing?" Her voice rose a full octave as Ferrin took a running start and lifted off the street.

The window she'd crashed through nearly a week ago had not been repaired, only shuttered with a board, which was easy enough to pry off as Soviel watched from the street. She tumbled through the window, dropping the board on the dusty floor. The room was empty.

"What the…" she said under her breath. She pushed open the door to the hallway. Nothing.

A sense of dread crept over her as she continued down the hall. The spiral staircase creaked beneath her feet, the iron of the railing cold beneath her clammy hands. There was no one downstairs. There was no one in any of the rooms along the hallway, the doors all hanging open. In fact, the entire downstairs had been emptied. Save for the bare table and six wooden chairs, there was nothing but dust.

The storage chests that'd been placed around the room were all gone, a few papers lay strewn beneath the table, as if the occupants had packed and left in a hurry.

Ferrin rushed to the door and undid the cross bolt, the chain and the lock to let Soviel in.

"What the hell, Ferrin?" Soviel hissed.

"What, you didn't pick up on that? Sounds like you're letting your skills dull, perhaps it's all the forbidden romance."

"You're insufferable," Soviel snapped, smacking Ferrin on the arm. They both seemed to sober at once as they took in the disarray of the room, and the emptiness and quiet of the house. "Where are they?"

They looked at each other with alarm.

"Did you check the office?"

"Not yet."

The door to Helene's office swung open without resistance. Ferrin half-expected to find a corpse sprawled across the desk, a note skewered to its chest with a list of demands written in blood.

All that remained was the desk, a stack of banking slips and some papers—forged, most likely—for potato exports.

"This is bad." Soviel's inhale was sharp.

Ferrin turned her head see what Soviel had found. The note was scrawled in Helene's bold hand, in black ink.

GET OUT. NO VACANCY.

"What does that mean?" Ferrin asked.

"We need to go," Soviel said, grabbing Ferrin's wrist and scurrying to the door.

"Sov, what does that mean? Is it code?"

"This base was compromised. We need to go."

CHAPTER THIRTY-SIX

"It sort of seems like there very much *is* vacancy. That whole place was empty," Ferrin pointed out as they hustled back to Soviel's rooms in the castle.

"It's a code, Ferrin. A concealed message. This isn't good," she huffed as she clenched her fists. They had just left her there. No wonder she hadn't spotted any of the other castle moles in the last few days, they'd *all* been pulled.

There must have been a leak.

But then why had no one come for her?

Soviel's heart was pounding as they rounded the corner and nearly ran straight into two of the Kingsguard. "Apologies," she said, letting the shy, nervous waver return to her voice, veil falling into place with ease. She dropped her gaze to the ground as they passed.

"Highness," one of them barked at Ferrin, "you're to come with us. Your father wishes to speak with you."

"Did he say why?" Ferrin asked, backing away a step. "I'm a little busy."

"He insisted." The second guard inched closer.

"Very well," she said with a resigned sigh bordering on the dramatic. "Soviel, will you see that my dress is taken care of and let Mr. Mazrihn know I will be expecting his delivery imminently?" Her eyes flared as she spoke.

"Yes, Your Highness," Soviel replied with a curtsy. "Right away."

"Very well, gentlemen," she said, letting the guards fall into step beside her.

Soviel could sense the buzz of fear just beneath Ferrin's skin. As soon as the guards were out of sight, she ran the rest of the way to her rooms.

She began strapping her knives to her legs with a set of buckle garters, accessible through the slits in her skirts meant to reach her pockets. In her desk, there was one precious vial of reagent that Nimhe hadn't managed to smash on the ground, and she tucked it into her pocket bag, along with a vial of sweet nightshade. The last of the sleeping spores she'd developed with Madame had been spilled on the floor when Nimhe ransacked the room. Too bad the little rat hadn't managed to inhale a lungful and pass out cold on the floor.

When she'd gathered everything useful she could think of, she ran out, heading for Lukas's cabin. If the king had found out about Ferrin's involvement in the prison break, she would be in serious trouble. They had to be ready to get her out.

Ferrin steadied her hands and took a deep breath as the big double doors to the throne room swung open and she was escorted in. The guards marched her to a spot a few paces in front of the throne, which was unoccupied.

"Well? I thought you brought me here to speak with my father."

"We did, Highness."

"Then where is he?"

"On his way."

The guards hadn't left her side. They remained stationed just behind her, on either side. That did not bode well.

"What exactly is going on here? I demand an explanation as to what could be so important to warrant this interruption of my day."

"Couldn't tell you, Highness, as I don't go around questioning His Majesty's orders," said the guard on her left with a dismissive shrug.

She turned around to face them. "I'm going to leave if you don't tell me."

"He said if you tried to leave that we were to prevent you from doing so by *any means necessary*."

She inhaled through her nose before squinting at them skeptically. "Right, that's unfortunate," she uncrossed her arms, backing away a step, "for you."

The closer guard grabbed for her as she fell backwards, weightless as the ring took hold of the air around her. She sent the first guard back with a kick to the face, her boot whacking into his jaw with a crack as she ascended to the high, vaulted ceiling. The second guard's eyes widened.

His rifle trained on her as she skimmed across the ceiling, reaching into her boot for the knife she'd hidden there. She threw it at his face. It clattered to the ground but not before the handle hit him on his brow bone. He dropped his rifle but immediately scrambled towards where it had landed on the floor.

"Fuck," she hissed, dropping to his level.

The shot nearly hit her. She didn't hesitate, grabbing the barrel before he could reload. She slammed the stock into his face with a crunch and he went down.

Panting, she turned to flee from the room, but the doors suddenly flung open wide and in stalked her father.

"Seize the traitor!" he commanded to the pair of guards flanking him. Before they could surge forward and grab her, two dozen more flooded into the room.

Her breath caught in her throat. Those *uniforms*. The soldiers now spilling into the room with their muskets primed were wearing bright blue, trimmed in red and cream—Bourjony's colors.

She didn't think, didn't look at his face, didn't wait to see what happened next. She turned and ran for the dais, vaulting up the steps to the hidden hallway she had seen Nerena use time and again. The door flew open and she launched herself through it, into the dark hallway.

She didn't think, she just ran, nearly knocking over a servant boy making his way to the throne room with a tea tray. The hallway let out near the kitchens, the light harsh on her eyes as she ran towards the nearest exit.

Soviel and Asha hustled through the central hallway of the castle, the latter with a shawl wrapped over her head and shoulders. Ash didn't quite know what to make of Soviel. Every time she thought she had her figured out, they'd run into a different guard or servant or lord and Soviel would shed her personality and don an entirely new one. It was uncanny.

She had burst into the cabin, cheeks rosy from rushing all the way there from the castle, and announced that Ferrin was in trouble, once again. Clearly, Ferrin didn't live her life here any differently from how she had lived it at sea.

They'd split up, with Lukas and Rhi going off towards the throne room, while she and Soviel headed towards Ferrin's rooms. They'd all meet back at the cabin and figure out exactly what was going on.

Another thing Ash didn't know what to make of was this *place*. The palace itself was opulent and glorious, of course. But why were there so many soldiers? It seemed like they were arriving by the wagonful.

"How could they already know Gill—I mean Ferrin—was involved in the prison break?" she asked.

"She stole the blueprints for the building from her father's office. That had to be it. Or maybe a guard recognized her and reported back."

"She did announce herself there. But still, how could they have gotten word down here so quickly? We traveled fast."

"A messenger eagle, probably. Besides, this may be unrelated. Something else is happening in this place," Soviel said. "I just don't know what it is."

"You think they're growing one of those monsters here?"

"More than that," Soviel admitted as they rounded the corner to Ferrin's hallway. "The people I work for disappeared. They left a message, but I haven't had time to decode it since Ferrin was taken. As soon as we get her, I think we should leave the castle grounds. Indefinitely."

Ash agreed. The place was giving her the creeps.

"What are we going to do if we find her and she's being guarded? I don't know if you noticed, but there're about a million soldiers prowling around this place."

"That's another thing, what are they preparing for? Why are there so many soldiers moving here? It's not the front, it's the most well-fortified spot on the whole damn island." Soviel seemed to be talking to herself at this point as she tried to make sense of what was going on.

Ferrin's rooms were empty, and so were Rhi's. Soviel and Ash exchanged a look as nerves unfurled in Ash's stomach. "Should we check somewhere else? I've got a bad feeling."

"Let's cover the ground between here and the throne room. That's where they took her."

"Right then, lead the way," Ash said.

The pit in her stomach only grew as they descended the stairway and heard voices approaching. When two guards rounded the landing, Soviel slipped into one of her many masks. Watching the shift in her aura was startling to see firsthand.

"Good evening, Royce," said Soviel with a coy dip of her head. Serpent's teeth, was she *blushing* on command? If Ash hadn't seen the change happen, she'd believe Soviel was sweet on the guard, but too shy to do much about it.

"Ladies," one of the soldier's tipped his hat to her.

As they passed them on the stairs, the second guard, a woman, elbowed the first. "Isn't that one of them?" she asked.

"Hang on, you two," ordered Royce.

"Is something the matter?" Soviel said, her voice registering high and light, brows raised with concern.

"You, lower your hood," the second guard jerked a finger at Ash.

She knew there was no sense in arguing. She was about to pull the hood down when Soviel laid a hand over her arm, stopping her. "My friend is ill, I'm afraid. I'm trying to get us to the hospital swiftly. Perhaps you'd care to escort us?" Soviel said hopefully as she stepped in closer to Royce. "There's so many new guards, I don't want to have to stop and check in with every single one of them—"

"Lower the hood."

"Cath, it's just two girls," Royce began to say.

"Are you saying women can't be dangerous? Did you just miss the entire debriefing about the pr—"

Ash didn't wait to see what else the guard was going to say. Not when she was close enough to snatch the guard's knife out of her belt.

"Dammit!" Cath swore, drawing her sword.

Soviel, who had been standing well within Royce's space, had yanked the musket out of his hands and clocked him in the face.

Ash twisted out of Cath's reach, the sharp edge of her sword grazing her shoulder with a sting. She went to block the next swing with the knife, parrying it back as she stepped up one stair, hooking her ankle around the guard's.

Cath lunged, and caught on Ash's ankle, tumbling back on the stone steps with a sickening series of cracks and snaps. When she rolled to a stop on the landing, her eyes were open, unseeing, and her neck was bent at an angle that was wholly unnatural. A wave of nausea rolled through Asha's body. She knew sometimes it was necessary, but she'd seen more than enough meaningless deaths in the last few weeks to last her a lifetime.

"Is he dead?" Ash gestured to the body, which Soviel had apparently decided to rid of its clothes.

"No, just unconscious. Here, grab her coat."

"We should kill him."

"I try to avoid that, I'm a healer."

"You also have a cover to protect, yes? If he wakes up, he's going to talk," Ash said, eyeing the lump forming on the unconscious guard's head.

"I'm not sure how much of a cover I have left," Soviel sniffed.

"Suit yourself," Ash nodded as she walked down the stairs to peel the coat off the dead soldier. *Cath.*

Shrugging the military coats over their own clothes, and taking up the guards' weapons, they continued on their way.

*   *   *

"There's no one here." Rhi's voice echoed through the empty throne room.

"Look," Lukas said, waving Rhi over to the suspicious smudge of dried blood on the marble floor. "Someone was dragged out."

Rhi's heart launched into his throat. "Do you think—"

"It could be anyone's," Lukas told himself as much as Rhi. "Where might they take her for disciplining?"

"My father's office perhaps? His private office. It's not far," Rhi said, gesturing with his hand.

"Lead the way, Prince," Lukas said, his voice cavalier as always, but his forehead was creased with tension.

Rhi's breathing quickened as he ran a hand through his hair. "This way."

They should have left then and there. Maybe then all of what came next could have been avoided. They could have fled the city, gone north to Avaree or Port Galan or hopped on the last boat out to Karlgiard.

The castle hallways were empty. So empty that, by Rhi's count, at least ten guards seemed to have deserted their posts.

They really should have left.

"This way," Rhi directed, pushing open the door to the atrium of the royal office. The waiting area was empty, and the door to the office was open. They exchanged a nervous look and when Rhi stepped into the office, he gasped. It was a mess, as if someone had been hastily searching for something with so much urgency, they couldn't be bothered to close a drawer. The desktop was strewn with papers and leather folios, and a well of ink had spilled, pooling in a dark mass on the fine wood.

"Alright, this is bad. We should not be in here," Lukas said.

Rhi was about to agree when he caught sight of a half-empty cup of tea that had gone cold. "Wait a minute—is that?" Rhi picked up the tea. It had a milky grey layer at the bottom that had separated out from the clear liquid at the top. "Luk, look at this. Tell me this is what I think it is."

Lukas took the cup and peered into its contents. He sniffed it. "That is definitely *popava* steeped into tea."

"That's what I thought. But that means…"

"What?"

"Someone has been slipping *popava,* or some strain of it to my father. He hates the stuff, he's strictly a stout and wine man. There's no way he's taking it knowingly."

"Why would someone drug him?"

"Mood altering? Maybe Nerena uses it to calm him when he flies into one of his rages. She had no problem dosing *my* wine with it."

"She dosed you?" Lukas asked.

"I'll fill you in later."

"Maybe she is slipping it in his tea and wine," Lukas mumbled as he swirled the cup around and dipped a finger into the cold tea. "It looks diluted. Whoever drank it likely wouldn't notice a thing."

"This just keeps getting more and more bizarre," Rhi breathed. "We absolutely do need to get out of here, though."

"Agreed."

They quickly and quietly exited the room, no less confused than they had been before. Rhi barely had time to react when the heel of a musket slammed into the side of Lukas's head. He started towards his friend, drawing the knife from his hip. Steel met wool and then flesh as he got in one good swipe before something clonked him in the back of the skull and he lost consciousness.

Soviel finally found Ferrin as she rounded the corner of the hallway between the ballroom and the kitchens. "Gods above, you're alright?" she whispered frantically, gripping Ferrin by the shoulders.

Ferrin nodded, trying to catch her breath. "We need to go. Th-there's soldiers here. From Bourjony."

"What?" Ash asked, dumbfounded. "Isn't Lindbarrow at war with Bourjony?"

Ferrin looked as surprised as Ash. "Not as of yesterday. Things have been tense, because of our alliance with Efel, but I suspect that may be changing as we speak. The soldiers don't seem to be attacking, per se."

"Alright, explain it when we get back to the cabin. The boys will meet us there."

They hurried out of the castle, carefully avoiding the wing that Ferrin had seen the contingent of soldiers gathering in earlier.

The air still hung thick with fog, despite the hour crawling closer to noon. The trio made a detour to the stables to move some horses out to the woods, in case they needed to make a hasty escape. Ferrin was looking around worriedly.

"What are you looking for?"

"Alick. He's not here," Ferrin said quietly.

"He probably left with the rest of them. Come on," prompted Soviel.

"Yeah, maybe," Ferrin said hesitantly, checking the office one more time.

They tacked up three horses and mounted, riding down to the cabin where Rhi and Lukas were likely waiting.

Soviel didn't wear breeches often, but she was glad she had tugged some on as riding at speed quickly came back to her. It wasn't something she found herself doing often. Once they were closer to the woods, they slowed the horses to a walk.

Ferrin exhaled a shaky breath.

"What *happened* in there?" Ash asked, anxious to know what was going on.

Ferrin fixed her eyes upon her horse's withers, uncharacteristically slouching in the saddle and looking utterly forlorn. "He knows. He must have noticed the plans missing. He knows and he was going to… I don't know what he was going to do, but he knows."

"We need to get out of this city by nightfall," Soviel said. "We should head north to Port Galan."

"Oh fantastic, another jaunt across the Barrian countryside, pursued by military," Ash responded.

"I'm sure you'll enjoy the scenery more this time," Soviel smirked.

"As long as there's more of those bright purple trees. Those were absolutely wild."

"What purple trees?" Ferrin asked.

"You know, the purple trees? Along the road and in the woods? With the little gliding squirrels?" She looked at her companions' expressions and her expression fell. "Which I clearly hallucinated when I was feverish," she said with a sheepish grimace.

"Your fever was high enough to cook an egg on your head, you probably saw all sorts of nonsense."

"That is some truly horrifying imagery."

"It's true, though," Soviel quipped, unable to fight the smirk forming on her lips.

"You did start mumbling about not letting Lukas steal your mints," Ferrin added.

"That's fantastic," muttered Ash. "I'm so glad my harrowing experience of falling gravely ill while imprisoned in a monstrous facility experimenting on people has been entertaining for the both of you."

Ferrin snickered. "Sorry, Ash. But purple trees? Surely you can admit that's at least a little amusing."

They reached the cabin, only to find it empty. Two horses were still untacked at the hitching post, and the windows were dark. "Hold up," Ferrin said quietly, halting and dismounting.

"Ferr—be careful," Soviel cautioned as she watched Ferrin pad slowly to the front of the house.

Ferrin poked her head around the corner, then peered in the window. She jerked her head down with a start.

Did she see something? Soviel wondered. And more importantly, had the something seen her? She and Asha dismounted as quietly as possible.

"Ladies," came a man's voice from the darkened doorway. It wasn't a voice Soviel recognized and the gentleman who stepped from the stoop was decidedly *not* Lukas or Rhi. He was dressed in a military coat, deep blue trimmed with red, white and a touch of gold.

Bourjony.

His dark gold hair was neatly pulled back from his pale face and tied off with a ribbon.

Ferrin, hiding behind the corner of the cabin, held a finger to her lips and met Soviel's eye.

He will recognize me and we'll all be done for, she seemed to say.

"Sir, can we help you?" Soviel said gently.

"Just dropping by. There's a fugitive out there somewhere tonight. You ladies best get inside before nightfall."

"A fugitive?" Soviel asked, her tone apprehensive yet curious. Ash said nothing, but Soviel could feel her tense beside her.

"Indeed," the man confirmed. His accent was Barrian, she noticed, not Bourjon. Her stomach curdled.

"We'll get inside and bar our door right away, sir."

"Who's the third horse belong to?"

"Oh, my husband. He's just gone to gather firewood. He'll be back any minute."

"Well, it sounds like you're in capable hands. I'll be off to warn the rest of the townsfolk, then."

Once he'd left, Soviel exhaled a shuddering breath, her hands shaking.

"I thought for a second he was talking about me!" Ash exhaled.

Ferrin popped back out of the shadows. "Are you two alright?"

"Yes, just having a small fit of the heart," Ash said, pressing her hand to her chest.

"Sorry," Ferrin winced. "He's only looking for me. I assumed he would leave."

"Ferrin, did you see his coat? That wasn't a Barrian uniform."

"I didn't get a good look."

"It was Bourjon."

"He didn't *sound* Bourjon."

"No, he didn't."

"We still don't know where Lukas and Rhi are," Ash reminded them.

"Maybe they got held up," Soviel said. "We should give them an hour before we go back up there to search."

Ferrin was wringing her hands nervously. "An hour. Then we go and search for them."

"Until then?"

"We prepare."

CHAPTER THIRTY-SEVEN

When Lukas woke up, he was dizzy. Consciousness trickled back slow as syrup, and he cracked his eyes open. He'd taken a hard blow to the head.

There was light streaming through the window, far brighter than seemed necessary, and he closed his eyes against it. Between his blurry vision and the dull thrum in his wrists, he could make out that he was shackled and chained somewhere in the castle. From the feel of the rough stones, somewhere in the older end.

With a groan, he forced his eyes open. His head pounded, and he fought the urge to let his eyelids droop shut again. Squinting around at the room, he could see it was round, built of rough-cut cobblestone walls and a wooden floor. There was a large window opposite the door, and its shutters were thrown open wide, letting in the damp, gray air of the afternoon. They were high up.

Across the room was a slumped figure, whose wrists were bound by a chain through an O-ring bolted to the wall.

"Rhi? Rhi, wake up," he hissed.

The shape groaned in response, shifting and turning to face Lukas. Rhi leaned limply off the wall, his hair grimy and plastered against his face.

"Rhi, *listen* to me," Lukas struggled to sit up. "They're taking the castle, I think it's the Bourj—"

The tip of a sword was pressed firmly to his neck.

"You. Up."

Lukas turned his head, his eyes still adjusting. The commanding voice belonged to a masked man, his coat a dark, saturated blue trimmed with crimson and cream, his breeches bright white, his boots shining and freshly polished. He had no accent indicative of Bourjon heritage; in fact, he sounded a lot like he'd been raised in Lindbarrow.

Holding his gaze, Lukas rose from the floor slowly, his head pounding. A second soldier appeared to unbolt his ankle shackles from the floor. They left the manacles on his wrists.

"Walk."

"I'm not leaving him."

"He swings at noon tomorrow. You will meet a quicker end this day. *Walk.*" The sword point pressed harder into his jaw, drawing blood. "Or die where you stand."

Lukas shifted his eyes to Rhi, who had since regained consciousness. *Get help*, he mouthed.

Clenching his jaw, Lukas staggered forward. There were about a half dozen more soldiers on the level below. "No use wasting a bullet on this one, sir." This voice carried the telltale fluid accent of Bourjony.

"Bring him down to the cellar, for the creature."

"What are you doing?"

"Puttin' a bag over 'is head."

"Do not bother, one more impure item to remove before the feeding," said the first voice. "Besides, the creature will suck the life from him."

"The Reezornemo can truly do that?"

"*Rasernemaud*," corrected the first voice, exasperated. "Imbecile."

"Can't you just shoot me?" Lukas mumbled under his breath. The bag went over his head anyway.

"She's been feeding down there for weeks. When d'you suppose she'll start manipulating the weather and all?" asked one of the voices as Lukas was ushered out of the room, the sound of a bolt sliding into place separating him from Rhi.

"Keep it moving, man."

They were descending a very long, twisting set of stairs. Between his dizzy head and lack of vision, Lukas wasn't sure how he managed not to fall face first all the way to the bottom of the tower. The three guards accompanying him steered him through another doorway, and onto flat ground again.

He counted his steps as they led him down hallways and stairwells, but it was of little use. A sense of dread crept over him as they moved lower and lower in the castle.

Another one of those creatures was growing in a pit beneath the castle. And once again, a bunch of guards were going to try and feed him to it. If he could manage to get away, he could come back and help Rhi escape. He knew they had been keeping him in the old citadel, which consisted of three tall stone towers at the northern end of the castle. Towers now crawling with traitor guards and Bourjon soldiers.

They made it another few turns before something happened. He could sense stone floor beneath his feet, a musket at his ribs, a hand clasped on his shoulder. Then, at once, all of those things disappeared in a tussle.

His face met the stone floor and the musket went off, not into him, as far as he could tell. He heard a series of muffled grunts, footfalls and blunt impacts as he tried to get his elbows under him. Then the bag was ripped off his head and the body of the Bourjon guard landed beside him, his hat knocked askew.

"Get the other one!" a woman's voice called. Seconds later, another tumbling sound erupted from down the hallway.

"Don't move," instructed a second, more familiar woman's voice. "Hands out." The butt of a musket slammed down over the chain between his manacles, separating them into two heavy bracelets.

"Come on, knock him out!" There was another thud, and things came into focus as Lukas watched Ferrin slam the heel of her musket into the second guard's head. She was wearing an ill-fitting palace guard's uniform.

"Ferrin?" Lukas squinted in confusion.

"Come on, up!" she grabbed him by the wrist, hauling him up. "Someone will have heard that shot. Let's go."

With a vice-grip on his wrist, Ferrin pulled him down the hallway, the others supporting the weight of the unconscious guard between them.

"Let me help—"

"I think not," Soviel grunted. "Not with that head wound."

They stopped next to a section of wall adorned with a potted fern, and Lukas felt a little ridiculous that Soviel and Ash, who were both about half his size, had gotten stuck carrying the soldier.

Skimming along the cobblestones with her free hand, Ferrin felt along the wall, pushing her fingers into a crack in the mortar. With a quick, reverberating jolt, a section of the wall popped forward, and she grabbed ahold of it, swinging it open on hidden hinges.

"In, in," she said hurriedly, holding it open. Her gaze flickered back to the hallway they'd come from, anxiously awaiting the hell-storm of guards that was sure to descend on them any minute.

Once they were all inside, she stopped Lukas, running a finger feather-gentle over the welt on his forehead. Her fingers were cool and light, but the touch hurt nonetheless "Oh, gods, Luk. What have they done to you?"

He winced. "I'm fine, really, help them carry. I'll be fine."

"Where were they holding you?"

"It's pretty foggy, but I'll tell you once we're safely *out* of this damn castle."

"What about Rhi?" she asked, turning as if she planned to storm off on her own in search of her brother.

"There's time—" he grabbed her by the hand. "They want to make it a public affair, which means we have tonight at least to rescue him."

The flight through the ancient tunnels beneath the castle was harrowing and tight, nothing like the well-maintained servant hallways. Despite the pounding in his skull, Lukas managed to keep his feet right and follow the women through the damp, dark hall, through cobwebs and worse as he wondered how close they were passing to whatever fell creature lay beneath the castle.

Once they were back at the cabin, Ferrin began pacing. Rhi was imprisoned somewhere up there, set to hang at the noon bells the following day, and they were cooped up in the cabin. She was going to crawl out of her skin.

What if he thought she had abandoned him again?

The soldier they'd knocked unconscious in the tunnels was tied up in a chair in the kitchen, his hands and feet strapped firmly in place to the wooden back and legs of the chair.

"The soldiers in the tower. They didn't all *sound* Bourjon. But they all had Bourjon uniforms on. And facial coverings," Lukas was explaining.

"Bourjon uniforms," Ferrin repeated as she worried a hang nail to the point of bleeding. "They must have been planning this for months."

Soviel nodded grimly. "I was gathering intel on those likely to defect. We never thought…" she shook her head absently. "We never thought defecting to *Bourjony* was even on the table."

"They had the crest and everything."

Ferrin approached Lukas. "Here." She picked up a bottle of liquor off of the table and pulled the rumpled cravat from her throat, balling up the end of the linen and soaking it. She touched his jaw lightly, silently directing him to tilt his head. He winced when she brought the rag to the bloody welt on his face.

"You should really let me take a look at that soon," Soviel said, tossing a bite of cheese in her mouth.

Ferrin stood aside, gesturing for her to go ahead.

"So if there's been a coup from within the military, then where are the rest of the guards?"

"I don't think it's a coup. My father has had a hand in this. Perhaps he's allied with Bourjony?"

"That doesn't make *sense*," Soviel huffed.

"Why else cause all these problems? He didn't get his way with Efel, so he's hedged his bets. Changed sides."

"I'm not sure. This could have come from within the army, separate from the king," Soviel countered. "Did he say anything strange when you saw him earlier?"

Ferrin shook her head. "We didn't speak. His guards seemed dodgy so I was on my way out as he came in. Called for them to arrest me, *then* a flood of Bourjon soldiers came in."

"But how was he with them? Did he command them?" Soviel asked as she wetted the cloth again.

"I didn't stick around to find out."

"Whatever has happened, Bourjony is here now and they seem *quite* comfortable," Lukas interjected, wincing as Soviel brought the damp cloth to his face.

"Well, where would the rest of the Lindbarrian soldiers be? Prejudices against Bourjony run deep among them, probably deeper than any lingering resentment against the Caels." Ferrin drummed her fingers on the kitchen table absently.

Ferrin shook her head. Soviel squinted as if puzzling out the answer. "My guess, if anyone escaped alive, they've deserted.

Headed north, or to the mainland. Most likely, any who outright resisted the overthrowing were killed or imprisoned."

"Or worse," Lukas said. "They have a pit monster here. One that's bigger than the one in the prison, or so some of the guards seem to think. They called it something—a Bourjon word. Rader, Raser,"

"*Rasernemaud*?" Soviel asked as she examined the wound on his forehead from all sides.

"That's it." He shifted in his chair, straightening. The broken chains around his wrists clanked against the wooden chair.

Ash entered, a few logs of firewood balanced on her shoulder. "Well? Did we wake up Dead-Weight yet?" she asked, jutting her chin in the direction of the tied-up soldier.

"Not yet."

"Hold still for a second," Soviel ordered Lukas.

Ferrin watched as she slipped some kind of leather pouch out of her stolen coat's pocket. She doled out two green little leaves and popped them into her mouth, chewing quickly before gingerly spitting them into her hand. She was probably the only person who could make spitting bits of green into her hand look somewhat graceful.

"Sorry," she grimaced sheepishly as she pressed the spit-paste onto Lukas's wound.

"This doesn't seem terribly sanitary," Lukas quipped.

"Perhaps if you were in possession of a mortar and pestle, I wouldn't have to resort to such barbaric methods."

"Fair."

Soviel did whatever it was she did that somehow drew the life energy out of the plant conduit and healed Lukas's head-gash.

"I'll never get used to that," he muttered as he touched his now-closed forehead. "Thanks."

A pang of envy sluiced though Ferrin's chest. She wished she could be the one to help him.

"Did I miss anything?" Ash asked in a whisper.

"There's a *Rasernemaud* in the castle. Apparently it's big and close to being able to decimate the land around it."

"Oh."

Ferrin shuddered, remembering the aftermath of a *Rasernemaud* she had seen on Rivalona years back. The temperature had shot up, trees combusting, the water near shore *boiling* as refugees escaped on a skiff. Hundreds of people had been displaced. The island had been a charred, smoking pile of rubble afterwards, only a smoking, bald mountain remained.

"What can anyone do against such a creature?" Ferrin asked no one in particular.

"It has to be killable. Doesn't it?"

"Mm-mm," shrugged Ferrin to indicate she didn't know any better than anyone else.

"What if we find the pit it's in and we take a few explosives…" Ash rested her thumb on her lower lip in contemplation. "Can it leave its pit? Does it have legs? Or is it just some creepy, sentient hole in the ground?"

"I don't know," Ferrin mused. "I'd never thought about that."

"How does it get there in the first place? And where does it come from?"

"All good questions," nodded Soviel. "I don't think they can *move* something like that. It has to be cultivated. I think. It had to have been brought here when it was very small, or maybe it was even born here. Maybe it comes from an egg, or something similar."

"Sounds like one nasty omelette," Ash muttered.

"Only one way to find out now," Ferrin's gaze drifted to where their prisoner slumped in his chair.

"I'll get a bucket of cold water," Ash said, a little too gleefully.

"Keep anything sharp in this cabin, Lukas?" Ferrin asked.

He cocked his head at her and snorted, as if to say *what do you think?*

Ferrin rolled her eyes. "Allow me to rephrase: *Where* do you keep your sharp objects?"

"Should be a knife-roll under the kitchen cabinet, a machete on the hook by the door and one under my bed. Also," He held up a finger in a *wait-a-second* gesture as he reached under the kitchen table, feeling along the flat underside. "Here."

With a *clink,* he pulled an entire short-sword from under the table.

She squinted from the sword to the table.

"And I suppose if you're feeling really adventurous, there's the kitchen knives."

"At the risk of ever having to dine here, I will abstain."

"Probably for the best."

Soviel ducked out to get some fresh water and to inspect the surrounding garden for anything useful. As soon as they were alone, Lukas's expression sobered.

"Do you want me to do it?" he asked.

Ferrin swallowed, looking at the array of blades on the table. She had never outright tortured anyone for information. Could she inflict so much pain on another person for her own gain? To shoot someone in defense, to fight someone was one thing, quick and messy and necessary for survival, but to spend minutes, maybe hours, personally, intimately stripping flesh from bone was another thing entirely.

She'd been on the receiving end a few times, and she knew it was a horrible thing to endure. But she was desperate. There were lines she was willing to cross for Rhi.

"No."

He nodded solemnly. "Just… don't push yourself too hard. There's a chance this idiot doesn't even know anything."

"I've got it," she said, her tone more forceful than she meant it to be.

"I know you do. I just don't want to see you lose yourself in it. Have you ever done this before?"

"Not exactly," she picked at a crack in the wooden table. Along the grain, a large sliver was coming loose, its point sharp. "But I know how."

"All I'm saying, Ferrin, is," he stood up and came around the table to stand next to her, his fingers brushing against hers as he took her hand in his. "Don't get lost in it."

"Oh, sit back down," Soviel ordered as she swept back in. "I want to examine your wrists. Anything to get those manacles off with?"

Lukas dropped back into the chair with a huff and extended his hands. "Nope."

"Right… well, let me look anyway," she said, placing a little bowl of water on the table. She began dabbing at the inflamed skin where the ropes had chafed his skin. "You do *not* want this getting infected. A few weeks ago, this boy came into the infirmary with his hand swollen to the size of a loaf of bread. All because he got a cat scratch he didn't clean up. Leone nearly had to take his thumb off."

Lukas grimaced. "Go right ahead, Madam healer."

The irony of what was about to occur in this room struck Ferrin. Soviel was working to heal Lukas's scrapes and bumps while mere feet away she herself would be inflicting injuries on another. Bile rose in her throat.

"Alright, Luk. Hope you don't mind your floor getting wet," Ash said, poised over the unconscious guard with a bucket ready to pour.

"I can't stop you now," he winced as Soviel continued prodding his head.

"Do you have any rosemary?" she asked.

"For healing?"

"No, I was planning on taking a break and baking some biscuits," Soviel rolled her eyes.

Lukas blinked.

"Yes, for healing, you dolt."

"Either way, no," he scowled.

"Ready, Ferr?" Ash asked anxiously, eying the guard.

Ferrin sighed, steeling her resolve. "Let's see what this gent has to say."

Soviel sat tending Lukas's injuries in the kitchen. It was quick work, and she was glad to have a distraction from the task Ferrin was undertaking in the next room.

"What do these do?" Ash asked from where she sat cross-legged on the table. She held up a vial of light purple petals suspended in translucent liquid.

"That's sweet nightshade, and it *will* kill you."

"Right, then," Ash said, tucking it back into the kit. "What about this one?"

"Gods above, Ash. Let the woman work," Lukas sighed.

"Sorry, I'm just curious."

"It's alright," Soviel said with a half-smile. "That one is just regular old peppermint. It helps with stomach aches, no healing-magic necessary."

"Oh."

"All done for now," Soviel announced as she stepped back from Lukas's head. "Do you feel dizzy at all?"

He tilted his head side to side. "Nope. All better."

"Excellent, you should eat something," Soviel said. "It's been a long day and it's only going to get worse, I'm sure."

Lukas nodded and went outside to the little vegetable garden. Soviel wasn't sure who planted the garden there, but she loved the idea of big, intimidating Lukas rooting around amongst tomatoes and flowers.

Hopping up on the table next to Ash, Soviel said quietly, "I'm nervous too."

Ash swiveled her head to look directly at Soviel. Her honey-gold eyes were wide. "You don't seem it."

"It's a talent of mine," Soviel said sardonically. "She's going to learn what she needs and be done with it. One way or another."

"I worry, though, that this is a little close to home. The captain who betrayed us was very skilled with interrogations. And he left her in a few situations not unlike this one."

Ferrin had mentioned her run-in with the olive-trade boss. Soviel had seen her scars, her *brands*.

"There was no way she was going to let any of the rest of us do this. Rhi is *her* brother." Soviel didn't mention the nearly visceral guilt that had been eating away at Ferrin since she realized how much her abandoning this place had affected Rhi. Sometimes her shame was nearly palpable, no matter her efforts to hide it.

Ash tucked her feet up and rested her chin on her knees. "I know. Ugh. Let's talk about something else."

"So. Khalim, huh? What's it like to grow up at the 'Crossroads of the World'?"

Ash's expression transformed into something between a grin and a nervous twitching of her lip. "Hot. And easy to get lost."

Soviel chuckled. "Well, where's your favorite place you've been?"

"Old Orini. No contest."

"As in…"

"Yeah, the pirate port. The rules are different there."

"Is that why you never went home?"

"I would have gone home eventually," Ash paused for a second, eyes narrowing as if realizing just then that she was getting very personal with someone she'd only met two days ago. Nonetheless, she continued. "By the time I was free of the merchants who'd captured me, I was hundreds of miles away, across the sea. And freshly employed on a pirate vessel."

"I can see the appeal," Soviel nodded, a little more wistfully than she'd meant to. She had always felt she lacked an anchor— she could fit in anywhere, but because of that, she never knew exactly where she *belonged.*

"Yeah, no one expects you to act or dress a certain way. Don't get me wrong, it's got its problems and its bad seeds, but everyone there is looking for the same thing."

"Which is?"

"Freedom, of course," Ash shrugged. "Freedom from class, from crown, from servitude without proper recompense."

She sounded not unlike some of those among the Caelish cause—those who wanted to topple the crown and *not* replace it with another, but rather with a new system. It was a point of contention at the base, or rather it was, before they had all vanished.

"Loyalty is to your crew, your ship," Ash continued. "They're who you're willing to die for, because they'd do the same for you. Half of them are ex-navy from all over who didn't like being forced into a fight for some fat monarch who'd never seen a hard day's work."

Soviel cracked a smile. "Ash, you and I are going to be good friends, I think."

Years ago, Soviel had been unsure what to make of Ferrin. She hadn't been so sure about whether to share her more… progressive views until she knew her much better. Of course, things had changed since then, and she knew Ferrin, princess or no, was on the same page. But in Ash, she saw a kindred spirit almost immediately.

The door swung open and Lukas appeared with a wicker basket of food.

"*Where* did that come from?"

"I have a storage cellar with some provisions," he said with an impish grin.

"That would have been useful information when I ate a horrible little green tomato earlier," Ash retorted.

"Here," he tossed her a block of hard cheese.

"Thanks," Ash said a little ruefully.

"How's it going in there?" he jerked his chin at the other room.

"Unclear. It hasn't been that long. Maybe one of us should go—"

Ferrin stumbled through the door and caught herself on the edge of the counter before throwing up on the floor. Thankfully, it was just water and bile.

"Shit. Are you alright?" Lukas was by her side, an arm around her shoulder, pulling her braid back and out of her face.

Her bloodstained knuckles were white as she braced herself on the counter, trying to catch her breath.

Soviel slid quietly off the table and went into the room where the prisoner sat.

The man was bloodied up. His thigh was bleeding badly, and bruises bloomed on his face. His ear was not fully attached to his head anymore. Soviel reminded herself that he was a traitor who had been part of a violent coup. He had chosen this path knowing it would lead to bloodshed of his own people.

But still, it was hard to look at him and know that her friend had inflicted most of those injuries. All she could do was hope Ferrin had gotten the information she needed, and now offer the man a gentle end. The sweet nightshade was heavy in the pocket of her stolen coat.

"Hi there," she said, approaching the counter where the bowl of water from earlier sat. She picked it up and stood before him.

"Get out of my face, bitch."

"It's alright, you don't have to talk. I'm going to clean up your wounds if that's alright. Mind telling me your name?"

"Scrablehouse."

"Well, Mr. Scrablehouse," Soviel said. "I can patch up that ear of yours quite easily. Your knee is going to hurt a little more, so I can just put a little soothing salve on it and bandage it for now. Care for some water?"

"It's Lieutenant."

"*Lieutenant* Scrablehouse," she amended.

"Yes, I would like some water," he grunted.

"Ferrin, would you fetch the lieutenant some water in a mug, please?" she asked.

The rest of the group were standing in the doorway. Waiting. Ferrin nodded, but she looked pale.

"No. No. Not her," he grimaced.

"Very well, then, *Asha*, might you please fetch a cup of water?"

"Hmph," the man grunted, watching as Ash approached with the water and wordlessly handed it to Soviel. Ferrin walked to the back of the room, where Scrablehouse couldn't see her, but Soviel could.

"Now, this is going to hurt a little, but I can make sure it leaves no scar," she promised. "Do you think while I do that, you can talk to me a little? It helps distract from the pain, like when you get a tattoo."

"*You've* gotten a tattoo?" his eyebrows shot up lasciviously.

"I might have," she shrugged.

"Where?"

"A gentleman does not ask a lady such a thing," she said primly before tying her hair back with a dirty strip of ribbon that had been around her wrist all day. "Now, how long have you been working for Bourjony?"

Ask about the general, Ferrin mouthed.

"Few months," he grimaced. "But some of the other men have been in contact for over a year."

"And they've been in correspondence with this general? He sounds important."

"Not sure about the general."

"Who then recruited you?"

"A Major Tierrault," he grunted again.

Behind him, Ferrin threw her hands up in silent exasperation. She must not have gotten that particular bit of information out of him, despite her efforts.

"You've met him, then?" Soviel asked a little absently as she ripped a strip of fabric from the hem of her shirt and began bandaging his knee. With every touch she willed him to calm, to relax. She felt his heart slow under her command as she drew energy from the bay leaves she kept in her pocket.

Scrablehouse nodded. "He's the one managing this operation."

She froze imperceptibly. Major Tierrault had to be *here,* on the grounds.

"Oh, my," she blinked honey from her lashes as she moved her gaze to his. He leered down at her as she tied off the linen bandage. "Do you expect to be promoted within the Bourjon army now that you're defecting to them?"

"Not sure. They promised us better pay, and keep for our families. And that they'd waive any legal issues we'd had with the Lindbarrian government."

"That's kind of them," she said wistfully. "You know, my parents were banished from their estate here after the Unification. They gave aid to the Caels."

"So did mine! I was only thirteen at the time—" he winced as the healing magic spread through the skin and cartilage in his ear, knitting the delicate ridge of flesh back together.

"So how did they get that awful creature in there?" she asked, no less casually than one might ask a dining mate to pass the sugar.

"No idea," he winced again. "It's been here far longer than I've been in contact with them."

"But how do you know that?"

"Stories, mostly." He inhaled a pained breath. "The older guards have always looked the other way. Especially those working the dungeons, making sure some prisoners never make it to trial. They're fed to the beast."

"That's awful," she said emphatically.

"I sure wouldn't want to go that way," he agreed, seeming to forget the position he was in.

"Well, Lieutenant," she said, standing and dusting her hands off. "That's about all I can do. Just get some shut-eye and drink some water."

She passed him the cup that she'd dripped a few drops of the sweet nightshade tincture into. An easy death, a gentle end. Whether or not he deserved such a thing, it wasn't for her to decide.

He drank greedily, and she left the room, ushering the others away from the threshold.

"*How* did you do that?" Ferrin asked in a hushed tone.

"A few tricks of the trade," Soviel shrugged, her energy depleted. "He needed a kind touch to give him reason to talk. He knew he was going to die anyway." She didn't have it in her to explain the methods of relaxing his body and mind with a few well-placed touches.

"Which trade, spying or healing?"

Her two jobs overlapped sometimes. Sometimes in a way that made one violate the other. Healing magic was to be used for just that—healing, helping people. And her work as a spy could require her to be ruthless, sometimes to do harm.

But she had never been good at being just one thing.

She tilted her head, pondering. "Both."

Ferrin's hands shook as she recounted to her friends what she had learned. Rhi was being held in a northern tower; no, she didn't know which one. They were planning to hang him at noon tomorrow. He was guarded by seven men in the room, and more below. He was being kept high up, which matched with Lukas's description of walking down a lot of stairs.

That left three potential hundred-plus feet towers. Each filled with Bourjon soldiers and defected Lindbarrian castle guards.

The embers in the fireplace were simmering at a dull glow as the sun finished its descent towards the horizon, the dark encroaching with a ticking chill. The orange glow from the dying fire cast ghosts of dancing figures on the walls. Soviel had closed the windows as the cool breeze rolled in.

Ferrin wordlessly grabbed a shovel from beside the fireplace and stalked outside to dig the grave. The soil was loamy and easy to move as she set to cleaving the ground. She wasn't sure how Soviel had managed to get more information out of the man with nothing but a few gentle touches and sweet words. One thing was for sure, she would never underestimate her again.

She wished they'd started with that method. She wished she hadn't had to do what she'd done. There had been a second where she'd heard Zare's voice in her ear, urging her on, telling her how best to manipulate the prisoner into talking.

But just as quickly, she'd flashed back to the time she'd been on the other end of an interrogation. She shook her head to clear her thoughts. Her goal was too important to get caught up in the blackening of her soul. It had long been a little tarnished, anyway.

"Are you alright?" Lukas's voice roused her from the storm brewing in her mind.

"I will be once we get Rhi out of there," she confessed.

He picked up the shovel leaning against the woodpile and began digging from the other side, the loose chains from his shackles clinking against the handle.

"We really need to get those off of you," Ferrin said.

"Yeah, I'm sure there's something inside we can use to pick the lock with."

They continued to dig in silence, working by the low-light of the oil lamp perched on the fencepost. At last, it was done, and Lukas called for Soviel and Ash to drag out the body.

They'd untied him and rolled him onto a thick, wool blanket, his eyes closed as if in sleep, and his arms crossed over his chest like a knight of old entombed in stone. He dropped into the shallow grave with little ceremony, and they covered him with earth as quickly as they could.

When they'd finished, they all sat inside devouring the cheese and hard tack from the storage. The fire was near dying, and Ash went out to grab a few more logs. Soviel excused herself to say a blessing over the grave.

"I have to remove any lingering ill magic, since he died at my hand," she explained morosely. "It's more complicated than that, but…" she waved a hand in the air as if she was trying to ward off evil, but was too tired to commit to it.

"Come on, let's try to get you out of those cuffs," Ferrin said, laying a hand on Lukas's forearm. He looked exhausted.

In the kitchen, she found the rest of the knives not used in the earlier events of the day and plucked one off the countertop. Lukas stood adjacent to her, the table corner between them as she took his hands.

"Hold still," she ordered, examining the manacles' closure.

"So," he paused, "do you have a plan?"

She bit the inside of her cheek, not meeting his eye. "Seven guards in the tower, more below. It'll take a lot."

"We have time," he said. "They won't kill him until tomorrow at noon."

Her stomach turned. "That's not the comforting sentiment you think it is."

He frowned. "I know. I'm sorry."

She wrapped both her hands around his. His skin was warm. "We don't have the numbers, and when they bring him out tomorrow, he's going to be so heavily guarded, we won't get near him."

"Probably true."

"So we do this now. We break him out tonight. We climb the tower and take them by surprise and shoot the guards before they know what's going on."

"Ferrin…" Lukas began, pulling his hand out of her grasp. He lifted her chin in one hand and gripped her shoulder with the other. "You're right that we need to get him before they move him tomorrow. But we can't climb that tower. We don't even know which one he's in. We would have to climb all three. Whoever took the climb would be totally exposed."

"If we knew which one he was in, though," she said without finishing her thought.

"But we don't, unless you know something else."

She shook her head absently. "No, but I can find out."

"What do you mean?"

"It's a long story, but I need you to trust me that I can find out."

"I don't like this. This seems like a bad idea," he rubbed a hand across his face. "Even if you find out, even if we can all climb up in one piece, he's chained up, maybe wounded, and surrounded by guards with muskets."

"To be honest I haven't figured that part out yet." The knife at her hip was heavy, and her eyes scanned over the arsenal on the table. She took another set of knives and slipped them into her belt. Then she took a pistol and shoved it in her waistband. "I thought I'd get an idea when I scout it out."

"Alright, then let's go."

"No." She backed away a step.

"You're not going alone." He grabbed her hand again, stepping closer. "We have a few hours *at least* to come up with something better, let's just sit and think it through. Hell, maybe Soviel can weasel them into letting us in the front door."

He was trying to diffuse the tension. She knew that. It didn't make what she was about to do any easier. "I need to go look, *now*. Once I see, I'll come back with a report, and we'll make a plan."

"Ferrin," his voice was firm as he stepped closer. "I want to get him back as badly as you do, but rushing in against an army with half a plan is going to get you killed. No matter what secret scouting idea you have."

She could feel the wind picking up outside, almost as if in answer to what she had to do. As if it was calling to her.

"I know what I need to do. I will not abandon him again," she said, her voice quiet but defiant.

"You shouldn't go alone. I'm going with you. Let me get some more ammo," he said.

"You're stalling me, Lukas," she said, stepping into his space. She laid a hand on the side of his face. His chin was rough with stubble, gold in the firelight. "Just sit tight, I'll be back within the hour."

"Back from where?" He widened his eyes in exasperation, unaware of the dagger she'd drawn as he drummed his hand on the wooden table, loose chains still clattering.

"I'm getting him back."

"Ferrin, *no*." His eyes were pleading, the beautiful angles and planes of his face golden brown in the dim candlelight. "They will shoot you on sight. No amount of secret passages or tunnels can make you untraceable."

She tightened her grip on the dagger in her right hand, while her left hand delicately curled around the back of his neck. In one swift motion, she pulled him in and crushed her lips to his, pressing against him as she spiked the dagger through one of the loops of his broken chains, anchoring him to the table.

She pulled away breathless, and gave him one last look as she backed away. "I'm sorry."

She ran out the door without looking back.

CHAPTER THIRTY-EIGHT

Soviel stood from the grave and wiped her hands off on the front of her already filthy breeches. The night had cooled off considerably. She wrapped her stolen coat tighter around her shoulders and looked up at the sky. The reality that her entire support system had vanished overnight with nothing but a cryptic note hit her with a wave of nausea. There was no backup, no one to swoop in with a distraction if something went wrong. It was all on her.

A second realization hit her—in all the commotion, she'd never bothered to apply the reagent to that note from Helene.

She rushed to the fence, leaning against the post as she pulled the vial of chemicals and the rolled up note out of her pocket. She unscrewed the cap and withdrew the little brush from the vial, careful not to be wasteful as she painted a thin film over the back of the note. It took a minute to work, but sure enough, a black scrawl materialized on the page.

In the dark, it was hard to make out exactly what was written. She squinted at the page and moved the lantern closer.

Ivy,

There's been a leak in the operation. Half our agents are compromised and power is about to change hands in the castle. We had to clear out.

Your cover is still intact, and we need it to remain that way. Do what you can to disappear quietly from the castle and come to Port Galan posthaste.

I have a job for you that may change the course of this entire operation, but it can only work if your cover remains intact. *Drop everything and come north. Leave word at the White Cliff and I will come find you in the city.*

Best,
Hyacinth

She read it and read it again. She hadn't expected it to be addressed to her specifically, but there her codename was. Black and bold across the top of the page. She exhaled slowly, shakily. Her cover was intact when Helene had written this. Anyone who may have put that at risk was now dead. She also had orders to report to Port Galan immediately.

Orders she was going to disobey, or at the very least, delay.

When the paper had at last dried, she rolled it neatly and replaced it in her pocket, along with the sealed bottle of reagent.

She went back into the house, only to find the sitting room empty. Hushed voices argued from the kitchen. Ash and Lukas were talking animatedly and waving their arms around. When she pushed the door open, they both snapped their heads up to look at her.

Lukas was chained to the table, a dagger staked into the wood through the open link of his chains, which Ferrin was supposed to have been getting him out of.

Ash wore an exasperated frown.

"What happened in here?" Soviel asked, looking from the chains to Lukas to Ash, and finally to the open door that led towards the castle grounds.

Lukas straightened and met her eyes. "Ferrin's gone."

The wind bit into Ferrin's face with a fierce chill as she hurtled towards the castle at a full sprint. Night had fallen dark and damp, no moon or stars to illuminate the velvety darkness that settled into every corner and crevice of the palace grounds. The fog hung like a theater curtain, thick and plush and full of anticipation.

The look of hurt and betrayal on Lukas's face when he realized what she'd done stuck like a brand on her mind. She shook her head to clear it, to focus. The grounds were practically barren; only a group of three sentries remained outside the main gate. She wouldn't be going anywhere near them.

She shot straight into the air and out of sight. Wet air pressed the loose strands of her hair to her forehead and dampened her clothes as she sent a prayer to every god she could think of and she sped towards the castle.

Her plan was murky at best, but all she needed to do now was scout. Once she knew where Rhi was, and in what condition, she would report back to the cabin and find a way to get him out. Sitting around was no longer an option. Saving Rhi was essential, at any cost. He was the one they needed, the one both peoples could rally behind in the face of Bourjony's declaration of war.

She wouldn't abandon him again.

Ferrin whipped around the castle to the north wing, where the three towers stood sentinel, facing the forests and crags that stretched far into the north. The first tower was lit from top to bottom. She circled it, peering in each window, careful to avoid the glow that might illuminate her and give her away. At its top room, guards dined at a rectangular table, some consolidating weapons into a stockpile. No sign of Rhi.

Circling to the roof, she slipped out of sight as a group of sentries patrolled the grounds far below. When they were gone, she set off to the second tower.

As she neared the highest window, she immediately caught sight of Rhi. His head hung limply, and he sagged against the wall, as if he'd been on his feet for hours. Apart from him, the room appeared to be empty.

She sped closer, trying to get a better look. The room *was* empty.

If the room was truly empty, they'd never get another opportunity like this. She circled around and touched down on the roof. She needed to think.

He looked like hell. There was no way he could free-climb down the side of the tower. Maybe she could let him take the family ring, and she could climb down...

She shook her head. She knew her limits, and climbing down one hundred feet of cobblestone was not something she was physically prepared for.

She circled the tower again. The room below and diagonal from Rhi's was empty and dark. If she remembered correctly, it was used for food storage in case of siege, from when the Three Tower Keep had been the safest place to weather a storm of invaders. If she could tie off a rope somewhere in there and let Rhi fly down, she could shimmy down fast enough to get away, provided no one saw her.

Nodding to herself, she resolved to find some rope.

"How did you not see her whip out a knife?" Ash threw her hands up in exasperation.

"I was *distracted*," Lukas gritted his teeth.

"Oh, I'm sure you were," Ash's tone was sarcastic.

"Don't look at me like that!"

"Alright, this is not helping," Soviel snapped her fingers in between them. "We need to formulate some kind of plan. Obviously rushing in after her is not a good choice."

"She *said* she was only going to scout."

"But knowing Gill—sorry, *Ferrin*—she's going to get one look at the situation and think she can just yank him out, no problems. And I'm still *very* confused about how she vanished so fast."

"She can fly," Soviel said softly.

"I'm sorry, she can *what*?" Ash said apprehensively.

Soviel nodded slowly. "It's true. She's going to fly around those towers and see which one Rhi is in, I'm guessing. If she stops to think, she'll come back here with the information before doing anything stupid, but—"

"She can *fly*," Lukas repeated, squinting at the knife stuck into the table. "How?"

"It's a long story, and not important right now. But if she's going to report back, it won't take long. So let's come up with our plan and if she isn't back in thirty minutes, we take action."

Ash eyed Soviel. Who *was* this girl? Why did she seem to know everything?

"I agree," Ash said. "If she's not back, I'll go look around. No one knows who I am, and I can slip in and out easy enough."

Soviel frowned. "I should—"

"You could be recognized. Despite your social witchery," Ash said, wiggling her fingers at Soviel, who frowned at the notion. "Besides, you said you have a cover to keep intact. Right?"

Soviel nodded begrudgingly. "At least let us give you the lay of the land. Lukas, you have a map of the grounds?"

He nodded and pulled the dagger out of his table, laying it flat. As he got up to get the map without a word, Ash could tell he was embarrassed. Something had happened between him and Gillian. Ferrin. Something right before she'd run out.

Soviel dropped into a chair, her brow furrowed, eyes narrowing in on nothing in particular as she thought. She looked exhausted.

"How?" Ash asked.

Soviel shook her head, as if clearing fog from her vision. "Something to do with a family ring. It grants the wearer the gift of flight. Apparently, it wasn't sapped by the weakening of magic and has been in her family for generations."

"Interesting," Ash nodded. "But it only works on her family?"

"I think so. She gave me a rushed explanation—yesterday? The day before? Gods, it's been a long few days."

"You're telling *me*," Ash agreed.

Lukas returned with a rolled up map. He unrolled it on the table; it was crinkly and old, and not entirely devoid of coffee and wine stains. It was a map of the palace grounds. In the bottom corner was a watermark of the royal archives, including the inscription *DO NOT REMOVE FROM PREMISES*

"Is someone going to come looking for these?" Ash said, eyeing the mark.

"I think we're well past that at this point," he said grimly.

At last, Ferrin found what she was looking for: a room filled with sleeping soldiers.

She landed gently on the window sill, which was wide enough for her to crouch on while she slowly eased up the window. One leg at a time, she climbed into the room. Rolling her feet with each step, she padded across the floor, holding her breath as she went. It was almost completely dark, save for the dim glow of the fire that had gone to embers.

One of these soldiers *had* to have something useful, dammit.

Tip-toeing around the edge of the room, she searched for shelves, storage of any kind. Her heart raced as she waited for a soldier to sit bolt upright and raise an alarm, bringing hell down around her.

She stepped on a floorboard that creaked and settled under her weight, the shrill sound reverberating through her bones. Eyes wide, she didn't dare move a muscle. Her heart thudded in her ears louder than the floorboard. A soldier shifted in his sleep. She stood, frozen for the longest minute of her life.

Finally, her hands stopped shaking and the room remained still. She closed her eyes for a precious second, one slow blink of relief. When she opened them, her gaze fell on a canvas tote tossed next to the door. There was a bundle of rope peeking out from one of its flaps.

She approached as quickly and quietly as she could manage, and pulled back the flap—the rope was thankfully thick. She couldn't tell how long, but it would certainly help make up the gap between the tower and the ground below. It would take her weight and she'd figure out the rest when the time came. Darkness would aid in covering her descent.

Once she was at the window, she looped the rope over her shoulder and around her waist, and stepped onto the sill. The wide windows must have been built back when Stormriders frequented these towers, it was almost too easy to step up onto the spacious sill and out into the sky. The wind took her up in an instant and then she was soaring towards the food storage room below Rhi's.

Still damp and stormy, the air plastered her hair to her skin. A bolt of lightning in the distance illuminated the landscape for a moment, and she nearly missed the shape of a figure above her before something tackled her from above, shoving her into the hard, stone side of the tower.

Ash was drumming what looked like an artist's pencil on the table, its middle between her two fingers, as the two ends rapidly tapped down on the wood. She realized it was probably bothersome, so she closed her fist around the pencil and stopped.

"So, how do you know all this stuff?" she asked Soviel.

Soviel, who was in her own world as she moved tiny measurements of some kind of powdered root into a capsule, barely managed a *"Hmm?"*

"All this plant magic," Ash clarified.

"Well…" Soviel said, frowning at the little vial on the table before leaning back to examine it from afar. When she seemed satisfied, she shifted her attention to Ash. "I had a teacher in the hospital. You met her. Madame Leone."

"Oh, the woman who helped me," Ash nodded. "And how long have you been able to do all this?"

Soviel squinted. "Five years? Maybe a little longer. I used to travel back and forth from Karlgiard, so I learned a little from my aunt before entering Leone's tutelage."

"Honestly, I wasn't aware there were still people out there with the ability for any of this."

Soviel met her eye with a half-smile. "I think magic is waking up. Slowly, of course, but with time, I think that more like me will emerge."

Ash concentrated on the glass of water in front of her, willing it to move, to spill, to jiggle. She was Akhatan. The desert people. That meant she should have some kind of affinity for water, did it not? Of course, nothing happened.

She tried not to pout.

"You think so?" she asked, folding her hands in her lap as she turned to face Soviel. The girl seemed so much more solid, more *real* with her sleeves rolled up and her brow creased with focus as she carefully measured the vials of plant matter before her.

"Madame Leone thinks so. She's been keeping an ear to the ground with some network. I'm not sure what they are, but she's mentioned sightings of people performing extraordinary feats. Usually in moments of danger. Like this one woman in the far reaches of the Yarian mountains, in Njorske. She was coming back from the river with fish—this was in the winter, mind you—and she comes back to find a *huge* bear in the middle of her village. There's a lot of bears up north, snow bears are the most vicious though. They hunt on the ice and blend in," she explained, pausing to adjust the cap on one of the vials.

Ash nodded, encouraging her to continue. She was intrigued to see Soviel launch into a long-winded story like this. It made her a little less intimidating.

"So she finds this big, white bear terrorizing her village, and it's got some children cornered in the yard outside the schoolhouse. She drops the basket of fish and it turns to her, snarling. And she lets out this primal *scream* of rage and terror and throws up her hands as it starts to charge her, and a wall of pure flame just erupts around it. Then one of the hunters was able to get into range and shoot it. The village was fed for weeks."

"So she was a flame wielder."

"Yes. Well. There's this old legend in my father's country about the fire wolves," Soviel went on. "Shapeshifters who could wield fire, strongest on the full moon. They could turn into huge, white wolves. The legend says that way back in the old days, tribe warriors became wolves to protect their people from the dangers of the far north."

"The far north *sounds* dangerous," Ash agreed emphatically, "and cold."

"Cold it is," Soviel confirmed with a little laugh. "Where I'm from is closer to the Veiran border. So the temperature fluctuates with the seasons, and we have actual summers. But when you get up to the ice caves and the Yarian mountains, it rarely thaws. It's all sky and snow and ice."

"Well, where I'm from, it's mostly sky and *sand*."

"I've never traveled south," Soviel admitted. "I'd like to some day," she mused.

"You have to! There's so much to see. You never run out of things to look at." Ash slid off the table. "But we'd have to get you a really big hat for shade. If you go out in the southern sun, you'll roast up like a tomato."

Soviel snorted. "Good point."

At that moment, Lukas came back into the kitchen, a bucket full of gunpowder under one arm and another weapons roll under the other.

"She's not back yet. It's time to move forward."

She had come out of *nowhere*.

Ferrin had just enough time to tuck and turn so she hit the wall with her back instead of her face as the assailant slammed her with the force of a boulder. She let out a pained grunt as all the air left her lungs. She was barely staying aloft. The two grappled as they scraped down the side of the building, the cold, wet stone hard and sharp even through her coat.

Suddenly they were falling—no, *tumbling*—through a window and onto the ground. She managed to kick free of the tall woman and scramble backwards towards the window. She stood to face her attacker, to get a good look at her.

She was tall and broad of shoulder, built like a warrior. Her pale hair was braided and slicked back with rain water and her eyes, entirely black, held a deep, inhuman rage. Her teeth were *pointed*.

"What are you?" Ferrin panted as she tried to regain her breath.

She heard the shot before she felt the bullet rip through her. A strangled sound left her as the momentum of the bullet threw her backwards, blood soaking her already-damp breeches. A hot, sharp pain lanced through her left thigh and warmth oozed outwards as she began to tip backward.

Just as she was about to tumble out the window to the ground far below, the woman lunged for her, grabbing a fistful of her shirt. She yanked her back in, and let her crumple to the floor in a heap. Ferrin buckled, yelping in pain as her knees hit the ground, jarring the fresh wound. She was slick with blood.

Ferrin's limbs went rag-doll-limp and her head went fuzzy. She tried to sit up but was met with a booted foot on her chest. She couldn't make a sound as the weight of the foot pressed down on her sternum and stars danced across her vision as the breath was forced again from her lungs.

"So," a male voice cooed in a tone deeply chilling. "This is the brat princess."

The man stood over her, clad in Bourjon colors with a black kerchief across the bottom of his face. His accent did not sound Bourjon. "Monroe. Off."

The blonde woman stepped back without a word.

"How unsurprising," he continued. "Sticking your nose where it does not belong. She was right about you," he whispered, removing the cloth from his face. "And you even brought rope for us to tie you up with."

"No—" she grunted. The sound came out of her mouth in a broken, choking breath as her voice failed her.

The soldier crouched beside her and brought the kerchief to her bloody thigh. "Oh, dear," he said, not sounding very sympathetic at all. "She's bleeding out. Must have hit an artery. Monroe, fetch the healer."

A healer?

The soldier standing over her was in his late thirties. In her state of delirium, she thought he looked a little like Danske, one of Zare's enforcers.

"Yes, the queen has told me *all* about you. Quite the annoying little shrew, it seems," he spat as he began to wind the rope around her wrists. It was abrasive and felt like it was cutting into her skin.

Her vision fogged. It was cold in the tower. So, so, cold.

"My mother?" she asked, desperately trying to blink away the fog.

"No," his nose twitched into a predatory smirk.

"Who are you?" she gasped.

His laugh was a sadistic purr. He cocked his head to the side, studying her. The ache in her thigh grew sharp and demanding and she realized he was digging his thumb into the wound. "Time to reunite you with your brother."

She couldn't feel her fingers anymore. And her focus…

Rough hands dragged her to her feet, every step jarring the musket ball deeper into the muscle of her thigh. The edges of her vision darkened as they dragged her up a set of stairs.

"In you go," he sneered, after opening a door. She was shoved through and caught by two soldiers as she stumbled and fell. "Where's that damn healer? We can't have her bleeding out before the execution."

Everything went black.

CHAPTER THIRTY-NINE

The ropes digging into her wrists stung and bit into her skin every time she moved as she regained consciousness. Warm candlelight hovered somewhere to her left. Or maybe her leg was on fire. It certainly felt like it.

The sensation in her thigh bloomed like a poisonous flower, blossoming deadly and sweet. Her eyes flew open.

"She's waking up!"

"Ferr!" Rhi's voice hit her.

"Hello, Highness," the soldier from earlier sneered. "Jorsin, are you done?"

As her vision cleared, she saw that the odd source of the burning sensation was a pale-haired soldier, no, a medic, kneeling before her injured leg. His hands glowed as he knitted her flesh back together.

"Hold still," the young man growled as he gripped the skin around the wound. It was like being shot all over again, the ache compressing into one focused spot as he closed the main vessel in her thigh.

She squeezed her eyes shut as she bit back the scream trying to tear from her throat.

"Why—" she gasped.

"Oh, don't worry, just need to stop the bleeding," the soldier above her winked. His accent was indeed Lindbarrian, not Bourjon. That confirmed it. The castle had been infiltrated long before this takeover. The mechanics of it were still blurry, but the guards and the army, or at least parts of it, had defected and were helping Bourjony to secure the castle.

"Who are you?" she croaked.

"Time for you to go back to sleep. Jorsin." He jerked his head at the healer, who waved his hand and sent her tumbling into oblivion.

When she awoke again, she was shackled by her wrist to a bolt in the floor. The skin on her wrists was torn up and inflamed from where she'd thrashed against the rope and she was propped up on a pile of straw that she wasn't sure had been there before. Everything felt awful. Her head pounded, her joints were stiffer than a corpse's and her body felt as if she'd been trampled by a stampede of farm animals.

She couldn't feel her leg.

The memory of what had happened and where she was began to come back to her, along with a surge of panic. Rhi was still chained to the wall across from her. He looked drained and exhausted and—

She *couldn't* feel her leg. A sob rattled loose from her throat as panic built in her chest.

"Ferrin," Rhi's strained voice whispered.

She was here to get him out. "Oh, gods," she squeezed her eyes shut. She didn't dare look down at her body. The fear of losing the limb was nearly paralyzing. "My leg. Is it...?"

"It's still there. It isn't bleeding anymore," he said. "You can't feel it?"

She blew out a long, shaky breath and sat up. She sighed with relief as she wiggled her toes. "It's starting to come back," she told him.

Rhi nodded, mumbling that that was good.

"Can you get out of those cuffs?" she asked her brother. He was leaning weakly against the wall.

"I'm not sure. They're really tight."

"Guards?" she asked, scanning the room.

"One floor down, and right outside the door," he warned. "They come in and out."

Ferrin nodded, blinking the liquid out of her eyes. "Rhi, listen to me," she said, trying to scoot around to face him. The pain that shot through her leg was blinding. "Get those cuffs off. Dislocate your thumb, break your fingers if you have to. Just get them off."

"And then what, Ferr? Fight off the entire outpost of Bourjon and traitor soldiers? No." Rhi shook his head, defeated. "We're trapped. You shouldn't have come back here. There's nothing to be done."

Her chest knotted painfully at the despair in his voice. "Rhiach, we need you. *I* need you. I will not leave you behind," she promised.

"Well, now we're both stuck here. And any hope of mending the rift torn between the Caels and Lundis will hang with us tomorrow."

"Rhi—"

"You should have fled the capital when you had the chance." He stared at the ground, shaking his head.

"Rhi, *listen*! I have a way you can get out, but you have to trust me," Ferrin explained quietly.

"How?" His voice was gravelly. Had they refused him water?

"I didn't exactly walk here," she shared, propping up on one elbow.

"Yeah, they dragged you in here half-dead."

"That's not what I mean."

"What are you saying?"

"You're not going to like it." She tugged their mother's ring off her hand. "Spit all over your wrists and hands if you can."

He looked at her askance but obliged, hocking back and snarling up as much saliva as he could muster, spitting it onto his hands.

"Good. Good. Try now."

He wrapped his hand over the first cuff, forcing it over his wrist. Ferrin could hear the crack as something moved in a way it was not supposed to. He gave a pained, stifled cry when the shackle stuck at his thumb, but with a sharp twist, it was off. He was breathing hard as he rubbed his now-free hand.

"Again. The other one," she instructed. He was already bruising on his left hand.

His face contorted as he yanked the second shackle off. It didn't catch like the first one did.

"Got it," he groaned, panting. A thin sheen of sweat bloomed on his forehead as he made his way over to her.

"Good," she nodded, swallowing the lump in her throat. "Good. Now take this." She pressed the ring into his hand. "You're going out the window."

"What?" he asked, completely perplexed. "Ferr, you've lost a lot of blood. Do you even know what you're saying? We're a hundred feet up."

"Take the fucking ring, Rhi. Put it on, jump out the window. Trust."

"You're not making sense."

"Rhiach, you remember mother's stories as well as I do. *Gwelie.*"

He looked down at the ring and snapped his eyes to her. "But I thought… the golden eggs—"

"Different version." She waved her free hand.

"But—"

"I flew up here."

"How?"

"Trust in *Strata*, as Gwelie did. She was our ancestor. *You will not fall.* The others are in Lukas's cabin. Go there, and get ready to flee the capital. If I'm not back by nightfall, leave without me."

"No. No way," he shook his head vehemently.

"I'll be alright. You're the one they're after. They won't kill me for spectacle without you. They'll probably use me as bait," she lied. "I'll figure my own way out."

"I won't leave without you," Rhi said, still shaking his head.

"Pass me that lantern," she ordered, jerking her chin to the unlit lantern on the shelf across the room.

"Ferrin."

"If you want me to have hope of getting out, you'll pass me the damn lantern."

He did.

"Great." She tucked it beneath her discarded coat, careful not to spill the precious oil. "Now go."

He looked down at the ring in his hand.

"If you stay, Rhi, they'll put your head on a pike by the gate." She set her jaw. There wasn't much time, she could hear the stairs below creaking under the weight of soldiers. "If I'm hearing right, you'd better make your decision fast. They're coming back up to check on us."

He swallowed, the look in his eye a mixture of fear and desperation.

"Have the horses ready. Remember what I said. Nightfall!"

He slipped the ring on and grabbed her head, kissing her on the cheek. In two strides he was out the window, falling. And then flying.

Squeezing her eyes shut, Ferrin forced herself to take three deep breaths. Now she was truly alone. Unable to fly, aching with whatever botched methods the healer had used to stop her from bleeding out, chained to the floor and about to be greeted by some very unhappy Bourjon soldiers.

The door burst open. Six men with muskets flooded in.

Ash was getting antsy. They'd begun laying traps an hour ago, in the dead of night. She'd almost stepped in one of them, but Soviel had shot out a hand and stopped her just before she ended up with spikes through her calf.

They'd scouted the edges of the grounds. Soldiers were *everywhere*. Ash had little skill with working under cover. She stood out, with her mix of boys' and girls' clothes, short choppy hair and boisterous energy, she wasn't usually suited to blending in.

But, out of the three of them, she was the only one who wasn't recognizable. A new face, she just needed to look the part. They'd found a way to tie back her hair, and Soviel had pulled a threadbare shawl out of Lukas's storage cellar that Ash was fairly certain was actually an ancient picnic blanket.

Now they lay shoulder to shoulder in the tall grass as the sun made its first appearance of the day. The dew drops shone in the spiderwebs like antique diamonds lost in an old forgotten trove.

"So, that entrance?" Ash squinted.

"Yes. Coup or no, the castle still needs servants to run it. You go in there, you keep your head down, and find a tray or a pitcher to carry and hopefully no one will question you. The wall I mentioned opens up with a push, and you can slip in unseen." Lukas nodded in the general direction of the side entrance. "Do you remember what I said about the passages?"

"Yes, 'Stay on the ones with the wooden floor. If you find yourself on the stone floor, you're in the wrong place and a horrible beast will devour you'. Thanks."

"How do we get them out of there?" Soviel gestured to the Three Tower Keep looming over the castle.

"We don't," Lukas's tone was grim. "Ferrin has to have some kind of plan to get them both out of the tower. We find them when they're on the run. We can only hope to cause a distraction big enough to give them a chance."

"Where is the prince?" the man from earlier—an officer?—grabbed ahold of her collar. She hadn't noticed the epaulette marking his rank earlier. The cold barrel of a pistol pressed into the soft flesh of her cheek.

"Good morning gentlemen," she said, her voice sounding distorted by the pressure on her cheek. "As much as I'd be delighted to have my brother's company in this state of confinement, I can't help you locate him. I've only just woken up."

"Liar!" The captain pulled back his musket and backhanded her.

She fell back into the straw pile, careful not to knock over her hidden lantern. Her vision swam with sparks as her heart pounded.

"Sit up," ordered a soldier behind her. His Bourjon accent was thick and nasal as he prodded her shoulder with his foot. "Now!" His voice rose and she caught the flick of his eyes, desperate for approval, at his commanding officer.

"Major Tierrault will be here soon. He'll have some questions for you," he spat.

Ferrin plastered on a sweet smile, though her tearstained face and trembling hands may have put a crack in her facade. "If this all-important major arrives soon, I'm sure he won't be happy that you let his most valuable prisoner slip through your grasp so carelessly," she said, closing her eyes and leaning her head back on the straw. Her calm front was so thin a veneer, she knew if she let it slip for even a moment, she'd descend into a state of terror she might not come out of.

"Gag her," he growled. "I'm sick of hearing her voice."

"Yes, Captain Clarings." One of the younger soldiers, who she recognized from around the castle, took a rag from his pocket and bent down in front of her, shoving it into her mouth. Try as she might to reject it, she was powerless to stop him. She groaned in protest.

A deeper fear began to take root in the back of her mind. A fear that they would do worse than gag her. The fact that one of the soldiers in the room appeared to be a woman offered her very little comfort.

"Quit your moaning," snarled the one standing to her left, the back end of his rifle prodding her in the leg where she'd been shot. She cried out, her vision bleeding black once more.

"Enough! She must be *conscious* when the major arrives!" the captain screamed at the young soldier.

"Yes, sir." He stepped back.

There was a rap on the door and Ferrin noticed a flicker of fear move through each of the soldier's faces. When the door opened, the man who walked in was nothing like what Ferrin had expected. The way the men seemed to fear him, she assumed he'd at least be older.

The major was no older than twenty-five. His face was finely featured, handsome, even. He was of medium build, all lean muscles, like a jungle cat. His features reminded her of Rhi, refined and confident. His jewel-blue eyes were cold, and his dark brown hair pulled back neatly.

The comforting familiarity ended as soon as he spoke.

"Gentlemen." He offered a curt nod. His voice was cool and calm, and while he spoke perfect Lindbarrian, the hint of his highborn Bourjon accent was detectable. He wore the same uniform as the rest, though the epaulettes on his shoulder were edged in gold, and his knee-high boots were polished to a shine. He wore no hat, and no face covering, only a black satin ribbon at the end of his short braid. "I was assured that *both* royal children would be here when I arrived."

"The boy escaped, sir," Captain Clarings said. In the presence of the major, his cruel confidence was reduced to that of a schoolyard bully who'd been caught filching the schoolmaster's pocketwatch.

"You let the boy escape?" the major asked calmly, flitting his eyes dismissively over Clarings. He showed no emotion. "You bloody idiot. Why wasn't he guarded at all times?"

"Major Tierrault, I did not think there was anywhere for him to *go*," he stammered.

"We had intelligence that the girl could fly, is it not entirely logical that that ability extended to the boy as well?" Tierrault snapped. His voice remained at the same level tone, even in anger. "This entire operation depends on him swinging from the front gates by sundown. I don't think that the rightful king of these lands will be happy to hear how your laziness has caused such a disaster."

"No, sir."

"Wait downstairs. I want you out of my sight," he said coolly, his sapphire eyes going icy.

Ferrin took this opportunity to size up the major. He conducted himself in a way that made her think he was no fool. He was intelligent, probably well-educated too. He was around six feet tall, and though he was no bulked-up brawler, he outweighed her by at least forty pounds. In her state, there was no way she could fight him.

Typically, she relied on being fast and witty to best larger opponents. But injured and lagging as she was, she knew her prospects were slim. Squeezing her eyes shut, she prayed to Haz, the Akhatan patron god of luck, to guide her.

If anything is getting me out of this, it's sheer, dumb luck, she thought to herself.

The major approached her with preternatural slowness. His movements were deliberate, calculated. "Now," he sighed, and sunk into a crouch beside her, pulling the gag from her mouth. "Why don't you tell me how you got your brother out?"

"I already told them," she said, holding his gaze. "I was passed out after being *shot*, and when I woke up, he was gone."

He studied her for a moment. "I can tell you're smart." He nodded. "I think you and I both know that you've got no plan, and you're stalling. Is that correct?" He raised his dark eyebrows ever so slightly.

"You're forgetting that I'm completely useless to you," she shrugged. "Publicly executing me will get you nowhere near the reaction you're hoping for. No one sees me the way they see Rhi."

"Oh, on the contrary, sweet Gillian."

She flinched.

"Yes, I know *all* about you. The queen, as well as my other informants, have told me of your very unique reputation."

"A-and?" Fear crept over her. Zare popped into her mind uninvited.

"There's no need for such modesty." He narrowed his eyes. "You've inspired the people more than you think," he said with an analytical tilt of his head. "It seems that they find both of you to be beacons of Caelish hope, particularly after your public opposition to your father regarding Taroch Forest."

She swallowed, trying to steady her breathing.

"They see it as a rallying cry against your father's pitiful regime. And against our new one." He sighed. "This might go one of two ways."

"Oh?" She waited to hear what he had in mind.

"Yes. First, the Lindbarrian people might split, half defecting to the ever-growing Caelish resistance, and half becoming part of the Bourjon Annex of the isle. The two groups will fight for a while, draining resources and causing more bloodshed for a year, maybe more. The Caels will eventually lose."

"Or?"

"Or you work with me, and convince the Caels to support the Divine Bourjon Cause."

"*Divine?*" she asked, unable to keep the mockery from her voice.

"King Avent is descended from the original King of the Gods. It is his destiny to rule all lands."

"Right, and I'm Queen of the Fairies."

He didn't laugh. "Bourjony will have these lands, one way or another. You and your people can be part of it, or you can be crushed beneath our feet as we take what is ours."

"Why? What could you possibly want with Lindbarrow? You already have coastline on the Meddemara and the Northern Sea. What could you possibly be gaining?"

"Not all advantages are for the purpose of trade."

Whatever that meant, she thought.

The realization hit her like a tidal wave. "*Bourjony* has been pushing my father to put distress on his people. Destabilizing the country at its roots."

"I knew you were smart. Now, are you smart enough to take my offer?"

Something she couldn't quite place twinkled in his eyes. Was it a challenge?

"What do you want from me?" she asked.

"I want you to broker a peace between the Caelish Resistance and the Bourjon occupation. The island would become a territory. An annex. You'd keep some sovereignty. Your brother was our first choice for this, of course, but since you've seen fit to do away with him…" He spread his arms out in an exaggerated shrug.

"Why would I do that? And what happens to the rest of us when you move in here with your troops?"

"Well, you'd pick a Caelish ruler. One Bourjony approves of, of course."

"You can just go ahead and shoot me," she shook her head. She needed to lay back down.

"You'll reconsider. It was you who fled the country during political crisis, was it not? Forgive me, but I do not believe your patriotic loyalties have been tempered so strongly these last months."

She didn't dignify him with an answer.

"Either way, I have to go teach someone a lesson. I hope you're in a more sociable mood when I return." His rapier hilt twinkled beneath his fingers as he stood. "You," he gestured to the large young guard by the door. "Watch her. The rest of you, come see what happens when you disappoint me."

CHAPTER FORTY

Ash was again sitting cross-legged and filling little paper pouches with gunpowder when it happened.

They'd been up all night, and the route out of the castle was as prepared with traps as three sleep-deprived people could make it. They'd stripped springs out of the couch, laid rope, and strategically left a weapon or two along the designated path. The horses were saddled, watered and ready to flee to wherever.

They were about to head out and make their way to the edge of the grounds before sunrise when a loud crash sounded just outside, followed by urgent and incessant knocking on the door.

Soviel slid off the table and moved to the window to peek out of the curtain. She recoiled in surprise and quickly stepped around to open the door.

"Who is it?" Lukas asked, rifle ready.

She opened the door and in poured Rhi, soaked, bloody and exhausted. He collapsed on the welcome mat.

"Strata's teeth!" Soviel cried.

"Shit," Ash muttered as she swiveled and hopped off the table.

"Help me get him in a chair," Soviel said, crouching next to the prince.

"I can stand," Rhi managed hoarsely.

Leaning on Lukas, he got to his feet.

"What happened? Where's Ferrin?" Lukas asked, helping him into a chair.

Ash grabbed one of the last clean rags from the kitchen and dipped it in the bucket of water they'd brought from the pump.

"She's," he coughed, catching his breath, holding up a shaky hand. A silver and ruby ring glittered on his pinky finger. "She's in the center tower. She gave me this and sent me to get help. She's wounded."

Ash felt her stomach twist and saw the flicker of panic in Lukas's expression.

"We spent the night setting up traps and were about to leave to try and get you both out."

"We need to hurry," Rhi said. "Some important major is on his way. He's heading up this entire operation and it doesn't sound like he has a reputation for being generous and lenient."

"I'm the one going in," Ash shared. "No one from here knows me."

"Alright, I suppose that'll have to work. But— we need a distraction."

"Set the food storage on fire?"

"Release all the horses from the stable?"

"No. But maybe we could use those as backup plans," Rhi said, seeming to contemplate Ash's suggestion about the horses. "Soviel, do you remember that storeroom we found full of tainted popava?"

"I still think we should have destroyed it."

"Yeah, but listen—there's some huge and horrible beast down in the tunnels, right? I was able to listen in on a lot about that. Apparently, it's at a pivotal point, and only needs to feed on a few more people before it's strong enough to devastate the countryside. Landslides, hurricanes, anything and everything. But it's still sensitive. Vulnerable. If you feed it something bad, it becomes sick."

"The shoes," Ash breathed. "At the prison, they had to take almost everything off the prisoners before the mass feedings.

Shoes, belt buckles, spectacles, jewelry, everything. Could we throw something like that down there?"

"Right! Sort of. What if we feed it something it can't process and it gets sick and dies? Something that huge is bound to make some noise. And we're ridding our enemy of two deadly weapons at the same time."

"We throw the popava barrels into the pit," Soviel nodded, catching on to Rhi's idea. "And blow them up."

"Right. But how?"

"There're tunnels that go into the castle starting at the oak tree by the gates. It's how we got in yesterday. We should be able to navigate well enough and be back out here to work the traps before Ash is out with Ferrin."

"Great, let me just—" Rhi tried to stand but immediately collapsed again.

"You're not going," Lukas told him, depositing him back into the chair. "You're going to stay with the horses."

"What! It's my plan, though!"

"Yeah, and you're the most-wanted prisoner in the land. Soviel and I will go through the tunnels and find the pit. Ash will go in and fetch Ferrin. Then we all ride out of here together. No one is getting left behind."

"You're sure there's a tunnel entrance up here?"

"Yes, I'm sure," Lukas whispered as he and Soviel crept towards the big oak tree at the edge of the grounds. There were sentries posted by the gate, but they were far enough away and the morning was dim enough that they didn't notice as the two interlopers crept by. "You're not the only one who does a lot of sneaking around the castle."

"I don't sneak, I blend," Soviel retorted. "You don't really strike me as one for stealth."

"If the occasion calls for it," he said.

"Once we're in the tunnels, we need to get to the normal servants' passages—the newer ones. That will lead us down to the wine cellar and then we just have to open the trap door," she explained. "Then we need a way to move the barrels back into the antechamber where the pit is."

"I'd really hoped I was done with trap-doors leading into death-pits for the week," grunted Lukas.

"Well, here's to hoping we can get rid of this one. Permanently."

"This way," he said, gesturing to the network of gigantic roots on the ground. Once they were beneath the earth, the air grew cold and damp, as if the tunnel were part of a cave system predating the ancient castle itself.

"So, you and Rhi really found an entire storeroom of popava?"

"It was only two barrels. In the wine cellar. But Rhi and I had a whole little adventure while you two were up north," Soviel said, batting a snarl of dusty roots out of her way.

"Sounds like it." He trudged after her. "What exactly is it you do again?"

"What has Ferrin told you?"

"Not much. She said it was secretive work of some sort. Gathering information and making connections for the Caelish cause."

"That's the essence of it," was all she said.

Lukas had the feeling she was holding back the full scope of her duties, but didn't want to press it.

"Here, this chamber ahead should lead us back into the servants' passages," he gestured to the right fork.

"I think we should blow up the pit. Beyond just shoving the barrels into it."

"And how do you suggest we go about doing that? And preferably without bringing the castle down on our heads?"

"I'm not sure, but I don't think it would take much to blow it up from its inside. The thing has a mouth, and if we can localize the explosion, it'll make the dose that much more deadly."

"The popava leaves, if dry, are quite flammable," Lukas considered.

"I've read about these things. We have to be careful not to get too close, we don't even know how far down it is. It could suck us in."

Lukas shuddered. How close to being 'sucked in' had he come back at the prison?

They reached the wine cellar and Soviel dropped into a crouch beside a rack of aging Merlots, feeling along the floor.

"Here it is," she said, just as the trap door swung open.

"How did you find this?"

She rolled her eyes at him. "It was a long few days."

"Let me guess: Rhi saw this trap door while he was down here with a nobleman or a merchant's son he was trying to impress with his knowledge of Efelian reds."

She cracked a smile. "Come on, let's get these things out of here before someone else starts poking around down here."

He peered over the edge of the hole. In the lamplight, he could make out two huge barrels, big enough to fit an entire person inside. Maybe more. "We need to find a cart, or a dolly, or something," he said.

"How are we even going to get them out of here?" Soviel wondered, sitting back on her heels to think.

"I can get down in there and lift, while you pull from up here?"

"Maybe," she squinted. Suddenly, she dropped into the hole with the barrels. Before Lukas could ask her what the hell she was doing, she'd vanished to the side, under the floorboards of the cellar.

"Oh," came her muffled voice.

"What? What's in there?"

"You should come and see this, Lukas."

"On my way," he said, dropping down into the floor. "I think I should mention that I really hate—whoa."

He held up his oil lamp. Extending out from beside one of the barrels was a track: two rails made of sleek metal running parallel into the dark beneath the floorboards above.

"What in the name of Bastar is this?"

Soviel shook her head. "It's a transport system."

"For what? Expensive wine?"

"No, look," she gestured. "It's not in use yet. Those carts look brand new. This is part of the big plan."

"Are those—" he squinted into the gloom. Light from above came through the floorboards in stripes. "Mining carts?"

"I'm not sure. Maybe." She shook her head again. "Whatever this is, it has to be related to the invasion."

Lukas looked around. "Do you think that track leads to the pit?"

"It might."

"We could put those barrels on a cart and see where we end up."

"Yeah, and end up wandering around down here forever," she pointed out glumly.

"Just a suggestion," he said, raising his hands in defense.

"Sorry. I'm just… thinking." With another shake of her head, she turned back to the barrels. "Let's get them up to the right level. The passage should be wide enough for us to roll them. I hope. We'll need an empty bottle or two, and some extra lamp oil."

Ferrin sat still for several minutes, heart pounding violently as she tried to figure out what she could possibly do to get out of here alive. She couldn't fly. She was too weak to make the climb. She wasn't even sure she'd be able to walk if she got her feet under her.

The skin of her thigh, visible through the huge tear in her breeches, was mottled red and purple where the bullet was sealed beneath her skin. For all she knew, she was still bleeding internally.

The lone guard had settled himself by the door, shifting nervously every few seconds. He was broad and tall, but his face betrayed his youth. She knew she couldn't fight him without some kind of advantage, not even on her best day. His hair was shorn to a close crop, and was a bland middle ground between blond and brown. His coat didn't quite fit, as if he'd been shoved into it right before the raid and there hadn't been time to make adjustments.

"You." Ferrin jerked her chin at the man-boy.

"What?" He looked almost startled.

"Where are you from?"

"Uh—" He looked like he was about to answer, but stopped himself. "That's none of your concern, prisoner."

Ferrin rolled her eyes. "I'm asking where you live, not for the tower keys."

He sighed. "Warrich. Just north of the old wall."

"Warrich," she repeated. "Big whiskey distilling city, right?"

He nodded slowly.

"Why leave? Seems like an alright place."

"No place is great for the youngest son of seven."

Ferrin nodded. "Sorry to hear that."

"My father almost lost his company paying taxes to the crown," he said, his tone full of resentment. "Then when he retired, he gave what was left of it to my oldest three brothers."

"So you joined our enemy to wipe out the crown?"

"At least they're not choking us with fees and taxes and collections," he snapped. "The Caels haven't stepped up to protect their own. Many were left with no alternative."

"And how do you know Bourjony won't do the same? Once they have what they want, who's to say they won't keep bleeding the people dry the same way my father did?"

"Well," he hesitated, blinking. "I could not afford to wait around for change."

"I'm just pointing out, one tyrant king can't be expected to be better than another. Everyone's heard the rumors."

"Rumors are rumors."

"Your blind faith in a man across the sea you've never met or lived under before is intriguing, I'll admit." She let her unshackled hand creep down to where blood crusted her leg.

"Easy for the daughter of a king to say."

"It's more complicated than that, you know."

He leaned forward. "Does your silver spoon tremble at the thought of starving peasants? At the families on both sides who are pushed to the brink of starvation by tax collectors? At the people on the coasts, neglected by their lords and left at the mercy of rogue corsairs and raiders?"

Ferrin sighed. "You're right, but that doesn't mean Bourjony is the answer. They're fanatical. Insane."

"Well, not everyone has the luxury of sitting around and waiting for a better option," he sneered, his voice tired.

She didn't know what to say to that. If there was no swaying this guard, then it was time. "I just think—" she emitted a sharp gasp through her teeth, followed by a yelp.

"What is it?"

"Oh—" She dropped back onto the straw, drawing on present and remembered pain.

"What? What's going on?" He stood, clutching his musket like it was a baby. "What is wrong with you?"

"My wrists—my leg—" she panted, shaking. "I think they're— infected."

"The wounds?"

"Please, can I have some-some whiskey?" she gasped violently.

"What? Why?"

"The major wants me alive. Do you really want to be the second person to disappoint him today?" she hissed through clenched teeth.

"Oh, gods," his voice shot up an octave. "I have some."

"Hurry," she whimpered as he approached, stopping a few feet away.

"Here. Uh… what do I do?"

"Pour it on my wrist, it'll disinfect it," she said shakily. The skin was indeed inflamed. But she'd rubbed crusted blood on the rope burn to make it appear worse, and an untrained eye might just fall for it.

The liquor stung her raw skin. She yelped, then asked, "Can I have some?" as she reached for the bottle with her free hand.

"What? No!"

"Please," she begged, imploring him with her eyes. "For the pain."

"Fine, one swig if you'll quiet down," he agreed, holding the whiskey up for her. She leaned up and kissed the bottle, letting the pungent liquor pour into her mouth. The burn made her wince, but she took a big mouthful, knowing she'd need the liquid courage.

"That's enough."

"One more, please," she slowed her breathing.

He hesitated for a moment, but then obliged. This time, she wrapped the fingers of her free hand around the neck of the bottle as she drank, tilting it further.

As fast as she could, she yanked it out of his hands and sprayed the whiskey from her mouth right into his eyes. He jolted back, and she didn't give him time to react before swinging the half-full bottle at his head with a loud crack. He collapsed to the floor.

Of course, they hadn't been daft enough to leave her only guard a set of keys. That's why she had her backup plan—the lantern oil.

She made quick work of dousing her hand in the oil and wriggling it out of the cuff. It hurt, but the pain was nothing compared to the sharp wave that coursed through her leg when she struggled to her feet.

She rifled through the unconscious young man's pockets. There was nothing of immediate use, save for his musket and knife. She took both and pulled off his coat, shrugging it on. Maybe it would offer her some kind of disguise.

She limped towards the door, leaning heavily on the wall. Every flex and movement of the muscle in her thigh sent searing pain through her leg. She wondered distantly if she was making the injury worse by walking on it.

When she reached the door, she halted, steeling herself and preparing for the chaos she was about to cause. She felt a pang of sympathy for the young guard she'd knocked out. With a deep breath, she inspected the door. She'd have to break the lock, or shoot it off, or…

She reached out and slowly tried the handle.

It wasn't even locked! Was luck on her side at last?

The soldiers on the other side weren't prepared as she burst into the hallway with the force of a hurricane. She clubbed one in the head with her newly acquired musket and hurled herself down the stairs.

A musket ball exploded into the stone wall inches behind her, shattering rock to dust. There was no time to stop. She half-ran, half-fell her way down the spiraling stairs, not daring to chance a look behind her as men and women in bright blue and red coats chased after her, flooding into the hallway and raising the alarm. They spilled into the stairwell from every door as if a dam had broken.

She tumbled down step after step, and it was all she could do to keep her feet beneath her, every step sending a lightning bolt of pain into her leg.

"Stop her!" came a cry from above. She hastened her steps, gritting her teeth in agony with each one. She could see the bright white light of the day seeping through the door at the bottom. Her feet could barely keep up with her as she tumbled down. Just a few more steps.

Behind her, the sound of leather soles on stone steps echoed closer, the swarm of guards flooding in from behind to devour her. She reached the door and morning air brushed her face. She stumbled out. A bullet buried itself in the ground steps away.

There were gunners on the roof.

The courtyard between her and the woods stretched long and barren. She would not make it if she ran. To her right, the main wing of the castle stood proud and tall. She might make it there. She might find her way into the tunnels and get out through the underground.

She looked back towards the woods, then at the castle, and made her choice. She took off running towards the palace she'd been dying to escape.

Ash watched from the inside of a topiary shaped like a swan. Guards walked the roofs with rifles at the ready. Soldiers stood sentry at every damned doorway of the castle. The tower had erupted into chaos only seconds ago, from what she could hear. She was still a long way across the courtyard.

She wished she'd studied the map more closely. There was too much empty space between her and the Three Tower Keep. To even make it to the next point of cover, she'd have to sprint across a good few-dozen paces of empty field, completely in view of the rooftop gunmen.

Muffled gunshots came from the center tower, followed by shouts. A few seconds later, the doors burst open. Ferrin stumbled out and looked around for a beat, her expression feral, before taking off towards the main castle entrance.

Ash's eyes widened. She had to get over there.

Bullets bloomed behind her as she flew across the edge of the courtyard, hugging as close to the wall as possible. Debris rained down from missed shots and the sand whipped into dust with each bullet that embedded itself in the dirt.

Ferrin ran faster than she'd ever run before. Faster than she had any business running with her injured leg, as if Strata herself aided her with each of the four winds, propelling her onward. The pain in her thigh dulled as a new surge of urgency coursed through her veins.

She made it through the door and into the foyer, pulling the Bourjon jacket closer around her shoulders and chest. She prayed no one would look too closely at her as she rushed purposefully through the halls, her heart and her breath loud as war drums in her ears.

Voices echoed up ahead, and she ducked into an alcove until they'd passed. Two soldiers and a man out of uniform. She recognized him from the Forest Council—the beady-eyed one.

"I was told we would be keeping our positions in the castle," he hissed. "King Henrik was to appoint me to Senior Council next week!"

"Henrik has outlived his usefulness," one of the soldiers said smoothly. "Now that things are underway, he cannot be trusted to stay... focused."

She recognized this soldier, too. It was one of Lukas's contacts in the palace guards. He was higher-ranking. A sergeant, or a corporal or something. She strained to hear the rest of their conversation, but it was drowned out by another round of shots from outside. The alarm had been raised throughout the castle.

If she didn't make it to the servants' passages soon, they'd be crawling with guards too.

Ducking out of the alcove with as much grace as she could muster, she limped a few steps down the hall. The rush of her escape was starting to fade, and she was growing woozy and achy all over again.

Thankfully, this wing of the castle was nearly empty. Perhaps her luck had not run out, and they'd pulled guards from this wing to aid in the search for Rhi. She could swear her own breathing echoed through the hall as she hurried along the carpet. Once she was in the passage, she wasn't sure what her plan was. She just needed to get out of sight. Fast.

But why hadn't the soldiers from the tower followed her into the castle? Surely they'd all seen which way she'd headed. She rounded a corner, almost there, and smacked right into the chest of Captain Clarings.

*   *   *

Well, they'd managed to get the popava barrels out of the mysterious hole in the ground. But turning them over had proved more troublesome than expected. One of the barrels had nearly crushed Soviel's ankle, and the other had sprung a leak, and now left a veritable breadcrumb trail of dried popava leaves behind them.

"This is less than ideal," she said in a massive understatement, eyeing the red-brown leaves.

"At least we know it's the right stuff," Lukas said with a shrug. "Since we didn't exactly check beforehand."

"Wait. Stop for a minute."

He obliged, stopping so he didn't run into the barrel she was rolling just paces in front of him.

"I want to collect a sample. So we can see if this is the strain that was being used on people. If I can learn more about it—" she mused as she stooped, removing the cravat from her neck to use as a makeshift glove.

"Here, take this," Lukas tossed her a little leather pouch.

With the linen kerchief, she managed to scoop up a cup-or-so of the stuff, along with the dust, sand, and other grime one might find on the floor of an aged castle's hidden hallways. "It looks like the base strain was the Veiran Red."

"Easier to get than Maraki Blue, these days. But not as mellow."

"I know, I grew up on the edge of a plantation."

"Right," nodded Lukas.

"I wonder if the use of this variant was intentional," Soviel mulled aloud, squinting at a little crushed blossom. Right, she thought. We're short on time. "Let's get moving."

They made it through the tunnel with minimal hassle. At one point, they nearly plowed into a Bourjon messenger as he rounded the corner too quickly. Lukas knocked him out, snatched his bundle of correspondence and pocketed it for later.

At last, they neared the pit. Or at least, Soviel assumed they did, based on the shift in the air. "Oh, gods, can you feel that?" she asked Lukas, breathing deeply. The pressure was sudden and impossible to ignore, like she'd been submerged in twenty feet of water with no warning. The temperature dropped and every hair on her body stood on end.

"It's colder," Lukas acknowledged.

"You don't feel it? The pressure?" she winced. Her head felt like an over-stuffed powder keg.

"No," he answered warily, watching her.

"Dammit," she seethed. It was her magic, being sapped and drained. It was the same unnatural and painful feeling she'd had when she'd healed Denison without the use of a conduit, but multiplied one-hundredfold. "Come on, we're getting close. Do you have the supplies?"

"Yep, right here." He reached into his coat and pulled out the empty bottle they'd taken from the wine cellar. "I hate to show my inexperience as a rabble-rouser, but I've actually never made one of these before."

"Don't worry, I have." Soviel assured him, squeezing her eyes shut, willing her legs forward.

"Are you alright?"

"Yes… It's just… I think it can sense me. My… life-magic. It hungers."

"That's not at all unsettling," he muttered.

"Hand me the bottle and a cloth."

He handed over the bottle and his own kerchief, if a little apprehensively.

"Can you see the pit?" she asked, taking the second, unlit oil lamp and pouring its contents into the empty wine bottle.

"No, but there's something at the end of this hallway," he told her. "I think it's a staircase."

"Ferrin mentioned a staircase—" Soviel gritted her teeth. "She said she felt a presence and that's when she had to run."

"Yeah, it lets out near the oak tree, where we came in… shit, are you sure you're alright?"

"No," she barked.

"Let's get this done and get the hell out."

She nodded and shoved her barrel forward, suddenly far heavier than it had been only moments earlier. Lalana, give me strength, she thought to herself as her heart thrashed in her ears, as if it could escape through her skull. They passed the staircase and continued along the hallway.

"Stop. Stop," she gasped when they were half a dozen feet from the edge. "This is close enough. Get the barrels in position."

Lukas obliged. Despite his generally intimidating appearance, his presence was comforting. Solid, honest.

With one hand, she stuffed the kerchief into the opening and shook it up, letting the oil saturate most of the cloth.

"Alright, on my word, shove like crazy." She set the bottle down, wiping her hands dry on her filthy breeches. "Let me just… light this…"

Another wave of light-headedness washed over her as she picked up the lantern, which still blazed. "If I pass out," she warned between labored breaths, "run like hell. Don't waste time trying to drag me out."

"No way. We're all riding out of here together." Lukas's voice was firm, unmovable.

She swallowed, nodding past the sharp, stabbing pain that had taken up residence in her head. She lit the cloth. Flames licked up the soaked material, illuminating both of their dirty faces in the oppressive dark.

"Ready, one, two…" she took a deep breath. "Three!"

Lukas heaved the first barrel, then the second, and they plummeted into the trench. Soviel hurled the flaming bottle with every ounce of strength she could muster.

"Run!" she commanded, though it came out as barely more than a grunt.

The pair turned and sprinted, stumbling as the pit behind them erupted in a roar of hunger, the tunnel devouring itself in a war of rock, flame and earth.

CHAPTER FORTY-ONE

"Hello, Highness," the captain's voice ripped through the space between them like a jagged arrow.

She gasped as he gripped her chin, forcing her to face him.

His face was bleeding, his head bandaged. *Oh, gods,* she realized, *his eye.*

Across his left eye socket was a white bandage, held in place by a strip of gauze wrapped across his forehead and around the back of his skull.

Had the major taken an eye as punishment? Her stomach lurched at the thought.

"Walk," was all he said.

There was nothing she could do as he pressed the barrel of a pistol to the side of her head and gripped her wrist, spinning her around. She squeezed her eyes shut for a moment, trying to gather herself, trying—mostly—not to cry at the feeling of defeat and hopelessness.

Be strong.

She'd been so close. She could see Lukas's face in her mind as she pulled away from him, skewering his chains to the table so he could not follow her. She could see every mistake she'd made since leaving that damn cabin.

"Keep moving." The tone of Clarings' voice made her skin crawl. It was full of hate and disgust and cruelty, and she would not give him the satisfaction of breaking down. She would die with her chin up.

"You cost me my honor, my rank, and my left fucking eye!" he spat as he shoved her into the wall.

She didn't say anything.

Breathe, breathe, breathe.

"And now, you're going to tell me how you got *him* out, before I return the favor." He poked at the delicate shell of skin and bone encircling her eye.

"He must have climbed," her voice shook. "I didn't see. I was knocked out."

"Not. Good. Enough," he growled.

"I swear it."

"Maybe so," he said, a dark and unholy expression on his hate-twisted face. "But, still, you cost me. So now it's time I settle our score."

"I can be of value alive," she stammered, the desperation in her own voice cloying and chilling to her ears. "The major will be displeased if you kill me. If you return me, he'll be impressed, he'll—"

She cried out as he punched her in the stomach. If he hadn't been gripping her by the shoulder, she'd have doubled over.

"I don't care," he grunted. "I no longer require his approval."

Her vision faded to black and she screamed as his knee dug into the bullet wound on her thigh. "I've been demoted, you see," he continued pressing. "Mutilated, and humiliated. Why shouldn't I do the same to you, who caused my suffering?"

From beneath them, the earth suddenly shook with a vengeance. For an instant, he was distracted. Ferrin took the opportunity to wrench herself from his grasp, bringing her knee up to his groin. She missed her target, but the effect was enough to put some distance between them. She scrambled back, tripping over her feet. He fell after her.

He growled—*growled*—as he launched at her, pressing her into the ground with his weight and crushing the air from her lungs. "Give me *one* good reason I shouldn't throw you to the soldiers in the barracks for sport. Let them kill you slowly." His voice was barely human. She was blacking out.

"I can think of a few," said a nearby voice.

I must have blacked out, she thought absently. Perhaps I've died and this is all in my imagination as I fade.

She watched as a blade sprouted from the center of his waistcoat, blood spreading around it. It twisted as it withdrew back into his gut. His grip on her throat went slack and he slumped forward. Blood and who knew what else leaking onto her from his body.

A figure stepped to the side and hoisted the body off of her. Wide caramel eyes looked down at her from beneath choppy brown hair. "Thank the gods you're still alive. Idiot!" Asha scolded, squatting down to help her up.

"W-we have t-to—" Ferrin gasped, still in the grip of panic, her throat raw.

"I know. Let's go."

"How did you get in here?" she croaked.

"Front entrance," Ash said, as casually as if she were discussing which route she'd taken to the alehouse.

"They let you in?" Ferrin asked with astonishment. "And Lukas was on board with this plan?"

"I had a rather convincing argument," Ash countered as she hooked an arm around Ferrin's waist, supporting her as they limped through the corridor.

"What?"

"Well, two things," Ash cleared her throat as they hastened their steps.

"Oh?" Ferrin winced as they rounded a corner, expecting another enemy to jump into their path.

"Well, first," Ash huffed, taking the brunt of Ferrin's weight. "No one here recognizes me."

"And the second?" Her voice was barely more than a rasp of air forming the ghost of the words.

"I can do a really good Bourjon accent," Ash said, in an accent that *might* have been Bourjon.

"You're joking."

"It's really gotten much better," Ash said defensively.

"Where are the others?"

"Rhi waits with the horses. Lukas and Soviel… well, that explosion was no coincidence, I hope."

A pile of dirt had saved them.

Apparently, the altered strain of dried *popava* leaves had been *extremely* flammable, and the burning bottle Soviel had tossed with the barrels had gone up in a far larger conflagration than anticipated. The blast had brought stone and timber down around them. They would have been burned alive had the earth not reached out a gentle hand and shielded them as they were flung down the hallway.

"Are you alright?" Soviel gave Lukas's shoulder a firm shove. His head was covered by his arms and several layers of dirt.

He turned and said something to her, which she could scarcely hear over the ringing in her ears. At least she knew they'd succeeded in killing the creature, as the intense, sucking pressure had subsided in her head.

Unfortunately, that headache had been replaced by a new one, left by the explosion.

"What?"

"I said 'I'm alright.'" He climbed to his knees, wincing. "You?"

"Yeah. I think we killed it."

"Let's get the hell out of here."

She wasn't going to argue with that.

They stumbled as quickly as their shaky limbs would allow back towards the gravelly little cave where they'd entered. If things had gone as planned, they had only minutes to get to the tree line and lie in wait to spring the traps.

"Come on, this door will take us closest to the woods," Ferrin said, pulling Ash by the elbow towards yet another entrance to the passageways. It was baffling how she'd never thought to use those hallways to get up to trouble in her childhood.

The door swung shut behind them and the tunnel went dark. They hurtled into the blackness, not knowing what lay ahead or below until light flashed behind them, spilling soldiers into the tunnel. Faint daylight illuminated their shadows, creating a collection of shapes like paintings on cave walls. The first men hunting monsters—primitive, angry figures, charcoal-black on rough rock, carved into the stone forever.

The girls sprinted, the might of harrow-hall at their heels for all they knew as they cut through the dark on a knife's edge.

"Stop them!"

"Fire at will!"

Bullets flew useless as falling stars, vanishing into the dark and ricocheting from the stone in brief sparks of bright white.

"Ow! Shit!" Ash swore. She must've been hit, but she didn't dare slow her pace.

They broke out into the light at the back of the castle, gulping down fresh air as they careened down the slope of the bluff. The midmorning sun was near blinding. From here, it was a straight shot to the woods. They could lose the soldiers in the trees.

"When I say so, split," Ferrin said as they ran, "Go left, I'll go right!"

"Are you insane?"

"There's a bog! Bottom of the hill."

From the corner of her eye, she could see Ash nod. A spatter of fresh blood stained the sleeve of her shirt as if she'd been grazed by a passing bullet, and she breathed heavier and heavier as they ran.

The jolting on her knees and thigh was nearly unbearable, but she shoved it aside as they tumbled down the hill.

"Now!" she yelled, releasing her hand from Asha's shoulder at the last second, skirting the edge of the narrow bog.

Anyone who'd grown up playing *Knights and Serpents* on the castle grounds knew about 'the swamp'. Once winter had relinquished its icy hold on the ground, and after all the snow had melted, and Lalana's spring showers had come to restore life to the fields and gardens, the water and mud pooled in the tall grass at the bottom of King Hill. It made a nasty, muggy bog for just a few months each year.

Unfortunately, she'd gotten stuck in it before. Fortunately, the soldiers giving chase didn't seem to know about it.

Asha pitched left, zipping across the side of the little bog, dodging a bullet. Ferrin veered right, lightning prickling at the back of her neck, like a thunderstorm was rolling in on the horizon. Again, that lightness came to her, propelling her forward. Despite the pain shooting through her leg with every step, she felt the swiftness of a rogue breeze carrying her onward.

"Bank right! Bank right!"

The soldiers at the front of the group had gone straight into the sinking mud. The remaining five barely had time to shift and circumnavigate the swamp.

The woods were within sight.

Thundering footsteps and shouts cascaded across the hills, though to Soviel's ringing ears they were almost undetectable. She watched from the underbrush as Ferrin and Ash sprinted down the hill, a small wave of soldiers in blue and red running after them.

Then she watched as the two girls split, as if they'd practiced it, and three or four of the soldiers on their tail went straight into the mud, unable to correct their own inertia. A few of the soldier's on their tail split, following them around the bog as the unlucky few were left struggling in the deep, spongy mud.

They were headed right towards the edge of the forest.

"Lukas, get ready!" called Soviel.

"Are we sure this will work?" Rhi's voice was nervous and tentative as he eyed the rope in his hand.

"As long as you don't pull it too early. Or too late. Or not hard enough," Soviel muttered to herself.

"What?"

"I said it'll be fine!" she repeated as loud as she dared, taking the tiny spyglass from her pocket.

Ash and Ferrin were approaching the woods fast. Ferrin's face looked pale and sickly. She was maintaining speed despite the limp on her left side. She looked close to vomiting. The soldiers behind them must have run out of shot, or perhaps they didn't want to waste the time it would take to reload as they pursued on foot.

Ash's face was frantic. The top of her shirt sleeve was torn and bloody; it looked like she'd been shot, as well. As a group, they were worse for the wear, and she hoped she'd have the strength to heal the most dire of their injuries. After getting close to the pit-beast, she still felt drained.

"Someone's going to have to carry her until I have time to fix whatever it is that quack healer did," Soviel grumbled under her breath. Rhi had described the way the healer had closed off the bleeding but not repaired anything, or even bothered to take out the musket ball.

"I will," Lukas said, slamming the first musket into his shoulder.

With a final deep breath as the girls neared the trees, Soviel loaded the ball and powder into the flintlock Lukas had given her. "Shoot first. Do not take any chances—if you hit Ferrin or Ash, I will end you," she promised. Lukas looked offended by the very notion. "When the girls are past and the soldiers reach the clearing, Rhi and I pull the rope. *Hard.*"

She hoped Ash remembered *which* two trees she was supposed to lead them between.

Rhi and Lukas nodded. Lukas crouched back onto the rock, waiting, while Rhi sunk into the thick branches of a towering evergreen, the trap rope slack and ready in his hands. Not a minute later, Lukas took his first shot. A guard went down. Two of the remaining guards giving chase stopped and fell into firing formation and reloaded. They took aim and fired. One shot went wide, the other embedded itself into the bark mere feet from Lukas.

Ferrin and Ash neared the woods, chests rising and falling like desperate bellows on the dying embers of a cold winter's fire. Another shot rang out. Then another. A second soldier fell. Lukas stopped to reload his guns.

"Come on, come on," Soviel muttered quietly.

They entered the tree line, four soldiers still behind them. Raucous as a stampede as they thundered through the trees.

"Now!" Soviel screamed at Rhi, yanking her own rope as hard as she could, her leg braced on a sturdy pine. A loud thump, followed by a collective '*oof*' sounded as they tumbled over. She could feel their weight in her arms as they hit the rope.

"Run!" Soviel called.

"Horses ahead!" Lukas shouted.

Ferrin could see the horses in the clearing ahead, four of them all saddled and ready.

She was leaning heavy on Ash now, more stumbling than running. They were close—maybe thirty feet away—when a shadow passed over them and something vulture-like slammed into the ground before them.

It was the woman from the tower. Ferrin had nearly forgotten her in the last few hours. She had been *flying*. And incredibly strong.

They skidded to a halt.

"You may have bested the foolish foot-soldiers, but I am far stronger than they could ever hope to be," she snarled.

"What *are* you?" Ferrin rasped.

"I was *made* to oppose you. I am one of many," she announced as she stepped forward.

Gods, she was *huge*. She looked like she could break a brick in half with one hand. If they had to fight her, Ferrin knew she wouldn't survive.

"Face me, and see how weak you are, let fate decide—"

A shot rang out and Monroe toppled over without ceremony. Ferrin panted, staring at the hole in her chest, then at Ash, who held a smoking gun in her other hand. Where had that come from?

"Well," she said, fighting for breath, "that was anticlimactic."

Then, her knees went out from under her and her vision went black just before she slammed into the ground.

"Help me!" Ash squeaked. Ferrin was now draped over Ash's shoulders, and the girl was struggling to hold them both up. It was a wonder she was managing it at all with the wound in her shoulder.

"I got her, I got her," Lukas assured his sister, scooping Ferrin's unconscious body over his shoulder. "Come on, we need to move."

"We need to hide so I can fix *that*," Soviel pointed at Ferrin's leg, which, through the tears in her breeches, was entirely discolored.

"They're still after us—"

"She will lose her leg," Soviel said stonily.

"Behind that thicket—be quick about it," Lukas said with urgency, straining to look back towards the castle.

They hurried behind the bush, Soviel's heart racing like a thousand war drums.

"Lay her down," she directed.

She examined Ferrin's left thigh. "Knife." She held her hand out and someone, probably Lukas, passed her a blade. Everything faded into the background as she leaned over the wound, slitting the leg of Ferrin's breeches wide open. She sucked in a breath. "They left the ball in. It's grinding against her bone."

She thought for a moment. There was no telling when they'd next have time to attend to it. It had to happen now.

"Cover her mouth, one of you."

"Why?"

"In case she wakes up," Soviel said grimly.

Lukas knelt next to Ferrin, sweeping her hair off her forehead, his brow furrowed with concern.

"Here goes," Soviel blinked. "Who has some alcohol? Whiskey?"

Rhi reached into his tattered coat pocket. "I have a half-empty flask."

"Give it here," she held out her hand.

Rhi passed her the little silver flask with the cap unscrewed. She doused the edge of the knife.

"Everyone, quiet!" she snapped. She had never done work like this out in the field. "I need to focus."

She let her power out, surging into the tissues to explore.

The work the healer had done was shoddy. She supposed it had just been a patch job to keep her from bleeding out before the execution. But in doing so they'd done further damage to important paths in the body surrounding the wound. She was bleeding internally again, and the ball of lead was still inside her thigh.

With a deep breath, she pinpointed the foreign object within the tissue, and pressed the blade over Ferrin's leg, slicing deep, and as cleanly as she could. Blood oozed out as she parted the flesh, fat and muscle. She stopped to splash the remaining liquor on her fingers before digging into her friend's open wound. She wrapped her fingers around the ball.

"Oh, gods—she's waking up," Lukas's frantic and distressed voice was a world away.

"Keep her still," she ordered him as she pulled out the ball, keeping it as even and level as she could, blood still gushing.

A muffled scream of agony pierced the woods as Ferrin's eyes opened.

"Do not let her move!" Soviel ordered. "This part will hurt the worst."

She held her hand over the gushing wound and focused her energy on the major blood vessel, willing it to close. She could feel the lower parts of the limb regaining their main source of blood, waking up after being starved of life for so many hours.

"Relax, it's almost done," Lukas said in a hushed voice.

The shrubbery around them faded, as if spring had come and gone, and winter was there to stay. A trade.

The muscle and connective tissue began to weave itself back into shape, a layer of raw, fresh skin covering it over. Soviel's fingers grew warm, and she could feel the life-magic spreading between them. Ferrin's face had contorted into a grimace as her body grew new flesh.

"That'll have to hold for now, but she needs more help. Medicine, a hospital," she explained, sitting back on her heels, breathless. She was thoroughly drained, and turned to Lukas. "Can you ride with her?"

"Of course."

"We can get to Port Galan in a few days if we make haste," Rhi spoke up.

"You don't think the Bourjon invasion will have reached them?" Ash asked.

"There's a Cael stronghold there. They won't fall as easily… I hope." Soviel shook her head. "My orders are to report there, anyway."

"Port Galan is our best option," Lukas agreed.

"You don't want to go home? To Njorske and your family's estate?" Ash asked Soviel. "Wouldn't it be safest for us to all leave the isle?"

She shook her head. "It's too far. And I don't want to drag my parents into another war. I have worked too hard here to give up now."

"We need to stay," Rhi agreed softly. "The Barrian throne is empty. I can't desert our people, I've always said I'd do better than my father. Now is my chance to prove it."

"He's right," Ferrin croaked as she strained to sit up. Her face twisted in pain and she stilled. "We'll go to Port Galan, join up with the Caelish, help gather forces, and strike back at Bourjony."

Soviel nodded. She hadn't realized Ferrin was still conscious. "Careful—that's still fragile," she warned.

"I know. Believe me, I can tell," she quipped.

"Well," Lukas nodded, glancing up at the sky, "We'd better get moving. It's a long way to Port Galan."

To Be Continued…

ACKNOWLEDGEMENTS

Wow, this has been a long time in the works, and it's weird to be writing this page, as it signifies that this book is well and truly done. I want to start by thanking Sam and Katie, the first people to read a ~very~ early draft of "Wayward as the Wind" all the way through. Your early feedback helped shape the book into what it is today, and I can't wait for you to see this new version! Thank you to my roommates of various eras throughout post-production who gave me thumbs-ups and thumbs-downs when I was agonizing over cover designs and title names
(I swear, that's the hardest damn part!).

Thank you to Steve F. and Aunt Elizabeth for sending me a pile of useful and entertaining resources on writing. To Hannah W., for reading all of my little scribblings on the carpool to swim practice when we were in Middle School, I hope you like this one.

Thank you to Professor Doherty for being the best English teacher with the wildest stories. Thank you to Tom, Distler, Bryan and Scott, for writing distance practices that had me in my own thoughts as I stared at that black line on the bottom of the pool for unending hours. Some of the most random ideas came out of those practices, which were typed furiously into the
notes app on my phone with wet fingers after practice.

To my parents, thank you for supporting me in this 100% from the beginning. You mean the world to me.

To Hector (and Cassie, but mostly Hector), thanks for screaming in the hallway every morning between two and five

AM for the entire winter of 2021-2022, and refusing to let me go back to sleep. Those were truly some of my most productive hours, so thanks little guy.

To those of you who got this far, thanks! I really hope you enjoyed reading this story, and that you'll like the rest of the series too!

ABOUT THE AUTHOR

Whitney Knowlton-Wardle was born and raised on Cape Cod, the flexed-arm shaped peninsula that makes up much of Massachusetts's Eastern coast. She studied Visual Arts at SUNY
New Paltz from 2015-2019, and spent a lot of time in the pool as a competitive middle-distance swimmer. Whitney now lives in Boston with her two cats, Hector and Cassie, and loves to spend time in the mountains and wilderness.

From a young age, she has loved to read and write fantastical stories full of long lost princesses, forgotten evils and anything with dragons and swords.

PENCIL HILL PRESS

© 2019 WHITNEY KNOWLTON-WARDLE

www.ingramcontent.com/pod-product-compliance
Lightning Source LLC
Chambersburg PA
CBHW031236310726
48971CB00004B/1034